ruin him

SCARLETT FINN

Also by Scarlett Finn

GO NOVELS
GO WITH IT
GO IT ALONE
GO ALL OUT
GO ALL IN
GO FULL CIRCLE

EXILE
HIDE & SEEK
KISS CHASE

WRECK & RUIN
RUIN ME
RUIN HIM

**THE BRANDED
SERIES**
BRANDED
SCARRED
MARKED

**FORBIDDEN
PREQUEL DUET**
ALL. ONLY.
ONLY YOURS

THE FORBIDDEN NOVELS
FORBIDDEN DESIRE
FORBIDDEN WANT
FORBIDDEN WISH
FORBIDDEN NEED
FORBIDDEN BOND

**BOMBSHELLS & BILLIONAIRES
(ROXIVERSE)**
NOTHING TO HIDE
NOTHING TO LOSE
NOTHING IN BETWEEN: ONE
NOTHING TO DECLARE
NOTHING TO US
NOTHING IN BETWEEN: TWO
NOTHING TO SAY
NOTHING TO GAIN
NOTHING IN BETWEEN: THREE
NOTHING TO YOU
NOTHING TO THIS PREQUEL: ONE WILD NIGHT
NOTHING TO THIS
NOTHING IN BETWEEN: FOUR
NOTHING TO DO
NOTHING TO NO ONE
NOTHING TO FEAR
NOTHING TO DENY
NOTHING TO BEAT
NOTHING TO THE WEDDING
NOTHING TO TELL
NOTHING TO IT
NOTHING TO SEE
NOTHING TO WIN
NOTHING TO OFFER
NOTHING TO PROVE

**LOVE AGAINST THE ODDS
STANDALONE COLLECTION**
SWEET SEAS
HEIR'S AFFAIR
RESCUED
MAESTRO'S MUSE
GETTING TRICKY
THIRTEEN
REMEMBER WHEN...
RELUCTANT SUSPICION
XY FACTOR

KINDRED SERIES
RAVEN
SWALLOW
CUCKOO
SWIFT
FALCON
FINCH

MISTAKE DUET
MISTAKE ME NOT
SLEIGHT MISTAKE

LOST & FOUND
LOST
FOUND

**THE EXPLICIT
SERIES**
EXPLICIT INSTRUCTION
EXPLICIT DETAIL
EXPLICIT MEMORY

TO DIE FOR...
TO DIE FOR TRUTH
TO DIE FOR HONOR
TO DIE FOR VIRTUE
TO DIE FOR DUTY
TO DIE FOR LOVE

**RISQUÉ & HARROW
INTERTWINED**
TAKE A RISK
FIGHTING FATE
RISK IT ALL
FIGHTING BACK
GAME OF RISK

ONE

ANOTHER CITY. Another shitty room.

The conditions didn't bother Tulsi as much as the fact that she was starting over. Again.

Vegas had been a bust. For about three weeks, Tulsi did her best to belong in the city that never slept. Getting a job there had been a major stumbling block. Turned out that learning fast was necessary for a life in hiding. Employment had come easier when she went off-strip and started to wear revealing clothes. Finding work had been only one hurdle; it wasn't the last she'd faced either.

Two weeks into her job at Heaven, a strip club where she worked as a server, her boss's advances became impossible to ignore any longer. Darnell, her employer, cornered her in his office and reminded her that all of the girls had to sleep with him at least once if they wanted to keep their jobs. He'd put his hands on her; men who did that didn't tend to live very long. So, Tulsi defended herself against the letch and then split in a hurry.

Going to the bus station with her meager earnings, she'd caught the first bus that was headed out of state. That was how she'd ended up in Florida.

Her short time in Vegas taught her a lot, so she wasn't

beginning at zero. Starting over in a new city was frustrating, no doubt about that; but she had a better idea of how to take care of herself.

Departing the room she'd been staying in for two days, Tulsi was careful to lock the door. One of the things she'd learned in Vegas was that regular motels were more expensive than the back street flophouses. A colleague in Heaven clued her in on how to locate the cheaper places.

Tracking down a similar flophouse in Florida hadn't taken long. All she had to do was seek out the roughest area of town and look for a building with open doors and a bunch of down-and-outs hanging around.

Making money was her primary goal. Slipping her key into her pocket, Tulsi's mission that night was to find a job. She didn't need to find a man, except that was exactly what faced her when she turned intending to walk down the hallway.

"You're new," he said to her, a smile on his face.

Though he appeared amiable and his warm smile genuine, Tulsi was suspicious. "Maybe you're new," she said and tried to sidestep.

He mirrored the move to stay in her way. "Amsterdam," he said, offering a hand.

She had no intention of shaking it or making friends. "That's not really your name."

"It's what they call me," he said, tucking his hand into his pocket. "Dam really, for short."

"That's nice," she said and tried to get around him again. When he persisted in blocking her route, she growled in frustration. "What do you want?"

"We're neighbors. We should get to know each other."

"If you want to get laid, I'm sure there are plenty of willing women down the block who'd take your money."

His smile grew. "You've got spunk."

"I've been told that before. Now get the hell out of my way…"

"A bunch of us hang out at a club downtown. It's called Fox Den… I can show you."

"Why would I want to go to a club with you?"

He shrugged. "Because everyone needs someone watching their back. I'll introduce you around."

Knowing a wider range of people could make it easier for her to get a job. If Tulsi didn't start earning soon, she wouldn't be able to afford the flophouse for long, which was a testament to her pathetic state. The place was the cheapest of the cheap. Tulsi wasn't accustomed to living under the radar. Even though she was willing to do practically anything, not having a social security number or employment history made legitimate employers suspicious.

Any of the less reputable places she'd entered were wary straight off the bat because that was their norm. Any new face could lead to trouble or be connected to a government agency, so they were hesitant to trust newcomers who had no one to vouch for them.

"What do you do?" she asked this Dam.

"I connect people."

He said it like he'd said it a thousand times and like it was a valid answer. But it didn't really tell her anything. Dam's statement reminded her of someone else's response when she'd asked a similar question. The occupation of the man in her memory wasn't really an occupation either. As soon as the thought of him entered her mind, she pushed it back down into the box where she'd locked all memories of him.

"What does that mean?"

"If you let me buy you a drink," he said, "I'll tell you."

It was around ten p.m., a good time to go job hunting. Everywhere was open and managers didn't have time to ask too many questions. Even though Tulsi had tried places during the day too, so far she hadn't come across any stores or coffee bars that offered discreet, i.e. cash in hand, employment.

"Just so we're clear, the last three men who touched me without permission ended up with a blade in them," she said, almost groaning at the sight of his interest brightening.

Hillam had been dead before she stabbed him and Darnell had only got an icepick in his arm, but they were mere details.

He tipped his head in a side nod. "Good to know."

"Lead the way."

Dam, as apparently people called him, seemed happy to have succeeded. But he wasn't home-free yet. In her experience, no one did anything for nothing. Having only been in town for two days, Tulsi didn't think anyone could have been spying on her. Not for long enough to learn anything valuable anyway.

Taller than her and built strong, it didn't take a genius to figure out Dam would be able to pin her down if that was his plan. But Tulsi was not as naïve as she'd once been. In the past, she'd managed to defend herself and wouldn't hesitate to do it again.

In a way, Dam having a sexual interest would put her at ease. Men did stupid things for sex; they went out of their way to get laid. Tulsi was practiced at resisting sexual interest. Fending off unwanted advances was part of her repertoire. Anything more sinister would be harder to handle.

Despite her history, she'd also learned not to judge someone based on appearances. Yes, Dam was capable and he had an ominous snake tattoo sticking out of his shirt that curved up the side of his neck. But the men that a woman had to be truly careful of were the ones who did everything they could to appear gracious and respectable.

"What's your name?"

"Sienna," she said, following him down the stairs to head for the wide entrance just beyond the front desk.

That was where Betsy spent her days smoking cigarettes and watching TV while waiting for tenants and potential tenants to come hand her money.

"You're not from around here?" Dam asked.

Tulsi didn't plan to be an open book. "Are you from around here?"

"Don't like answering questions about yourself?"

"Has it been your experience that people do?" she asked. "Whether I answer or not, you'd have no way to know if I was telling the truth."

They continued to the corner. Dam put an arm around her to guide her across the street. Tulsi chose to assume that the maneuver was absent, just a kind way to communicate. While they were outside at least. If he'd tried that when they were alone, she'd have a different reaction.

Until she knew more about his motives, she couldn't put up too many barriers. But that didn't mean she'd let him take liberties. Being suspicious was becoming a way of life. It wasn't easy being out on her own. Dam had been right that having someone watching her back would make life easier, except she wasn't sure she'd ever be able to trust anyone to do the job for the right reasons.

"I bet you have a story to tell," Dam said as they carried on walking.

"Not one I'll be telling you any time soon," she said. "But I'm a great listener, if you want to talk."

Tulsi wasn't offering an ear to be kind. If he talked about himself, she would learn more about him, and it would put a stop to him asking questions. Answering questions was her biggest pet peeve. It never used to be that way. In the past, she hadn't been suspicious and careful when telling people about herself. But then, no one asked her questions that could lead to her being dragged to her death.

Not being herself anymore was the most difficult thing to wrap her head around. Who she was couldn't ever exist again. Although Tulsi sometimes felt like her ex-self on the inside, she had to live a double life, never telling anyone the truth.

It was exhausting and meant she had to be aware and switched on all the time, ready to bolt at any second.

"I'm going to guess you're running from something," Dam said, apparently not paying attention to her offer.

Stepping away, Tulsi moved out from under his arm. "Why do you say that?"

"Most people are running from something. Sometimes it's just themselves. Other times, something more serious is on their tail." He left a silence that he probably expected her to fill. She didn't. "You gonna give me a hint?"

"Maybe I came for the weather," she said.

He bobbed his head in agreement. "Possible. Some people do. But those people don't stay somewhere like

Betsy's. And if you're looking for a rich sugar daddy, you're not dressing right at all."

Her dress was skintight and cheap, in that regard, Dam was right. If she wanted some rich guy to take over her life and pay for everything, she should go for a more sophisticated look. Some rich guys liked the skanky look, but not usually for more than a night.

"There are better towns for that," she said. "Actually, I came because I heard you had good coffee."

He laughed. "We do. Yep, good coffee."

"You must have been here a while if you're saying 'we.' How long have you been here?"

"On and off for years," he said. "I head south in winter."

"A lot of people do. You still haven't told me what you meant by connecting people. You're a headhunter?"

Any headhunting he did wouldn't be for a reputable organization. Even she wasn't naïve enough to believe that.

"You could say that," he said. "People need something, they come to me. I get it for them."

"Right. Just offering a public service."

"For a price," he said. "I travel a lot. Visit different cities. Learn what people have. What people want... Means I have access to a network that a lot of people have use for."

"Someone needs something and you know someone else who'll get it for them. For a price, no doubt."

"It's like a finder's fee, that's all."

"So that's why you walk up to random people and introduce yourself."

"Good way to expand my network," he said.

That he wasn't trying to sell his approach as altruism actually made her feel better. Dam wanted to know if she could be of use to him. If he could hook her up with steady employment that would be great, but she wasn't sure what she could offer in return.

On the bus into Vegas after fleeing Merchant's, Tulsi spent a lot of time thinking about the future, about what it would take to survive. It was at that point she'd decided that sex was off the table. Her decision was about protecting herself, sure. But it was also a reflection on her feelings about the act. Nothing good came from sex. It brought out the worst in people.

It drove men to act out their primitive desire. Women weren't always any better. Knowing the power it gave them over men, some females used it to take advantage of others. Even if there wasn't something underhanded about the exchange, it was still a negative experience, leaving those who engaged in it either heartbroken or violated. There was no reason for Tulsi to put herself in that position ever again.

Someday, if she ever managed to get settled somewhere, she might change her mind. But she doubted it. Living in hiding, disguising herself as someone else, wouldn't lead to honest and truthful relationships. Knowing that at any time someone could jump out to take her down, Tulsi couldn't risk trusting anyone with the truth. So, if a man didn't know who she was, how could she be intimate with him in anything other than body?

"You've gone quiet," Dam said. "It's just up the block."

A dozen yards further on, he slowed to direct them through a covered double entrance. From beyond, she could hear music. To the left were booths where payment was supposed to be made. To the right was a coat-check place. Dam waltzed straight on past both, putting an arm around her again as he opened the internal double doors in front of them.

The music coming from a DJ booth to the far left was almost deafening. A dance floor was down a few steps and laid out in front of where the lights were flashing around the DJ. Her companion took them the opposite way, along a raised walkway that led to an area filled with booths and tables.

Dam waved at some folks as they passed, but didn't slow in his journey to guide her to a booth in the far corner, next to the bar. That the booth was empty seemed odd, but ten was still early in a lot of circles. Except the rest of the club was busy, which led her to wonder if Dam frequented this place so much that the booth was reserved for him.

"What do you want to drink?"

He'd suggested a drink when they met, but she wasn't

ready to trust anything that he put down for her to consume. Still, she was intrigued and wanted to know more about why Dam had picked her out.

"Why don't we share a bottle of something," she said so as not to insult him with a flat refusal.

Their eyes met. He knew exactly what her offer implied, this guy was perceptive. "I don't drink wine," he said. "But I'll get you something still in the bottle if you want." She nodded. "Smart."

He left the booth to cross to the end of the bar a few feet away. The whole corner was quieter than the rest of the space. A curtain hung on the wall running between the end of their booth and the short part of the bar where Dam stood. The bartender came straight over to Dam and the pair began to talk.

The curtain interested her. It didn't seem to conceal powder rooms and didn't fit with the more industrial feel of the rest of the decor. The sign on the lintel above the curtain said "private" in white letters that glowed under a black light, making them pop. Someone wanted to keep drunk patrons out of there.

It could just be a storeroom or an employee area. Tulsi was still thinking about it when Dam came back with their drinks. Her bottle was sealed, as promised, and he put a bottle opener down beside it.

"Least I know for sure you didn't agree to drink with me because you wanted sex," he said as she opened the bottle.

"If I wanted to have sex with you, there would've been no point leaving Betsy's," she said, tasting the wine cooler. "We both have beds there."

"I have a bed here too," he said, tipping his head up to indicate above them. "Few folks I know stay in the rooms upstairs... So, if you change your mind..."

He put a hand over hers, which she immediately pulled away. "And we were getting along so well," she said without disguising her judgment.

He laughed. "No sex, okay, I get it. I'll make sure to tell the guys... I might know a couple of women who'd be interested, if that's what floats your boat."

"I can float my own boat," she said. "I don't need any help from you."

Settling back in the corner of the padded seat, he considered her. Tulsi glanced his way at his narrow assessing gaze. If he was trying to be intimidating, he was failing. The lack of answers was growing tiresome. If this guy wasn't going to help her, she could better spend her time trawling bars and clubs for work.

"Either you've got a guy or you're running from one."

"Is this what I have to look forward to?" she asked. "You going to spend the whole night tossing guesses at me?"

"If you'd just tell me—"

"The point is, I'm here," she said, twisting to face him. "And if you want me to help you, you have to help me."

He crooked a brow. "Ah, that's why you came along. You need something."

"Doesn't everybody?"

"And that's what makes my life so much easier. What do you need?"

"Work," she said because it was no big secret. "I need an income."

"That is something I can help with. What are your skills?"

"I'm dynamite in bed," she said, keeping her tone and expression flat.

He laughed again. It was a nice sound. For almost a month, Tulsi had been alone. Even before that, she hadn't had a chance to relax and just have fun not since… Thoughts of him made her eyes close. She couldn't keep doing it to herself. Tulsi couldn't let herself live in the past. Even just thinking of him distracted her from the present. Given that she never knew who could be watching her or attempting to track her down, Tulsi couldn't take the risk of being oblivious.

That was his word. He'd said she had a nasty habit of being oblivious. It was a habit she was trying to break. While he'd been around to be aware for her, she hadn't needed to be. But he wasn't around. Not anymore. He never would be again.

"You don't strike me as the kind of broad who needs

a pimp," he said, leaning forward to lay a forearm on the table, scrutinizing her again. "I can set you up if you do, but I can't say I recommend it… Pimps don't usually like women who think for themselves."

"Good to know you're not a complete idiot."

Lifting her bottle to her lips, Tulsi tipped some alcohol into her mouth before drawing her eyes around to find he was smiling again. A friend. It was sad that she was so tempted by the idea. In Vegas, the other girls at Heaven had been nice. Most of them anyway. Some were more vocal than others and some weren't fans of anyone they saw as a threat.

But being a server, Tulsi didn't spend much time backstage, which was where the women really bonded. Then Darnell had put his hands on her and she'd been running… without a friend in sight.

A friend would be great. But she couldn't trust Dam, not yet.

"I'd be happy to serve drinks," she said. "I have some experience with that."

"There's no table service in here, but I know a few places that might be interested in someone of your… figure."

"I don't do topless."

"Course not," he said, smirking. "I can get you into a job that will pay your way in Betsy's and leave you with some money at the end of the month… Places with the best tippers."

As much as that sounded like a dream, she knew better than to accept anything that was too easy or seemed too good to be true. "In exchange for?"

"I don't know yet," he said. "Usual price would be something in the corporate dating world."

"What does that mean?"

"Business men come into town, they want company… someone to show them around…"

"Didn't we just clear that up? I'm not interested in being any kind of escort. Corporate or otherwise."

"There are a bunch of jobs in that arena. Some women just date, some offer company for other women, some—"

"Put me down for a no," Tulsi said, taking another drink from her bottle before putting it on the table. "If that's all you've got…"

He put a hand on her leg to prevent her from sliding out of the booth. "Wait now," he said. "Never leave after the opening offer. We'll always be able to work something out."

Tulsi thought of another man from her past. One who preferred to use implication than to be frank. Even though Dam hadn't used any kind of sleazy tone, she was still suspicious.

It was on the tip of her tongue to call him out. Perhaps the sales pitch was all just some ruse, or maybe he gave women hope only to snatch it away as some kind of sick fetish. Before she could open her mouth, a shadow darkened their table. Both of them turned toward the huge guy who blocked her end of the booth.

The stranger tossed something down onto the table. "This is a piece of shit. I want my money back!"

Dam raised a flat hand. "Calm down, Bogey. Geez, can't you see there's a woman present?"

"I don't give a fuck," the giant guy snapped. "I want my damn money! You vouched for this piece of crap. Now I have a whole fucking box of this shit that's not worth dick."

Impressive, it seemed the guy was trying to squeeze in as many curse words as possible. While Dam tried to calm the infuriated guy down, Tulsi turned her attention to the thing he'd thrown onto the table.

Picking it up, she examined the leather and metal cuff. It didn't appear expensive. Turning it over, she discovered a mechanism on the underside, attached to a piece of sheared metal. That meant there should be another piece. Sure enough, on the table there was a blade, only about an inch and a half wide. With both pieces in front of her, Tulsi realized what she was looking at. The cuff concealed a weapon… or it was supposed to. Apparently the blade had snapped right off. It wasn't difficult to see why when she inspected it more closely.

"The solder was weak," she said, still examining the piece. "Looks like they used a soldering iron, which isn't right for something of this size… You'd be better with a torch… or a laser weld."

Silence fell over the men, which brought her attention upward. Dam's smile was slow to rise, but it glowed with appreciation.

"There you go," Dam said, turning back to the looming guy. "My new associate here will fix them up for you."

Tulsi shook her head and pushed the pieces back onto the table. "Oh, no… No, I—"

"She's modest," Dam said, sliding along the seat to put an arm around her. "Bring them back, we'll get them fixed for you… Free of charge."

Bogey eyed them both, probably unsure if he could trust her or Dam, who'd provided the substandard product in the first place.

"I'll bring them back tomorrow… I want them back fast," Bogey said and stomped off.

She was still watching him when Dam smacked a kiss to her temple. "Think we found your calling."

"No," she said, pushing away from him to slide down the booth. "No, I can't—"

"Sounds like you can."

Doing anything that was remotely related to her previous business could spell disaster. But her skill for jewelry making was really the only one that she had. It would be more lucrative than serving drinks. Another plus? It could be done in private, so she wouldn't have to worry about being recognized. Especially if Dam was doing all the face to face work.

"I don't know."

"I'll get you all the kit you need," he said. "Make me a list… Do you know how high demand is for discreet weaponry? Talk to me about this and we'll work up a pricelist."

"And how much of that do you pocket?"

"Twenty-five percent," he said. She lowered her chin to set her disapproval on him. Dam laughed. "Okay, twenty."

"Ten."

"Let's split the difference and call it fifteen."

She thought about haggling more, but Dam was going to be a valuable ally. Tulsi didn't want to risk pushing him too far.

"Fine."

He raised his bottle. "To the beginning of a beautiful friendship."

Finally allowing herself to smile, she picked up her bottle too. She'd come out on the hunt for a job and had found one. Tulsi just hoped it wasn't one that was going to reveal too much of her former self. If it did, termination would mean a lot more than starting over in another new city.

TWO

A BEAUTIFUL FRIENDSHIP was right. Dam might have appeared from nowhere and made her suspicious, but Tulsi had come to rely on him. Not only had he built up her reputation and kept work rolling in, but he'd supported her acclimation to her new life.

The day after their initial meeting, he'd revealed what was behind the curtain in Fox Den. Well-lit and quieter than the bar outside, the room had a bunch of couches and a card table set up for the men who hung out there.

In the back corner were the stairs that led up to the bedrooms Dam had spoken about. They weren't luxury, their quality was about the same as Betsy's, but they kept everyone together. Dam's adopted gang was full of people with different skills and trades. Many of the newer recruits were uncertain and suspicious; those who had been around a while were more relaxed.

Dam didn't live at Fox Den year round. But when he came south for the winter, it was his usual haunt. As it turned out, he didn't sleep at Betsy's at all. His people paid for a room there when they had meetings with associates that they didn't want to take to their base. At Betsy's, Dam also kept an eye out for new drifters coming through who might help his cause. Hence how he'd found her.

The booth where Bogey had accosted them was an extension of the den behind the curtain. An interview space as Dam liked to call it. Somewhere they could take people to introduce them to the building without drawing them into their private space.

After just a couple of days, Dam invited her to stay at Fox Den. The cost was about equivalent to Betsy's and it did have an advantage over the flophouse. At Fox Den, Tulsi had access to a communal—often messy—kitchen. Given that Dam had set up her work bench in the room behind the curtain, living at the club made sense. Tulsi could work as late, or as early, as she wanted to and never had to worry about walking home alone at night.

Dam had also become her defender. None of the Fox Den guys had overstepped the mark in the way some men from her past had, but they didn't mind flirting with her. Any time Dam thought one of them might be getting ideas, he'd step in. It had been his suggestion that Rook, one of the other guys, teach her how to throw a knife. Apparently, her newest friend hadn't forgotten what she'd said about putting blades in men. Rook was proficient, an expert, and he was a good teacher too.

Tulsi didn't exactly have a lot of free time, but she enjoyed learning a new skill, so didn't mind staying up late. It was good exercise too. She'd started to run again as well. The beach was much better than her old trudge in the gym. Even though there was a room upstairs at the club full of gym machines, Tulsi preferred to be outside. Nothing in the gym matched and she wasn't sure any of the equipment had been bought legitimately, but it was there for them to use.

After living in Fox Den for two months, Tulsi's time with Dam was coming close to its end. They hadn't talked about him leaving, but it was coming. She had no idea what her reaction would be when he told her he was going. If he even told her. Dam joked about hating goodbyes and how it was dramatic to just disappear. Each day for the last couple of weeks, Tulsi had woken up dreading getting up. She feared being told that he'd slipped away in the night without saying goodbye.

Rook didn't go anywhere, as far as she knew, so she'd have one defender if she stayed. But staying in one place for too long might not be smart. This life on the lam thing was taking its toll. Any time she relaxed and felt herself drawn closer to the people at Fox Den, she'd get a harsh slap when a thought from the past snuck through her defenses.

That night, the club was in full swing. The bass of the music carried past the curtain as it always did, but she paid more attention to the men behind her playing cards. Tulsi's focus was on the piece that she had to get finished. There were only a few more joins to make then she would leave it to cool.

Thinking that she might ask Rook for a few lessons that night, she hoped to get to bed before the club closed. Dam was at the card table with the half dozen other guys who'd already gone through a keg of beer.

"Patch," Dam called out. "Get over here and show these guys who's boss."

She smiled, but kept her focus on the two pieces of metal and her weld. The magnifying glasses offered her protection and let her look at the minute pieces without straining.

"You still owe me fifty bucks from last week," she called out without turning around. "You better not lose my money."

"Don't panic. I'll just swipe it from one of these guys after they pass out like I usually do," Dam said. She knew enough to laugh, but one of the newbies obviously glared because Dam laughed too. "Geez, Salt, I'm kidding, man… Patch, tell him I'm kidding."

"He's kidding," she said, putting down her laser. "Or he paid me to agree with him."

Dam laughed again. "Shit, babe, you trying to get me in trouble?"

"Gotta get my kicks somehow."

From the response at the card table, she guessed that everyone was friends again. Salt wasn't really that touchy, usually, but he was one of the guys not completely at ease yet.

"This is a private party," Dam said. "Back out the way

you came."

Wouldn't be the first time that a drunk wandered past the curtain looking for a restroom or to snoop. Obviously, whoever had come in wasn't getting the message because Dam cranked up his anger and spoke again.

"Yo, buddy, what do you want?"

"Her."

One syllable. That was all it took to rattle her whole world.

A thorn of sheer joy pierced her first. Just the notion that it could be true was enough to excite her endorphins. Yet, a background prickle of awareness reminded her to be cautious. The pessimism wasn't welcome. Tulsi wanted her fantasy to come to life. She'd never let herself believe that it would and yet…

Slowly raising her attention, Tulsi caught sight of the last person she expected to see. In her dreams, in the night, her subconscious cried out for him. In the day, when she had her wits, Tulsi never let herself think of him. In fact, she'd chastise herself for being so juvenile as to expect some kind of fairytale ending.

Allowing herself to think of him without regret for the first time, Tulsi absorbed the moment. The truth infused her senses. He'd come for her. Somehow, he'd freed himself from the clutches of Merchant's men and crossed the country to get to her. It was incredible. That he'd even thought to begin such a daunting mission was flattering. That he'd battled through and somehow found her was plain miraculous.

It was unbelievable. Wreck. Her Ruin… Her next inhale caught in the back of her throat. Struck dumb, she probably could have sat there staring into his fierce feral gaze all night.

The sound of someone cocking a gun distracted her.

"No," Tulsi said, rising to her feet and opening a hand out to stall the men behind her. All the while, she kept her focus pinned to the man standing just inside the room.

"You know this guy?" Dam asked.

It took her a score of seconds to find her voice. "He's my Ruin."

Saying the words kicked her into action. Bounding away from the table, she couldn't get around it fast enough. Tulsi rushed to her ruin and threw herself against him.

Grabbing for her in return, he lifted her clear off the floor. "Nymph," he breathed the word into her hair.

It was so quiet that the others wouldn't have heard it, but the edge of vulnerability in that single word brought tears to her eyes.

"You came for me," she said, tightening her arms around his neck. "I never thought... How did you find me?"

Tulsi squeezed him tight. She feared ever having to let him go. Yet, she missed his eyes, the sight of his face. The memory of both had been her precious touchstone since fleeing the scene of her crime.

She lost track of time, and guessed maybe he did too, because he didn't reply. They just stayed there, locked in each other's embrace, absorbing each other again.

Clutching his shoulders, Tulsi pushed back to find his gaze, searching for an answer to her question.

Wreck put her back on her feet. "Want me to leave?" he asked, his scowl darkening.

"No!" she said. A whisper of her incredulity escaped as a laugh. "Definitely no."

Staring into him, she still struggled to believe that he was really there in front of her. Wreck seemed content, looking down at her. There wasn't as much wonder in his gaze as she imagined bled from hers, but he'd known this moment was on the horizon. Tulsi hadn't believed for a second that he'd track her down. But there he was. He'd come for her.

"I've got a room in the city," he said.

The obvious hint that he wanted them to be alone was no surprise or disappointment. The idea had occurred to her too.

Tulsi grinned and leaned closer. "I have a room in the building," she said and grabbed his hand. "Come on."

Dragging him to the other side of the room and up the narrow, walled-in staircase, Tulsi didn't miss a beat. She pulled him along the shag pile carpet circa 1977 that was so bare in some places, the boards beneath were visible.

Shoving open her bedroom door, Tulsi got him inside and closed it fast. She could hardly believe it. Hardly believe he was there. But if this was a dream or some kind of drug induced haze or concussion, she didn't want to wake up. Not before she got the chance to taste him again.

As Wreck surveyed her modest room, which must have been decorated around the time the shag carpet was installed, Tulsi moved in close. Picking up his hands with hers, she laced their fingers together so they were standing palm to palm.

When his intimidating stare landed on her, she couldn't be anything except thrilled.

"We both have our hands," she murmured. "It's been a while, huh?"

"Nympho," he said in a low, rumbling tone.

The mention of the pet name made her smile widen.

"I can't believe you came for me," she said, pushing closer to inspect the darkness in his eyes. "Did you come here for me?"

"You think it's a coincidence I showed up?"

She relaxed and shook her head. "A dream maybe."

He took one of his hands from hers. With curled fingers, he caressed her cheek until his digits came to rest beneath her jaw. "Always were a dreamer."

"What happened to your rules?" she asked, in a semi teasing tone. "You said no lovey stuff." He didn't respond, just continued to admire her. "And I said no. You said if I did that, you'd never touch me again."

"Never heard you."

Her smile grew. If that was true, he'd ask when she said it or he'd deny that she had. If he intended to follow his own rules, just the admission that she'd said no should be enough to make him back off.

But the man in front of her wasn't interested in backing off. His fingers unfurled to curl around her chin. Tightening his possessive grip, he forced her head further back.

"Wreck," she whispered. A shiver went through her just at the sound of his name. Tulsi closed her eyes as her fingers drifted downwards to curl around the buckle of his belt. "I need you… Satisfy my craving."

"My little addict," he murmured, sinister and satisfied. "You want it."

"From you," she said, arching closer. "Dreaming about you hasn't been enough." Tightening her hold, she retreated, pulling him deeper into the room. "I don't have a bathroom or a vanity for you to put me on…"

Snatching her waist with a crushing grip, he spun her around to face the bed and dipped to force her head aside with his.

Digging his teeth into the side of her neck, he sealed his lips and sucked hard. The painful pinch of his mark would definitely bruise. Instead of hurt or horror, Tulsi drowned in the rushing hormones of a desire that made it almost impossible for her to stay upright.

Wreck continued to mark her as he unzipped her pants. He worked them and her underwear down from her hips.

He was going to do it; he was going to have her and Tulsi had no intention of stopping him. She raised her arms to let him remove her top. As her hair tickled her back again, he unhooked her bra. There was barely time to free her arms before he shoved her down on the bed face first.

His tee-shirt was gone by the time she rolled over, then he was bending down to unlace his boots. Soon as he stood up to toe them off, his eyes landed on hers.

They were free. Together. It was more than she could have wished for. Until he'd appeared, Tulsi scolded herself any time she thought of him. Admitting they would never see each other again was too painful a conclusion to reach over and again.

If she was going to wake up, she wanted to take advantage of every lucid second.

Parting her legs, she pointed her toe to trail it up the front of his jeans as he unfastened his belt. She got a flashback to the first time they'd shared a shower… the first time she saw him in all his naked glory.

Her lips were about to ask if he remembered when he

dropped onto the bed on top of her. The weight of his incredible body smothered hers. For a second, she couldn't breathe, then a sensation she hadn't felt in months swamped her. Safety. Tulsi felt safe.

"You searched for me," she murmured, coming to terms with what a task that must have been. "You found me… My Ruin."

"Your Ruin," he breathed the bassy words against her lips a fraction of a second before he kissed her.

Sinking into the warm bliss that enveloped her, Tulsi looped both arms around his neck, ready to take her time.

Wreck wasn't so patient. All of a sudden, he straightened both arms to rise over her. He wasn't taking his time to enjoy their reunion. He flipped her over, grabbed her hips and forced her onto her knees.

"Ruin—"

He yanked her back as he drove forward, impaling her hard, just like he had their first time together. All thoughts and words disappeared from her mind as her head sank down low between her straight arms that braced her weight.

"Jesus fucking Christ, Nymph," he growled, hissing the words as he stretched her for his pleasure. "Damn."

It was impossible not to be flattered by straining his control. Maybe he'd forgotten how good it felt to be inside her. Tulsi had remembered how incredible it felt to be with him, but even she'd lowballed the pleasure her pussy felt to be filled with his cock.

Their first time had been rough and fast. This time he withdrew and advanced at a slow pace. Either he was testing her or enjoying being in a familiar home.

"Baby," she said, reaching around to slide her fingers over his on her hip.

The moment she began to rise, he folded himself over her to graze his teeth on her back through her hair, forcing her to bend again.

The contact kicked him into gear. He propelled himself deep into her, hitting her far inside. Tulsi gasped in a high pitched squeal of pleasure.

"Fuck," Wreck said, fucking her faster. "Goddamn."

After another gasp, she got into the rhythm with him. "Feel good, baby?"

"Primo pussy, Nympho…Shit, you take it good."

"I want it bad," she answered through panting breaths.

"You do," he said, slamming into her. "Fuck, my Nymph."

He'd never claimed her before. In the haze of passion things were said that meant nothing. But she didn't care. She wanted him to mean it and let herself believe he did. With adrenaline and lust coursing through her at lightning speeds, she could convince herself of anything.

"Shit! Oh, fuck, Wreck," Tulsi exclaimed, heaving in a breath. "Oh, I fucking missed you."

Bruising her hips in his strong, capable grip he tugged her back. "I'm right fucking here."

She slid her hand down her side. Wreck surprised her by anticipating what she needed. Smacking her hand away from her body, like it almost offended him that anyone else should touch her, Wreck took power of her.

Coiling his arm around her body, he kept working his cock in and out of her as he toyed with her clit.

"You remember who's in control," he growled, bowing over her again. "Right here."

The pressure on her clit pushed her into a powerful orgasm that tightened each of her muscles. She didn't breathe for half a minute, not until a desperate need to inhale engulfed her. Opening her mouth wide, Tulsi drew in as much oxygen as her lungs could hold and liberated a long scream.

The echoing sound of her climax came just moments before Wreck's growl that signaled his release.

She hadn't had time to catch her breath before Wreck let her go. He didn't lie down or even sit in her eye line. So although her heart was still pounding like a freight train riding down the tracks at top speed, she turned over and flopped onto her back.

Her lover was sitting at the end of the bed with his back to her. She wriggled down the mattress and pressed the sole of her foot to his spine.

Breathing out, Tulsi basked in her ecstasy. "Baby?" she said, but got no response. "There's so much I have to tell you."

Seeing Wreck again wasn't just a shock to her carnal self, it was a shock to her emotional self. To the very stability of her existence. Tulsi was no longer a stranger to herself. The identity that she had left behind in Merchant's blood wasn't a myth anymore. Wreck knew her. They knew each other. A part of her ex-self was alive again. Not scared and confused, she could hold onto her bond with Wreck. No matter what anyone knew about her or what secrets she kept, the truth of her being would always exist in her ruin.

"You trust me."

His words were so flat they were almost monotone. Tulsi wasn't sure if he was stating fact or asking for confirmation. Wreck didn't turn to look at her, so she got no clue from his expression.

"I've been staying here a while," she said, choosing just to absorb his words rather than react to them. "I make a little money rigging accessories with weapons… I'm good at it…" When he said nothing, she worried about where his mind was. "I'm sorry I left the way I did. I know you must be mad about—"

"I'm not mad," he said, twisting around to lay a hand on the bed to meet her eye. "Not at you."

Tulsi didn't quite know what that meant. He flipped over and ascended the bed to lie on his side next to her.

"We can make money here," she said, stroking the back of her fingers up and down his chest. "Not a bunch, but at least it's safe… Dam probably won't be around much longer. We could go with him when he leaves, if you want to."

"Where's he going?"

Pushing one of his legs beneath hers, Wreck trapped her between his strong thighs. Once he had her secure, he rolled onto his back, putting her on top of him. The position reminded her of the first night they'd slept together.

"Don't know where he goes," she said, brushing her lips left and right on his torso. "He travels around, widens his network… I'm sure he'd take us along with him."

Wreck put a hand on her head to push it down against his body. "You trust him?"

"He looked out for me… I would never have found this place without him."

"What'd it cost you?"

Rising, Tulsi crawled up his body. His hand slid through her hair and down her back. She kissed him.

Keeping her eyes closed after she parted from him, Tulsi whispered, "I choose you." Opening her eyes, she sought his. "Do you remember the first night I said that to you? I was as sure then as I am now. I will always choose you, Wreck." He didn't react, but that just reminded her how much she loved the intensity of his gaze. "Thank you."

"For?"

"Coming for me," she breathed out and sank down to tuck her head beneath his chin. "I missed you… My Ruin."

Every muscle relaxed. Just being near him was incredible. She was safe. For the first time since she'd last slept in his arms, Tulsi finally felt safe.

THREE

IT COULDN'T HAVE BEEN much after that thought Tulsi fell asleep. She did remember some sleepy middle of the night sex, which was probably why she woke up wearing such a broad smile. Her smile faltered at the discovery she was alone in her bed. Quick to jump up and seek any sign he was still around, she relaxed a little when she noticed his belt on the floor.

The accessory was hardly a guarantee, but Tulsi picked it up after putting on her robe, and kept hold of it as she departed the bedroom. The hallway got light from the window at the very end. But it was the sound of the radio in the kitchen that attracted her attention.

Dam was the only one in there when she rounded the space where the door should be.

"Morning," she said, twisting to check the time.

"That all?" Dam asked, leaving the counter with his coffee to sit at the round table in the corner by the threshold.

Wearing a frown, she peeked at him as she retrieved a mug to pour her own coffee from the pot. "All?"

"You know how long I knew Foxy before he trusted me to vouch for his lodgers?"

Tulsi licked her lips and sipped the coffee. "Uh… no.

I never asked."

She joined him at the table.

Dam swept his cup around as he propped his elbows on the table to lean toward her. "Hint: it wasn't two months."

Foxy was the nickname of the guy who owned the building. The club was his main interest, though he dabbled in some illegitimate ventures too. Profits from those ventures could easily be cleaned through the club. That was what Dam told her anyway. She and Foxy weren't exactly close.

Tulsi exhaled a laugh. "What are you talking about, Dam?"

He eyed the belt in her other hand that was resting on the table. "Your booty call."

"Where is he?"

The question better have an answer she liked or else she'd sound like a moron for even asking it.

"Shower," Dam said.

It was tough to restrain her smile and sigh of relief. "He's not a booty call," she said, drinking more of her coffee.

Dam locked his attention on her and waited. After a few seconds of silence, he prompted her. "You've gotta give me more than that if you're thinking about asking him to stick around."

Tulsi shook her head. "I'm not sure he wants to."

His brows rose and he sank back in his chair. "Well, Patch, you still got some surprises in you… Dragging guys to bed hasn't been your bag… Fact, you've been all about keeping them at bay."

On a half shrug, she hid her mouth behind her mug. "We have history."

"No shit," he said, almost laughing. "Guys and me could hear you scream over the sound of the club."

It wasn't so easy to hide the smile that Dam's revelation inspired. "If it wasn't for him, we would never have met."

"I'll be sure to thank the guy," he said. "If he plans to talk to any of us anytime soon… Kinda a rude fucker."

Pushing her lips to the side, Tulsi knew it wouldn't be right to laugh, but her smile just wouldn't go away. "I can't argue that," she said when she trusted herself to speak. Dam wasn't amused and wasn't doing a thing to hide it. "Look, Dam, I…" Reaching across the table, she opened her hand. It took him a moment to lean forward and slide his over it. "If it wasn't for him, I wouldn't be here. I wouldn't be anywhere. Yeah, he's… unique, but he's mine."

Dam blinked in surprise. "Yours?"

"He wouldn't have come all this way if he didn't want to patch things up."

Her friend's head began to bob. "He the guy you were running from?"

She shook her head. "No… He's the guy I abandoned when I had to run… I murdered a guy… A guy with connections."

That was more than she'd ever confessed to Dam. Sure, there were times he got close with his guesses. But it wasn't exactly a difficult thing to figure out when she was so against sexual advances.

"And your booty call knows about that?" She nodded. "If you two are so coupled up, how come he didn't run with you?"

Thinking about it for a second, Tulsi couldn't come up with any vague way to explain it. "It's complicated."

"Ain't it always," he said and slouched in his chair again. "Patch, you gotta be careful."

"I don't," she said, picking up her cup. "Not with him."

Dam frowned again. "You don't? What the hell, babe. Have I taught you nothing? Always watch your six. Always."

"That's my job."

Wreck's voice made Tulsi smile, she tucked her chin lower and hid behind her coffee mug. He didn't give her much time to enjoy the tingles his presence caused. Sweeping her hair into a fist, he twisted it once and again, forcing her head back.

"Good morning, my Ruin."

"Ready to go?"

The fact that she was in her robe drinking coffee sort of suggested that no, she wasn't ready to go anywhere. But

Tulsi didn't have time to say anything because Dam spoke up.

"Listen, dude, I'm sure you've got a great sob story. But Sienna is going nowhere."

Still looking at him upside down, Tulsi smiled when Wreck's critical gaze descended to her. "Sienna?"

Shoving her cup onto the table, Wreck's hand loosened from her hair when Tulsi leaped from her chair.

She hooked his belt around the back of his neck and used it to pull him down.

Taking another shot at their greeting, she kissed him. "Good morning, my Ruin."

He let her kiss him again, but the judgment in his glare stayed potent. "We're going. Grab your shit."

Tulsi took her time about slipping his belt through its loops. Wrapping her arms around him, she pulled herself close and managed to stay that near as she finished sliding the leather through denim.

"She's got a life here, jerkoff. A life, a job, friends."

That Dam and Wreck couldn't get along would be a stumbling block. Tulsi owed both of them so much.

"Way I hear it, you're gonna be on the road soon."

"Maybe," Dam said. "Maybe not. That's my business."

"And this babe is mine," Wreck said, slinging an arm around her shoulders to hold her against his body. "You don't gotta worry about her anymore."

"Funny 'cause that's been my job for the last couple of months. Guess you couldn't hack it for her."

Wreck tensed, so Tulsi immediately pressed both hands to his torso and twisted to look over her shoulder at Dam. "You two shouldn't waste your time pissing each other off. I'm the only one allowed to do that." When Dam laid a glare on her, she smiled. Showing him and then turning it up to her lover who was scowling, Tulsi was pleased to have broken their focus from each other. "I vouch for both of you… That means neither of you can hurt the other without breaking my word, and neither of you want to do that."

Maybe they did, but she was going to show her faith in both of them and hope that was enough to keep them from killing each other. Easing back, Tulsi took her time about fastening Wreck's belt. Once she was done, she stepped back and pulled out the chair she'd vacated to offer it to her lover.

"What do I tell Foxy?" Dam asked.

Wreck sat and picked up her coffee to down the rest of the liquid. Tulsi took it from him and went to the coffee pot to refill it.

"Depends if we're staying," Tulsi said, glancing at Wreck. "Are we staying?"

"No."

"Okay," she said. "I guess Foxy doesn't have to worry about it."

"And your outstanding orders?" Dam asked.

Tulsi took the fresh coffee to Wreck.

Propping a hand on the back of his chair and the other on her hip, she sighed. "Good point." She slid her hand from the chair onto Wreck's shoulder. "I have orders to finish."

"Give 'em their money back," Wreck said, putting the cup down and twisting to hook an arm around her waist to pull her onto his lap.

"And that does shit for her rep," Dam said. "Sienna's actually respected around here."

"He's right," she said, scooping her hands under Wreck's when they started trying to find her thighs beneath the edges of her robe. "Dam has a rep too. If it wasn't for his word, I wouldn't have got anywhere down here."

"What do you need?" Wreck asked.

"A day," she said in the direction of her shoulder. "Maybe two."

"He can't stay here," Dam said. "I'm sorry, Patch. He's a stranger."

"So was I. You took a risk on me."

"If you stepped out of line, me or the guys could've taken you out in a snap."

Wreck was a different ballgame altogether. The threat level around her was low. Most of the guys would be able to break her if they had to. After seeing her work with Rook, they understood she was capable of defending herself. But since moving in, she'd built up trust with the Fox Den gang.

No one knew what Wreck was capable of. Even Tulsi hadn't seen him working at full capacity. She trusted the man she sat on with her life and more than that, she'd trust him with any of her friends' lives. But she had to show Dam some respect and at least try to put him at ease.

"If you want to hurt him, all you have to do is hurt me," Tulsi said. "I'm the weak link. That's the key to keeping him in line."

"Nymph," Wreck growled, clamping both arms around her narrow waist.

"What?" she asked, again talking to her shoulder. "You're not going to hurt anyone around here. Dam wouldn't hurt me by choice. If he feels threatened, he needs some way to get through to you. It's not like you'd let anyone hurt me."

"If he tries, I'll break his neck."

"There we go," she said, presenting both palms in front of her and smiling at Dam. "Now you can both focus on that... Finishing my orders works in both of our favors, Dam. If you really want me to go over to Betsy's—"

"Like I'd leave you out there exposed," he grumbled. "You're safe here... Least you were before the booty call showed up."

"You know, I think you two probably have a lot in common." Still, neither man seemed in a hurry to stand down from their hostile positions. "Both of you have a flexible view of morality... You're both intelligent... Street smart... loyal—"

"Okay, Little Miss Fixit," Dam said. "I'll can it so long as that guy remembers whose town this is."

"Keep your damn town," Wreck said. "I came for my woman. When I leave, she comes with me... for me."

Tulsi didn't let that one linger for long. "You could be useful to each other."

Dam crooked a brow. "I got enough muscle on my books."

"Fine," she said, pushing Wreck's arms open so she could rise to her feet. "Don't say I didn't offer."

As she spun around, intending to go back to her

bedroom, Dam questioned Wreck, "You got skills?"

Tulsi froze.

"I don't work for free."

"No one does," Dam said. "Tell me what you do."

Jumping around, Tulsi clamped a hand over Wreck's mouth and pulled the back of his head against her stomach. "Please don't ask him that question."

The kicker was, her reaction raised Dam's intrigue. "Why not?"

"I just got him back," she said, trying not to let the depth of her vulnerability show. "Let me enjoy him a while before everything collapses again."

Curling his fingers around her wrist, Wreck drew her hand down from his mouth. "I don't answer to fuckers like you."

"If you think I'll let you stroll out of here with Sienna without knowing you can take care of her—"

"What's it to you?" Wreck asked.

Usually, he wasn't so chatty. Either something had changed since she'd last seen him, or Dam's suspicion was provoking him.

"We look out for her here."

"All I see is you," Wreck said. "Missed your chance if you were playing the long game."

Tulsi took a second to figure out what Wreck's statement implied. It was the narrowing of Dam's focus on the newcomer that clued her in.

"So much for everyone getting along," she muttered.

"I don't know anything about this guy. Don't even know his name."

"Wreck," Wreck said. "You got some shady friends, Amsterdam… No one is safe with you."

"Sienna is," Dam said. "If you really know who I am, you should know that."

"And if you had a damn clue who she is, you'd know she doesn't need you."

"Can we please—"

"She was safe 'til you showed up," Dam said, shooting to his feet.

Panic surged through Tulsi when Wreck got up too. Her love could kill in seconds and without breaking a sweat, she'd seen it.

"No," she said, rushing around him. The men stayed on their sides of the table, staring each other down. "Maybe I should cook something. Who wants some eggs?"

"Want to burn the place down?" Dam said, still glaring at Wreck. "You know better, Si. You made everyone sick last time you cooked."

"That was an accident," she said. "How was I supposed to know that the ham expired?"

Wreck's heavy hand landed on her shoulder. "You've gotta pack, Nymph."

"What happened to giving her two days to finish her orders?"

"She doesn't need you anymore."

"I take fifteen percent."

"Ah," Wreck said. "So she's your moneymaker? Sure you want to hang around for this asshole, baby?"

"He's not an asshole."

Dam didn't seem to hear her defense. "We work together. Help each other. We're close. Real close."

Not as close as that clandestine tone suggested. Tulsi couldn't understand why Dam wanted to tread that route. Wreck wasn't exactly the jealous type. Though, she couldn't really say that for sure. Their time together had been brief and marred by so many obstacles, there was no way to know the truth of how he'd react to another man showing an interest in her.

"You think?"

Her focus quickly switched from Dam's implication to Wreck's subtle amusement. "Wreck," she murmured as she turned to face him.

But he wasn't interested in looking at her, he was fixated on Dam. "We've lived together for two months. I think I know her pretty fucking good."

"You're a goddamn nobody."

"I'm somebody to her. She trusts me."

"Know her so well," Wreck said, that glimmer of

amusement in the back of his throat again.

"Yeah. Yeah, I do."

"You don't even know her real fucking name!"

Silence settled around them after Wreck's words stopped. Tulsi didn't want to turn, she didn't want to look at Dam. Sure, she could argue that he hadn't given her his real name either, but that was no secret. Dam had never lied about his name being a nickname. While she hadn't ever claimed Sienna to be a nickname, she hadn't offered the truth either.

Figuring there was no excuse, and because she didn't want to face her friend, Tulsi moved around Wreck. "Excuse me."

Walking out of the kitchen, she stayed quiet on the return to her bedroom. She didn't even know what to do. Didn't know what to think either. There was no time for her to figure anything out. Almost as soon as she closed the door behind her, it opened again.

"We don't gotta stick around for that dickwad." Wreck stormed past her and began to open drawers. "Where's your bag?"

Her head began to shake. "You don't even care, do you?"

He slammed a drawer and turned his glare to her. "What?"

"Dam is my friend. He's my friend. He's done a lot for me. Why did you have to—"

"Tell him the truth? He doesn't have a damn clue who you are."

"He knows more than you do," she said, storming across to him. "He's right. I have lived here for two months. I've been safe. Looked after. Protected. Yeah, maybe it was you who told me how to get out, but it was the gang here who kept me from going insane... Do you know how scared I was being out here on my own? I was alone, Wreck. I had nothing."

"I told you what it would be."

"That I would never be myself again," she said on another nod. "I know."

"You took off."

"You wanted me to," she said, raising her arms. "You told me to run!"

He closed his eyes, but turned his head toward the light coming from behind her pale closed curtains. "You did right. You did what you had to."

The anger and frustration were gone from his words, but they did leave her wondering. Tulsi had been so sure of her feelings for him. She'd never doubted them. Even in this minute, it was no secret that he was more to her than she'd ever been to him. Except... he'd come all this way. He'd tracked her down.

Wreck wasn't exactly a big talker; he never had been. But this act. Showing up for her, to claim her, it revealed so much of what he felt for her.

Creeping closer, she took his hand from his side. "If we're going to do this... if we're going to be together..." He brought his gaze to hers, so she hazarded a small smile. "You've never had a woman..."

So many people had been eager to tell her how unusual she was in Wreck's life. Only now was Tulsi beginning to see what that would mean for their relationship.

"I've had plenty of women, Nympho."

"Sex," she said, keeping her eyes on his as she unbuckled his belt. "You've had sex with women... You've never had a relationship with one."

"Women make men weak," he said, his jaw tight.

It was possible that he resented falling for her. Loving her would give him a weakness. Hadn't she just told Dam that? Tulsi was weak for him, but trusted his strength. Wreck had fought against ever having responsibility for a woman. After what had happened to his sister, she understood that need.

He'd done the hard part by bringing them back together. Tulsi recognized that it was her job to keep them together. Wreck was no pro when it came to patience and compromise. She'd guide him as best she could and forgive him as, she knew, he'd often need her to.

FOUR

OVER THE COURSE of the next couple of days, there was a lot of sex and talking… More sex than talking… A lot more sex. Enjoying each other whenever they wanted was a novel freedom they both embraced. It didn't help that Wreck had nothing to do other than glare at people. Her friends at Fox Den were wary of him, so to keep the peace, Tulsi kept him out of their way as much as possible.

So much of her time was taken up with entertaining her lover that it became a mad dash to get her work done. Night on the second day had already crept in by the time she finished the last order.

The city was buzzing and the club was beginning to fill. Wreck had taken her bag from her bedroom stating that he was going to put it in the car. Tulsi hadn't even known that they had a car, though it made sense that he'd have acquired it some time. He'd disappeared for a few hours that afternoon, so she assumed that was when he got the vehicle. Though it was just as likely he'd had it all along; they hadn't been outside together.

Figuring it didn't make sense to ask questions, Tulsi let him take control and said she'd meet him outside. All that left her to do was say her goodbyes. Something that she hadn't been looking forward to.

The last couple of months had flown by. She hadn't appreciated just how close she'd gotten to the Fox Den gang until she had to leave them.

Most of the guys were upstairs and brief in their goodbyes. She went to Dam's bedroom, hoping to find him there. When Tulsi couldn't locate him anywhere upstairs, she descended to the lower floor hoping that he'd be in their common room.

At the bottom of the stairs, Tulsi was disappointed. Rook was there, sharpening his knives, as he so often was. He didn't look up, and yet somehow knew she was there. Not only that, but he sensed her mood too.

"Didn't really think he would stick around, did you?"

Rook was older than every other guy she'd met staying at Fox Den—by more than a decade. Still, she didn't ever underestimate his capabilities. The guy was no slouch. Even his age wasn't a disadvantage. Some of the other guys might be quicker or stronger, but Rook never feared them. He had more than enough wits and smarts to triumph over anyone who tried to take him on.

Tulsi would like to think that she wasn't as predictable as Rook's question implied. But she knew better than to question the man's intelligence.

"You know I was worried he'd split without saying goodbye to me," she said, wandering in Rook's direction. "I never thought I'd be leaving first."

Rook drew in a long breath and slid lower in his chair. "Dam's been good at what he does for a long time… Makes him forget what the fight is like."

Tulsi wasn't sure that she understood what that meant, but dropped into the low chair next to Rook's, holding the long woven strap of her purse in both hands.

"I'm grateful for everything he did for me," she said. "I wanted to tell him that myself… Maybe I should wait to—"

"The boy won't be coming back," he said. "Not for a while."

Did that mean Dam had left to head north? It was

possible that her departure just happened to coincide with his. But it was also possible he'd got the jump on her and scurried off to avoid saying goodbye.

"You think he'll forgive me?"

Rook stopped sharpening the blade to peer her way. "You'll never find out, will ya?" he asked and returned to his sharpening. "Don't matter anyway. Your new fella won't let your paths cross again."

"He's not like that," she said, almost tired of defending Wreck.

Her lover wasn't warm and fuzzy, but she'd never known the Fox Den gang to judge someone so fast or so permanently. It didn't seem to matter what she said. They wouldn't give him a chance, not even for a minute.

"A man sees the competition. He recognizes it."

"Competition? No one is in competition. It's just juvenile. One man doesn't like another wandering onto his territory. Dam didn't have to leave. Wreck and me will be out of town tonight… If he was so sure he never wanted to see us again, why didn't Dam stick around to say that?"

"Us," Rook said. "Dam doesn't want to see you as an us. That's the damn problem."

Trying to understand, she pressed her lips together and shook her head. Tulsi thought that she'd made headway. That she'd become somewhat more worldly over the last few months, since walking into Teal's. So much had happened that her views on several things had changed. There was no denying her general wariness level was higher since her ill-fated date with Kieran.

"I know that Dam doesn't want me to be hurt. And he doesn't know Wreck. He probably can't understand how I can be so sure about a person who just appeared from nowhere. But it wasn't like that. It isn't like that. Wreck and I… It's hard to explain. I knew from the second I saw him that there was something special about him. That he would be special to me."

"Mm hmm," Rook said like he understood, but also like he knew more than she did. The older man could be humoring her, but he wasn't known for sugar-coating anything. "Sometimes that's what it's like."

Suspicious, she narrowed her eyes on him. "Why do I feel like you're not really agreeing with me?"

"I am," he said. "You just gotta remember sometimes it's like that for other people too… Other people who might be looking at you."

Angling his chin her way, he made eye contact. It was obvious he was trying to tell her something. Maybe it was just the sleep she'd missed since Wreck had wandered back into her life, but she wasn't getting it at all.

Tulsi had never asked Wreck what he thought when he first saw her. But damn sure it was going to be a question she'd be putting to him as soon as she got the chance.

"We went through something together," she said. "Wreck and me… If it wasn't for that, we would never have got together… I never expected to see him again."

"That why you never told Dam about him?"

"I never told anyone about him."

And Tulsi had never intended to. Leaving Merchant had been a smart choice. After what she'd done to him, there was no way she'd have survived facing Baines and the others. Waiting for Wreck would've been suicide for both of them. If Wreck had been present when Baines went for her, he would have stepped in. The night they'd met, Wreck had shielded her. No reason to believe he wouldn't do the same now that they meant something to each other. Baines would've been mad enough to take them both down. She couldn't have done that to the man she loved. She wouldn't want to do it to anyone.

The choice to murder Merchant was hers. If there were ever consequences for that action, she'd take them. Tulsi only realized after the fact that by fleeing she'd saved Wreck and possibly Rowdy too. Taking away their chance to make a fatal choice to defend her meant they both survived. More than that, they'd obviously flourished.

Without Merchant navigating the pieces on the board, it was likely his crew had disbanded. Baines may have kept it together, but he didn't have the same gravitas as Merchant. Maybe Wreck and Rowdy had taken the opportunity to grab Kieran and split.

She'd tried to ask Wreck about what happened. About Rowdy. Seeing one without the other felt odd. It wasn't like she'd never been alone with Wreck before. Yet, she'd somehow expected to see the friend not that far behind her lover.

The conversation hadn't gone anywhere, but that was no shock. She'd made the mistake of asking while they were naked in bed together. Wreck never took long to ready himself for another round. It was impossible to inhibit his need for her while he embraced their freedom. He could have her any time he wanted her. No one was watching or setting out rules. There was no voice telling them no or issuing orders.

Tulsi couldn't be upset or mad with him having such a craving for her. During their initial ordeal, she'd doubted their chances of getting out alive on plenty of occasions. Yet, somehow, they had won their liberation and were together again. It was more than a dream come true. She couldn't apologize for her happiness. Not even to Dam.

Rising to her feet on an inhale, Tulsi wrapped the strap of her purse around both hands. "If you do see him again," she said. "Thank him for me."

"You could write him a note."

She shook her head. "He's made his feelings clear. If he wanted a speech, he should've stayed to say goodbye." Bowing over him, she kissed Rook's cheek. "Thank you for helping me out… I appreciate it."

As she stood up, he reached down the side of his chair to pull something out. "Don't forget what I taught you," he said, sliding the knife he'd been sharpening into the sheath he'd produced.

When he held it toward her, she blinked in surprise. "What's that?"

"Strap it to your ankle," he said. "Inside your boot."

Rook had taught her how important it was to secret weapons on her person. Given that it had been her job to equip people to do that, she couldn't disagree. Slipping off her boot, she raised her foot to the arm of his chair and attached the strap to her ankle before putting on her boot.

"Thank you," she said when both feet were on the floor again.

He nodded once. "Keep your head up."

Tulsi took comfort in the advice and shared a brief smile with him before heading out. The club was busy. The music loud. But she paid no attention to the revelers. Her life was becoming something new. What it would end up like, she had no idea, but as long as it was with Wreck, she'd be okay.

Once Tulsi got outside, she scanned the street, seeking her ride. In the shadows of the building opposite, she caught a glimpse of him. As he was hanging in the mouth of an alleyway, his build was more obvious than his features.

No doubt the darkness was comforting to him. It suited him. The shadows were his natural habitat.

Shirking her wounded feelings and bruised ego caused by Dam's disappearance, she tried to focus on the future. As she crossed the road, Tulsi put a bounce into her step and kept her attention on Wreck. It was only as she got closer and could better see him that she noticed he was talking on a cellphone. He'd been pacing, which she thought was odd enough. His stride wasn't hurried, but stressing wasn't typical of him. Wreck was laid back and ready for anything, anytime.

Tulsi had never seen him on a phone before either. Even since he'd showed up at Fox Den. He'd never used it in front of her or shown her that it existed. Maybe it was another recent procurement or it had come with the car.

When Wreck turned to pace in her direction again and detected she was there, he stopped walking. His lips moved, but she didn't catch any words. A second later, he hung up and stuffed the device in his pocket.

He came marching over and slung an arm around her shoulders.

"Who was that?" she asked. "Was it Rowdy? I would've talked to him."

"You got everything?" he asked, grabbing her purse as he gave her a push toward a sedan parked in the alley.

"Yeah."

"We're not coming back here."

That much was obvious even without him stating it.

He opened the back door to throw her purse inside and then climbed into the driver's seat.

"I've never seen you behind the wheel of a car," she said, putting on her seatbelt as he roared out of the alley.

He hadn't put on his own seatbelt. Wherever they were going, he was in a rush to get there. Or maybe he was just desperate to put distance between her and Fox Den.

Getting used to being with a man who didn't like talking would take some time. But Tulsi wasn't averse to making herself heard.

"You should be careful," she said, keeping her head lower than his chin when she reached all the way across the vehicle to get hold of his seatbelt.

"I'm driving."

"I know," she said, clicking his seatbelt into its slot. "That doesn't mean there aren't maniacs on the road… You did hear me tell Dam that I wanted to enjoy you for a while."

Still no response. He just focused his perpetual scowl on the road ahead. No matter that happy glittering colored lights flanked their route or that everyone outside was in a cheerful mood. Wreck still scowled.

"Where are we going?" she asked, figuring he'd have to answer a direct question. Apparently, that assumption was wrong. The question stayed in the air unanswered growing stale, hanging between them with a gathering mass. "Wreck, you can't ignore me forever. Are you mad about something? Is something wrong?"

He'd been fine before he disappeared that afternoon, but had been in a crappy mood ever since he'd come back. It was possible he didn't appreciate having to wait for her to finish her work before they began their new life.

But this was it. They were together with endless possibilities stretched out in front of them. He couldn't be mad that they were in this position. If he hadn't wanted to be with her, to make the effort with her, then he shouldn't have sought her out.

"No," he grumbled the syllable yet it looked like his grip on the steering wheel was tightening.

"Talk to me," she said, trying to soothe him.

Reaching across the center console, she rubbed his thigh. "I know it's going to take you a while to get used to this, to being in a relationship, but the only way we'll work is if we both try… You can't fuck it up." Her smile was meant to encourage him. "All you have to do is trust me."

He glanced at her, just for a split second, but at least it was something. "You're a good girl."

Curling her fingers, she pressed her nails into the denim of his jeans. "Wait 'til we stop tonight and I'll prove that's not true… Not completely anyway."

"You see the world as black and white."

His tone wasn't teasing. His scowl hadn't relaxed. Something lingered beneath his tough façade and it wasn't something she recognized. In the past, when they'd been together before, she'd been able to tell when he was aroused, when he was angry, when something was bothering him. Somehow, Tulsi suspected that what he was holding back was a combination of all three.

"I see us as black and white," she said, knowing that her views of morality were much more flexible than they'd been before meeting him. "I told you that I choose you. You can take that to the bank. I will always choose you. What we are is solid. I have faith in you. I trust you. This is unshakeable." He glanced at her again, so she smiled and gave him another squeeze. "I love you, Wreck… I know that it's not easy for you to say and I don't expect you to. What you've done… bringing us back together. That is how I know. How I know that we're going to make it… I don't underestimate what you did for us. You put us back together… Even though I don't know the details I—"

"Can we just drive?" he snapped. "Just put some miles on the rubber?"

In their relationship or literally on the road? Tulsi wasn't sure and it wasn't like him to snap at her. Settling back in her seat, she kept stealing glances his way. After a few minutes passed, she spoke again.

"Remember when I told you that looking at you made me feel safe," she murmured, wrapping her arms around herself. "I feel safe here, Wreck, but I don't feel secure… You were always honest with me. Always told me the truth. Whatever you're afraid of—"

"I'm not afraid of shit."

Tulsi couldn't believe that. Not when it seemed he was too on edge to look her in the eye. "Even on that first night, the way you talked to me, the way you looked at me… I didn't have to be confident that you wanted me. It felt so… natural. If you're afraid to want me the way you did then, why did you come for me?"

At least a mile went by before he responded. "You should sleep," he grumbled. "I'll wake you when we stop."

Maybe he would. If he didn't want to talk to her, Tulsi didn't put much faith in him waking her soon. He could drive for days if he had to.

She trusted him, she did. But then, more than ever, she got the sense he didn't trust her. The start of their new life wasn't shaping up to be plain-sailing. Though, where they were concerned, that shouldn't come as any surprise.

FIVE

THE SENSATION OF his curled fingers drifting down her cheek roused Tulsi from her sleep. Turning toward the caress, she smiled and kept her eyes closed. If it was a dream, she didn't want it to end.

"If I could bottle the way you make me feel, I'd be rich," she murmured.

The tip of his thumb touched her lips for just a breath before his mouth took its place. Waking up to his kiss made her feel like the richest woman in the world. Tulsi couldn't wait to get used to being awakened in this way every day.

The ferocity of his kiss grew until he scooped a hand around the side of her head to pull it up. With his other hand on her cheek too, he cradled her head, angling her so he could deepen the urgency of his kiss.

Tulsi pulled back. "Whoa," she said, blinking her eyes a few times to unfog her thoughts. "Someone has something on his mind."

With some effort, Tulsi managed to focus on what was beyond the windshield. Only a few of the exterior lights attached to the side of the low building worked. In spite of the crappy illumination, she quickly figured out it was a motel.

She laughed and flattened her skirt on her thighs. "We're so close to a bed," she said. "Guess you don't want to waste any time warming me up in there."

Leaping out of the car, it was only when she got onto the porch that Tulsi remembered her purse and bag were still in the vehicle. Wreck was out of the car, locking it up when she bounced back down to the concrete of the parking lot.

"I need to get my stuff."

"Later," he said, storming over to grab her hand. "Gotta get this over with."

"So romantic," she said, frowning his way.

If Wreck wasn't in the mood for sex, there was no need for him to force it. She couldn't think what she'd done that would make him feel like sex was a chore. His mood hadn't lifted since their sort of argument at the start of the journey. Sex was usually something they agreed on. If that was tainted, Tulsi wasn't sure what they'd have left.

Wreck pulled her onto the porch and marched past one door to open the next. Swinging her around, he thrust her inside.

In one jarring second, everything became clear. Her excitement about what lay ahead died in an instant. Cold, hard, disgusting fury clashed with the realization that she'd been betrayed.

There was no other explanation. The expressions on the faces of the two people already in the room revealed the truth. Wreck hadn't come for her because he loved her. She was his mission.

It didn't even occur to her to turn and exclaim they'd been found. Tulsi didn't think to call out to Wreck, to tell him to run or scream because they'd been tracked down.

The truth was obvious. From the initial shock, everything slowed down. Playing the last few days through her mind in a split second, clarity came to her like ice-water cascading down her spine. This was why Wreck had been distant. Why he hadn't wanted to talk or confess his love. Their future together was non-existent as far as he was concerned. That was why he didn't hint at it. He didn't come to her for love. He came to her for Baines.

Baines himself wasn't there, which might have been a positive. But Tulsi would've picked him over the man who was in fact present. He hated her more than almost anyone else. He'd had cause to despise her even before she'd murdered Merchant.

"Pretty, Pretty, Pretty…" Coombs said, strutting her way. "Ya didn't think it was gonna be that easy, did ya?"

Did she? Whatever she'd been through in the last few months hadn't been easy. Though it would be a cakewalk compared to the reckoning ahead.

Svana laughed. "I can't believe you really did it! Wreck, you are amazing!"

Coombs reached for Tulsi's face. She tried to jerk away from him, but that brought her up against the man at her back. Her betrayer. Gritting her teeth, she tolerated Coombs caress, only because it was the lesser of two evils.

She couldn't believe her naïveté. Tulsi never thought herself idealistic and didn't even consider herself much of a romantic. But she'd thrown herself into the reunion with Wreck like it was some sort of meant to be forever love.

Vomit threatened her throat. Her body fought against her urge to scream and throw up. What she really wanted to do was beat the shit out of everyone in the room. Including herself.

"Don't paw at her. Let her adjust," Svana said, sashaying across the room to nudge Coombs out of the way.

The blonde pushed out her lower lip in a pout that was probably supposed to suggest sympathy. Whether it was genuine or not—most probably not—Tulsi wouldn't be letting her guard down any time soon.

"I wanna see," Coombs said, crowding in behind Svana, his glee unrestrained.

Svana curled a finger around a loose section of Tulsi's hair. "I feel bad it had to be like this," she said, combing her fingers through the same section. "You were kind when we met. We're friends."

"Friends?" Tulsi said, thinking that couldn't be further from the truth. If Svana was in cahoots with someone like Coombs and running Baines' errands, she wasn't someone Tulsi wanted as a buddy. "What the hell is going on? What do you want?"

Svana blinked in surprise and her gaze shifted to the man standing behind Tulsi. "You didn't tell her?"

"Tell her what?" Wreck growled from behind her back. "I don't have a damn clue what he wants from her."

An incredulous laugh sputtered from behind Svana's lips. "You have no imagination, Wreck, baby."

Keeping her nausea at bay was an ongoing struggle for Tulsi. Hearing anything from the man who'd deceived her or the woman with more faces than outfits didn't settle her stomach.

"You can't make me stay here," Tulsi said, hoping she'd be able to get past Wreck.

Again, her assumption was proved wrong. Coombs made a tutting sound and produced something from his rear jeans pocket. The moment Tulsi registered what the narrow black plastic was, her nausea curdled.

Gritting her teeth, Tulsi settled her rage on Coombs. "I will not let you touch me."

"I don't have to," Coombs said, surprising her when he held the zip-ties out to the man behind her.

"What the hell is…"

Wreck took the ties from Coombs and grabbed her hand from her side. Tulsi tried to pull away, she tried to struggle, but it was pointless. Even in the times he'd used his strength against her to arouse her, Tulsi hadn't been naïve to his capability. Wreck's ability to overpower her had never been in doubt. Yet, he was reinforcing his superiority and pissing her off at the same time.

Svana and Coombs moved out of the way as Wreck forced her across the room to the space between the two double beds.

"You're a fucking bastard," Tulsi hissed at him when he whipped her around to face him. The prick wasn't even looking at her. He kept his focus on the zip-ties as he fastened them around each of her wrists. "Enjoy it, did you? Every fucking second you spent inside me knowing you were working for them." He tugged her hard, jerking her hands toward a thick metal bar that held the lamps to the wall. "God, I should've listened to Dam…" She closed her eyes, marinating her disgust in anger. "He was right. We don't know each other at all. We're nothing… Fuck, you always said this ain't real." Her venom enhanced her revulsion. "You should've just snapped my neck. Got it over with. Did the sex not at least earn me that?" Nothing. He didn't react at all. "You're going to hell, you fuck."

His gaze rose to hers. Whatever Tulsi thought she read, she dismissed. Wreck was a cold, calculating brute, for sale to the highest bidder. Death didn't scare her as much as what could come before it. But she would never say that aloud. Tulsi would never let herself beg for mercy… She wouldn't give them the satisfaction and wasn't sure she'd ever trust anyone enough to reveal any truth of herself again.

"Hey, now, don't leave us out of the fun," Svana said, sidling up behind Wreck to slide her fingertips up his arm. Peeking around him, the blonde smiled. "We'll treat you good, Tulsi. You don't have to worry."

Coombs snickered. "Treat her good, 'til the boss gets hold of her."

The boss? Baines had to want her strung up. Memories of the broken Alexis returned to Tulsi's mind. The murder she'd witnessed hadn't risen in her mind for a long while. By all accounts, Alexis was a favorite of Keaton, one of Merchant's competitors. If Keaton was anything like Merchant, Alexis must have been used to a violent and erratic life of subjugation. Despite enduring such a horrific existence, Baines had pushed the poor woman beyond her limit. By the time the thug put a bullet in her head, Alexis had been truly traumatized and defeated.

"Weren't you going somewhere?" Svana called back to Coombs, still stroking Wreck's arm. "I'm hungry."

"You want me to leave you alone with these two?"

"I don't need protection," Svana said. "Get outta here."

Tulsi couldn't see Coombs as he left the motel room, though she did hear his muttering. The moment he was gone, Wreck turned to stalk away from both women. Svana came in closer to cup Tulsi's face.

Tulsi pulled away, but the woman persisted. "Get

your hands off me."

"I don't know why you're mad at me," Svana said. "I didn't abandon you."

Sneering at the blonde, Tulsi wondered what Svana's statement implied. "You think I abandoned you?"

Svana shrugged. "You did say I could get out, didn't you?"

"I was a prisoner, just like you," Tulsi said. "I didn't have a damn clue where you were. I didn't even know if he'd let you live. I asked about you, I tried to see you—"

"You gave up on me," Svana said. "The minute he started to treat you good—"

"Good?" Tulsi spat, growling as she got into Svana's face. "He put his hands on me. He pushed me down on that goddamn desk and swore to have me."

"You should've let him have you."

"Why?" Tulsi asked. "Because that's what you do? You let men take anything they want from you just because you want an easy life? I would rather die than let any man touch me against my will."

"That's immature. You let them take so they feel superior, so they feel in control. Men need control. But we're the ones who have it. We are what they want."

The flawed logic left Tulsi incredulous. "If we have no power to say no then we have no power. If they take whenever they want, without consent or apology, they do have control. You give them your power."

Svana scoffed. "You're the one in cuffs, honey." She held up both hands. "I'm free."

Tulsi bobbed her chin in the direction of the door. "Then walk out. Go on. Walk out of here." Some of Svana's smugness faded. "Yeah, you won't go anywhere. You tried that once and he brought you back. He put that leash back on and you're back to where you started. Worse off probably; Merchant at least had some affection for you. According to you anyway. What does Baines do to you? What does he make you do?"

"Baines?" Svana said, breathing out a sound that was half-laugh, half-disbelief. Her conceit vanished to what could only be described as compassion, though the expression only lasted a second or two. "You think you killed him, don't you? You think he's dead."

"Stop," Wreck said somewhere in the background.

Neither woman paid him any attention. Svana might be unreliable, maybe even cruel, but she was the first person to give Tulsi the truth. It was a horrifying one, but it was a truth that she hadn't even considered.

"Oh my God," Tulsi whispered. "Merchant is alive."

Svana nodded. Just a subtle gesture, but enough to confirm it. "He's recovering, it hasn't been easy on him... Baines is at his side twenty-four, seven."

"Nilsson," Wreck barked.

The blonde twirled around, pasting on a smile and strutting away. Tulsi searched the carpet. It was unbelievable. She'd stabbed him and knocked him out. There was blood. So much blood. There had been blood everywhere and...

"He's alive," she whispered.

If anything, facing Merchant was a more horrifying prospect than standing in front of Baines. For one thing, the threat had just doubled. She would have both of them to deal with. Each would have their own reasons for despising her. Both would no doubt have their own unique brand of sadism to practice.

Because she assumed that Merchant was taken care of, Baines had been the only one she'd feared. Finding out that Ilias wasn't dead, more than that he was still in charge, it changed everything. Everything that she had thought about his men disbanding, about the operation falling apart, it was wrong. Everything was wrong.

SIX

SVANA'S IRRITATING LAUGH encroached on Tulsi's reverie. As much as she wanted to re-order her thoughts to figure out what might be waiting for her at the other end of this journey, she couldn't help but watch the beautiful blonde slithering up to the man Tulsi had once considered her safety.

Ironic. While watching Svana rub herself against Wreck, Tulsi accepted how wrong she'd been about that man too. Wreck wasn't her great love. He wasn't even her friend. Like a wolf creeping into the flock, he had entered her home in the guise of a man she'd once known. The sad thing was, he hadn't even bothered adopting a disguise. Tulsi had known that he was a wolf, capable of being ruthless, vicious even. Whatever he'd put Putnam through was a testament to that.

Remembering how he'd screwed her against the bathroom door before walking out to take Putman apart, Tulsi wondered how she had managed to miss the truth of him. Wreck hadn't even lied to her. While they'd been together, he'd told her that she was nothing to him. He'd told her they weren't real. That they didn't have a relationship; that she was a distraction.

"Forget morals and boundaries," she murmured to herself, watching Svana tiptoe backward while unzipping her dress.

The blonde had a figure most women would kill for. Like the models in the magazines and the centerfold stars, Svana was a wet dream come to life. Feeling almost removed from the moment, from the world, Tulsi observed the slant of the seductive woman's eyes, and the glisten on her pouting lips.

Svana was superior to her in many ways. She obviously had the trust of Merchant and Baines. That much was obvious by the freedom she'd been granted. The woman was probably only there as a distraction. Whatever her purpose, Svana didn't face the same fate that Tulsi did.

But in one way, Tulsi was superior to Svana. Even if Svana and Wreck had been intimate a thousand times, there was one thing the pert blonde seemed to have missed.

A laugh warmed her lips. "You have to be more aggressive," Tulsi called across the room, looking only at Svana. "Don't be subtle and flirty, he responds to direct… to a woman who doesn't need permission."

Somewhere along the way, some part of their intimacy had to be real. Sure, Wreck had never held any feelings for her. Not above the belt anyway. But his cock hadn't lied to her. No way. Maybe it had lied in the last couple of days, maybe he was faking that he was interested in having sex with her to get her compliance. Screwing her had been a great way to avoid answering her questions. But his dick hadn't been lying in that hotel bathroom all those months ago.

"No permission…" Svana said, unhooking her bra. As it dropped to the floor, Svana took Wreck's wrist in her grip. He tugged it back, which made the blonde giggle. "You need me to be in control? I can do that."

Svana reached for Wreck's belt, but he jerked away before her hand could make contact.

"Aww, honey," Tulsi said. "You know he doesn't like to be touched, right? You gotta do better than that… Got any more of those zip-ties?"

Wreck glared her way, Tulsi just bobbed her amused brows.

"You can have both of us," Svana said.

"Cut it out," Wreck snarled, storming away to drop into the chair at the end of the bed.

"We have time to play," Svana said with a pronounced sway in her hips as she approached Wreck again.

Wreck didn't even look at the woman. The last thing Tulsi wanted to witness was Wreck being intimate with anyone else. Still, there was something amusing about Svana's seduction. Raising a leg, the blonde draped herself across Wreck's thighs, sinking down in his lap to rock against his hips.

"Bite him," Tulsi said. "He likes that."

Svana exhaled a sound of arousal and ran her hands into his hair, trying to tempt his head back, presumably so she could go in for a kiss. The ferocity with which Wreck grabbed her wrists to thrust her away surprised both women.

"Touch me again and I'll rip your skull from its skin," he growled and threw Svana to the floor.

The woman hit hard. Tulsi's mouth opened, not to speak, she just hadn't expected Wreck to be so rough with the youngster. Turned out she didn't know much of anything about the man she'd shared her body with.

Wreck kept glaring down at the almost nude woman on the floor. When Svana got to her knees, he offered no support or help while she clambered to her feet.

"You know what will happen when I tell Merch what you just did?" Svana spat his way, stomping over to her discarded clothes.

"Call him," Wreck snapped, grabbing a phone from his pocket to throw it across the room at the blonde. "Do me a fucking favor. Call the fucker."

Svana jumped out of the way of the device. "I'll wait. Give you some time to come to your senses," she said, tossing a glance Tulsi's way while fastening her bra. "Coombs will want to have her… he will…"

"Won't happen," Wreck said.

Tulsi wasn't sure that she liked being discussed while in the room, but it did give her a chance to learn some more.

Svana gritted her teeth and let out a frustrated screech. "He shares me with any damn man he wants, why is she so different?"

There was more than a little resentment in that question. Made sense because Svana was right. Tulsi hadn't been shared among the men who worked for Merchant. She hadn't been asked to have sex with them. Svana had.

"I still have my power," Tulsi said. "You gave yours away."

The blonde glared. For that comment, Tulsi deserved the blonde's malice. True though it was, Svana was so young and had lived such a horrible life that she hadn't learned self-respect or pride. Her mother hadn't taught her those lessons. Neither had the men who used her for her body over and over again. Even in spite of Svana's superior position in this situation, Tulsi still felt pity for her. She would endure humiliation and subjugation, even eventual death, rather than submit willingly to men like Merchant and Baines.

"None of this would be happening if you had just been smart," Svana said, swiping her dress from the floor. "You did this to yourself, Tulsi Tern."

"I had a little help," Tulsi said, looking at Wreck who stood with his back to her at the end of the bed.

"Your precious Wreck turned out not to be so perfect after all," Svana said, walking closer. "You didn't tell me you were sleeping with him."

"Why would I?" Tulsi asked. "Wasn't your business."

"Yes, it was! I told you things… I said things about him—"

"I didn't lie to you."

Tulsi remembered the moments she'd spent with Svana in the hotel where they'd met and the motel afterwards. For a time, the blonde had considered Wreck might be working both sides. Wasn't a leap given what he'd done over the last couple of days. He *had* been working both sides. It just so happened he wasn't working to her advantage.

"You did! You did lie to me!"

"Okay," Tulsi said, leaning back as the bitter Svana bore down on her. "So I didn't tell you that I'd fucked him when you were admiring his cock. You should've figured it out when he put his boot into the skull of that fucker in the back of the van. Really?" She squinted. "You didn't figure it out then? Guess the blonde seeped through to your brain."

"Doesn't matter now, does it?" Svana said, folding her arms, the dress still hanging from one hand. "He's not sticking up for you now, is he?"

"No," Tulsi said, accepting that truth stung more than anything Svana could give to her. "Like you said, that's on me. I never should've trusted him."

Svana's smile twisted in triumph. "Guess you're not so smart."

"Never claimed to be smart," Tulsi said. "Turns out my gut is not so reliable when it comes to men…"

"You know what they'll do to you," Svana said, opening up her dress to step into the fabric. "When we take you back to Merchant… he has plans for you. He's had a lot of time to consider how he can punish you."

"Punish me? What about his punishment? Who's gonna punish him?"

"You stabbed him!" Svana said in a squawk of disbelief. "You put his own dagger through him and knocked him out!"

Hearing it repeated made Tulsi smile. "Yes, I did. And if I get the chance, I'll do it again."

Svana shook her head. "You will never get the chance to hurt him again."

"Don't put money on that," Tulsi said, hitching her chin.

Svana scoffed. "How would you hurt him if he chains you to the wall? You can't. He won't let you."

"Then he learned his lesson," Tulsi said, ignoring Wreck who crossed to the phone he'd thrown at Svana to pick it up. "If he dares to put his hands on me, I will kick and scream and struggle until my last breath. Anything he puts near my mouth will feel my teeth ripping through it… I will not submit to him. To anyone."

Shaking her head, Svana zipped her dress and folded her arms again. "You are so naïve."

"I was," Tulsi admitted, nodding her head. "But I get it now."

"It?"

"Last time I was concerned about others. I made decisions based on the collective. I made assumptions. Now I have proof, truth, that the only ass I have to save is mine. And if I have to burn down the whole damn building with me and everyone else in it, that's what I'll do."

It seemed that Svana didn't believe her from the way her brows rose. "You'd kill yourself?"

"Give me my hands and I'll prove it," Tulsi said, doing her best to point a finger the blonde's way. "But I warn you. I won't go first and I won't go alone."

The confidence in Svana's expression faltered. "You would kill me?"

"I would kill anyone who got in my way… You think you're so smart, Svana, but there's a lesson you haven't learned."

"What?" Svana asked, shaking her head to make her hair trail down her back.

Obviously, she was trying to regain some composure. Tulsi wasn't sorry that she'd unsettled the woman.

"The only victory is the one you take for yourself. No one gives it to you. To win, you have to take care of you and only you," Tulsi snarled. "Fuck every other soul on the planet. You have to be vicious. Play both sides. Do what you have to do. Whatever you have to do. Forget morals and boundaries. Know your goal. Have one and achieve it no matter the cost."

The blonde laughed and exhaled. "You're crazy."

Maybe she was. As Svana turned to walk away, Tulsi noticed Wreck's chin move in her direction. The subtle move was followed by him turning just enough to see her. Although she didn't exactly want to look into his intense eyes, she wasn't going to give him the satisfaction of shying away.

Her gut told her to scream at him. To swear and curse him to hell. He could have come to retrieve her without having sex with her. Wreck chose to be intimate with her, probably as the cherry on his sick, sadistic cake. He knew they'd be coming here. What he planned to do. All along Wreck had been planning to take her back to Merchant.

Why had he slept with her? As another way to

humiliate her or was it more basic than that? He had an itch and she hadn't hesitated to scratch it for him. It could be that he got his kicks from betraying her. Maybe it was some kind of sick, twisted fetish to draw a woman in, gain their trust, and then abandon them. Not just abandon them, but throw their blind trust back at them.

She had been blind. So blind. In a return to her self-loathing, Tulsi cringed at how she'd thrown herself against him, how quickly she'd dragged him up to bed, how she'd dismissed Dam's concern. Tulsi was almost sure that she'd laughed at Dam when he voiced reservations. If she hadn't laughed outwardly, she sure had been in her head.

Dam warned her to be careful and she'd flat told him that she didn't have to be. Her eyes closed again. What she wouldn't give to be back at the Fox Den. But, if nothing else, at least this had taught her that the mooning and pining had been inappropriate. Wreck wasn't a great love that she'd abandoned. He was a man who'd been waiting for a chance to betray her. He was smart to run the mission as a marathon. He got some sex and still got to betray her at the moment that was most profitable to him.

If he wasn't leading her to her death, Tulsi might acknowledge his skill. As it stood, she wasn't feeling magnanimous enough to be impressed.

The motel door opened and Coombs came inside carrying a bunch of food bags. Tulsi didn't expect to be fed, though the drifting scent did awaken her hunger. That was just something she'd have to get used to.

"Chow time!" Coombs declared, taking the food over to the TV unit.

Svana went over to join him and they began to hand out the food.

With her hands on the bar of the lamp, it was difficult to turn all the way toward the room. Still, Tulsi didn't want to twist in the awkward position all night. Keeping her hands up, she sat on the nightstand between the beds and slid as far back as she could to reduce the strain on her arms.

Svana took food to Wreck and went back to retrieve her own. From the corner of her eye, Tulsi noticed Wreck raising the box a fraction. Was he looking at her? Was he really offering her food?

"Fuck you," she sneered, without caring that Svana and Coombs looked over.

"What's she been saying?" Coombs asked, coming toward her while scooping some rice into his mouth.

If he thought he was taunting her with food, he underestimated how much she hated him and his boss.

"She's been saying you're going to rot in hell," Tulsi said. "She's been saying that you are a cretin who deserves a long, slow, painful death. You and your associates… This is sick."

Coombs smiled. "Pretty, you don't even know what that word means yet. Merch is gonna shit himself when he hears what we've done."

"We?" Tulsi asked. "You did nothing. As fucking usual. You just traipse around following orders. You're no one."

"Proud of your boyfriend for fucking you over?" Coombs asked, just as cocky as she remembered him.

"Proud of myself for putting a knife in your boss. I don't give a damn about any of you."

"We don't give a damn about you," Coombs said. "'Cept we've got bets on how long it'll take you to break."

Tulsi didn't doubt that he and his cronies were exactly that sick. That Wreck was included in that group would take some getting used to. Despite how he'd hoodwinked her, she still acknowledged that Wreck was on a different professional plane from Coombs. The latter was just a sniveling goon, only capable of doing what he was told. Wreck had been so good that even while telling her the truth that he had no regard for her, she still convinced herself that he did. It was a great act.

"Sure you do," she said. "Gonna let me in on the action?"

"You got nothing I want."

"Aww," she said as he turned to walk away. "I had something your buddy Hillam wanted."

Coombs stopped walking. Tulsi had no reason to keep Wreck's confidence anymore. Except it was in her interest for people to think that she had the ability to do whatever was necessary to protect herself. That was the only reason she was keeping the secret. If it turned out to be advantageous to drop the bombshell later, she would. It might not be such a bad thing to tell Merchant the truth. That could lead to Wreck having to answer a few questions of his own.

Slowly, Coombs turned around. The hatred in his glare encouraged her. Yes, she silently said the word in her mind, coaxing him on, eager to provoke him beyond the limit of his control.

For good measure, she showed him a proud smile. "He was drunk, you know," Tulsi said. "Slobbering, disgusting prick got himself hot watching twisted porn… Real depraved shit no real man would watch… He asked me to suck him off, asked me to fuck him. I laughed in his face." Coombs showed his teeth and began to creep her way. "The bastard couldn't even walk straight. It was sad really. The sick fuck only got as far as he did because he knocked me out. Probably by mistake. Doubt he could even get it up. He was pathetic. Pitiful. Killing him was sport. I could've just waited for him to pass out. But I enjoyed it… I enjoyed seeing him die. Enjoyed how his warm blood spilled over me."

Coombs gave her exactly what she wanted when he smacked her in the face. Tulsi smiled as she turned her head back to stare into his hatred. Witnessing how much he loathed her gave her a real opening. If it was a choice between this and going back to Merchant's torture, she'd take the first. Coombs wouldn't be difficult to trigger and if he killed her, he'd actually be doing her a massive favor.

"You bitch."

"Bitch who took your tragic friend's life from him," she said, leaning in to get closer to his face. "I'd have sliced his dick off and made him eat it if your boss hadn't walked in when he did. Hillam was worthless. Useless. Idiot wouldn't have known how to pleasure a woman if his life depended on it. Clumsy fool was asking to be put out his misery. I did him and the damn world a favor."

Coombs lunged forward, dropping his food to grab her neck in both hands. As he squeezed and the pain of his grip became crushing, Tulsi got a rush of desperate relief. Her body wanted to fight to live; her mind wanted freedom from what lay ahead.

The possibility of freedom vanished when Wreck got hold of Coombs and dragged him off her. Wreck swung around to throw the fucker onto the floor, putting himself between her and the others.

"Touch her again and I'll finish you myself," Wreck snarled down at the man Tulsi couldn't see much of.

"You forgotten what's at stake?" Svana snapped.

Wreck thrust a hand Coombs way. "He was not part of the deal. He touches her again and I'll do what I have to. Merch wants her in one piece."

Svana exhaled and sank into the chair. "Long as that's all it is… He won't want to hear you're playing favorites… I'd hate to have to tell him that you're not onboard like we thought."

"I'm onboard," Wreck growled. "Would I have brought her here if I wasn't?"

Svana shrugged. "Don't forget your loyalties."

Whatever that meant, Wreck accepted it and walked away, stepping over Coombs on the way.

Tulsi was in a mess. In something that wasn't going to be over soon. She had to be careful. Provoking Coombs was a good idea—she'd just have to ensure there were fewer witnesses the next time she made an attempt at freedom.

SEVEN

COOMBS WASN'T RELUCTANT. After food, Coombs produced liquor from another bag and began to drink with Svana. It didn't take long for the laughing pair to become amorous. Listening to them making out was repulsive; Tulsi had turned her back on that. Hearing them fuck was enough to make her retch. She couldn't imagine how any woman could give herself to someone like Coombs. Not that Svana was much of a prize when she was drunk. Emotional outbursts, slurring and falling over weren't top turn ons.

It didn't sound like Svana even made it through the first round. After some moaning and squealing, Svana went quiet while Coombs continued to rut over her. As if that spectacle wasn't bad enough, keeping her back to Coombs and Svana meant the only place Tulsi could look was at the other bed.

The light in the room was out, no one had ever bothered to put it on. But there was light from outside, enough that she could see Wreck when he lay down, locking his fingers behind his head. He closed his eyes. Tulsi envied how he could so easily shut out the noise of the couple screwing just inches away from both of them.

Once the lascivious sounds died, they were quickly

replaced by Coombs' snoring. Seemed everyone was at ease enough to sleep. Everyone except her. Tulsi wouldn't be able to sleep even if she wanted to. Lucky that she didn't want to.

Sitting on the nightstand again, she folded her legs in front of her and counted slowly, giving the others in the room time to fall asleep. Without thinking too much about her plan, which could lead to her chickening out, Tulsi slid a hand into her boot. Moving her lips, keeping the rhythm of her silent counting, she was careful to be quiet while pulling Rook's blade from its sheath.

Still counting, she inverted the weapon in her palm, so it pointed at her. After that the task was easy. Slipping it under the plastic on her wrist, she ignored how the tip dug into her forearm causing a little bead of blood to form. Rook always kept his weapons sharpened to perfection, but she adjusted the angle and kept on going.

Just a few seconds later, the blade cut through the plastic. Refraining from shouting out her delight, Tulsi scanned the room to ensure everyone was still asleep. With one hand free, it was easy to cut through the second tie.

With the knife still in her hand, Tulsi slipped off the nightstand. In almost complete silence, she set the door in her sights and started toward it. There was nothing there for her. Nothing to hang around for. Turning the handle, she closed her eyes in relief when it opened. Tiptoeing out, she glanced back only once. One last look.

Wreck was still asleep. They were parting and this time it was on purpose. He wasn't the man she thought he was. Her tainted memories weren't reliable. Yet, some part of her wanted to say goodbye, so she allowed herself that final look.

Closing the door on her farewell, Tulsi wasted no time in turning to stride down the walkway. She didn't know where she was going, but had to put distance between herself and anyone associated with Merchant.

If only she knew where Dam was. Finding him would be difficult… and probably reckless. As her relationship with Wreck proved, she wasn't a great judge of character or others intentions. In fact, she downright sucked at it.

Going down the stairs at the end of the walkway, she glanced up and down the road ahead. Catching sight of a line of what appeared to be vehicle lights in the distance, she figured that was the highway and her easiest route for escape. It was dark, so she couldn't see the whole way, but it couldn't be more than a mile or two.

"You'll freeze."

The sound of his deep voice made her spin around. Wreck was there, just a couple of feet away at the top of the stairs she'd just descended. He'd been asleep. She was sure… but obviously not. Again, her ability to judge anything about him turned out to be terrible.

He tossed something her way. Although Tulsi caught it, she didn't know what it was until opening her palm to look.

"Car keys," she whispered and turned her frown up to him. "What are you doing? What is this? A trap?"

He shrugged. "If that's what you think."

"Why let me walk out if you knew I was going?"

"Don't go south, they'll expect that. Go west. Avoid Vegas. Avoid any big cities for a while."

Shaking her head, she exhaled her disbelief. "Yeah, like I'm going to do whatever you say."

He'd been the one to advise her on how to disappear the last time. Following his advice gave him an advantage in tracking her down.

"There's a gun in the glovebox. It's loaded," he said, ignoring her contempt. "I already put cash in your bag, it's still in the trunk."

Now Tulsi had no idea what to do. It had to be some kind of trap. Either she took the car and they tracked her or she didn't take it and walked out to the highway, which would give Wreck enough time to rouse the others and capture her again. No doubt they'd be thorough about searching her for weapons this time. They hadn't bothered before, but probably assumed Wreck had cleared her… somehow.

"You're fucking with me," she said. "You wouldn't bring me here and then let me go… What's your plan? Shoot me as I walk away?"

"I don't need a weapon to kill you," he said, plain as

day. "If I wanted you dead, you'd be dead."

"Am I supposed to thank you, is that it? Believe that this is some insane change of heart, that suddenly you're so sorry for leading me back to them?"

"My heart doesn't matter and I'm not sorry."

"No, course not," she said, tossing the keys up and catching them in her palm again. "I'll dump the car by the highway. I won't let you track me beyond that."

And as soon as she could, she'd turnaround from whichever direction she headed in first. Switching up rides as often as possible, Tulsi would get herself completely lost, which should help prevent anyone from following her… quickly anyway.

Going back up the steps, Tulsi walked back the way she'd come, checking out the cars, trying to remember which one Wreck had brought her in.

"They have Rowdy." The statement made her slow to a stop. "I didn't fuck you over for fun."

He'd fucked her over because Merchant pulled the same play he'd used to keep them all in check the last time.

"What did they do to him?"

"See for yourself."

Turning around, she didn't expect him to be holding a phone toward her, but he was. A phone not unlike one Merchant had handed to her once. Walking over, she took the phone and touched the screen. It lit up to show a cell like the one she'd met Styx in.

Except instead of seeing a man on the floor or in a chair, she saw one chained to the wall with his arms stretched over his head. She was just able to make out through the blood and bruises that the man was Rowdy. His hair was longer than when she'd last seen him and he only wore a pair of grubby jeans, but it was him, no doubt.

"Oh my God," she whispered, seeing how her actions had caused an innocent man to suffer. "Blood for blood."

Just like Rowdy had told her Merchant operated. Closing her eyes, she thrust the phone back toward Wreck and he took it. That scene was too much. Tulsi had no idea what to make of it. Was it real? A setup? She didn't know. Though, it did make sense that Merchant wanted someone to pay for what she'd done. He was the kind of man who had to lash out at someone.

"Baines put all of us in cells. For weeks. We didn't have a fucking clue what happened… Later we were hauled into Merchant's office. He asked questions… questions about you."

About where she'd go or where he'd find her? Tulsi was beyond trying to figure out what was in Merchant's mind, though it was obvious he wasn't going to let her crime go unpunished. Baines had told her once that Merchant never forgot.

"He wasn't happy. Told us we'd face a firing squad… He put one in Kieran and was about to put one in Rowdy, so I told him I'd find you… I bought time. I'm not sorry. I did what I had to do."

Time. He'd given Merchant a last hope. A chance. While Merchant kept Rowdy as insurance, he sent Wreck out on the road to track her down. So she was his ticket to freedom. His ticket to saving his friend. Except…

Looking at the keys in her hand, she frowned. "Why give me these? If everything you've said is true, you don't take me back to him, he'll kill Rowdy… he'll kill you too."

He shrugged again. "He'll kill us anyway… After he does, you'll be alone with him."

"You'll be dead, you won't care."

Not that she assumed he'd care in the first place.

"I'll be dead. Rowdy will be dead. He doesn't get to have you too." Her attention ascended to his, but she just couldn't figure him out. "I had to get to you, to tell you he was looking. You're not safe so long as you're in the country… You have to find a way to get out. Don't go back to anywhere you've been."

Establishing herself in Fox Den had been difficult enough. Tulsi didn't relish the idea of starting a new life as a nobody without a history. She didn't have the first clue how to get out of the country without a passport… and wasn't sure she had the courage to travel on a false one.

Wreck spoke again. "I know a guy, Otis—"

"No," she whispered.

"He can get you a passport and—"

"No," Tulsi said again and took a step toward him, her determination burning from her. "Tell me why I should believe you. Why I should trust you ever again? You could've told me all of this at Fox Den. You didn't have to bring me here to them."

"We had a chance, a slim one that Styx could work something out for you. If I got back to Rowdy in time, I might have been able to… Doesn't matter. You're not safe here."

"And Rowdy?" she asked. "If what you showed me is real, Merchant will kill him, probably as soon as he hears I left." Wreck's lips narrowed, but he nodded in resigned agreement and lowered his attention. "You won't even have a chance to say goodbye. A chance to tell him what happened."

"Rowdy knows," Wreck said. "He'll know what happened. Won't matter if I'm there to say squat. Dead is dead."

But for a man who lived with the guilt of his sister's death weighing on him every day, Wreck would be ruined by carrying the responsibility of his best friend's murder too.

"He'll think you failed," she said. "That you couldn't find me."

"If I didn't find you, Merchant would still have hope," he said. "He wouldn't kill Rowdy. He'd lose his only way to control me."

Because even if Kieran was still alive, Wreck wouldn't have any reason to risk himself for the man who meant nothing to him. The man who'd gotten them all into this mess. While Rowdy was alive, he had his friend to answer to. Without him, Wreck would have no one to support him. In many ways, Rowdy was Wreck's guide through life. Without him, Wreck would have no one to be his conscience, no one to slap him into line when he needed to be told what was what.

"If all you're going back for is to die," she said. "Why go back? Why not leave right now?"

With her? Was that what she was saying? Was she asking him to run away with her?

He shook his head and slipped his hands into his

pockets. "Rowdy won't die because I failed. Rowdy will die because I made a choice… It's one I have to own."

He chose her. Shock made her mouth open. While she let that reality sink in, Tulsi tried to decide what it meant and why what he'd said was an answer to her question.

"You want to die," she murmured. "You *want* Merchant to kill you."

"I don't want to die," he snarled, glancing toward the motel room door that was further down the walkway. "I don't want Rowdy to die either. But it's what's gonna happen."

"Because you're letting me go," she said, looking at the keys again. "That's what you're doing. You're going back to face Merchant without me, knowing that he'll kill you because—"

"Maybe I finish what you started."

What she'd started? There was so much anger in Wreck. She understood why. Rowdy once told Kieran that Wreck didn't like to be blindsided. Even though he'd seen this train wreck coming, he'd been unable to avoid it. Wreck was not the type of man who enjoyed being helpless.

"You want Rowdy to know that you'll follow," she said. "Merchant will tell Rowdy his plans to murder you before he kills him."

"Maybe… I won't abandon Rowdy, no matter what that means for me."

"It means death," she said, stating the harsh truth. "Even if you do manage to kill Merchant, Baines won't let you walk away."

"I'll take down as many of them as I can," Wreck said, meeting her eye. "That way there'll be less of them to follow you."

Her. He was sacrificing himself and his best friend for her. It was more than she could comprehend.

"Is this a trick? Are you lying to me for—"

"What? Sympathy? Fuck your pity," he asked and snorted. "If I wanted you back at Merchant's, I'd toss you in the car and take you there. You know that, Nymph. You know I'm stronger than you."

Yes, she did. She knew that if he wanted to

overpower her, if he wanted to hogtie her or pin her down, he could. Tulsi had a knife in her boot. Even if she got to it, he'd be skilled enough to take her down.

"Make me understand," she said, narrowing the space between them by another step.

He shook his head. "I can't. It's not in me to explain it."

"That's not good enough, damnit," she said, growing frustrated. "You've known Rowdy most of your life. You two are strong. Your loyalty to him wouldn't be broken for anything. Not for anything. Why wouldn't you sacrifice me if it meant freeing him? You think Merchant will kill you both, but you don't know that. Not for sure. He could stick to his word. You take me back to him and maybe he'll let Rowdy live. You don't take me back and he will kill your best friend for sure." Wreck tried to turn away, but she caught his arm to stop him getting too far. "Your best friend. Rowdy is your best friend. He's your family. The only love your sister ever knew beyond you."

"Don't you think I fucking know that?" he hissed, tossing her grip away from his arm. "Don't you think this is tearing me apart?" He backed away from her, rage contorted his face. "How the fuck do I choose? Maybe one of you will live. *Maybe*. And the choice is mine? Only fucking mine. My best friend or the only woman I ever loved? How the fuck does a guy figure that shit out?"

The only woman... Tulsi couldn't breathe. For a second, she forgot everything and just focused on those words. Love? Wreck loved her... She tried not to let herself believe it. The bastard had led her to Coombs and Svana, he'd planned to take her back to Merchant... He'd betrayed her.

EIGHT

NOTHING MADE SENSE.

Even when Tulsi told herself that he was full of shit and just toying with her, she couldn't figure out his motivation. Wreck had always been a straight shooter. Always. He told it like it was. She couldn't figure out why he'd choose that moment to start lying.

He was handing her keys to a vehicle, telling her how she could arm herself, and funding her escape. In spite of the knowledge that aiding her would guarantee his and Rowdy's deaths, he was sending her away.

"Say it," she said, entitled in the way she closed the space between them again.

Meeting his eye, she kept her determination fierce despite the conflict ripping through him.

"Tuls—"

"Say that you need my help."

His blink of surprise cleared the signs of his inner battle. "What?"

"I don't know if anything you've said is true or not. And I will not fall for some eleventh hour claim of love. No way. The words are too easy to say." She took a deep breath and pushed her shoulders back. "But I won't take the risk that what you've said about Rowdy is true. If he really is paying for what I did, that's unacceptable. I take responsibility—"

"Like you did for Hillam?" Wreck asked, ire in his tone. "That was my crime to—"

"Axton Wrecker, this is where we are," she said, surprising him again with how she asserted herself. "You and me standing here right now. This is zero. You want a chance at saving your friend, you need me… I want to hear it. I want to hear you say that you need my help."

Wreck shook his head once. "Merchant will torture you."

She smiled, not out of pleasure, but as a signal to how she'd changed since they met. "A lot can happen on a journey to Ilias Merchant's compound." Touching his chest, she drew a slow finger downward. "Don't tell me you've forgotten our last journey."

One of his eyes narrowed more than the other. "You hitting on me?"

She took a step back. "You have forgotten. I'm Tulsi, not Svana. When I want something from you, I don't ask for permission to take it." Tulsi didn't trust him. Not a chance. Playing with him, keeping him guessing was the best way to try and hold some power. He reached for her face and she reversed further. "You, on the other hand, shouldn't expect permission from me any time soon."

But he didn't retreat, she didn't really expect him to. With one long stride, he brought himself up against her. The step down to the parking lot was right at her heels. Not only did Tulsi spurn the idea of shrinking from him, she also didn't want to step down. Wreck already had a height advantage over her, she wouldn't give him more.

Grabbing her arm, he hauled her closer, holding her teetering on the edge of the step. "Taunt me with that pretty mouth, Nympho," he growled. "I dare ya."

"If I open these lips for you, it will be to scream bloody murder… How would that screw with your plans?"

"If you won't look out for yourself, I won't do it for you."

"Sure you will," she said, raising her chin higher.

"You threw Coombs off me today, didn't you? That's what a man does for the woman he loves."

It was difficult not to be amused by the tension in his jaw. He didn't like to be teased and there she was mocking him for his confession. Maybe it was true, but Tulsi wouldn't let herself believe it just because some corner of her inner female psyche wanted to own this capable man.

If he loved her, that made him vulnerable, not only to being hurt by others, but to her. He wouldn't like that and she wouldn't be sure he wasn't just using her hormones against her without proof. So far, bringing her to Merchant's minions was the only thing he'd done. That wasn't exactly convincing as a measure of his devotion.

"You wanted him to hurt you," he spat. "You're so fucking stupid. He woulda killed you."

Snatching her arm from his grip, Tulsi had no choice except to go backwards. Instead of just accepting that she had to be a step lower than him, she turned and strode away across the parking lot.

Assuming that he would follow her, she didn't look back. She didn't hurry either. Having a man like Wreck on her heels, scurrying after her, was empowering in itself.

Even though she didn't have confirmation he was there, she tipped her chin toward her shoulder to talk over it. If he wanted to know what she was saying, he would have to trail after her.

"Think about it," she said, her words slow and sure. "If you had a choice between going back to a place where you knew you'd be raped and tortured, or doing something to get yourself a quick death, what would you choose? No, wait…" She pointed a finger upward. "I know exactly what you'd choose because that's exactly the plan you just told me."

"Stop fucking around," Wreck said, grabbing her arm to whirl her around.

Tulsi was enjoying playing with him. It didn't seem he shared the sentiment. "I'm not fucking around, I'm telling you how it is. Coombs is a meathead, easy to provoke. I don't know the deal between him and Hillam, but I know how much he hated me after *I* killed him."

"*I* killed him," Wreck said.

Tulsi pushed onto her tiptoes to whisper up at him, "I know. I was there."

When she tried to spin around to march away, Wreck didn't let her get more than a quarter turn before he hauled her back. "Quit walking away."

"I haven't heard the words," she said. "Tell me you need my help and maybe I'll think about sticking around."

Wreck didn't let her go when she tried to get her arm back. "I won't let you stick around."

Something almost sinister consumed her when a sly smile rose to her lips. "I don't need your permission for anything." She leaned in even closer, imagining her gaze could match the intensity of his. "I gave you a choice before. I almost gave you my power. All my power… I won't make that mistake again. With my help, you have a chance of getting out of this alive. I could even get Rowdy freed too… But I will not work under you. I will not trust you to make my choices… You want my help? We work as a team. One more lie and I'm gone. Anything you know, you share with me."

"And anything you know?"

She raised a brow. "A woman is allowed to keep a little mystery. You'll just have to trust me."

Containing her laugh wasn't easy, so she curled her lips into her mouth while he considered what she'd said. He could tell her to go to hell, but if he did, and she went, Rowdy would pay the price for Wreck's pride.

He let her go and shook his head. "If you're with him, I won't think straight. I can't do what I have to do if you're in trouble."

Opening her hands at her sides, she presented herself to him. "I have been in trouble since the night we met, Wreck. And look, I'm still standing."

His focus narrowed. "What happened in Vegas?"

Obviously, he knew she'd been in Vegas. He must have tracked her from there. Though she couldn't begin to figure out how he'd got it so right, asking him would hand him a power that she didn't want him to have. Not yet.

"I grew up," she said, thinking about how her skills

had developed since the fated night she'd gone out with Kieran. "I can't make you any promises. I won't. There's a chance all of us will wind up dead. With my help, there's a chance your friend will make it. That's all I can say."

"And I say you need to get the hell out of here."

She shrugged. "Okay."

Passing him to go back toward the motel, she pressed the button on the key to unlock the vehicle doors. It helped that the lights blinked. Tulsi adjusted her trajectory and took a few steps that way.

But she didn't put too much distance between them before stopping to turn back to him. "Before Merchant slaughters him, if you get the chance, make sure you tell Rowdy that you pissed away your chance to save him. Don't know which it is pride or fear. Whichever it is, you make sure to tell him you were too much of a pussy to step up."

Tulsi didn't need confirmation when she turned to strut in the direction of the car. There was no chance that Wreck would let an insult like that pass by. When he caught up, he grabbed her and hauled her around to throw her against the side of the car.

"Say that again," he growled between gritted teeth, rage emanating from every pore.

Tulsi reached up to touch his jaw. Slowing her words to make sure there was no equivocation, the moment would be crucial. "You, my despicable Ruin, are a pussy."

His hand rose, his fingers curling into a tight fist as his jaw ticked. "I should tear you apart."

"You can't," she said, taking less pleasure in her next statement. "Not if you really love me… If you love me, you would die before you'd ever consider hurting me in anger."

Tulsi had said that to him once before. She'd said it with complete conviction, which wasn't something she had anymore. Strange thing was, she didn't fear him. Pressing his buttons, riling him, it didn't make her afraid. With Coombs there had been an iota of fear, not that she wanted to admit it, even to herself. But Coombs was capable of killing her. That was a given. Wreck didn't want her dead. He wouldn't kill her. Even in the face of everything, somehow she still knew that.

Looking into him, witnessing the wretched conflict ripping at his insides, she understood his torture. "You should protect yourself," he said.

"From? I'm not afraid of pussies."

The side of his fist slammed down on the hood of the car just over her shoulder. "I am no pussy."

"No?" she said. "'Cause you were all ready to go riding in gung-ho to sacrifice yourself and Rowdy for me. Damn, baby, if I couldn't take care of myself, I wouldn't have made it through the last few months. We're in this shit because I took care of business myself. I didn't tuck tail and give up like a pussy."

The line of his mouth flattened. The light in his dark gaze piqued her interest. Not only did he seem aroused, and impressed too, but there could even have been a hint of pride in there as well.

"You'd risk your life for mine and Rowdy's?"

"Only because I started this."

They'd ended up under Merchant's control because of Kieran's mistake. But if she hadn't stabbed Merchant and fled, Rowdy wouldn't be strung up on his wall. Wreck wouldn't be thinking about giving up his life either.

"Okay," he said, his hands relaxing.

She turned her head to tip her ear his way. "Uh, what was that? I didn't hear the words."

Opening his rough fingers, he drove them through her hair to scoop it away from her ear. He bent down to murmur the words millimeters from it. "I need your help, wicked little Nymph."

Tulsi didn't think he'd ever said those words to anyone, she couldn't imagine it. Some of her nerve faltered when he pulled back just enough to meet her eye. When she couldn't look right at him, her attention fell to his mouth.

Damn him for still having the power to intoxicate her. Tulsi had been so strong and sure, so confident that she was almost cocky. Now all she could think about was the last time she'd tasted him, in the car they were leaning against. The way he'd kissed her. He'd owned her. He'd known they were about to walk into the motel room and she was about to learn the truth. That was what the kiss was for. It was his goodbye.

Socking his chest with the heel of her hand, she made him back off, just a little. "I can't believe you marched me in there to them."

"Merch had to know that we'd got you. He'd keep sending us 'til we got you."

"You," she said, poking a finger into his hard torso. "Do not have me. You will never have me."

"Never?"

The confidence in his arrogant smirk made her sock him again. The prick could read her arousal. It wasn't her fault, he'd seen her turned on too many times for her to deny he'd recognize the expression.

"You didn't have to have sex with me, you know," she said, thrusting her hands down her shirt to flatten it out. "At Fox Den, you could've been a gentleman. You knew I'd never consent if I knew—"

"I was on Merch's mission?" he said, scanning her figure. "Exactly why I didn't tell you."

Maybe that was true. Believing in them made her more compliant. "You thought I would abandon you," she mumbled, figuring out why he hadn't been honest. "You thought you'd tell me about Merchant and Rowdy and I'd split... That I'd leave you both to your fate."

"Couldn't gamble."

That sentiment was sad. Tulsi exhaled, realizing a truth that even with her new understanding of the man, she'd still hoped was genuine.

"You don't love me," she said, touching his arm. He frowned at her, but she hazarded a pitying smile. "You can't."

While she was simply accepting the truth, he seemed challenged by it.

"I can't?"

"If you did, you'd understand how far someone would go for the person they love."

"You think I wouldn't do anything to keep you safe? I've killed for you. I was ready to die for you... to sacrifice the only person who ever meant squat to me."

"But you can't trust me... Not so long ago, you were

my strength. The only thing that got me through… I trusted you in every corner of my very being because I was just so overwhelmed by what I felt for you. My love for you burned my soul. It kept me safe. It was all I had of who I was and all that mattered about who I'd ever be."

NINE

SHOWING A SIMPLE smile, Tulsi laid a gentle hand on his cheek. After just a second, she left him to go around to the trunk. Popping it open, she unzipped her bag to learn he'd been honest about putting money in there.

"Not so long ago?" Wreck's question made her look up to see him approaching the back wing of the car. "Fall out of love with me in a day?"

A whole day hadn't passed since his betrayal. "Maybe… Not like you would know how easy it is to fall out of love. You've never fallen into it."

Leaning over to snag her wrist from inside the bag, he dragged her across to stand in front of him.

Snatching her head in both hands, he bent to align their eyes. "You don't want me to love you."

She exhaled a laugh. "There was a time that was all I wanted."

"If your crazy plan works… If we go back to Merch together and somehow get out of there alive… you'll believe it then."

Raising a shoulder in a casual shrug, Tulsi tried to make out it meant nothing to her either way. The truth was, she didn't have a clue what to think or what she wanted anymore.

"If we get out of there alive, without a posse on our tail… I'm going back to Fox Den."

Wreck straightened up. "Amsterdam."

"He was right," she said. Wreck couldn't contradict that. "I laughed at him when he told me to watch my six… If I hadn't trusted you—"

"Did you fuck him?"

"What does that matter?" she asked, incredulous that his focus was on sex. "What does it matter if I fucked every guy I met from here to kingdom come? You've probably had Svana hanging off your cock for weeks."

Tulsi tried to return to the trunk, but he pulled her back. "I told you to stop fucking walking away."

"Stop pulling at me," she said, twisting her arm, straining in her futile attempts to free it from his grip. "Let me fucking go."

Instead of doing as she asked, he grabbed her chin in his other hand and yanked her forward to force her against the back passenger door. Tulsi fought and kept on fighting even after he pushed his mouth to hers. His fingers squeezed her arm and around her chin, he wouldn't give her any freedom to move. Still struggling, Tulsi refused to let herself kiss him back.

At least until he thrust his tongue into her mouth. Hating herself for being so weak, it only took a few seconds for the strength of his entitled tongue to coax hers into responding. For half a furious minute, they fought, entwined and desperate in their need to both love and hate.

The sensation of him relaxing his pressure made her spit his mouth from hers and turn away.

"You fuck," she hissed, her head snapping around so she could pin a glare on him. "You have no fucking right—"

"You got that blade in your boot," he said, releasing her arm to stroke her hair away from her face. Her locks were still caught in the grip he had around her chin, but his rough caress was about ownership, not comfort. "Show me you know how to use it."

"Don't tempt me," she said.

"Why didn't you use it? You could've put it in Svana, in Coombs… in me…"

"Never makes sense to let the assholes know what you can do," she said, mesmerized by his mouth, thinking of the time he'd said those words to her.

The slant of his lips was definitely proud this time. "That's my girl."

"You wish," she said, following her spite with lust.

Grabbing his face to pull his mouth down to hers again, she took from him. Tulsi wanted to hate it. To hate him. Walking away would ensure her safety. For a while at least. Wreck had been honest with her early in their relationship, before sex was ever a part of it, she'd asked him straight how this would work out. She asked if she would always be living with the situation hanging over her. He hadn't bullshitted her. He'd been honest. Maybe too honest.

Back then it meant something to her, it made her feel something. These days, she couldn't imagine living life like she had before. Even if by some miracle Tulsi did survive the ordeal, there would be no returning to her store to live a quiet life again.

Wreck tore his mouth from hers. Panting in their fervor, he pushed his forehead to hers while shoving her hair away with both hands. She didn't open her eyes, Tulsi wanted to feel good for as long as she could. The chances were both of them would be dead within weeks. If they were, she wanted something to remember in her last moments.

Only when he withdrew did she open her eyes. Confused and still in a haze of lust, Tulsi stayed there against the side of the car, watching him retreat, his gaze gobbling up every inch of her.

"Get it," he said. "Get the blade."

"What?"

"I'm no gentleman."

Meaning he wanted her? Tulsi bowed as she brought up her leg, just enough to retrieve the blade from the sheath strapped to her ankle. Wreck grabbed the end of his tee-shirt and pulled it up to reveal his delicious torso.

He smacked his other hand against his bare chest.

"Put it in here. Put it in deep."

"What?" she asked, licking her lips. "What are you—
"

"Didn't I already prove I don't hear the word no from you?" he snapped.

His anger mystified her. Tulsi was the one with a right to be angry. But angry or not, she understood what he was saying.

"If I kill you," she said. "How do you know I'll go back for Rowdy?"

His dark eyes were less aroused than they were menacing when they next met hers. "Trust."

This was the moment she had to make a choice. If Tulsi wanted her freedom, wanted to punish him and free herself from obligation, all she had to do was put the knife in him. Rook had sharpened it, the blade was capable. So was she. Hillam's blood hadn't made her squeamish; she hadn't hesitated to hurt Merchant or Darnell when they forced her hand.

"Do it," he barked. "Do it or I'll have you. Nothing else will stop me."

Nothing but death. Shoving herself away from the car, Tulsi drove her thumb under the tee-shirt he'd gathered high on his chest. Gripping it tight, resting her fist on his body, she took over. Wreck opened his hands at his sides. He wouldn't fight or resist. Was he doing what she had done with Coombs? Begging for a quick death?

Tulsi wouldn't let him sneak away from life so easily. Even if he wanted to be punished for his betrayal, she wouldn't grant him a simple reprieve. She wouldn't be so direct or so merciful.

Yanking the tee-shirt, she thrust the knife up behind it and sliced through the fabric. "Show me what you want," she breathed. "Ruin."

He lunged forward, casting the material from his shoulders. Reaching behind her, he pulled open the back door of the car. Tulsi wasn't sure how he moved so fast. Somehow, she ended up on her back in the rear seat of the car, her legs open around his hips in a flash.

Wreck said nothing else. Asked for no permission. He pulled his cock from his jeans, shoved her panties aside and surged into her hard. Her whole body convulsed around his. It arched up as a desperate breath filled her lungs.

Like a jackhammer working overtime, Wreck didn't savor the tense moment. He fucked her hard and fast right there in the parking lot. Meters away from the room where he'd betrayed her, Tulsi was giving herself to the man who'd imprisoned her heart.

For all the anger and upset the day had caused, she couldn't bring herself to hate him. She wanted to. Wished that she could. If she could switch off her feelings then it wouldn't be so difficult to be sensible.

"Oh God," she groaned, unsure if she was mad at herself or falling harder for the man who pushed into her deep. The bastard planted his arms on either side of her head, forcing her to look up at him. "Fuck you."

Surging down, he caught her lip in his teeth. Biting into her, he dragged his own mouth free. "That's right, baby," he panted. "Fuck me… You still fucking want it, Nympho. Can't help yourself."

Smacking his shoulder, she couldn't argue his taunting when she'd done the same thing to him just a few minutes before.

"This is for me," she said. "Not for you."

Rising up, he hooked his arms under her legs to force them higher, giving himself a perfect angle to rub the head of his dick against her g-spot. "For you," he purred too damn proud of himself.

"Fuck you," she said again, writhing against the delight shimmering through her. "Oh, fuck, Wreck… Baby—"

"I got ya," he said, dropping down to press his mouth against hers.

She didn't even know what it meant. Any of it. The kiss. The sex. What did it mean for them? For what would come next? If nothing else, she'd learned that it wasn't always such a bad thing to live in the moment.

What did resentment and sulking get anyone?

Coombs could walk out of the room, catch them screwing and put a bullet in both of them. They could die in minutes. It didn't take Tulsi long to conclude she'd rather die after having an orgasm than deny herself one for the sake of spite.

Pulling back, Wreck began slamming into her again. Hooking a forearm around her hips, he did all the work of moving her body with his. It was possible he just wanted to heighten his own climax, but surrendering to the bursts of pleasure exploding within her, Tulsi's lips curled into a smile.

Wreck's eyes didn't leave hers. Thinking of all the times she'd looked into him before, Tulsi gave herself over to the sensations surging through her body. The man at the bottom of Teal's stairs had given her the thrill she'd always sought. The man who'd ordered her to keep him warm had given her safety. This man, whoever he was now, he was in torment. Both of them were riding into the unknown.

Yielding to his own climax, Wreck gritted his teeth, maybe to keep himself quiet. They were both done, but they didn't part. He kept on looking down into her.

TEN

TULSI RAISED A TIRED arm to flatten a hand on his chest. "I'm hungry."

Without saying anything, he nodded and retreated out of the car. She only half watched him scoop something from the ground, assuming it was the car key. After it was in his hand, he folded her legs into the backseat and slammed the door.

She continued to lie there, staring upside down at the window above her head. There weren't many visible stars; the artificial light from the motel blocked most of them. She just breathed and stared at the sky. The trunk closed a few seconds later. It had been open the whole time they'd been screwing. Being robbed was the least of their worries.

The driver's door opened and Wreck got in. When the engine started, she shifted her head on the backseat and noticed fabric on his shoulders. Obviously, he'd retrieved another tee-shirt from the trunk.

Forcing herself to sit up, Tulsi grumbled and ran her fingers through her mussed hair. "Where are we going?"

"You're hungry," he said, glancing at her in the rearview mirror.

Picking up her hips, she wriggled her skirt back into

place and righted her panties. "Won't they wonder where we are?"

A glint of metal in the foot-well drew her eye. Her knife. Huh. Tulsi had been so out of it that she hadn't thought about the weapon. Checking the blade in the flashes from the street lights outside as they drove past them, she was satisfied it wasn't damaged.

"If they wake up," Wreck said. "They'll notice."

Tulsi slid the knife back into its sheath in her boot. "And you're not worried about that?"

"I was alone with you in Fox Den… I'm their ticket to accessing you."

She scoffed. "Yeah, so you like to think."

Unconvinced, he glanced at her in the rearview again. "While they've got Rowdy, they know I won't bolt."

"Except you were ready to let me walk," she muttered. His previous comment caught up with her. Confusion brought a curious frown to her face. "Why did they let you come to me in Fox Den?"

"Didn't want to spook you. I told 'em it was better to draw you out than storm the place."

Tulsi nodded. "'Cause Dam and Rook would've killed you all."

"Got alotta faith in that guy."

"Dam never screwed me over."

"You don't know that… Guys like him can't resist."

Tulsi grabbed the shoulders of the front seats to clamber over into the front beside him. "Can't resist what?" she asked.

"Doing what comes natural."

That didn't explain anything. Tulsi wasn't sure that she wanted to know what he was on about. "You think he would've screwed me over because he screws everyone over?" Wreck shrugged. "Shows what you know. Dam is a good guy. Yeah, he knows how to turn a profit, but he does it by looking out for people, finding out what's mutually beneficial."

She flipped down the visor to open the mirror but couldn't see much in the dim illumination of the car. Wreck's head turned her way. Tulsi didn't bother to return his look, even when it lingered.

"Did you fuck him?"

Again with the sex questions.

Slamming the mirror cover shut, she threw up the visor and twisted her whole body his way. "How is that your business? I told you, the sex wasn't for you, it was for me."

"Right," he said, switching his focus back to the windshield.

"Doesn't matter. We're not doing it again anyway."

"Right."

The hint of amusement in that tone raised her hackles. "I mean it, Wreck. We are not having sex again."

"'Til the next time."

"Are you trying to piss me off?"

"Baby, you love it. You know you love it."

"What I feel doesn't matter. It's all we do. All we do is have sex over and over again. It's the whole way you process emotions. You feel something, turned on, angry, love, whatever, and that makes you want to take something from me."

"You love to give it."

"Didn't I just say that didn't matter?" she asked, hating how he got her so frustrated. "Yes, okay, the sex is great. It's amazing, incredible. Does that make you feel better?"

"I never had a problem. You're the one with the problem."

Frowning, she folded her arms. "Hmm, and I wonder why that could be. Maybe if we hadn't been so focused on having sex in Fox Den, I might have actually been able to pause long enough to figure out Rowdy was in trouble. Maybe instead of screwing me senseless, you could've taken a breath and told me that Merchant was alive. Why didn't you tell me he was alive by the way?"

"Figured you could do without the agro."

"Oh great, yeah, and this worked out so much better."

"You were gonna find out eventually," he said, concentrating on the road. "I gave you a few extra days of ignorance."

"How did you know I wouldn't flip out?"

"Took it better than I thought you would."

She exhaled and sank into her seat, holding her head in both hands. "He's alive," Tulsi groaned, sort of just coming to terms with it. "Oh God, he's alive."

"I don't get it," Wreck said. "You were fucking him for weeks. How come you flipped when you did? What did he do? Stick it in your ass?"

"Would you stop?" she asked. "Just stop making assumptions about me. It's insulting."

"Assumptions?"

"Yes. You assumed I would bail on you if I knew the truth. You assumed I would save my own ass and leave Rowdy to die. You assumed that I was still in love with you."

"You are."

"Wreck, I swear, this is not the time to tease me."

Tulsi couldn't assert that he was wrong; her emotions were all over the place. The idiot was right that love didn't vanish quickly. Even while resenting the shit out of herself for it, she couldn't just turn off her feelings for him. If everything he'd told her about Rowdy was true, that wasn't the time to abandon the man she loved or his best friend.

His hand slid over the center console to grip her knee. "I wanna know."

Recognizing that he was being serious, she glanced his way. "What? What do you want to know?"

"I want to know what he did to you. I wanna know everything. What you went through in Vegas? What happened with—"

"How did you know I was in Vegas?"

"You did what I told you to do. After I said I could track you, they told me when you split. The time was on the video."

Clearing her throat, she tried not to show her discomfort by squirming. "Have you seen it?"

He shook his head. "Merchant wouldn't show it to anyone… Even Baines hasn't seen it."

That surprised her. She'd presumed Merchant would

show everyone to really get their blood hot. Being told what she'd done was nothing to actually witnessing what had transpired. Nothing on that tape would work to her advantage.

"Baines didn't watch when Merchant was recovering?"

"Merchant is the only one with access to anything that goes on in his office, on the whole top floor I think."

Having argued that her intimate life wasn't his business, Tulsi didn't want to give away too many details. But she had asked him to tell her everything, so she had to show a willingness to do the same.

"We never slept together." He glanced her way again. "Merchant and me, we never had sex."

"I don't get it. The guys who saw you in the office—"

"Merch liked to make out that we were screwing. As long as we weren't actually doing it, it seemed smart to play along."

"But the night I was in the office…"

"We did other stuff."

"What other stuff?"

"You want a blow by blow?"

The scowl on his face provided an answer to that question. The idea of talking Wreck through her every encounter with Merchant wasn't palatable to her either.

He turned the car into the parking lot of a burger place by the highway and switched off the engine.

"Wait here," he commanded and slammed out of the car.

With a deep breath, Tulsi took advantage of the chance to gather herself in the precious seconds that she had alone. Merchant was alive. That was one possibility she hadn't considered, but it only made it to second place in her list of most prominent thoughts. The first was much more agonizing. Rowdy was in pain. The man who'd been honest about his lack of trust in her was hanging from a wall because of her actions. Chained. Tortured. Abused. All because she hadn't wanted to open her legs for a thug.

On a slow blink, she watched Wreck go into the burger place and walk up to the counter. She'd opened her legs for him. Wreck was a thug. Why was he so different to Merchant?

Looking at him wasn't helping, Tulsi licked her lips and averted her gaze. That's when she saw them. The keys were in the ignition. Wreck had left her alone right next to the highway with the car keys. A bunch of bikers were crowded around the end corner of the burger place. Probably just a rest stop for them to snag something to eat, but they were talking, laughing, comparing the sound of their engines.

The noise from that ruckus would be enough to cover the sound of her turning on the car. It would hide her escape… if she chose to make one. Tulsi had been honest with Wreck. He needed her help. The only chance of saving Rowdy came if she played along. If she didn't, and ran away, Wreck would have no choice except to go back to Merchant and admit her escape. His failure.

She breathed out. Tulsi wasn't going to run. For one thing, she could've done it from the motel parking lot. Wreck hadn't stood in her way. Out there, it was a little different. Wreck was a couple of miles away from the motel. It would take him time to get back there to tell Svana and Coombs what had happened. Those minutes would be vital in her escape. Tulsi could floor it on the highway and put some distance between them.

Living with that decision would be impossible. How could she abandon Wreck so soon after he'd asked for her help?

Tulsi wanted to love him. She did love him. It would be easy to tell herself the opposite, but she couldn't help herself. In truth, his actions were understandable. Okay, so maybe it would've made more sense for him to tell the truth at Fox Den. In that safe place, she could've asked Dam and the others for help. But this love thing was new to Wreck and it wasn't like he'd received a warm welcome from the Fox Den gang. Given that, he had no opportunity to trust them.

She hadn't been lying that once upon a time the thing she'd wanted more than anything else was for him to love her.

Tulsi didn't know what to think anymore. She didn't know what to do. He'd referenced her "crazy plan" when she didn't have any kind of a plan. Tulsi was more used to taking Wreck's orders than coming up with a strategy on her own. Whatever they did, they would need to figure it out together.

The last few minutes that they'd spent in the car, talking, felt more real than any of the time they'd spent together at Fox Den. Wreck had been carrying the burden of Rowdy's torture as well as the knowledge of what he planned to do to her. That conflict must have pressed hard on his conscience. Every second he probably questioned himself about the right thing to do.

Tulsi would question herself in the same situation and couldn't come up with an answer on what she would do. She was lucky in that she didn't have a best friend. Her mother was dead and she had no other close relatives. All she had was Wreck. But if it came down to a choice between him and say her mother, because they had been close before her death, Tulsi didn't know how she would make that choice. Or how she would live with it.

Since finding out the truth of their situation, it felt like Wreck had relaxed. Maybe that was a false perception, but it felt like the man she'd fallen in love with was with her again. The barriers that had existed between them in Fox Den and the car trip after were gone. Wreck had been trying to hold himself away from her, maybe trying to convince himself that he could sacrifice her. Whatever it was, he'd made a decision, a choice, and that choice had been to let her go. To sacrifice himself and his best friend to let her live.

How could she know that and still doubt his feelings? The sense of betrayal that had consumed her upon walking into the motel room and seeing Coombs with Svana was still too raw. Any time she tried to look past it, Tulsi remembered how naïve and stupid she'd felt for handing Wreck her trust without question.

Instead of being a dope in love, she should've asked more questions. Basking in reconnecting with her man had tempted her into ignoring that they didn't have the same security as before. In spite of her misgivings, she'd trusted him.

It would take time and being more careful was top of her list. Letting her guard down could be fateful. Yet, since slipping out of the motel room, since he'd revealed the truth, Tulsi could feel the cocoon of Wreck's security settling around her again.

One of them, or all of them, could end up dead. Whatever happened, Tulsi would know she was no coward. She'd been the one to stab Merchant. If anyone had to face the consequences, she would be the one to do it.

ELEVEN

WRECK HAD COME back to the car with the food. Tulsi said nothing about the keys in the ignition, but she did make a point of staring at them as he got back in. If he'd wanted her to bail or disbelieved her word, his test had given him his answer. He could trust her. Being cautious about handing over her trust didn't mean she was interested in screwing him over.

They didn't say much as they ate. It pleased her to see Wreck eating too. He hadn't eaten much of the food Coombs had brought back to the room and he'd expended a lot of energy in the parking lot.

"Guess there's nothing left to do but go back," Tulsi said after Wreck returned to the car from tossing their trash.

He shook his head. "I can't."

"You can't, what? You're not going to make me walk all the way back there, are you? It's cold."

That was sort of a joke since the temperature had been his objection when he'd first stopped her in the parking lot.

Laying his hands on the steering wheel, he curled his fingers slowly until he was squeezing it tight. "I gotta know."

"Know what?"

There were so many possible answers to that

question, hazarding a guess could open a new can of worms. Tulsi didn't want to just start talking and hope to hit the mark. There was a good chance her mouth would never stop once it got started.

Angling his chin her way, he stared through the darkness. "What happened that night?"

Without asking, she knew which night he meant. Immediately, she began to shake her head.

"No," Tulsi said, more sure of her refusal than anything else. "No, you don't want to know."

If this was all a con and he didn't love her, it didn't matter if she gave him every gritty, disgusting detail. Yet, something in her just knew it wouldn't be smart to tell him the whole truth.

"I fucking know what I want," he said, twisting to glower at her. "We're not going back 'til you tell me."

"Fine," she said. "I will walk." But as she grabbed for the door handle, the sound of him locking all the doors stalled her. Glaring his way, she shook her head again. "You don't want to know, Wreck. Trust me." He just raised his brow, though that didn't take the threat out of his stare. "Okay, fine, he tried to have sex with me. I didn't want to have sex. I said no, he ignored me, so I stabbed him."

"I'd figured that much out on my own."

She opened her hands. "So what the hell? What else do you need to know?"

For a few seconds, it seemed like he wasn't going to say anything else. He didn't make a move to start the car or to speak. The strength in his jaw tightened. That tension wasn't going to go anywhere on its own. He needed to know something or needed to say something. Whichever it was, Tulsi was going to be patient.

Eventually, he spoke, his focus on the dials of the car. "I watched what those fuckers did to Sienna. I watched them torture my sister. Rape her. Over and over again… And I did nothing."

Shit. Him opening up about the trauma of witnessing his sister's demise was the last thing Tulsi expected. Wreck hadn't even been the one to tell her the story. Rowdy had clued her in as to how the pair met and the incident that changed both their lives.

Sympathy rose inside her. Tulsi reached over to put a hand on his. "Wreck—"

"No," he said, snatching his hand away. "It's the fucking truth. Yeah, I was a dumb kid. Yeah, there were more of them and yeah, they tied me down so tight I couldn't move… I still have the fucking scars…"

He had plenty of scars. Most were small, she'd never questioned him about them, but she did like learning the patterns on his body. Hearing the story of those on his wrists and ankles, helped her to know him better, but it didn't give her any comfort.

"Ruin," she whispered, stroking his thigh.

One good thing came from being in such a small space. Anywhere else, he wouldn't have accepted solace from her. In the confines of a car, he had nowhere to go. His muscular form didn't give him much space to pull away.

"I walked away from you, Nymph."

It wasn't like him to sound so… broken. He was a guy who felt guilt. For some reason, he thought it was on him to shoulder everyone else's problems. He took responsibility for what happened to his sister and for what happened to Rowdy. Now he was taking responsibility for what she had done to Merchant.

"You didn't walk away," she said, recalling her thought when Merchant was pinning her down. Wreck had just left the room before Merchant got amorous. "You had no choice. Merchant was there. Baines wanted you out. I gave you no sign that I wanted you to stay. None."

"I waited," he said. "When you walked in… I waited for you to give me something. Some goddamn signal that you wanted him taken down."

She remembered that too. How he'd stood in front of Merchant's desk with his back to the bastard. Tulsi hadn't been sure why Wreck had switched his focus to her, but she had wondered if he was waiting for an order or permission.

"Then what would've happened? I made a point of never, ever giving you any reason to think you had to step in for me. Not there. Not at Merchant's. They'd have killed you. No one's life would be better without you in it."

Wreck shook his head. "I didn't even know how much I needed you until you were gone," he murmured. "I'm not that guy. Not the guy who gives a shit about who I screw… I told you we weren't real… Crock of fucking shit."

"You convinced me," she said, hazarding a smile, though he wasn't looking at her anymore. "I knew you felt something for me, but that pissed you off. Rowdy told me about Sienna because he didn't want you to feel responsible for me. You were not responsible for me… You still aren't."

The way his eyes rose to hers betrayed just how little he believed that. "If I wasn't, I'd leave you to the dogs."

She shrugged. "Could still happen. We have no way to know how this will play out. One thing I can tell you for sure is I make my own choices. I could've chosen to let Merchant take what he wanted. We wouldn't be in this mess if I had… It's not like I'd be the first woman to just lie there and detach my body from my mind. You'd be amazed the things we women figure out during obligatory sex." He didn't flinch, yet somehow she read his mind. "I am not obligated to have sex with you. Never have been… Being with you never helped me figure out a dang thing."

No way Tulsi was that good at faking. No woman could be that good at faking. Any time Wreck was inside her, she lost her mind. Being cool or aloof would probably make her more mysterious, but Tulsi just didn't have the skill to restrain herself.

His shoulders loosened. "Nymp—"

"Wait a second, is that what you think we were? That I was humoring you all those times we had sex? Why would I do that?" Something Merchant had said to her came to mind. "I have an ability to sense power." Sitting back, she was happy to shove away from his thigh. "You prick. Yeah, that was it. I thought *this guy will fall for me 'cause I'm just so irresistible and I'll be home free.* Fuck you."

"What happened to 'stop saying fuck me'?"

She wasn't dissuaded. "This is different. I'm the one saying it."

"Fuck me any time you want, baby. For any reason you want."

"I won't justify myself or what we did before. I know why I had sex with you and it wasn't for freedom. If it was, I wouldn't have left on my own, would I? I wouldn't have walked out of that apartment to go to Merchant. I'd have expected you to do something to help me. Instead, the only thing I could think walking out of there was that I didn't want you to move a muscle. I was terrified you would get hurt."

Probably wasn't wise to admit so much truth given the uncertainty of their relationship. But Tulsi was being honest, nothing else she could do.

"I fucked you because I wanted you…" he said then lowered his volume like he was almost ashamed to admit what he said next. "Don't remember ever wanting anything more. I'm a fucking asshole."

That was sweet, in a Wreck kind of way, but she wasn't going to soften. "So you didn't care why I wanted you?"

"No… I wanted you, that's what I cared about."

"You said you didn't."

"I should've known better," he said, chastising himself. "What the fuck? Getting mixed up with that weasel's girl… Asshole."

Tulsi was definitely over people assuming she was Kieran's property. Instead of fighting it, she decided not to give it the time of day.

"Yeah, you were pretty dumb… But that's that. Over and done with now."

Hoping that they'd said enough to appease Wreck's curiosity, Tulsi waited for him to start the car. But he didn't.

Obviously he wasn't yet satisfied. "Did he hurt you?"

Tulsi exhaled a frustrated groan. "Wreck," she said. "It's in the past, let's just leave it there."

His deeper curiosity landed on her when his attention swung her way. "Why won't you tell me?"

"Because I don't want to," she said. "I don't want to relive it and I don't want you to either."

"When we get back to Merchant, anything could

happen." She nodded because there was no guarantee of what would happen any time. "If he shows me the tape…"

"He wouldn't do that. Not if he won't show Baines." Thinking about Merchant's reluctance to show his lieutenant the crime, Tulsi couldn't suppress her own intrigue. "I wonder why he won't show Baines… You think he's embarrassed?"

"That you got the drop on him? Maybe."

"Not even I knew what I was going to do. There was no way for him to anticipate that I'd—"

"Hillam," Wreck said. "Any guy who knows what you did to him has gotta have a death wish."

She smiled. "What *I* did… Why do you think I never told anyone the truth? Not a bad mark to have on my record."

"You're welcome."

She sighed. "I know what you're trying to say. You're telling me that you'd rather know now than have Merchant be the one to tell you. You don't like to be blindsided. If he says something you don't like and you flip out…" Wreck stayed still, which confirmed her theory. "The video won't tell you any more than I've already said."

"What about him? What will Merchant tell me?"

She couldn't imagine that he'd ever be so dumb as to tell Wreck the truth. He couldn't… He wouldn't… would he?

Wreck's presence, or what Merchant thought was her reaction to being near her ex-lover, was what had caused the man to snap. But he wouldn't tell Wreck that. Why would he? Merchant couldn't admit that he'd been turned on thinking of her having sex with Wreck. That was the reason he'd been so adamant that he wanted her.

But that wasn't Merchant's only interest in Wreck. Merchant had brought him up before that final night too.

"I don't know why exactly, but you intrigue him," she said, thinking it was only right that she give him the heads up. "At one point, he… he sort of implied that he wanted you to stick around… that he wanted *us* to stick around."

Wreck frowned. "I don't get it."

She shrugged. "I don't either, not really. He asked me what I knew of your reputation… He'd done his research on me and figured out that I wasn't affiliated with any of you, other than Kieran, who he didn't see as any threat… rightfully… He said you had no roots, but he wanted to offer both of us a home with him."

Another scowl formed on his face. "I don't know what the fuck that means."

Tulsi scanned the parking lot around them, noting the bikers were getting ready to depart. "Just telling you what he said."

"Tell me what he said the night you stabbed him."

Frustrated, Tulsi struggled to restrain her annoyance. "Look, Wreck, there's nothing I'll say that will make you feel good. You trust me enough to leave the keys in the ignition, but not to make this decision? I already said you're not responsible for my actions and you're sure not responsible for Ilias Merchant's either. We can sit here all night in silence or we can go back to the motel room and try to save your friend. Choose."

Set in her determination, Tulsi presumed Wreck would yield if she just stopped talking, so that was exactly what she did. Wreck's inexperience with conversation couldn't be working in his favor. The guy said he got results. He'd broken Putnam; Rowdy had told her everyone broke under Wreck.

Not her. No way. Tulsi wouldn't break.

Except… she wasn't great at just sitting in silence. Damnit. Her scheme backfired. After maybe five minutes had gone by, she peeked his way to find his focus completely on her. It didn't appear that he was going to break and give up any time soon.

"If you love me…" she said, softening because in a battle of wills, they were probably as stubborn as each other. "Trust me."

Appealing to his devotion was a last-ditch resort that she didn't think would work for a second. He surprised her by reaching over to scoop a hand around her head. Pulling her across the center console, he pressed a long kiss to her mouth.

Still holding onto her, he stayed close. "I will find out and if he's the one to tell me, I won't be responsible for my reaction."

She smiled as he let her go and started the car.

"You're responsible for everyone and everything else, but you're not taking responsibility for your own actions?"

He hooked a hand around the back of her headrest to swing the car around in a backwards U-turn. "He put his hands on my woman without permission from either of us," he said, gunning the engine as they roared out of the parking lot. "Every second he lives is borrowed time."

Tulsi had told herself in the past not to be flattered or turned on by his brutish talk and behavior. But every time, she got a flutter of a thrill when he spoke like that.

TWELVE

WHEN WRECK GOT her back to the motel, he took her inside. Instead of fastening her to the lamp again, he pushed her down on his bed and took off her boots. He removed her ankle strap too and tucked her weapon into her discarded boot. Tulsi objected to being in his bed, even as he stripped down to his underwear and got in beside her.

It wasn't easy to argue with a gruff man like Wreck while trying not to wake the slumbering, slobbering idiots in the next bed. Once he locked his legs around her, Tulsi gave in. His entitlement might have been insulting, but it was also sort of arousing.

She'd sleep better lying down without the zip-ties than she would attached to the lamp. Exhaustion would mean being sluggish and could lead to bad decision making. That could also be her last night of semi-safety for a while, so Tulsi chose to take advantage of it.

She hadn't figured anything out by the time he started prodding her in the morning. Her protests to being woken up were ignored. Still half-asleep, Tulsi had no real awareness of where they were. It took a particularly long kiss and a little expert fingering to rouse her. Only then did she recall where they were and what was going on.

As she started to argue again, Wreck boosted himself off the bed and dragged her onto her feet. He was already in his clothes, which didn't make sense because she remembered him stripping the previous night.

"Wreck," she hissed as he hauled her into the bathroom. "Jesus, what is the rush?"

He turned on the shower and put his hands to the back of his neck to drag off his tee-shirt. A bunch of stuff, that had to have come from her bag, was laid out on the vanity. Clothes for both of them, toiletries, everything she'd need to get ready for the day. Her boots, and presumably her knife, were on the floor beneath.

"Get naked."

"Get naked?" she said, turning away from the vanity to see he was already in the buff. "What the hell do you think is going to happen here?" He answered her question by unzipping her skirt and dragging her top off over her head. "Wreck, I—"

He picked her up off her feet and put her into the shower. Still in her underwear, she squawked, but he was right there behind her, peeling it away from her body.

Both his arms came around her once she was naked. As his hands slid up and down her body, he pushed her head aside with his to kiss her neck and shoulder.

"I said no more sex," she said, pushing at his hands. "No more sex, Wreck."

To make her point, she spun around, but quickly decided facing him was a mistake. The damn man was difficult to resist in his full naked glory. His defined body was one thing. His obvious arousal was another.

"Just a quick fuck."

"No," she said, turning away to fumble for the soap.

"We gotta be back out there before those fucks wake up."

Wreck had taken care of her whenever Merchant's goons were around. After one of their first nights together, he'd rushed her to the shower to make sure no one else took the opportunity to be alone with her while she was naked and vulnerable.

Even recalling their easier days didn't change Tulsi's certainty. His care was no longer just about looking after her, he wanted to get some too. If she gave in without getting some vital information, he'd have no reason, or opportunity, to tell her later.

She licked her lips. "I can't give it up until I know you'll be honest with me."

"Honest? What the fuck was last night?"

That was still a mystery to her too. "You have to give me something."

"I'm trying to," he said, taking her hips to pull her body back against his erection.

"Something more than that," she said over her shoulder. "I need to know what Merchant said about me, what to expect when I get there. Where is Baines? What about the others? Teal and Delray? And you haven't said a thing about Styx… Is Merchant still trying to track his missing shipment?"

The doubts that Styx had put in her mind about the shipment were still prominent. Merchant may have been playing a game or trying to start a war. With his more recent issues, like her stabbing him, that game had probably slithered down his list of priorities.

"Chances of getting some when we get to Merchant are low," he said, shoving her sopping hair away from her shoulder.

Spinning around to grab hold of his dick, Tulsi yanked him her way. He didn't object to her shameless claim.

Instead of pleasuring him, she glared. "Anything you know, you tell me, remember that? One more lie and I'm outta here, Buster."

She'd just said it last night, so he damn well better remember. This was a chance to show him that she was serious. Tulsi had to regain her faith in him, she had to. If he couldn't prove that he respected her and that this wasn't some elaborate game, none of them would survive. Tulsi needed him to treat her as a partner; to know they would follow each other's lead.

After a frustrated exhale, he spoke. "Baines is with Merchant. Teal and Delray went a different way. Merch sent the five of us out together. When I knew for sure where you were, I gave them a bullshit story and sent them back north."

"A wild goose chase?" she said, which he acknowledged with a blink and a nod.

"Plan is to hook up with them before we go back to Merchant's."

"How did you know where I was? That you had definitely found me."

"I knew, but it didn't matter if I found you, I was getting pissed with them."

"You're pissed with everyone," she said, not buying a sudden impatience. "You're always pissed."

"Pissed now because I'm not getting any."

"Wreck," she said, easing closer while sliding her wet hand up and down his cock. "You're gonna learn there's a lot more to keeping your woman happy than fucking her."

"I'm figuring that out," he muttered, his attention ascending.

He might be irritated at her or fed up of talking, but he wasn't running away. Though that may have had something to do with her hand on his shaft. Tulsi had lessons to learn too, such as how effective it could be to play nice in order to get what she wanted.

Touching her lips to his chest, she enjoyed the water warming her mouth as she caressed him. "You once told me I should manipulate you with sex any chance I got... You told me to make you earn me, remember?"

"And you wonder why I don't like talking?"

Giving him a squeeze, she kept kissing. "What did Merchant say? What am I going back to?"

"He doesn't tell me his plans," Wreck said and groaned when she set a foot on the side of the bathtub and jerked his dick closer to her pussy. "He still wants you."

"Like sex wants me or something else?"

"Fuck, babe, I don't have a damn clue."

Merchant hadn't shared much of his thinking with her when she was living just meters away from his office.

Being with Wreck in the shower reminded her of when they first got intimate. It was difficult not to trust him when she had once relied on him so much.

Her mouth drifted to the edge of his chest. She breathed against him and then went further. Opening wider, she sank her teeth into his arm and bit him hard. Something about him brought out the urge in her. Even as his hand drifted down her hair and hers moved faster on his cock, he didn't resist. It had to hurt, she bit him with more force than she ever had before, and held on for longer.

One truth kept coming to mind. Merchant would kill her. Whatever he wanted to do to her before that final moment was a mystery, but there was no doubt that she wouldn't be getting away with her life.

She could run, probably should, but if she did, Rowdy and Wreck would die. Just because Tulsi didn't want that on her conscience didn't mean she wasn't afraid of what she might have to endure.

Releasing her bite, she leaned back to look up at him. Wreck pushed her soaked hair from her face.

"I do love you, Wreck. I know it's nuts. I know I shouldn't. I know you're an asshole… but I love you."

Most people would probably just accept the sentiment.

Wreck wasn't so easily satisfied. "What happened to busting my balls?"

"This might be our last chance to be alone. That's what you were trying to tell me, right?"

"So you're saying goodbye." His arousal vanished in a heartbeat and was quickly replaced by anger. "What the fuck!"

It wasn't like Wreck to raise his voice; he was more of a growler than a shouter. His rage was underlined when he leaped out of the shower, and away from her caressing hand without getting relief.

She wasn't sure exactly what had just happened. Left alone in the spray, it took Tulsi a second to realize he'd abandoned her. Shoving the shower curtain out of the way, she tilted her head out of the water to watch him pace in the small bathroom.

"Wreck?"

He stopped and flipped around to glare her way. "I will not let him hurt you… He won't—"

"What? Fuck me?"

The probability was high that sex was on Merchant's list. If nothing else, it was a way to exert his power over her. To prove that she had no rights while under him.

Something broke the height of his tension, but it wasn't any kind of calm. "What the fuck are we doing, Tuls? If going back means watching him hurt you, watching him…" His teeth clenched so tight that his jaw ticked. "He might as well just fucking kill me."

Wreck was no actor. Not that she doubted his ability to be silent and brooding if the moment called for him to keep his mouth shut. But a display of emotion was not his MO. It had to be genuine. The man who had tried his best to avoid being intimate with her, falling for her, telling her anything personal… there he was standing in front of her, showing her that just the idea of her being violated was enough to break him.

"Come here," she said, straightening her arms toward him.

Wreck came over and took her waist to lift her over the edge of the tub. Once she was on her feet, she swiped her wet hair from her face and set her sights on him.

"Nymph—"

"When you love someone," she said, cutting him off. "Their problems become your problems. Their joy becomes your joy. Their vulnerability becomes yours… I knew what I was getting into last night. I've lived with Merchant. I know that his patience is thin, that he doesn't like to be disrespected. I also knew there wasn't much chance of me making it out alive."

"There's no—"

"But that wasn't what I focused on. That wasn't what hurt the most… There's little chance of you making it out alive either. But you know what? If he's going to kill you, killing me will be a relief…" The word seemed simple until she had to verbalize a sensation that she'd been living with for months. For a moment, she faltered while trying to find the right words. "There's something about being in love that leaves you… halved. Something about dividing your power and your sense of identity. When you're with that person, it can be freeing… exciting. The last few months, even though I thought we would never be together again, I always got some comfort knowing you were still out there… hoping you might feel something for me."

"Babe—"

"Let me say this," she said because it wasn't easy to put this truth on a plate for him. "You felt that you had to make a choice, me or Rowdy. Either way, there was a high chance you were never walking away… Knowing that the man you love is going to sacrifice himself…" Tulsi's emotions were all over the place, so it wasn't easy to articulate them for a man who wasn't used to dealing with feelings at all. "Put it like this, after you told me the truth, it became a choice for me too: abandon you or die with you."

Letting go of her waist, he backed away. "You asked me to leave with you."

"Yeah, but I knew you wouldn't… Like you said, you wouldn't abandon Rowdy. Your loyalties become mine. We're going back to get Rowdy out. That's what we have to focus on. It's not about us anymore. It's about him."

From the expression on his face, it was easy to deduce that he didn't understand. "You're sacrificing yourself for my oldest friend?"

She shrugged. "He's your only friend. That makes him pretty special…" Taking a deep breath, she turned to the mirror. "Of everyone in this situation, he's the most innocent." Which was sort of ironic given he'd admitted to doing time in jail and not being as wholesome as she'd teased him about. "Kieran got us into it, but he's not to blame for this. We are."

Looking at him over her shoulder, Tulsi recognized the moment he came to terms with her conclusions. "I should've made you keep your hands off," he said, approaching to put his arms around her shoulders.

Their reflected eyes met. "If you had, we wouldn't be in this mess. You said that to me once."

"Yeah, and you said I didn't have a choice."

She smiled and curled her hands around his forearms. "You were attached to the wall. You didn't… I was naked, hot for you…"

A shiver of weighted arousal set low in her gut when his eyelids grew heavy. Without a word, he loosened his arms and slid both hands down her body to take hold of her hips. Picking her up from the floor, he set her on the vanity. Tulsi knew exactly what he wanted, how he wanted her, and knowing that could be their last chance to be alone, she let herself feel exactly as she had their first time together.

THIRTEEN

POUNDING ON THE bathroom door broke their solitude. It really did seem like a return to their early days. Tulsi pulled away from their kiss to show Wreck her smile, but he was less amused.

"I gotta get you out there," he said, pushing her hair from her temple.

After their sex on the vanity, they showered together. Although they were dressed, Tulsi hadn't wanted to waste a second with blow-drying and the noise could've woken the others prematurely. Somehow, they'd ended up lying on the floor together, just kissing and touching each other.

Of course she was still mad and hurt that he had walked her into a trap. But anytime she thought about pushing him away, Tulsi imagined their last moment together. It would be soon. Too soon. She didn't want to live in that moment with any regrets.

She'd also have to endure whatever sexual torture Merchant wanted to subject her to. Her time with Wreck may be her last chance to ever enjoy intimacy.

"Get the fuck outta there!" Coombs hollered through the door.

Wreck gritted his teeth and tossed a glare toward the

door. "I really wanna fuck that guy up."

"Later," she said, stroking his cheek to draw his mouth back to hers. "They can't know we've talked."

Her statement was as much a question as anything.

Wreck nodded in confirmation. "Merch set rules. Prick."

"Rules?" she asked, lowering her brow.

"Your dick better be in your pants, asshole!" Coombs shouted.

Wreck crooked a brow. "Like that one."

"You weren't supposed to have sex with me?" she hissed. "What the hell? You might have told me that."

Pushing away from him, she started to get to her feet, so he followed, hauling her up with him. "You wouldn't have given it up."

"Yeah, 'cause I have so much loyalty to Merchant," she said, straightening his shirt while eyeing the bulge in his jeans. "You better get rid of that."

Checking herself out in the mirror, Tulsi wasn't encouraged. There was obvious stubble burn on her chin and her lips were swollen like she'd spent the morning making out… which she had.

Wreck smacked her butt. "Stop flaunting your ass."

She'd been leaning toward the mirror to check the damage on her face and hadn't thought about how she was presenting her ass to him. It was almost funny that when she sought him out she found him turning his back on her. Maybe that was the only way to ease his hard-on. Tulsi was proud of her power over him, even if it could get them into trouble.

The stubble burn reddened her skin, so she slapped at her cheeks a few times, hoping it would just appear that the water of the shower had been hot.

"Let's get out of here," she said when Coombs started hammering the door again.

Taking her shot, Tulsi smacked his ass and then linked her fingers through his. Her swat surprised Wreck, which gave her another chance to smile.

"Babe," he said when she went toward the door. Drawing her back, contrition was written all over his face.

"I've gotta—"

"You've got to use them, don't you?"

On the vanity, under everything else, the ominous zip-ties had lay there, heralding their reality. Just the notion of them brought out her anger, but she couldn't express it. They were playing a dangerous game already.

In her defense, Tulsi hadn't known that sex broke the rules. Wreck had, but apparently he was willing to endure Merchant's punishment just to have her again.

"I don't—"

"It's okay," she said, letting go of his hand to retrieve the plastic from the vanity. Holding them toward him, she offered her wrists. "Do your worst."

"For you, not to you," he said, but took the plastic and did his duty.

At least he'd been nice enough to fasten her hands in front of her rather than behind. The plastic cuffs weren't tight enough to mark her skin, which was another reason she'd rather Wreck attach them than Coombs or anyone else.

"Remember we hate each other," she whispered when his hand landed on the lock.

He nodded once and grabbed her thumbs in one hand. Bowing again, he surprised her by offering one last lingering kiss, despite Coombs rising infuriation on the other side of the door.

As they parted, Wreck ran a crooked finger down her cheek. The single moment of appreciation vanished when a scowl clenched his features. Then he was unlocking the door and dragging her out of the room.

Tulsi did her bit by pulling back and growling at the man leading her. "God, I can walk on my own you know," she said, fighting Wreck who walked past Coombs without looking at the guy.

"What the fuck you doing with her in there?" Coombs demanded.

Svana was seated in the middle of the bed she'd shared with Coombs. The blonde was completely naked, but didn't seem to notice. "If she gets to shower with you, I definitely do."

Wreck didn't respond to Svana. He pulled Tulsi to the lamp she'd been attached to the previous night and fastened her to it again.

"You guys have got to come up with some new material," Tulsi said, shaking her hands.

Wreck didn't acknowledge her either. While she couldn't do anything about him ignoring her, Coombs could. Even knowing that the guy wasn't the brightest bulb in the pack, Tulsi was still surprised when he marched up to block Wreck's way.

"Answer me, asshole. I'll tell Merch you—"

"Oh, go cry to your mommy," Wreck said, putting a hand on Coombs' face to push him out the way.

"Wreck…" Svana called in a beckoning tone. "While he's in the shower…"

He didn't even bother checking her out even though the beauty was trying to arrange herself in a sultry pose.

"I'm outta here in ten minutes," Wreck said, opening the door. "You wanna come, be in the car."

Leaving the room, he marched out onto the walkway, but didn't close the door all the way. It might have been a mistake, but he wasn't a guy short on strength. If he wanted to slam out the room, he would. Leaving the door open would let him still listen to what was going on inside… or hear her call for him if she had to.

"You fucking him?"

It took Tulsi a second to realize that Coombs was barking at her. "What?"

"You tell me the fucking truth!"

"Why?" Tulsi asked, propping herself on the nightstand, which left her hands above her shoulder. "You got yours last night, didn't you?" Drawing her eyes away from the fuming idiot, Tulsi smiled at Svana. "Must feel good. Apparently, I'm on a sex embargo, but you can screw any man you want… Merchant must really value you. You're *so* powerful."

Her sarcasm was enough to disgruntle Svana who kicked the sheet from her legs and pounced out of bed. "If we tell him you're screwing Wreck—"

"What? He'll be mad?" Tulsi asked and then laughed. "I put a knife in the guy's gut! I think he's already there."

Coombs and Svana shared a look. Seemed that she'd made a good point. Fucking Wreck might make Merchant mad with him, but that wasn't her problem… as far as these two were concerned anyway.

"Get in the shower," Coombs said to Svana, trying to exert control over someone.

Svana pointed her nose in the air and strutted off. Coombs gave Tulsi one more glance over and then he went to follow.

Tulsi breathed out when she found herself alone. Coombs was going to fight against Wreck all the way. She understood that he was threatened by Wreck's superior masculinity. Though it didn't seem smart to provoke a guy who was already so close to losing it all.

Concern came with her sigh. Losing it all. Wreck was close to that. If anything happened to Rowdy before or after they returned to Merchant, he'd have given her up for nothing. Her love would be reckless… She was already worried he'd be provoked into acting out. Without Rowdy in the picture, it was unlikely he'd find any cause to restrain himself.

Just like she'd thought during her first spell living at Merchant's pleasure, if Wreck acted in any way to protect her, or fought against anyone trying to hurt her, Merchant wouldn't hesitate to give the order to injure or kill him.

Whatever she had thought when making the decision to go back, one thing Wreck had said was right. If Rowdy died and Wreck reacted, causing his own demise, she would be alone with Merchant. Alone. There was no time limit. No hope of rescue. She'd just be alone and at his mercy.

Death had never been something she coveted, but without anything to live for… Tulsi wasn't sure there was any other way out of this, for any of them.

***

BEFORE GETTING ON the road, a lot of time got wasted.

Svana wasn't an easy woman to please. While sitting cuffed in the back of the car, Tulsi thought it would be much easier to treat Svana as a prisoner again. Every time it seemed they were going to get going, Svana thought of something else to do. She wanted a jacket, then she wanted a blanket. The blonde rearranged things in the trunk while Coombs dashed off to get her a soda, then she wanted water.

Wreck sat in the driver's seat, hands on the wheel, ready to leave. His impatience was growing, as was hers. They were the two in most danger, the two with ulterior motives, secrets to keep. Yet, they were the two most ready to make progress.

"You could just throw it in reverse," Tulsi muttered. Wreck's eyes met hers in the rearview. He didn't give much away, so she just shrugged. "Just a suggestion."

Svana was doing something at the trunk again. Tulsi didn't even care what it was. Coombs was coming back along the walkway with a couple of bottles of water.

He held up the bottles to show Svana. The trunk slammed and then the pair were getting in the car. Finally.

Svana had a purse and her blanket, there was something else under it, but Tulsi was beyond caring.

"Would've been quicker to ship me in a crate," Tulsi said.

Wreck threw the car into reverse and got them going. Svana took water from Coombs and vocalized her displeasure with his choice. That seemed to set the mood. They were on the highway, a dozen miles from the motel before anyone spoke again.

No surprise it was the young blonde. "Where did you go?" Tulsi had an idea that the woman was talking to her, but she didn't take her attention from the side window. "After you hurt Merchant and ran away, where did you go?"

"Who cares?" Coombs said from the front. "She's a coward. She ran away like a coward."

That made Tulsi's attention slink around. "A coward who stood up for herself," she said. "Your boss had no right to touch me. No right to say the things he did."

Svana just huffed. "You say *I* have no power; you

don't even get it."

Apparently what Tulsi had said to her the previous night was still bugging the woman.

"I get why you do what you do," Tulsi said. "I know you think it saves you from other pain and I get that. We're just not the same, you and I."

"You've got that right."

Svana wasn't shy about tossing her things to the middle seat or sliding forward to curve her hands over Wreck's shoulders. He sat straighter, away from her caress.

"Touch me again and I'll leave you on the side of the road."

Another huff puffed from Svana's lips when she dropped against the backseat again. "I think you're gay… He has to be gay."

Tulsi smiled and slid her focus to the passing highway again. "If that's what helps you sleep at night."

Glancing back, she caught sight of Wreck's eyes in the rearview for just a split second.

Svana sighed. "No man has ever refused me."

Because she was young and gorgeous and willing. In a way, Svana's upset was understandable. All her adult life, she'd been taught that her value was in sex. Wreck's lack of interest in taking advantage of what Svana saw as a gift, perplexed the youngster. Her desire for Wreck was understandable too. The more he said no, the more Svana probably wanted him—just like a child whose parent said no.

"Maybe he's just not interested in Merchant's seconds."

"Then he wouldn't want you, would he?" Coombs said. "Don't you worry, beautiful. Real men love you."

Tulsi didn't dare look at the rearview again. If Wreck was looking her way, she'd never be able to contain her laugh. "Yeah, Coombs," she said, the laugh teetering in her throat. "You're a real man… So real that your boss has to order women to sleep with you."

"Merchant doesn't order me to sleep with anyone," Svana said. "He loves me."

"Right," Tulsi said.

"He does!"

The woman's naïveté was infuriating and made Tulsi flip around. "If Merchant loved you, it would make him sick to have another man's hands on you. If you loved him, you'd be jealous of the way he felt about me. You'd have wanted to kill me, not be giving me advice on what life with him was like… You have no fucking idea. No fucking idea what someone would endure for the person they love!"

Coombs laughed and shifted in his seat. "Unlucky schmuck, get yourself mixed up with some bastard since you bailed on Merch?" His laughter rose again. "Can't wait to tell the boss that, I'm betting he skins the fucker."

The only thing Tulsi had thought about was how ridiculous Svana was being: she hadn't considered how her words might impact those she'd left behind at Fox Den. Wreck had told her that he'd come to retrieve her on his own as it was smarter. He hadn't revealed what Coombs or Merchant knew about where she'd been.

If Merchant sent anyone back to Fox Den, she'd be devastated. The people there had helped her, they didn't deserve to be punished. Anyone who asked questions about her would quickly be told about her relationship with Dam. Tulsi knew it had never been more than friendship; Merchant wouldn't believe that.

First Rowdy and now Dam. Men who touched her against her will ended up with a blade in them. But men who didn't weren't exempt from her trail of devastation. Sinking deeper into her seat, Tulsi began to worry about the body count. People could die, they would die, because of her. She didn't have the skill or the power to save all of them.

Dam had left town before her and Wreck. At the time, she'd been upset that they hadn't said goodbye. Now she saw that it was the best thing he could've done. Her heart hurt. Tulsi hadn't foreseen how her actions had the potential to hurt others.

All of a sudden, she understood Svana's point of view and began to wonder if she was the naïve one. If she'd just shut the hell up and let Merchant do what he wanted, they wouldn't be in this position. Lives wouldn't hang in the balance. She was death. To anyone who came into contact with her, Tulsi was a bad omen.

FOURTEEN

TULSI DIDN'T SAY anything else. Even if someone tried to draw her into a conversation, she kept her mouth shut. Nothing she could say would make anything or anyone better. Since her realization, Rowdy had dominated her thoughts. Imprisoned and in pain, the man had no control over what happened to him or why it was happening. Wreck's best friend had no hand in the events that led him to where he was, yet he was suffering anyway.

Wreck told her his friend would know how the situation would play out, even if they never saw each other again. Tulsi kicked herself for not questioning what he meant. It broke her heart that Rowdy may be resigned to his fate. Did he know that Wreck's plan involved never seeing him again? If she had vanished when Wreck ordered her to flee, Coombs would've spilled the beans on her escape at the first opportunity.

In that scenario, Wreck would be useless to Merchant. He wouldn't be able to track her down or tempt her back, Tulsi would be clued in on the plan, which would lead to her being more vigilant. Just the news of an escape alone could be enough to make Merchant kill Rowdy. He'd be alone. With no one to swoop in and save him. After putting himself on the line for both of his brothers, neither of them would prioritize him. It broke her heart.

They drove all day and instead of stopping, the guys switched positions, so Coombs drove for a while. From mutters she overheard, it seemed Teal and Delray had moved on somewhere else, which delayed them meeting up.

Although she was sick of gas station food, Tulsi didn't refuse it when Wreck tossed a pre-packed sandwich in her lap. Merchant wouldn't exactly provide her with the best haute cuisine when they got back to him. Tulsi couldn't afford to be fussy.

The same went for sleep. After the sun rose and Wreck was back in the driving seat, she drifted off. Her slumber lasted until the car lurched to the side. The sudden move jarred her from sleep. Blinking into the brightness of the car, Tulsi lifted her head from the sill of the window and yawned.

"Where are we?" Svana asked.

Wherever they were, it was a populated area. Tulsi wouldn't say they were in the thick of a city, but they were definitely off the highway, which meant their destination was nearby. A motel came into view as Wreck took them around a corner.

Figuring that was where Teal and Delray were holed up, Tulsi groaned and stretched. With more goons lying in wait, her day was about to get a lot worse. Those goons came with hands; hands she'd have to avoid in more ways than one. Wreck's prophecy of their chances at getting time alone was proving to be on the money.

Her own prediction was right too; Wreck drove into the new motel parking lot. There was still light left in the day. If they took advantage of it, they'd pick up their colleagues and get back on the road. Wishing for that meant wishing to get back to Merchant faster, but Tulsi didn't want to spend time in the motel with Merchant's goons. Merchant wasn't an appealing prospect either. Talk about being stuck between a rock and a hard place.

She'd told Wreck a lot could happen on a journey to Merchant's. It had last time, but this trip seemed to be flying by.

Wreck pulled into a spot near a half-open door. At first, she didn't think anything sinister about the door being ajar. Seeking any positive, Tulsi was relishing the chance to stretch her legs. Being cooped up in the back seat all day yesterday and last night had left her muscles achy. Her stomach growled too. She had no idea what time it was. Lunchtime? Maybe dinner? Could be either, but her body was in need of nourishment.

Everyone else began to move like they anticipated getting out of the car. Everyone except Wreck.

"What's wrong?" Tulsi asked, breaking her self-imposed speaking ban on instinct. Something about his posture got her attention. "Wreck, what's wrong?"

"There's blood on that door."

Whether he thought about the others in the car or just answered her, victim to the same kind of reflex that had made her speak, Tulsi didn't know. The concern in his tone was ominous. Coombs and Svana stopped moving too and they all looked toward the open door. By Coombs and Wreck's responses, Tulsi assumed the number on the door matched the one they'd been given by their associates.

Even if it wasn't the thugs' room, the bloody stain on the doorframe suggested someone was in trouble. Inspecting the scene, she leaned closer, noticing a narrow smear of blood on the pale blue door too.

"Should we check it out?" Tulsi asked, unnerved by how creepily quiet everything seemed to be, both inside and outside the car.

"You should stay put," Wreck said, taking off his seatbelt and opening his door.

"I'm checking it out," Coombs said, hurrying to catch up after Wreck got out and slammed his door.

The eager idiot's pathetic attempts to out-man Wreck would be laughable if Tulsi wasn't so terrified about Wreck walking into potential danger. Without blinking, she kept her eyes on that door as the two men entered the room. Once they were gone, she held her breath.

"They better come back out of there," Svana said

with a waver that suggested both concern and irritation.

Tulsi couldn't think to retort, her worry was zeroed in on one spot. The tension vibrated through her, which was probably why she jumped when the driver's door opened. A man she had never seen in her life got in and hit the button to lock all the doors.

"Buckle up, ladies," he said, adjusting his mirror and grabbing the wheel.

The car began to reverse, fast, and then they were out on the road again.

"What the hell?" Tulsi said, pounding on her side door, desperate to signal Wreck.

Nothing worked. She grabbed the door handle, but the door was locked. Even pressing the button to lower the window did nothing. Svana was screaming and kicking at his seat, but whoever he was just kept on driving.

"Shout and scream if you want," he said. "Don't give a damn… You can fuck with me sure, but I'm the one driving."

As if proving the point, he sped up and turned in the direction of the highway.

"What's going on?"

"Doesn't fucking matter."

"It fucking matters to me," Tulsi retorted. "Who the hell are you?"

When their eyes met in the rearview, there were no warm fuzzies exchanged, he was all glare. That wouldn't scare her into silence, not when she was used to seeing a glare just as intense above her while she screamed in orgasm. Wreck didn't frighten her and she would not let this guy think he could either.

"You should be thanking me, Pretty," he said. "Merchant would've killed you… after he'd had his fun."

"Forgive me, where are my manners?" she said, but he didn't react to her sarcasm.

"Is he saving you?" Svana asked. "Oh my God, is he the guy you fell in love with?"

Svana wasn't helping. Her idiocy only served to piss Tulsi off. "Do you think if I knew him? If I loved him? That

I would be so angry? If we were in love, we'd be happy! Do I look fucking happy?"

Snapping with such venom was enough to shut Svana up, at least for the moment. Having not expected such an outburst, the youngster shrank back. It was interesting, she controlled men with sex. That was how she'd kept herself alive, giving men access to her body. That wasn't a remedy which would ever work with Tulsi.

"I thought you two got along."

Whoever he was, he knew something about her. He must have learned what he knew from or through Merchant's people. Calling her Pretty betrayed that.

"Just tell us what you want," Tulsi said. "Who are you?"

It suddenly occurred to her that Wreck wouldn't know what had happened. She'd realized that he'd notice her gone, but he wouldn't know why or with who. He could think that she'd set him up, that she was abandoning him. If that was the case, he'd believe that she was ready to let Rowdy die.

"Not on Merchant's payroll," the driver said, snapping her from her devastation.

Setting a frown on him, Tulsi fought to contain her urge to slit the bastard's throat. As much as that would give her momentary pleasure, they were on the highway, going the speed limit, she noted from the dials she could just see in front of him. They'd go careening off the road if she killed him, so his death would come only moments before her own.

"Tell me what you want," Tulsi said, half nodding at Svana. "Between the three of us, we can work something out."

Svana would be willing to suck the guy off, Tulsi was more inclined toward murder… She wasn't as expert in the art as she'd once thought, she could do with the practice.

A sinister sort of smile tipped up the corner of his mouth when he next glanced in the mirror. "You can't give me what I want, Pretty."

"Svana might," Tulsi said, without hesitating to offer up the willing woman. If Svana was willing to open her legs for Coombs, she had to be willing to open them for anyone. "She's young. Pretty. Perky."

"I can be anything you want," Svana said, sliding to the edge of her seat and reaching around to stroke the driver like she had with Wreck.

This guy didn't object or toss her hands away. All Tulsi could think about was how close Svana's hands were to his throat and how easy it would be to strangle the shit out of him with the seatbelt. With both of them pulling—

"Sorry, sweetheart," the driver said, still letting Svana's hands roam. "I'm not that easy."

"I'm good," Svana purred. "Very… very good."

The guy just shook his head. It frustrated Tulsi that she couldn't see the guy's face to read his expression. Arguing and panicking wasn't getting them anywhere. She needed to know more if she wanted to try reasoning with him.

"Okay," she said and exhaled. "You don't work for Merchant. Who do you work for?"

"Me," he said. "Quit asking questions."

"Where are you taking us?" Svana asked.

That Svana picked up the questioning made Tulsi smile. The driver had told her not to ask questions, he hadn't said the same to Merchant's swan.

"Home."

Home? Time for more panic. Did that mean to Merchant's? If Tulsi went back there without Wreck, there would be no one to barter for Rowdy's release.

"No," Tulsi said, shaking her head. "No way."

She started pounding at the door again, rattling the handle, kicking at it as best she could.

"Relax," the driver groaned. "You gotta trust me, Pretty."

Tulsi spat out a laugh. "Trust you? Are you fucking kidding me? You just abducted me!"

"From guys who were taking you back to their boss." Again, his eyes met hers in the mirror. It was just a brief flash of… calm. Was that his way of telling her to be calm? Was he telling her that they weren't going back to Merchant? "You know, you got a set of balls to go with that fuck-me figure, Pretty."

Her jaw loosened, just a little, as the words bounced

around inside her skull. Styx. Those were his words. Sinking back, Tulsi stared at the seat in front. Wreck had made a comment about Styx trying to get her out. This could be his plan. Except Wreck implied that plan had fallen through.

"What do we call you?" Tulsi asked, calmer but none the wiser.

"Ripp."

Svana gasped and leaped back, pulling her hands away from their driver; going so far as to pull her heels up onto the seat as if she was trying to get her whole self as far from him as possible.

"What?" Tulsi asked because it was obvious the name meant something to the youngster.

Svana was shaking her head. In all the time they'd known each other, Tulsi had never seen the youngster so shaken. The woman had been kidnapped, raped, and gone through God knew what when she returned to Merchant the last time. Yet, the mention of this guy's name was the thing that put the fear of God into her.

"He's... he..."

The stuttering frustrated Tulsi so much that she considered slapping the woman to her senses.

"What you know about me, baby?" Ripp asked, though there was little emotion in his voice.

The guy wasn't boastful about his reputation. Didn't seem sad or angry that Svana had an idea of who he was.

"Keaton," Svana whispered, her wide eyes landing on Tulsi who pointed at him.

"This guy works for Keaton?"

Styx wasn't that great at planning if his big idea was handing her to Merchant's competition. Especially since the guy would think she was something special to Merchant, who was eager to hunt her down. Everyone thought they'd been intimate, that they'd been a couple. A sudden image of the woman Baines had murdered flashed across her mind's eye.

"Shit," Tulsi said, understanding Svana's urge to push back.

After eavesdropping on her conversation with Styx, Merchant had repeated that comment about her fuck-me figure. Ripp, or someone else, may have heard it from him.

Baines had murdered Alexis, one of Keaton's lovers. One of his favorites. If Keaton wanted her, it could be as payback. As willing as Tulsi was to die for Rowdy's freedom, she didn't want to die for nothing. If Keaton got his hands on her, she would die, and Rowdy would still suffer. Wreck would still die. He'd have failed to return her and with her dead, there would be no way to give Merchant what he wanted.

"Once upon a time," Ripp said, but not as a beginning.

Svana twisted around and lowered her volume. "They're related, I think, I don't know, Ripp worked for him before, but now there's like... I don't know, there's like a blood feud or something."

The youngster didn't even take a breath, she was freaked. Whatever she knew about this Ripp guy must have come from Merchant or his men.

"That's enough backstory," Ripp snapped. "Keep your fucking mouths shut. We've got a few hours of road in front of us. Don't want you two yapping the whole way."

Settling back, Tulsi figured this situation could go one of three ways. Either Ripp wanted to dump her on Keaton's doorstep for his own reasons, or this was somehow connected to Styx. The third option was Merchant; she didn't want to think too much about that possibility.

If Ripp and Keaton were blood enemies, it stood to reason that he'd want to help Keaton's nemesis. But what would delivering her to Merchant get him? Money maybe. Except Merchant's men had her, he didn't need to pay a cent to them.

Unfortunately, her choices were limited. While speeding along the highway, cuffed and locked in, Tulsi had to hold her breath and be ready to react to whatever they faced at the end of the road.

FIFTEEN

DARKNESS FELL FAST… or maybe her mood just made it seem that way.

Tulsi hadn't closed her eyes for more than a second. Sleeping while Wreck was in the driving seat gave her a confidence that was only a distant memory now that Ripp had taken over. Svana had fallen asleep a while ago and Tulsi envied her peace. It had occurred to her that she could quiz Ripp while the youngster was unconscious, but she didn't want to take that risk. It wasn't difficult to fake sleep and Svana's loyalties changed with the seasons. Trusting her could be suicide.

Though it was night, Tulsi didn't mistake where they were. Ripp had said home. As they drove through the city, Tulsi recognized it as Merchant's home. To her relief, Ripp didn't go to Merchant's building. But having been told that Keaton owned a building at the other side of town, she didn't relax.

Nothing was made any clearer when they headed toward a once commercial district. Ripp slowed to turn down a narrow road, closed in on both sides by corrugated metal. The pot holes bounced them up and down, but only for a short while. At the end of the alley, the whole area opened up to a wide concrete yard filled with girders standing up in columns.

She was still trying to figure out where they were when Ripp did a U-turn to tuck the car in next to a building, one which was much smaller than the vast yard out back.

"What is this place?" Tulsi asked.

"Old lumber yard," Ripp muttered.

She hadn't really expected an answer, so was surprised to get one. He turned off the engine and released the locks to get out. Grabbing at her door, Tulsi pulled the lever just as Ripp opened Svana's side and snatched a handful of the woman's hair.

Svana's instant scream stole Tulsi's attention. With the door open and one leg out, she was ready to make a run for it. Except Ripp had woken the blonde with more than a tug on her hair. Holding a beautiful, but deadly, curved blade against Svana's throat, Ripp made eye contact with her.

Tulsi didn't even think about getting her first real look at him, his threat was too overpowering to ignore. He didn't even have to say it. The point of that terrifying blade was primed to rip the youngster's throat right out.

"Get out and come around this side," he said, the bass in his voice deep.

The knife in her boot imprinted itself on more than her skin. Tulsi thought about pulling it out and turning it on him, but she couldn't let Svana die for another of her choices. Whatever she did, someone was always hurt. Someone else. Svana might be a bitch or she could just be young and naïve. Whichever it was, Tulsi was already living with the possibility of Rowdy and Wreck's murders on her conscience. She didn't need to add any more weight to that.

Doing as he said, she got out of the car and walked around the truck to join them. Svana was stooped forward in a crouch, her hands around Ripp's in her hair. Ripp kicked the back door shut and took his knife from its threatening just long enough to slice through the plastic connecting Tulsi's wrists. Freedom? Ripp was giving her freedom… Nothing about the scenario was adding up.

The knife quickly went back to Svana's throat and

Ripp dragged the objecting blonde toward the building.

Because their car was parked beside it, Tulsi couldn't see inside. It appeared to be a concrete structure with a small single story wing attached to a huge warehouse type space. She assumed either the door was up or it had been taken.

Still trying to figure out what was going on, she tensed when they rounded to enter the warehouse. Another car was parked there in the center. Halting immediately, she got the sense that this was less of a final destination and more of a handover point.

Ripp towed Svana toward the vehicle, but Tulsi stayed on the threshold, waiting for her eyes to adjust to the darkness. A few seconds in, she registered a figure moving out of the shadowy far corner.

"You're late."

That voice. She knew that voice.

"You're fucking welcome," Ripp said, throwing Svana down to the ground next to the car.

"What's she for?"

"Two for one."

"Dick."

That voice. Who was… the figure emerged and her trepidation became relief.

"Fuck," Tulsi whispered.

"That all you got for me, Prize?"

A smile leaped to her face as she started to cross the space. He didn't move, so she picked up the pace, running right at him.

"Styx," she said, leaping up to throw both arms around his neck.

Squeezing him tight, Tulsi knew it was crazy that tears warmed her eyes. They didn't even know each other well. But whatever his involvement, Styx wasn't Merchant or Keaton and as far as she knew, he didn't have any plans to kill her.

"Okay, yeah," he said, putting her back on her feet and pushing her aside to zoom in on Svana, who was still cowering on the floor.

"What do we do with her?" Ripp asked.

"Kill her," Styx said like it was no big deal.

"You're the pro."

Styx took a step forward like he actually planned to end Svana's life.

Tulsi planted a hand on his chest and got in the way. "No."

Styx's eyes narrowed on hers. Grabbing her arm, he spoke to Ripp. "Give us a sec."

Dragging her across the room, Styx planted her in the corner and blocked her in with his body, laying an arm on the wall above her head.

"She's seen us," Styx said. "Together… She knows too much."

"I don't even know what's going on," Tulsi hissed back. "I need to know more than that before I think about killing an innocent woman."

"No worries," he said, stepping back and linking his fingers to invert them as he straightened his arms to crack his knuckles. "I'm the pro."

Lunging at him, she snatched a handful of his shirt to haul him back to her before he could turn around. "I wouldn't ask you to do it if I wasn't willing to do it myself."

The edge of his mouth reacted. "So cold, Prize," he said, doing a bad job of containing his admiration. "Shame your Wreck's a goner."

That changed the urgency of the situation. "What? What do you know?"

"I know that he was damn sure about going down with his buddy."

Tulsi shook her head. "Neither of them are going to die." He frowned. "I'm going back."

Pushing him aside, she tried to walk away.

Styx caught her arm and yanked her into the corner again. "Oh no you're not."

"I am," she said, determined. "I won't let Rowdy die for my mistake."

Styx showed a new side to himself when he crouched to get in her face. "Only mistake you made was leaving the guy alive," he said. "That was amateur hour."

She couldn't deny that. At the time, all she'd been able

to think about was getting out of the building in one piece.

"Even if I'd killed him, this wouldn't be over," she said, maintaining the hissing whisper of their conversation. "Not for me."

"Only reason I'm still around is for you," Styx growled. "You saved my life once, I'm returning the favor… whether you like it or not."

Frustrated and angry, Tulsi could think of no reason to keep the secret anymore. "Merch made that up. I had no idea that you were his big important meeting before they dragged you into his office. Even after they did, I didn't know who you were until he told me."

That news was supposed to surprise him, to knock him for six so he'd back off.

Styx didn't so much as twitch. "He was going to kill me in that room. He didn't because of you. Doesn't matter if you said a damn word."

At the time, Styx had been sure that Merchant was going to kill him. Tulsi couldn't argue that her presence had changed that plan because the truth was, she couldn't say for sure.

"Okay," she said. "Whatever. I free you from your bonds, whatever. Take off while you can, I'm going back."

Ducking down, Tulsi went under his arm to start toward the exit.

"Won't change anything," Styx called after her. "You walk in there, he'll never let Rowdy go free. You'll give him everything he wants and he won't have to give anything up." That was true enough to make her slow. "You know I'm right… You need a broker."

Stopping, she took a breath before spinning around to look at him again. "Are you offering?"

Before he could respond, another voice sounded behind her. "Nobody fucking move!"

Tulsi recognized that voice too. No delay, no need to think. Despite not being able to see him, she immediately identified the owner of those words. Styx's hard expression betrayed that he wasn't expecting another arrival, and he definitely didn't appreciate the intrusion. He didn't wear concern; anger was the only thing written on his face. As she turned, Tulsi noticed that Ripp's features were just as unimpressed.

"Oh my God," she exhaled at the sight of her friend in the doorway, holding a gun out in front of him.

"Who are you gonna shoot?" Styx asked.

"Dam," Tulsi murmured, swallowing to moisten her throat. "Put the gun down."

"Get over here," Dam demanded.

She did start moving toward him, but slowly. No one in the room deserved to die, not on her behalf, certainly not only minutes before she planned to walk out.

"Put it down."

"I knew it was fucked up," Dam said, his gun trained on Styx. "I told you not to trust that guy."

"Yeah, you did," Tulsi said. "Please put the gun down."

"We're getting out of here."

"Yeah, okay," she said, creeping closer. "We'll go, you don't need to hurt anyone."

His gun swung in Ripp's direction. "He kidnapped you. I saw it. I saw you screaming at the window."

Oh God, Dam had been watching. That was no accident or coincidence. Everyone assumed he'd left to avoid a goodbye. But he hadn't gone as far as they thought. He'd been following her. Following them.

"There's a lot going on here, okay?" she said. "I'm not sure of it all myself yet, but—"

"You know, Styx, you're a fucking disappointment," Ripp said. "Everything I heard about you is bullshit, isn't it?"

"What about you?" Styx asked, drawing her focus around. "Mr. Underhand Backstabber, ain't you supposed to see plays like this coming?"

"Another ex-boyfriend? How in the shit am I supposed to know how many guys she's fucking? You said Wreck was it."

"That's the intel I had."

"Si, we gotta go."

The whisper from Dam helped Tulsi to re-focus. He

was closer, still aiming the gun at Ripp.

"You followed me from Florida, didn't you?" Dam didn't answer. "Dam, that was stupid. So stupid. You don't know how much danger you're in now."

"He's the one," Svana said, sitting on the concrete in front of Ripp. "The one you fell in love with?"

"'Nother plot twist," Styx said. "Wreck know that? 'Cause I bet he'd shake my hand for taking this guy down."

Whipping around, she lost the reins of her anger. "Didn't you just tell me that Wreck was as good as dead? Good job impressing a corpse."

"Hey! I don't give a goddamn about impressing anyone," Styx snapped, marching her way. "You are the most fucking annoying woman I have ever met! You don't know what's fucking good for you, do you?"

"Oh, and you think that you're going to educate me? Hardly, asshole. Ripp's right, you are a disappointment! I never thought for a second that you'd be the kind of guy to run scared. Geez, I'd be better off with Kieran than you!"

When he got close enough, Styx grabbed her and spun her around, slamming her back against his body. Tulsi gasped in surprise. His forearm closed tight around her throat while his other arm supported it. He'd threatened her life once before. She hadn't expected him to do it again, not when he'd apparently gone to such lengths to save her from Merchant's reach.

"Put the gun down, fucker," Styx growled. "Or your girlfriend goes bye-bye."

"Let her go!" Dam snapped.

The gun went off and Svana shrieked. Styx didn't relax, so Tulsi hoped that meant he was okay. Yet, his grip tightened further. Grabbing for his arm, she tried to pull it down, but he just clenched harder.

"Put it down!"

Dam stepped back and held up both hands, pointing the gun in the air. Bending his knees, he put the weapon on the ground and stood up straight again. "Don't hurt her. Let her go."

Her friend had relinquished his control to keep her

alive. At least that's what Dam thought. Styx thrust her forward out of his grasp, but caught her shoulder to steady her.

Tulsi was quick to turn and slug his stomach while rubbing her throat. "Asshole, you should've killed me."

"Why's that?" he asked, a glimmer of a smile on his face.

"If there's one way to keep Wreck alive, it's to give him a target."

Styx actually laughed. Turned out, the reputed murderer had a sense of humor. "Think I couldn't take him down?"

"I'd like to see you try."

Dam distracted her from Styx amusement. "What the fuck is going on here?"

"He's right, we need to figure this out," Tulsi said.

Styx wasn't laughing anymore. "What do you need?"

"You'll help me?"

"No promises."

"What about her?" Ripp asked.

Yes, Svana. The curious blonde may be on the ground, but her ears worked just fine. From the intrigue on her face, it was obvious she was trying to come to some conclusions of her own.

SIXTEEN

NO MATTER WHAT Svana did, she always got herself mixed up in something. Tulsi could identify with that. Even though it wasn't exactly the woman's fault she'd heard some damaging information, they couldn't take any risks by showing her too much compassion.

"I don't trust her," Styx said.

"Neither do I," Tulsi said because it was the truth. Killing Svana was a little more than she was ready for, but they had to keep control of her as best they could. "You got rope?"

"Maybe," Ripp said.

"Hogtie her and toss her in the trunk."

Styx was the one to move. The car in the middle of the space must have brought him to their location, so it made sense that he was the one to open the trunk and pull out a coil of thin rope.

"We're taking orders from her now?" Ripp asked.

"You can piss off," Styx said, going to Svana. It took little effort for him to pin her down despite her wriggling and complaining. Holding her down, he glanced up at Ripp. "You wanna back out the deal?"

"Please!" Svana called. "I can help! I'll help, I promise!"

No one paid much attention to her pleas. Ripp

answered Styx's question by crouching to help him with the tying.

Tulsi was watching them when Dam came up at her side, the gun loose in his hand. "We should get out of here."

Her friend deserved an explanation. He deserved something for all he'd put on the line for her. Offering a smile first, she unfolded her arms to put them around his neck.

After kissing his cheek, she pulled his ear to her mouth. "Thank you for coming to save me."

"Doesn't look like you need it," he said, tucking the gun into the back of his waistband when she let him go. "You want to tell me what's going on?"

"You really followed me?" she asked, letting the gravity of that gesture sink in.

"I figured you'd need help eventually," he said. "Something about that guy just wasn't right."

"Well, you were right about that," she said as Styx and Ripp lifted Svana into the trunk of the car and slammed it shut. "Something wasn't right… but we're going to make it right."

Styx and Ripp were striding toward them. The noise of Svana kicking and cursing rumbled from the trunk of the car behind them.

"We should gag her," Ripp said.

Tulsi smiled. "Where's the fun in that?"

Styx put a hand on her shoulder. "She'll quiet down in a minute."

"She will?"

He nodded. "Oxygen's a scarce resource back there. She'll get tired fast." Angling her head, Tulsi regretted not having enough time to learn more about this enigma. "Trust me, Prize. I know what I'm talking about."

"Don't doubt it."

"What's the play?" Ripp asked, showing little patience for shooting the shit.

Scanning around, Tulsi was pleased to find a door to the shorter section of the building. The wall next to it had a window, through which they'd be able to see the vehicle. The glass was cracked and dirty, but it was enough.

She nodded that way and led the group toward it. Putting some distance between them and Svana's listening ears was just smart.

Going inside first, she waited until the trio of men were inside and then closed the door as best she could. The hinges were rusted, so it didn't go all the way into the frame.

"The play was to get you out," Styx said before she was all the way turned around. "I get you away from Merch and hook you up with—"

"Otis, I know," she said, remembering what Wreck had said about getting her out of the country. "Not interested."

Surprise flashed on his face. "Not interested? You know how many asses are on the line for you?"

"I'm more aware of how many asses will be sacrificed for what I did. I put a knife in Merch. If anyone should pay for that, it's me."

"Whoa, wait," Dam said. "This is about the guy you killed?"

"Turns out that I didn't kill him," she said, folding her arms again. "I didn't know that. Svana was actually the one to tell me."

"Wreck didn't tell you?" Styx asked. "Shit, all this time you thought—"

"Doesn't matter what I thought. What matters is how we fix it. So, here's what I think—"

"Let me read your mind," Styx said with little expression or intonation. "I go back to Merch, tell him I heard someone is holding you. That person wants to do a switch: you for Rowdy."

"Something like that," she said. "How did you get out tonight?"

On a loose shrug, he inhaled. "Merchant sent me out to take down a shithead who missed his last few payments."

"Let me see your hand," she said, opening hers toward him, he laid his on it. There wasn't a mark on his knuckles. Turning a discerning eye up to his, she was curious. "When Wreck comes back from work, he comes back with scars."

"I'm more direct."

Tulsi dropped his hand. "You meant take him down like…"

The slow ascent of one side of Styx's mouth left him wearing the unmistakable pride of amused accomplishment. "Told you I'm a pro."

She couldn't believe he was so loose and calm about ending someone's life. Still, they didn't have the time to dwell, so she shook off her discomfort.

"Right," Tulsi said, licking her lips. "We should get bang for our buck. Do they still have Kieran?"

Styx recoiled. "I am not putting my ass on the line for the weasel."

"Seconded," Ripp said, scowling at her.

She didn't waste a lot of time waiting to explain her logic. "Do they still have him?" Styx nodded. "Getting Rowdy out doesn't matter if they still have Kieran. He'll go back for his brother. Wreck will go back for Rowdy. So…"

"The weasel fucks up the plan."

"We'll put your name on that list too," Tulsi said, then had a thought. "If you're out alone, Merch must trust you… He doesn't associate you with me and what I did?"

"We didn't know each other before. You and me. Merch didn't pull me in after you split. I've been working for him, gaining his trust."

Could trusting Styx be a mistake? Thinking for a moment that this could be a double-cross, Tulsi shirked her doubt when she remembered the mess he'd been in when they met.

"Wreck said the plan for you to get me out didn't work out."

"It didn't," Styx said. When he blinked, his eyes went from her to Ripp. "Until I learned something useful. This is the upgraded plan."

Looking back and forth between the men, it didn't take a genius to read animosity. "What did you learn?" she asked, but no one answered. "Whatever you learned was about Ripp and now you're using that to blackmail him into helping us."

"Something like that," Styx answered.

"Doesn't make him a very sure bet."

Styx exhaled another sort of laugh. "Prize, for fuck sake, nothing is a sure bet here." He didn't pause for breath. "I don't want to be on the list."

"You don't… Wait, what? Why?"

"Not believable for one thing," Styx said. "Someone's holding you and he'll only trade you for me and the brothers?" He shook his head. "I didn't work so hard getting the fucker's trust just to blast it apart with a rookie move like that."

"But I don't—"

"Listen, babe," he said. "I'll worry about me. If you're going back, you shouldn't go back alone. Who will be in there with you after Wreck and the brothers split?"

It was hard not to be humbled by the question. Styx was offering to risk his life to be there for her.

"You already saved my life," she murmured.

"No, I didn't. Your life wasn't at risk when Wreck was around. In with Merch, it will be. Besides, you did more than save my life that day. You've been saving it every day since."

"How did—"

"With your advice," he said, getting closer. "Don't be useless." Curving a hand around the side of her neck, he gripped her to give her a slight shake. "If you're useless, he has no reason to keep you alive… You reminded me of someone… Someone I haven't thought about for too long… Since hearing those words, I have gone out of my damn way to make myself as useful to him as I can."

"This could be your only chance," she murmured. "To get out."

The knowing twist of his lips intrigued her. "I've got an ace card, baby, don't you worry about me."

Without turning around, his attention shifted in Ripp's direction. For a second, she didn't get it. Styx had learned something about Ripp and he was using that to blackmail the guy. Something—

Her mouth opened in a silent gasp. Styx pulled her forward to press a kiss against her hairline, probably as a signal she should keep her mouth shut. Although Tulsi didn't know it for sure, he was implying that he knew something Merchant might want to know. Something he could use at the eleventh hour before the executioner's axe swung his way.

The missing shipment had brought them all together in the first place. Ripp had to know something, or he had to be responsible for it somehow. If that was true, Styx was playing a risky game keeping the information to himself.

"If you want me to put my ass on the line with Merch," Ripp said. "I need something."

Backing away, Styx completed their circle again. "Something other than your life?"

"Try it, asshole," Ripp growled.

"Once we're through with you."

"We don't have time for this," Tulsi muttered then raised her voice. "If the plan wasn't working out, did Wreck know… does he know what's going on?"

Styx shrugged. "Probably not."

On an exhale, she backed off. "Oh, well that's just great."

"I figured he'd be fine with any plan that got you away from Merchant."

"Maybe. But that wasn't the plan anymore. I already told him that I wasn't going to walk away, that I wasn't going to abandon him. Except that looks like exactly what I did!"

"Who cares?" Styx said, opening his arms. "You're going to sacrifice yourself. To a life of wonderful rape and brilliant torture. He'll be out. Him and his buddy, so what does it matter? You're never going to see Wreck again anyway."

Just like that. The simple words that were thrown at her with such ease smacked her in the chest and took the wind out of her.

For a minute, Tulsi couldn't move, even her eyes wouldn't leave Styx. A slow understanding calmed him as he probably figured out what had stunned her into this stupor.

"Babe—"

"No," she said, batting his arm out of the way when he tried to reach for her.

Staggering back against the door and flattening a

hand on her torso, rubbing the area around where her heart was supposed to be. She couldn't feel it anymore. It had to be in there, but in light of the truth Styx had delivered, it became simply a practical vessel, she had no other use for it anymore.

"He'll want Svana back too," Ripp said. "I'm guessing."

With his concern still alight, Styx was slow to shift his focus. "Doesn't matter. After Wreck and the brothers are out, let her go."

"She'll tell him about this."

"Probably," Styx said. "But it won't matter. If Tuls isn't already dead, she'll want to be. I've been there…" A few seconds of crushing silence passed. "Okay, I better get back. No point putting this off, right?"

"Wait," Dam said when the rest of the group began to break up.

Everyone waited for him to say something, but he seemed to be struggling.

"Great input," Styx said, grabbing the door to pull it open.

Tulsi had to hurry out of the way to give him and Ripp space to stride on out.

Dam took the chance to get in front of her. "You're going to kill yourself."

"I'm not suicidal," she said, at peace in a strange way. "I did something wrong. He did something wrong first, but… I won't let others be punished for something I did."

"Let me do something," he said. "I gotta know someone he owes a favor to. Tell me more about him."

"This one won't matter," she said. "I wounded his pride." Her jaw tightened as she drifted into a memory. "I know how valuable a man's pride is to him." Forcing herself to focus on Dam, she smiled and touched his cheek. "He wants to hurt me. I made a choice. It's time to stand up for that choice."

She tried to follow Styx and Ripp, but Dam pulled her back. "There's gotta be another way. Something I can do."

Searching his need, she felt sympathy, but there was only one thing he could do for her. "There is something," she said, which awakened his hope. "You won't want to, but—"

"Anything," Dam said. "I'll do anything."

"Get a message to Wreck," she said. "Tell him this isn't his watch and I don't expect fair. No regrets. It might have taken time, but we found each other and I'm grateful for that. No matter what."

Dam considered her for a few seconds. "You really love him."

Maybe he didn't want to hear it, but she had to be honest. "I really love him."

Dam frowned. "I don't get it. He took you to them… When I saw you going in that motel room with him, I didn't know what to think. I was gonna be patient, wait until I knew for sure you were in danger… When I watched you together in the parking lot—"

"Oh my God, you were there? You were watching us?"

A sort of contrite smirk slunk onto his features. He might want to be sorry because that was the decent thing to do, but he wasn't sorry, not completely.

"I thought when you got in the car and left that you were going. I followed, but you just went to that burger place then back to the parking lot."

They'd had sex in the back of the car before going to the burger place. "Oh my God," she said again and let her head fall into the crook of her thumb. "You were watching us when we…"

"Not my happiest moment," he said, putting an arm around her. "You really went at it."

"Oh God," she said again and pushed him out the way as he laughed.

Ripp was alone with the still tied Svana on the ground at his side. The car roared to life and Styx began to back out. The plan was in motion. It was only a matter of time. Styx would deliver the message and then…

In the months between the stabbing and Wreck discovering her, Tulsi hadn't considered seeing Merchant again. She'd thought he was dead and wasn't sorry or grieving.

Knowing that she would never see Wreck again, that

was something else. Something that was going to take longer to get over.

SEVENTEEN

DAM WENT TO GET some food. Tulsi had been happy to go, but Ripp pointed out that Merchant's men were crawling all over the city. Keaton's too. It would take the wind from Styx's sails if Merchant got word she was wandering the city on her own. More than that, if his goons got the drop on her, they could haul her in front of their boss and really screw them.

While she and Dam had their conversation in the office, Ripp and Styx had arranged their next meet. The plan was for Styx to tell Merchant he'd been approached about the exchange of Tulsi for the brothers and Wreck. Merchant would have to decide if the terms were acceptable. If they were, Styx was to return to the guy at midnight to arrange the trade. That was what Merchant would think anyway.

At midnight, Styx would come back to the drafty old lumber yard to let them know if it was a go. In the meantime, all they could do was wait.

In one of the oddest moments of her life, Tulsi was sitting on a cold concrete floor, leaning against a damp wall with Ripp sitting next to her. Svana was tied up in the office space they'd had their impromptu meeting in.

Tulsi was sick of the silence. "You came to get me

and Svana because Styx couldn't be away from Merchant too long?"

He nodded once. The intel Styx gathered from Merchant's was being fed to Ripp. By listening in on conversations or asking straight questions, Styx must have ascertained that Wreck and Coombs were hooking up with Teal and Delray. Learning their location wouldn't have been tough.

Styx and Ripp could've exchanged information and made their plans in clandestine meets. Doing Merchant's dirty work gave Styx an excuse to get out. How the pair met in the first place was a mystery for another day.

The blood on the motel door was Ripp's way of separating the group. Wreck had left her in the car to go inside alone. Well, with Coombs trailing behind him, but she guessed it was agreed Merchant's minions were fair game. If Ripp needed to put a bullet in Coombs, none of them would've lost any sleep over it.

Divide and conquer. Smart. With Wreck being unaware of the upgraded plan, he'd have put up a fight for her. Ripp wouldn't have risked his own safety. He needed a way to ensure none of the allies were injured.

"Was the blood a setup?"

He inhaled. "Only had to kill one of them."

People were dropping like flies. Being surrounded by so many men willing to kill would've once been an anomaly. These days, it was her normal.

Not that it mattered, but she asked. "Which one?"

"The white one."

Teal. Hmm. Tulsi didn't feel any kind of remorse about that. The guy had touched her up once and had lured Kieran into Merchant's net. Hardly a saint. Despite that, he'd been low on the list of those she would like to see erased from existence.

The silence reigned again. It stretched out, dragging and catching on every second.

Tulsi couldn't stand the silence; it made her itch. "So..." she started. "You're related to Keaton?"

"Nephew," Ripp answered.

She bobbed her head. "You don't get along?"

"Used to."

"Long story, right?" she said and he offered a single nod. "The best ones usually are. My mom died when I was twenty-one. Never knew my dad and—" His eyes cut to hers, his glare was easy to decipher. "You don't care." The next single move of his head was a shake. Silence… More silence. Tulsi was too damn edgy to be quiet. "You got a girlfriend?"

His answer wasn't instant. Ripp waited before responding, just long enough for the air between them to shift. "Nope."

Slow to take his fingers from his lap, he pointed one and touched her thigh. Drawing it upward, it was obvious he assumed her question was a prelude to something else.

"Uh," she said, putting a hand down on his. "I don't think so."

"Whatever. We've got time to kill," he said, getting up from the floor. "Not like I have standards."

"Oh, thanks," she said, clambering to her feet. "So you'd screw me to pass the time even though you're not attracted to me?"

Ripp wandered across the room. "Better that way, right?"

His attitude to the opposite sex revealed so much more about him than any answer he could give about his family.

"Your uncle fucked you up good, didn't he?"

He about-faced and leaned against the opposite wall. "What's your story?" he asked. "Don't believe anyone just walks into their death without some part of them wanting it."

Tulsi's chin rose. "That your story? You just waiting for your uncle to kill you?"

He snorted a semi-laugh. "If either of us wanted that, we'd have done it years ago."

"So you still love him?"

Ripp shrugged. "Gives me purpose. Death's a gift compared to some of the shit we have to go through." Something she didn't really want to think about at that moment. "I bet you wouldn't be so worried if Merchant was going to feed you a quick bullet… You're thinking about what else he'll put in you."

To deny it would be insane. No one would believe another person if they denied being afraid of rape and torture.

Still, Tulsi pushed her shoulders back, forcing her determination out. "I'm doing the right thing."

"And where has that ever got anyone?" he muttered.

Silence. Tulsi couldn't explain why Ripp intrigued her so much. With his uncle being the only family he admitted to, and no girlfriend, it seemed that he lived a lonely life. Maybe that was why she pitied him more than she feared him. He had nothing to lose, nothing except the war with his uncle. Obviously that war wasn't about winning. Ripp didn't want to simply conquer his uncle, if he did, he'd have nothing else to live for.

"You got any friends?"

"Trying to save me?" he asked. "Save your breath. I'm happy… No, I'm twisted and bitter and angry. But I'm cool with that."

Cool with hatred churning him up. Tulsi couldn't believe that. But it was all he had to live for.

"What did he do to you?" she asked, realizing that was the question she really wanted answered. "What could he have done that's so bad? What could he have done to make you hate him that much?"

Everything about Ripp hardened and cooled; he turned to stone right in front of her. It took another five seconds before his attention slid her way. From all the way across the room, he managed to chill her blood.

Lucky for one of them, that was the minute the headlights of Dam's vehicle cut across the empty yard outside. Both of them went to meet him when he drove into the warehouse and stopped where Styx had been parked before he left.

"Anyone see you?" Ripp asked when Dam got out with the food bags.

"No," he said, glancing between them. "Why? What's wrong?"

"I'm gonna check," Ripp said, snatching a food bag

and stomping out of the warehouse.

"What is—"

"Just leave him," Tulsi said. "Let him go."

Dam handed her a food bag. "He's a real nice guy. Laid back, you know? You have some real interesting friends, Patch."

They were on their way around the car, but he paused, which made her look back. "What?"

"Tuls," he said. "That's what the other guy called you. That your name?"

"Tulsi," she replied. "Tulsi Tern." She faltered. "At least, it was. I don't know who I am anymore… I'm not sure that it matters."

Dam tipped his head toward the car. "Want to sit inside? It's warmer."

It didn't make any difference to her, so she followed him to the back. He opened the door, allowing her to get in first.

"Leave the door open," she said as he was about to close it. "So we can hear if Svana goes anywhere."

He didn't object and did as she asked. Each opened their food bag and began to eat. Tulsi couldn't remember feeling awkward with Dam. It wasn't awkwardness that was between them even then. Stealing glances at each other, they both continued to eat. She could almost feel the tension of him restraining himself.

"Just say it," she said, brushing her hands together, then seeking a napkin in the bag.

"Say what?"

"Whatever is stuck in your craw," she said, raising her brows at him. "I know you, Dam. You always have something to say. Always have an opinion."

"You know my opinion on this. It's suicide. Plain and simple."

"Maybe," she said. "But even though you're a guy who makes his living on the wrong side of the law, you still know the difference between right and wrong. This is right."

"Why? Because you hurt the guy? If he was forcing himself on you, he deserved it."

"Yeah," she said on a nod because it wasn't like she disagreed. "He did. Damn right he did. But he doesn't care about fair or what he deserves. He's punishing a man who did nothing to him. Punishing a man who he only imprisoned in the first place because of another man's actions."

Dam peered at her. "You care about this guy?"

"Yes."

"You love him?"

"No," she said, breathing out. "It's not like that. It's…" Dam deserved an explanation, but Tulsi hadn't been the best at making herself understood recently. "Wreck loves him."

That just confused her friend more.

His puzzled expression made her laugh. "Dam," she said, taking his hand. "The Fox Den guys, the ones you really care about. How would you feel if one of them was being punished for something you did?"

"This guy is your Fox Den."

"No," she said, taking his hand. "You are my Fox Den. All of you. I adored you all and had great fun living with you. Being around you guys, it was… the closest I've been to being part of a family for a long time. Fox Den was a home. One that meant a lot to me."

"Then why leave it to come back here?"

"When I left, I didn't know I was coming back here."

"He lied to you."

His anger might come from a righteous place, but it was misdirected.

Pulling his hand to her lap, she forced him to look at her. "Even if he'd told me the complete truth, I still would've come back with him."

"And where is he now, huh? He fixing to leave you to the slaughter?"

"Wreck knows how I feel. I already told him that I was going to do everything in my power to get him and Rowdy out of this. Believe it or not, they're both innocent… this time anyway. The only thing Wreck did was fall in love with me, but that wasn't wrong. I wanted him to fall for me, I dreamed about it."

While saying the words, Tulsi realized she'd hardly dreamed since Wreck had returned to her life. Before then, she would dream of making love with him almost every night. Something about his presence must have calmed those urges… maybe because he'd been fulfilling them in reality… not that he ever would again.

Her attention fell. Dam brought it back up with a fingertip. "You really love him?"

She nodded. "And it's important to me that you give him my message. He's going to feel responsible for this and I don't want him to self-destruct. You have to make sure that he doesn't go after Merchant or try anything crazy. If Merchant hurts him, or gets his claws in again, all of this will have been for nothing."

"If he gives himself up—"

"He could walk back in and offer himself to Merchant. Merchant would hire him, in a heartbeat. But he wouldn't free me in exchange for him. He wants his pound of flesh."

"And you're going to give it to him," he said, squeezing her knuckles. "Goddamn, can't you see how much that pisses the rest of us off? You're all calm and in control, but you're making the rest of us feel powerless."

She smiled. "I know. If Wreck was here, he'd say the same thing."

"But you're going to do it anyway."

"I am," she said, putting her food aside. "I don't think Merchant will waste a lot of time on this. Styx could come back any minute."

Sliding backwards, she opened the other rear door.

"Tulsi," Dam said, getting her attention. "You've got balls, babe."

She grinned. "As so many men like to tell me." Shifting back his way, she kissed him once. "There's one other thing." He waited for her to elaborate. She hesitated, not quite ready to say goodbye, but there was no alternative. She kicked off her boot and propped her heel on the shoulder of the seat in front of him. Unfastening the knife holster from her ankle, Tulsi held it toward him.

He licked his fingers clean before taking the sheathed knife. "That looks like—"

"Rook gave it to me," she said. "I can't take it in there. I don't want Merchant to get his hands on it… You'll get it back to him, right? Tell him I kept my head up, but nothing could save me from the inevitable."

"This feels wrong," he said, laying the knife on his leg above his food.

"We'll all feel better in a day or two." She slid along the seat toward the open door. "I have to get my stuff out the other car. Keep an eye on Svana."

The men should feel better because they'd be free from their bonds, Dam included. Once she was in Merchant's possession, he would be free to go where he liked, do what he liked. Wreck, Rowdy, and Kieran too. They'd all be free of her and that was the safest they could be. Tragedy poisoned anyone who came into contact with her. The least she could do was liberate those she cared about.

EIGHTEEN

CURLED IN THE FETAL position in the backseat of the car she and Dam had eaten in, Tulsi tried to sleep. Waiting was driving her crazy, making her restless. Styx words haunted her. *"You're never going to see him again…"*

Wreck had rejected her attempts to say a proper goodbye in the shower. Just the suggestion that they'd have to drove him into a rage.

The last time his lips touched hers was just before he'd opened the bathroom door to Coombs. The bastard. Tulsi had a new reason to despise the idiot who'd interrupted their peace. Even knowing those were likely their last moments together, it hadn't really sunk in. Not until Styx smacked her in the face with his words.

Thinking of Wreck, especially while they were apart, was standard. In bed, at the end of the day, she'd often speculated about where he might be and what he could be doing. Then she'd slip into sleep and he'd join her in a carnal fantasy. No more.

In Fox Den, she'd reminded herself over and over that she and Wreck would never see each other again. This time it was different. Death was on the horizon. So close that she could almost feel her heart slow by the prospect, Tulsi was ready to succumb.

Ripp was right, she was afraid. In any other circumstance, she'd probably opt for suicide over giving herself to a man intent on torturing her to death in ways she probably couldn't even imagine. Tulsi had been proud of her imagination most of her life, but it was becoming a curse.

She wasn't sure of the exact time until the rising sound of a vehicle coming closer gave her a clue. They were waiting for Styx to show up. Merchant had to agree to the switch, he had to. He had no reason to continue holding Rowdy. Except to control Kieran and Wreck. It all came down to what he wanted more. Did he want to control the brothers and possibly get his shipment back or did he want her?

Tulsi felt sick. Shifting onto her back, she stared up, and rested her bent knees on the backrest. She feared closing her eyes. That was the truth. She feared living a nightmare in reality. The reason for her insomnia was that simple, she was terrified to meet Wreck in her dreams. With her trepidation about what Merchant had planned, her imagination was an enemy.

Light from the approaching car died before it finished its arc around the interior of the warehouse. The direction of it betrayed that the car was parking next to the one she was in.

Styx.

Closing her mouth, Tulsi inhaled through her nose and told herself to sit up. Nothing happened. Not until she heard his voice.

"Where is she?"

Grabbing the top of the seat, Tulsi braced just a second before the door beyond her feet opened. "My Ruin," she whispered.

He thrust an open hand her way. With her gaze locked on him, she slid her palm over his and Wreck's fingers closed around hers. He yanked her from the back of the car, but her feet didn't touch concrete. Curving an arm around his neck, she joined it with the other when he let go of her hand. Wreck cradled her ass in both hands and moved to kick the backdoor shut as she tilted her head to seek his mouth.

Tulsi hadn't wanted their last kiss to be their last. On

their first night of intimacy, she'd begged him to be the last man she chose for herself. Nothing had changed. She'd said that she would always choose him.

As her legs wound around his hips and he turned to press her body against the side of the car, her love for him lit so bright that it heated her heart. Even though they were closed, her eyes were wet. Tulsi didn't care. She didn't care about herself, didn't care about Merchant, didn't even care about torture. Wreck was her gift. Whatever higher power was out there, it had granted her one final wish.

Ripping his mouth free from hers, Wreck had to let go of her ass to push her hair from her face and hold her back as she sought his mouth again.

"Kiss me," she pleaded. "Ruin."

"Did he hurt you? Nymph, are you hurt?"

She shook her head. Her tears streaked her cheeks. It was only then she realized Wreck had been wiping the moisture from her face.

"Is he going to do it?" she asked, opening her eyes to read his concern. Her tears were still slipping from her lashes. Tulsi didn't know if they were tears of fear or happiness that they'd got one last chance to see each other. "Will Merchant trade?"

"Yeah," Wreck said. "He will, baby."

Relaxing into a smile, her shoulders dropped on her exhale of relief. "I love you."

He took a step back, pulling her legs from around him so her feet dropped onto the floor.

"We're not saying goodbye," he said, taking her hand.

Styx, Ripp, and Dam stood on the opposite side of the car between them and the office. There wasn't time to speak to them. Ignoring the trio of guys, Wreck pulled her out of the warehouse and kept on going across the yard until there was serious distance between them and the building.

Yanking her past the nearest iron column, Wreck moved in close, pinning her back against it.

"Did you see Rowdy?"

Wreck shook his head. "No. There wasn't time."

Damnit, she'd hoped that the friends might have the

opportunity to see each other. It would do a lot for Rowdy's spirit to see Wreck. Enduring the pain would be much easier if he knew there was light at the end of the tunnel. Wreck could've found a way to tell him that they would be free soon.

Deciding not to dwell on that, Tulsi was happy that the men would be together and away from Merchant soon.

"When is the exchange happening? Do you know? Rowdy will be—"

"Are you sure you want to do this?"

Tulsi didn't expect the question. "Yes," she said, wondering why he was asking. "I told you we were going to get Rowdy out of there. When Ripp snatched us, I was terrified that he'd take us to Merchant and we'd lose our bargaining chip. But it's worked out. It's worked out great."

She smiled, but his concern didn't go anywhere. He was dealing with a pain of his own; it was written all over his face. Laying a hand on his jaw, she tried to comfort him.

He put his hand on top of hers for just a second before taking both her wrists. Wrapping her arms around to her back, he held her there. "I…"

"What, baby?" she asked.

The awkward position hurt her arms, but it was a price worth paying to be so close to Wreck again.

His jaw ticked at the same time his brow strengthened. "I don't know if I'm strong enough for this."

That he might be too weak for anything was laughable. "Course you are, baby. You're the strongest man I know. Don't focus on me, forget about me. Focus on freeing Rowdy. That's what I think about if I get scared. After this trade, both of you will be free and you can go back to how your life was before I walked into Teal's. Life will be exactly like it was."

Shifting her wrists into one hand, he used his free hand to tuck her hair behind her ear. "Life will never be like it was."

"I'm happy I got to see you again," she said, focusing on the reassurance of his body heat merging with hers. "I wanted to tell you I was right." One of his eyes twitched in question. Tulsi grinned. "You were the last man I chose for myself. Merchant can kill me if he wants, you ruined me for every other man."

"Tuls…" he started, his gaze searching her. "I love you."

The words he forced out on an exhale weren't easy for him to say. He'd been the one to assert that they wouldn't say goodbye. His declaration proved his belief that she was going to die. Wreck was saying his goodbye.

Widening her smile, Tulsi tipped her chin higher, pushing her crown into the metal behind them. "I know and that's why we're going to free your friend. It's why I will give my life for yours. And I do expect you to mourn, no other women for at least a year… Two if you really want to prove your devotion."

She tried the joke to keep things light. The situation couldn't be more serious, but she wouldn't act nervous or scared in front of him when he was already dealing with guilt. Only one could survive, her or his best friend. Making the choice would kill him, which was why she'd taken it out of his hands. Tulsi didn't blame him for where they were and she didn't want him descending deeper into the darkness that had lived in him since losing his sister.

"You are the strongest person I know," he said, the back of his fingers drifting across her cheek. "You've really made your decision to do this?"

"Yes," she said. "So it's pointless to talk about it anymore. What's the plan? Should we go over everything with the guys?"

They could make plans together, but after the exchange of prisoners, Wreck's part of the operation would be over. As far as she was concerned anyway. Rowdy would need to recuperate and it would fall on Wreck to get his friend through his rehabilitation.

He linked their fingers together and drew her away from the column to guide her back toward the building where they'd left the others. The three guys were loitering not far from where they'd been before. Styx stood facing the side of the car that Dam was leaning against. Ripp was between them facing the entrance, so it was him who nodded their way when they reappeared, alerting the others to their return.

"That was quick," Styx said. "And quiet… Thought your last time would be more… vocal."

Tulsi let her head fall to the side as she and Wreck stopped with the group. "We weren't having sex, thank you," she said. "What's the plan? When's the meet?"

"Two hours," Styx said. Her surprise must have shown on her face. "He wants it over with and I figured less time means less opportunity to plan a double-cross."

That made sense. "Okay, where?"

"Construction site across town, Ripp's got the address."

"'Cept Ripp can't do the exchange," Ripp said, glaring at Styx.

Obviously that had been the debate while she and Wreck were outside.

"You're afraid of Merchant?" Tulsi asked. "If your life's mission is to fuck with Keaton, I think Merch knows who you are."

"That's not why," Styx said.

She was still trying to figure out the why when Wreck spoke. "What the fuck is he doing here?"

"He's the guy." Styx said, jerking his thumb in Dam's direction. "The guy who tried to save her."

Tulsi didn't need to look at Wreck's face to know he was pissed. Sure, his grip on her hand tightened, but she didn't really need that signal either.

"Wreck's right," she said, stepping closer to her ruin. "You should probably go, Dam. It's safer for you to stay as far away from this as possible."

"Actually, we figured he's our guy," Styx said.

"Our guy for what?"

"I'll do the exchange."

"No!" she said almost before his words left his mouth. "You are not facing Merchant."

"Merchant won't do the switch himself," Styx said, then looked at Wreck for confirmation. "Least I doubt he will."

Wreck shook his head.

"I don't want Dam involved," she said. "It's too dangerous."

"There's a bounty out for Ripp," Styx said. "Merch's guys see him, there won't be an exchange, they'll just scoop all of you up."

"A bounty? Why would Merchant have a bounty out on you?" she asked Ripp. "If you spend your time dragging Keaton down, I'm surprised you're not his best friend."

"Ripp was the guy talking to Kieran the night before the shipment went missing," Styx said.

"Hey!" Ripp objected.

"The deal was I don't tell Merchant."

Though he was clearly pissed off, Ripp accepted that technicality.

"Why were you talking to Kieran?"

"Needed the time and the place," Ripp said. "Your friend is an easy mark."

Tulsi wouldn't argue against that. Kieran didn't know what was good for him most of the time, he wasn't great at big picture decisions. Ripp had shown her that he could be an intimidating guy. Approaching Kieran and pressuring him would be enough to get Ripp what he wanted with the least amount of effort.

"Why do you care about Merchant's drugs?"

Ripp exhaled his impatience. "They weren't Merchant's, he intercepted Keaton's shipment."

"So you were stealing them from your uncle?" Though she wasn't sure of his reasons, Tulsi doubted he was being altruistic in taking such a large shipment off the streets. "Do you deal them yourself? That amount of drugs can't be for personal use."

"I just like hiding them from people," he said. "Pisses them off."

"You can only piss them off if they know it was you. Your deal with Styx suggests you don't want Merchant to know."

Ripp's gaze narrowed on her. Tulsi figured he wouldn't be having that conversation with her if she didn't have so much loyal muscle nearby. "If Merch kills me before

I can crow to Keaton…"

Ah, so Merchant was incidental. Collateral damage in the war between uncle and nephew. Somehow, Tulsi got the feeling that Merchant had been caught between the two family members many times in the past.

Understanding what had happened to the shipment was one mystery solved. But that did pose another; her focus switched to Styx. "I thought you didn't know his name."

"I didn't," Styx said. "But I saw him with Kieran. One night I was out, chasing down Merchant's client when this guy tried to jump me."

So that was how they'd met. Styx had seen Ripp with Kieran, something Merchant would like to know. Styx could've pursued Ripp and taken him in to Merchant. That would've earned him beaucoup brownie points. Instead he'd recruited Ripp, made a deal to conceal what he knew, and saved Rowdy's life.

"Why did you jump him?" Dam asked.

"None of your damn business," Ripp said, obviously disliking how the focus had switched to him.

"He's looking for the guy who killed Keaton's girlfriend," Styx said. "Figure she was a double agent."

Keaton's girlfriend? His favorite. Alexis… she was feeding information to Ripp, did that mean he cared about her? Tulsi looked up at Wreck who glanced down. They were there when Alexis was killed. They knew exactly what happened.

"What?" Ripp asked. "What the fuck do you know?"

Their exchange hadn't gone unnoticed. "None of *your* damn business," Wreck answered.

"You know what happened to Alexis?"

"Were you in love with her?" Tulsi asked.

"We don't give a damn, Nymph," Wreck said, but she wasn't taking that from the man who was supposed to know what love felt like.

"And we're not telling him a goddamn thing until we don't need him anymore," Styx said.

Another part of the deal? Thinking about it, she realized it made sense. Ripp wouldn't worry about a threat on his life, not as much as he would about valuable information. At any time, he could walk away knowing that Styx wasn't free to track him down while working Merchant's cases.

So that was the deal. Ripp was to help them and in return, Styx wouldn't tell Merchant about Ripp's involvement in the shipment going missing. Once all was done and they didn't need Ripp anymore, Styx would provide information about Alexis.

Except Styx hadn't been there when Alexis died. Either he was bluffing, or he'd learned something about the murder from Wreck or the brothers.

"I was out of town," Ripp said. "Looking for her. I got wind that one of Merchant's men had taken her… that she was dead. Started hunting the fucker a while back."

Wreck squeezed her hand. "Ripp is the guy we were on the lookout for the last night, when Merch…"

The old enemy. Tulsi wondered at Ripp's sanity. If he hated Keaton so much, it would probably be smart to ally himself with Merchant. Except, men who believed they were powerful liked to control everyone around them. Ripp didn't strike her as the kind of guy who would take to being controlled.

"I don't need this shit," Ripp said, stalking around the front of one car, probably aiming for the other. "Tell Merch, I don't give a damn."

They still needed Ripp even if he couldn't do the handover. They needed him to keep the secrets of their meetings as well as deal with Svana who was a thorn in their side.

"Rowdy stepped up for her," Tulsi called out. "Alexis. He stepped up for Alexis." Ripp stopped and slowly turned his head to look at her. "We were there the night she died. That's why Wreck and I looked at each other. Rowdy spoke up for her. Tried to save her."

A few seconds of tense silence passed.

"Who killed her?" Ripp eventually asked.

Using his grip on her hand, Wreck pulled her back to step in. "We'll tell you. If you stick around, see how this plays out."

Ripp considered each of them. "I won't do the handover."

"Dam will do it," Tulsi said, accepting that he was the best man for the job.

Being the one to give her to Merchant also protected the Fox Den gang. It would prove that he was callous and had no feelings for her. So even if someone tried to tell Merchant that she had an affair while on the run from him, Dam's actions would contradict any claims that they were in love.

"Why would I trade you for them? I've never met these guys."

"Business," Styx said.

"Merchant won't ask," she said.

"She's right," Styx said. "And even if he does, you just tell him you're paying a debt or returning a favor or whatever. Doesn't matter, you know Merch wants Tuls and you had access to her… Rowdy is more valuable than her anyway." From the corner of his eye, he must have noticed her reaction because he turned her way. "In business. He's stronger. Has more experience."

"I'm not offended for me," she said. "I'm offended you think he's more valuable than Wreck." She didn't like the way that Styx's attention popped up to Wreck's. "What?" When no one answered, she let go of Wreck and moved around in front of him. "What is it?"

"I'm not part of the deal," Wreck said. "I'm not leaving Merchant's. The deal is for Rowdy and Kieran only."

NINETEEN

TULSI COULDN'T BELIEVE IT. After all she'd gone through, all her hopes and her conviction vanished in a heartbeat.

"Like hell you're not part of the deal," she asserted. "If you're not part of the deal, I'm not going back."

"Look around, Nymph," Wreck said. "Any guy here could drag you back there. Kicking and screaming only makes the scene more real."

"Damn you and more real," she said. "Why would you go back?" Flipping around, she set her anger on Styx. "What the hell did you do?"

"Wasn't me," he said, holding up his hands in surrender. "When I drove in Merch's garage to park up, your boyfriend and his buddies had just arrived back."

That would've put them a good hour or two behind her, Svana, and Ripp. "What took you so long?" she asked Wreck.

He growled Ripp's way. "We had a body to get rid of and a car to boost."

So Teal really was dead. Ripp had been telling the truth. That gave him another reason to be reluctant about the handover. Delray would've seen Teal's killer.

She frowned at Ripp. "If Delray knows you killed Teal, he'll tell Merchant that you were the guy who kidnapped us."

"I covered my face," he said. "I'm not an idiot."

Scrutinizing him and then Dam, she had to admit that they were similar in build, so they should be able to pull off the deception.

Tulsi looked to Styx again. "What does it matter that they were just arriving—"

"Wreck and I spoke before I saw Merchant."

Damnit. That meant her love could alter the plan in any way he wanted to. She sighed. "And he told you he didn't want to be part of the deal."

"Helped," Styx said. "He's the only one Merch would've hesitated to give up... He's got a real hard-on for your boyfriend."

Tulsi knew that, though she didn't like to think about it too much. "I won't do it," she said, shaking her head. "I won't go back in there without knowing that you're safe and you can't be safe in there."

Wreck didn't flinch. His steely eyes remained fixed on hers. There wasn't a glimmer of reluctance or contrition in them. "Before you started calling the shots, the plan was I'd die with Rowdy. Why do you think it changes because you're in his place?"

Tulsi couldn't work out which was more infuriating that he'd made a valid point she couldn't argue or that no matter what she did, she wasn't able to save his life.

Struggling to contain a growl of frustration, she turned to stalk away from the men. She paused, staring out at the columns in the yard. In the shadows of night, they were beginning to resemble towering headstones.

There were more than enough of them out there to account for every person Merchant employed. Tulsi's declaration that she would consider suicide, but wouldn't go down alone, had been prophetic. The problem: her strength came from knowing Wreck would be free. She would die for him, no questions asked, but taking him down with her... She hadn't factored that in.

"How do you know Rowdy won't come for you?" she called, still twenty feet away from the men behind her.

"Rowdy's fucked up," Wreck said. "It'll take him weeks to get back on track. We'll be long dead by then."

Odd consolation, but consolation all the same. "What about Kieran?" she asked, spinning on the spot to regard the men again.

"He'll give us the weasel," Styx said. "Guy's useless to Merch anyway. He's useless to everyone, I figure Merch's sick of him. Wasn't like he needed much persuasion."

Tulsi could believe that. She was sick of him and she hadn't seen him for weeks. "So you're going back to Merchant to tell him we're on?" she asked. "Then in two hours…" Her attention floated to her friend. "Dam takes me and Svana to the rendezvous. And then what?"

Like Wreck said, Rowdy was fucked up. In her version of what was supposed to happen, Wreck would be there to support his friend. In this updated version of the upgraded plan, no one would be there to support Rowdy. Learning that Wreck's mindset hadn't changed was a blow. He'd planned to die with his best friend, but they'd assured his freedom, so Wreck planned to die with her instead.

"We'll look out for him," Dam said, volunteering himself and Ripp with a nod.

"I don't play nursemaid," Ripp said.

Dam wasn't dissuaded. "Not even for the guy who tried to save your girl?"

The reminder of that truth grated on Ripp; she could tell from the way he worked his jaw and folded his arms. "I was promised goddamn information."

"Once Wreck and I are under Merchant it's unlikely that we'll survive."

Tulsi wanted to believe that somehow her love would be smart enough and quick enough to find a way out. But, in truth, once she was gone, his fight would leave him too. Wreck wouldn't try to save himself; he wouldn't worm his way out. He coveted death because he couldn't handle failing in what he saw as his responsibility for her. No matter how many times she told him that she wasn't his responsibility, that she made her own choices, he didn't hear her. Wreck seemed determined to shoulder as much burden as possible.

"Rowdy can tell you everything," Styx said. "If he was there, he'll know it all."

"We need a safe house," Dam interjected, talking as though it was a done deal. "Somewhere we can go that they won't find us. Doesn't have to be fancy. Somewhere warm, somewhere dry."

By the way he scanned their current environment, she understood he was offering a not so subtle hint that the lumber yard wasn't suitable.

An idea struck her. "Yes," Tulsi said. "You need somewhere they won't think to look for you. Somewhere warm and dry with indoor plumbing and basic medical supplies."

"Got somewhere in mind, Patch?"

"Actually, I do," she said on a smile. "Go to my place."

"Your place?" Ripp asked, his brows rising.

"Merchant already knows everything he wants to know about me. If they've tossed the place, it's done. There's no reason for them to go back. They know I'm not there. I'll be with Merchant. My store is on the first floor, my apartment's on the second. There are two bedrooms and the living room couch pulls out. It's already stocked with linen, towels, everything you should need. I'll write down the address." She paused. "As a plan B, if they come looking for you or you find yourself in trouble with no place else to go, call Bradley Hershel. I'll write his number down too."

"Your ex?" Wreck said.

"He has various properties and the cash to hire security. He'll also be able to afford the best medical minds, if Rowdy needs help." Wreck's disapproval went nowhere. "Like I said, it's a plan B. Isn't it better that they have the option?"

Wreck shrugged, unhappy with her suggestion, but he didn't argue it. There was no comfort in winning that battle when she could almost hear Wreck reminding himself that he wouldn't care about her ex after they were both dead.

"What about the swan?" Ripp asked. "Giving her to Merchant is a bad idea."

"Agreed, but what else can we do?"

"Use her as a bargaining chip," Styx said. "Ripp keeps her locked up until we're through, then we let her go."

"That might work," Tulsi said, thinking that she should take some time to talk to the woman who was probably doing her best to eavesdrop. Taking the risk that Svana had picked up on anything was too big a risk when the stakes were so high. They couldn't give her back to Merchant... yet.

"What about Putnam?" Tulsi asked setting her sights on Wreck. "He freed her when she wanted out. Merchant dragged her back... Maybe we should give her what she wanted... I'll talk to her. If nothing else, we should keep her away from Merchant until this is over with. Finishing us will be glory enough for him; he'll have won. Svana's tales won't matter after we're gone. He won't have a reason to pursue Rowdy. There will be no one left to torment."

There were so many details, so many things to remember, so much that she still had to say. Tulsi's head was spinning even though she did her best to appear composed. She needed to relax. She needed to breathe. What she really needed was some serious time alone with her man in a safe environment, but that would never happen.

"I don't know how long Merchant will keep me before he kills me," she said to Dam. "Could be a day. Could be a week, a month."

"Or a year," Ripp muttered under his breath.

That was a thought she didn't want to dwell on. Any notion of torture was difficult enough without considering the potential duration of the experience.

Choosing not to respond to Ripp's comment, she continued with her instructions to Dam. "Do not let Rowdy come back here. Merchant will use him if he gets the chance. Don't let Kieran come back either. If he comes back, his brother will follow, and then we'll be right back at square one."

"You guys are putting a lot of faith in the idea that this guy is gonna do what I tell him," Dam said, though he didn't appear too concerned.

"Rowdy's a mess," Styx said. "I know how those bastards treat the prisoners in their cells, and Rowdy's been putting up with that shit longer than I had to. He won't be thinking straight. He probably can't even walk the length of himself. Even if he wants to come back, he won't be able to, not for a while. But she's right, don't let him talk any of you into coming back. Wreck and me will be in there, we'll do what we can for Tuls."

Styx could've taken the opportunity to flee. He'd said he was staying to watch her back, but with Wreck staying, he didn't technically need to do that.

"Merchant still thinks we hate each other," she said to Wreck.

"That's good," Styx replied while her lover stayed silent. "Keep it that way for as long as you can. So long as he thinks that, he won't try to use you against each other." He moved to a more central spot of the group. "If Merch wants to hurt you or wants you to do something and all he has to do is hurt Wreck to get it, he'll keep on doing it."

Styx made a good point. He'd managed to activate her imagination, which conjured scores of ways Merchant could use their love to his advantage.

"He's an asshole," she said, rubbing her temples. "Why does this have to be so complicated?"

"It's not complicated," Ripp said. "Styx and Wreck go back to Merchant. Dam here takes you to the rendezvous, switches you out for Rowdy and the other guy. I'll hang back and watch your asses. He and me will take your injured birds back to your old nest and you get to die at the hands of the man you stabbed in the gut. Easy."

Ripp just tied everything up with a neat bow. Still she was uneasy. Once they were at Merchant's, all Tulsi had to do was play the bitter and twisted role of the scorned girlfriend, a woman betrayed. She could manage that. It was unlikely she would even see Wreck after Merchant had her. But nothing was a certainty, so they had to take advantage of the opportunity to say everything that they had to say while they had it.

"I need to talk to Svana."

Still tied up in the office, the young blonde would be pissed off to the max. Tulsi doubted she was afraid, if they'd wanted to kill her, they would've done it already. If Svana had gleaned anything from their conversations, she would be champing at the bit to reveal all to Merchant. All Tulsi needed to figure out was if the blonde was smart enough to listen to reason.

Tulsi opened a hand to Dam. "I need my blade back, just for a minute."

"Gonna cut her loose?" Styx asked.

Dam crouched to retrieve the knife from the sheath that was strapped around his ankle under his jeans.

Tulsi took it when he stood up to hand it over. "Temporarily. I need to find out if she's interested in saving herself. Do we have any duct tape?"

"Probably in the car."

"Can you find it? We'll have to put her in Ripp's trunk and keep her away from the exchange. We can't risk her screaming or being heard by whoever Merchant sends."

Styx offered a nod and a two-fingered salute.

"What are you going to say to her?" Dam asked.

"I'll give her a choice. She has to stay our prisoner for a while. After that she gets to decide if she wants to be freed or returned to Merchant."

Tulsi didn't wait for objections or reactions. She turned to march toward the office. The youngster was getting a choice while she felt merciful. Whatever Svana's decision, Tulsi wouldn't let the blonde beauty ruin their plans or risk any more lives. This wasn't a game, it was an Olympic event. Those at an elite level were determined to win. Medals and money weren't what lay on the other side of the finish line. Tulsi was going to die, but before she did, she planned to do everything in her power to ensure those left behind didn't suffer at Merchant's hands. He'd win his battle with her, but her death wouldn't herald the end of the war. His victory would be short-lived; hers would be eternal.

TWENTY

FORCING OPEN THE heavy office door, Tulsi stepped inside and used her whole body to push the door back into its frame. Svana was on her side in the middle of the floor, facing away from the entrance.

Tulsi sighed. Fortunes changed so quickly. The innocent weren't safe and the guilty could triumph. Nothing was certain.

Just a day ago, Svana was in a position of power holding her captive with Coombs, now she was the subdued prey.

Walking around her slowly, Tulsi examined the woman, waiting for a sign of awareness. Her eyes were open, but she didn't give any signal of being conscious anyone else was in the room. That or the youngster was just out of fight. Tulsi could identify with that sense of futility. Even if Svana wanted to fight, what would be the point? Ripp was bigger than her and faster, and he wasn't the only guy out there anymore. Dam had been joined by Styx and Wreck was present too.

Continuing around the prisoner, Tulsi tightened the circle of her trajectory and came to a stop just behind Svana. She breathed for a moment, preparing herself in case the blonde lashed out. Svana could have a weapon, although Tulsi doubted it. There weren't many options for concealing a weapon in such a skimpy outfit.

She crouched down and used her knife to cut through the rope, giving Svana control of her limbs again. Tulsi backed off to prop herself against the narrow sill on the internal window.

Svana needed a few seconds to realize that she was no longer bound. She rolled onto her back and then sat up to work the rope from her wrists. Her back was still to Tulsi, but the youngster spoke anyway.

"Are you going to kill me now?"

"Maybe," Tulsi said because until she got a measure of the woman, she wasn't going to give too much away. "Depends on you."

Svana twisted to peek over her shoulder. "On me?"

"What's the story with you and Putnam?"

On an exhale, Svana shuffled around to face her captor. "He probably thinks I'm dead."

"Maybe," Tulsi said. "You heard what we've been talking about out there?"

The youngster wasn't easy to read. She didn't go straight for innocence and didn't pull her attention away. "If you're going to kill me, just do it."

"Wow," Tulsi said, folding her arms, being careful to keep the sharp blade away from her skin. "For a second there, you almost sounded like me."

She tried to hazard a smile, but Svana's narrow eyes betrayed she couldn't figure out whether to be comforted, angry, or scared.

"I know you think I'm an idiot," Svana said. "You don't like me."

"I never said that. We're not the same, Svana, that's all."

Sorrow came into Svana's demeanor as she toyed with the rope. "Wreck's in love with you, isn't he?"

"Hopelessly," Tulsi said. "That should reassure you. He was being faithful to me when he rejected you, that's all."

"I don't care about that," Svana said. "He's hot, sure,

but…"

Seeing the youngster despondent, Tulsi's head tilted as she wondered what was hurting so much. Didn't take long for her to figure it out. "It's the love, isn't it?"

"You were right." Svana sighed and tossed the rope from her hands. "If Merchant loved me, he wouldn't share me."

Tulsi couldn't argue against that. The only love she'd known was with men who wanted fidelity, even if they weren't willing to give it. "Merch is a complicated man, not too easy to figure out. Maybe he's just different than other men. I was angry. I said what I said to hurt you."

"You were right. You were." Looking up, Svana met her eye with a renewed kind of determination. "Merchant doesn't love me. He's a sick bastard who can't love anyone… If you go back there, he'll torture you… We can't let you go back."

To not be suspicious of the sudden turnaround would be insane. Still, Tulsi smiled. If the youngster meant it, then the experience of being a captive had led to an awakening, one she needed. But if Svana had heard the plan, this epiphany moment could be a ruse in order to get her freedom and warn Merchant.

"I have plenty of people worried about me," Tulsi said. Wreck and Dam were on that list, maybe Styx, probably not Ripp, but at least he was on their side… for the moment. "I came in here to figure out what we should do with you."

The shrinking fear Svana adopted was fake, one element of the innocent youngster's persona. If she hoped to provoke sympathy, she didn't have to work too hard. Tulsi already felt sorry for her. Pulled this way and that, Svana had never made choices for herself. From her mother right on through to Merchant, people had been using the beauty her whole life.

"Do you love Putnam?" she asked because he was the only one Tulsi was on the fence about.

He'd helped Svana escape before. No way would he risk doing something so dangerous if he didn't have feelings for the blonde.

"He was kind to me."

"Yeah, and he almost lost his life for the trouble. I can't let you go now because I don't trust you. But if you trust me, you will be released soon."

"Soon?"

Tulsi shrugged. "I can't tell you exactly when."

"So you came in here and cut the ropes just to tell me I'm not free."

"No, I came to give you a choice."

Svana frowned. "What choice?"

"I'm going back to Merchant," Tulsi said. "Tonight. If he asks about you…"

"If he asks about me, what? Why would you go back there?"

"It's complicated," Tulsi said because there was no point in telling Svana everything.

Beyond the fact that Tulsi didn't trust her, she also wouldn't be swayed. So no matter Svana's opinion, nothing about what happened next would change.

"What he'll do to you, that is complicated," Svana said. "When he snaps, when his anger takes over… I've been a target for him and I never stabbed him… He'll kill you."

That seemed inevitable. Once Tulsi was back there, Merchant would either kill her on the spot or toss her into one of his cells. Escape would be impossible with his men crawling all over the building. Without a weapon and probably in a weakened state from the semi-starvation Merchant liked to inflict on his prisoners, Tulsi wouldn't stand a chance.

No doubt Styx and Wreck wouldn't be allowed within twenty yards of her. So even if they managed to get a security pass or a key for the door of her cell, they wouldn't know which one she was in. By the time they found her, Merchant would've mobilized his people to take the men down. Tulsi might not even know it, she wouldn't know when her love fell unless Merchant delighted in sharing the details.

The more she thought about the possibilities, the more her anxiety rose. Although she kept reminding herself that there was no way to know what would happen, Tulsi's imagination enjoyed speculating on what one or all of them would endure.

"We can tell him that you're dead."

Svana looked up, struck by a bolt of surprise. "What?"

"Either we tell him that you're being held and we see what he does or… we tell him you're dead, which might give you a better chance of surviving." Crazy but true. "If he thinks you're dead, he won't send anyone after you like last time. We won't be able to hide you." Because Tulsi would be dead. "So you'd have to be careful. Being out there on your own can be tough. But it's that or we return you to Merchant."

The blonde considered the choice for a dozen seconds. "Can I think about it?"

Tulsi shook her head. "You can have a few minutes, but no more than that."

If they were going to tell Merchant that Svana was dead, Wreck and Styx had to know that was the line before they returned to Merchant. Her group of allies wouldn't have another chance to get their story straight. All of them had to know if Svana wanted to be declared dead and they'd have to come up with a line on how it happened.

The blonde was still in the middle of the floor when Tulsi hauled open the door to rejoin her friends. All of them turned to watch her cross the space.

"She's thinking," Tulsi said.

"She gonna think fast?" Styx asked. "We gotta get on the road."

"I know," Tulsi said, giving the knife back to Dam.

As soon as he had it, she began to walk backwards, out of the group again. Some of them were probably confused about where she was going, but when she raised her arms and opened both hands to Wreck, they probably figured it out.

"We don't have time for that," Dam said from behind Wreck who was already walking her way.

Fixing her gaze on him, Tulsi smiled when he sped up. Stalking to her, he grabbed her waist to pick her up. Her arms and legs twined around him as her mouth nuzzled at his. Her lover read the signals, he knew her inside and out, knew what she needed from him.

He carried her out of the warehouse and around the single story building to the front where it was protected by the corrugated wall.

When her back hit the wall, she took her arms from around him to lay her hands on his face. "Please reconsider, love," she murmured, needing to take one last shot at getting him to safety. "No one's life is better without you. You should be alive. You should be—"

"A person needs something to fight for. To live for."

Spouting her words back at her didn't earn him any points. "You shouldn't listen to me. I didn't know what the hell I was talking about back then… We know that he wants to kill me, but you still have a chance. It wouldn't be fair to—"

"I told you to never expect fair from me," he said, squeezing her waist to give her a shake. "What do you think I'll do if I see him hurt you? If I hear he's hurt you?"

Her imagination grabbed at those questions and ran wild. "Then why are you coming back?" she asked, slipping her hands under the leather of his jacket to dig her nails into his shoulders. "You're walking into your tomb."

"Our tomb," Wreck said. "If there's any chance I can get you out of there…"

"No," she said, shaking her head. "My Ruin, he gets to do whatever he wants to me. This is for Rowdy, we're doing this for Rowdy."

"After Rowdy is out of there, he'll be safe. There's still a chance—"

"There's no chance," she said. "He'll lock me up, away from you. You have to toe the line, make him believe you don't care about me."

But Wreck didn't lose any of his determination. "I'm gonna take down those bastards from the inside."

"No, you're not," Tulsi said, brushing her nose across his. "You do that and Merchant will kill you… or worse."

"I don't care about torture."

"Yes, you do," Tulsi said, touching her lips to his. "I don't want you to see it."

"See…"

Raising her chin, she met his eye. "Merchant will make you watch. If he thinks you care about me, he'll make sure you're there to see it."

Gritting his teeth, his lips narrowed. Memories of Sienna's rape and murder still haunted him. Merchant would give him a chance to relive that horrific day if he got even a hint that Wreck still cared about her.

"I won't abandon you," he murmured under his breath.

"Oh, my Ruin," she sighed and touched her mouth to his again.

Grabbing the back of her head, Wreck's fingers curled until he gripped her hair tight. Deepening their kiss, he forced his tongue into her mouth, showing her his determination with the power of his domination.

Tears left her eyes again, but she didn't let them distract her from his kiss. Tulsi could accept death if that was the consequence of what she had done. She'd accept it to save Rowdy who was innocent of her crime and of Kieran's.

Losing her love, admitting that his death would follow her own was the only thing making her hesitate. But it didn't matter. Whether it was her or Rowdy, Wreck wouldn't walk away. He couldn't save himself; he wouldn't. The night he'd lost his sister had imprinted itself onto him. He'd stuck by Sienna then, even though it hadn't been his choice. Wreck was forced to witness the demise of his only family. The single night had changed him; he carried it with him. To that day, it influenced his decisions.

At the same time Tulsi began to loosen his belt, Wreck got hold of her skirt, yanking it up to her hips, out from between them. She got his jeans open and held him tight to guide him inside her. With one push, he sank himself deep. Tulsi breathed out her ecstasy. As she forced her heavy eyelids to rise, she noticed he was watching her.

Pulling back and pushing in, her love was moving his hips, uniting their bodies for the last time. He slid an arm under her ass for support and to tilt her so he could drive deep into her. Tulsi was mesmerized by the love she read in him, consumed by the heat of their desire. The wetness on her face didn't register until he began to brush away her tears.

He couldn't ask her not to hurt. By returning to Merchant, Wreck was breaking her heart. She understood that urge, his need to be near when she lost her life, but it would ruin him. Both of them knew it. Piling her death on with what he felt about losing his sister, he'd be broken. Maybe that was why he was indifferent to the prospect of his death.

Urgency began to build low in her gut. This was the last time they'd be alone. The last time they'd be together. Weeping for the death of their relationship, the death of their chance for a future, Tulsi couldn't deny that their joining was bittersweet.

Not so long ago, she'd been in bliss imagining that they could wake up together every day. But they would never wake together again. After he walked away from her, they would never even be close again.

Wreck had been right about fair. None of this was fair and she shouldn't have expected it to be. Merchant was wicked in the most despicable of ways. To think she'd once considered the prospect of being with him was sickening. It nauseated her just to think of his kiss let alone acknowledge that she'd once thought him skilled.

"My Ruin," she whispered, grabbing for his shoulders beneath his jacket.

Seizing her ass in both hands, he showed his resolve in his crushing grip and the way he propelled her hips to his, joining them hard and fast.

Her eyes closed again. Even though he was still scrutinizing her, she let herself focus on their bodies, on the sensation of him filling her up and withdrawing. The sweet heat of friction spoke to her soul. His skill fired her hormones, they begged him to stay within her always.

They didn't have always. This was their always. Nothing would come after this. That moment was her last living moment. Tulsi would never feel again. She wouldn't let Merchant hurt her or pleasure her. Without words, she gave Wreck permission to activate her emotions and endorphins any time he wanted. Knowing that he would never be allowed to touch her again, Tulsi handed herself over to his desire.

A burst of tense pleasure released its pressure. Her mouth opened in a yelp of orgasm that Wreck quickly stole with a kiss. Although they were supposed to be there in secret, there was nothing secret about what she felt for him. It was difficult to remind herself that they hadn't secured Rowdy's release yet. Part of her wanted to die right there, with Wreck inside her on the cusp of his climax. No moment could be happier and yet this was the saddest moment she'd ever endured.

Wreck released himself within her. With him still deep inside her, Tulsi opened her eyes and laid a hand on his cheek. His breath clouded hers as the short pants of his need subsided.

"I love you," she whispered. "And I still don't regret finding you."

He touched her lower lip with a fingertip. "I'm sorry, Nymph."

Though her tears still hadn't dried, she smiled. "That's not what I want to hear from you. This isn't your fault."

"If we'd kept our hands off, we wouldn't be here now."

"What did I tell you about inevitable?" she asked, guiding his hand away from her mouth.

Putting her hands on his chest, she slid them up under his jacket again. Instead of nestling them in his warmth, she pushed the leather down as far as she could. With his grip still on her hips, it could only go as far as his elbows. But that was enough.

Bowing forward, she tipped to the side and opened her mouth to press her teeth into his upper arm. That was their feral sign of love. She didn't bite him as hard as she had before, but she wanted him to have something, a reminder before their demise that they were a part of each other.

When Tulsi released him and sought his gaze again, she thought he was more at peace.

He brushed her hair from her face. "I love you, Nymph."

Finally the words, plain, simple, and perfect. She

smiled and put both arms around him to hold him. It was something she hadn't had a chance to do enough. Though she could probably say that about everything. Tulsi wanted a chance to be with her man in so many ways, yet they only had seconds left.

Clasping her head in both hands, he stepped away from the wall to let her feet drift back down to the concrete beneath them. His kiss was soft at first, but it built to something more desperate, something more permanent in a heartbeat. Wreck didn't want to leave her. As much as she was against him going back to Merchant, he had to face a more ominous truth. He could hope for a quick death. Hers wouldn't be so merciful.

Pushing her hair back and wiping the tears from her face, he eased away from their kiss to look into her one last time. When his hands dropped to his sides, Tulsi threaded her fingers between his. It was over. It wasn't their choice. But this was their last and now it was finished.

As much as her will fought against the need to leave that moment, she began to move, backwards at first, and then she turned to lead him around to the warehouse again. After they crossed into the building, she let him head back over to the guys while she went to the office door.

Straddling the threshold, she kept her regard for Svana brief. "What'll it be?"

Svana sat there hugging her knees to her chest. Yet, when she looked up, she didn't appear meek. "Tell him I'm dead."

Tulsi smiled. The swan had made a smart choice. She hadn't chosen the easy life, being in hiding alone wasn't simple. But it was better than submitting to Merchant, who wouldn't have much use left for her.

Each had their role to play.

An engine started behind her, Wreck and Styx were getting ready to leave, they'd just need word about Svana's choice and then they would be gone. The curtain was rising on their tragedy, and it was more important than ever that they all remembered their lines.

TWENTY-ONE

SITTING NEXT TO Dam in his vehicle, it was impossible not to be vigilant when the tension was so high. They needed the handover to go without a hitch. Rowdy needed it. Tulsi and Dam scanned the construction yard, waiting for something to change. Ripp had it a little easier. He was parked a block away with the duct-taped Svana in his trunk. They weren't taking any chances.

Rowdy was the most important thing to focus on. Once he was safe, they could relax. Before that, they had to assume Merchant planned to screw them over or that something would go wrong.

"This doesn't feel right," Dam said.

Incomplete structures and scaffolding stood around a central concrete courtyard. The boards around the perimeter of the site formed a barrier, giving them privacy from anyone who may be passing on the street. Not that there were many people loitering in the wee hours of the night.

"It wouldn't feel right to let an innocent man die," she said, remaining alert. "That's what I'm focusing on."

"I've never met this guy. Why will he trust me?"

"He'll be in no state to give you crap," Tulsi said. "And whatever happens, you and Ripp have to keep him safe.

Kieran will bug the shit out of you. I wouldn't wish him on you if I wasn't backed into this corner. He'll want to do something stupid. You have to keep a close eye on him. If you have to tie him up and gag him to keep him away from Merchant's then do it."

"Why would he want to go back?"

Tulsi didn't know that he would. Kieran could be a selfish being; she hoped he kept on being that way after being liberated. Knowing Kieran, he'd do the absolute worst thing possible, which meant he'd suddenly decide to grow a set.

"It's a long story," she said, glancing around the shadowy location.

They'd killed the headlights on driving into the site that wasn't padlocked shut. The wide wooden gate was temporary while the construction crew were building. But it had been open on their arrival, which made Tulsi uneasy. Dam had been smart enough to park parallel to the central concrete area, but had turned the car first. If they had to make a quick escape, they could floor it and get out.

Putting the lights on could signal to someone on the outside that they were there. With their luck the way it was, all they needed was some nosey neighbor or passer-by to call the cops. The whole thing would go to shit if police showed up to investigate what was supposed to be a deserted site.

No buildings overlooked where they were, though there were buildings on the same block. She supposed, and hoped, that they were workplaces rather than homes.

Guessing who Merchant would send to do the handover only fed her rebellious imagination. Since making her decision to return, Tulsi's mind only seemed satisfied when it was tormenting her.

"Tell me," Dam said, she glanced his way. "Tell me the story." Tulsi went back to studying their environment. "It's not like we have anything better to do."

"I was on a date with him," she said. "We go to the same gym. He'd been asking me out a while. I said yes when I couldn't come up with another excuse."

"He was your boyfriend?"

"No," she said on an exhale. "On our first date,

Rowdy called him." Tulsi took a deep breath. "I didn't know what was going on, but we left the restaurant. Instead of letting me go home, he took me with him to meet his brother... and Wreck. Turned out that Kieran owed Teal some money; they were going to pay that back. What we didn't know was Merchant had lost a shipment of drugs; he accused Kieran of stealing them. Merchant had a bounty out for Kieran. Baines, Merchant's number two, was at Teal's. They locked us up... That night was when this started, all of this."

"What did Kieran think of you hooking up with Wreck?"

"Far as I know, he never found out. I don't know. I don't really care. If it wasn't for Kieran, none of this would be happening. There's a reason people call him a weasel."

Blaming Kieran wasn't exactly fair. He hadn't asked to be locked up. Wreck had told her that someone put a bullet in him on Merchant's order after she fled. He'd probably endured his own hell in the past few weeks. Rowdy was his brother, Kieran wouldn't enjoy seeing him in pain, or not seeing him at all.

If he was smart, Kieran would curse her name. He should hate her. Rowdy should too. But she couldn't dwell on that. Once they were free, she would be imprisoned and they wouldn't see each other again.

Tulsi was beginning to feel the fingers of impatience clawing at her throat. A flash of headlights from the direction of the entrance made her straighten up. As cover, her wrists had been duct-taped together after they were done taping Svana's mouth.

"Put it on," she said, turning to Dam, shoving her hair out of the way.

Before leaving, they'd cut a length of duct tape for her mouth too. The corner of it was stuck to the dash. Dam exhaled probably to remind her that he'd been against the plan to silence and bind her. But it had to be believable.

If Tulsi was his prisoner, he wouldn't risk her escaping. Most of Merchant's men knew she liked to talk, so taping her mouth to shut her up was definitely credible. Making her look like a true captive was only one reason for the tape. The other was to remove her ability to say anything smart to whoever was doing the handover.

The headlights died as the sound of a vehicle rose. It trundled closer until it came into view in the wide space Dam had used to turn. Tulsi began to worry that the other vehicle could turn and block them in. The car did turn, and she tried to figure out who was inside when it stopped. Before she could decipher any features, the vehicle backed up to stop at the perpendicular side of the central concrete square.

Having a clear path was a break they needed. Both cars had the ability to leave in a hurry… or to block the other in if they were quick enough.

"Game time, baby," Dam muttered, checking the gun he had tucked into the back of his pants.

Taking a weapon was both smart and dangerous. At the lumber yard, she'd tried to dissuade him, but he was doing them a favor. If a weapon made him feel safer, she couldn't argue against it.

Baines and Delray got out the front of the car. Tulsi drew a long breath in through her nose. Suddenly, her memory of Alexis reared its head. That poor lifeless woman lying on Teal's floor, her eyes wet, a circle of blood on her forehead. Not long after Alexis' demise, Tulsi had wondered if she'd end up the same. She never in a million years guessed she'd be walking into the enemy's lair by choice.

Baines opened the backdoor and reached inside. Delray went around the hood to help his boss with whatever he was doing. They both did something and then jumped back. Delray retreated to slam the door just as the rear one closest to them opened and Coombs got out.

Great, three of them. Baines and Delray bent down. When they stood, they were dragging something between them.

Rowdy.

His head was bowed. While he was on the other side of the car, it was tough to make out if he was dead or alive. Tulsi swallowed hard. Presuming it was a given, they hadn't been specific about wanting him back alive. When they pulled him around to the front of the car, relief hit her like a tidal wave. Although he was shirtless and barefoot, Rowdy was trying to take his weight, trying to walk. It was unlikely that anyone had told him what was going on. He probably assumed his life was about to be ended.

Coombs joined his associates. They came a few steps closer before tossing Rowdy down to the ground in front of them. Tulsi wasn't thinking straight. She didn't think about Kieran or his absence. All she cared about was the man with his hands bound at his back and the pain he'd endured for her.

Grabbing for the door handle, Tulsi pulled it hard, but nothing happened. They'd locked the door. With her mouth covered, she couldn't call out. Instead she swung around and hit Dam's arm to gesture at the door.

"There's only one of them."

If she had to kill Kieran herself just to prevent Rowdy from coming back, she'd find a way to do it. Dam was still scrutinizing the men, so Tulsi hit him again, not hard, just to get his attention. He breathed out and opened his door to get out, though he stayed behind it.

"Where's the other one?" he called.

Baines said something to Coombs, who then retreated to the car, going in the direction of the trunk.

Tulsi was making as much noise as she could, trying to get Dam's attention. He didn't acknowledge her, but slammed his door and came around to her side. As soon as the lock popped, she yanked the door handle again and shoved the door open, which probably sent Dam backwards too. She wasn't supposed to like her captor and couldn't think about one friend while the other was so broken.

Tulsi ran around the door and Dam to head for Rowdy, who'd managed to get onto his knees. Probably before he'd even registered that anyone was there, she flung herself down, scratching up her knees as she slid toward him and looped her bound wrists around his neck.

She wanted to tell him that she was sorry. Wanted to beg his forgiveness and assure him that it was all going to be okay… All except for the death of his best friend. Regretting the duct tape, all she could do was hold him.

"Tulsi?" he croaked.

The difficulty of that dry word revealed how little he had used his voice. After denials and asking for mercy that was refused, he wouldn't have had anything else to say to Merchant's thugs. In that cell all alone, he probably only saw another person when they came in to give him water.

Her arms were still around him when she leaned back to look in his eyes. That was Rowdy, definitely, he was in there. Even if he did appear surprised to see her. His frown suggested an anger that she couldn't deny him.

Everything he'd been through was because of her— since she'd stabbed Merchant anyway. Rowdy had been in jail when Sienna, his great love, had been raped and killed. He'd been powerless to help her. His brother had drawn him into a plot that almost got him killed and forced him to do someone else's dirty work against his will. Then she'd stabbed the man in charge, and he was punished for it. He'd endured so much.

Pulling him forward, she felt his weight wobble, but brought his head to her mouth anyway. The duct tape remained between them, but she couldn't show him her remorse any other way. Holding him as tight as she could, she buried her face against his neck, offering him a sympathy and compassion that he probably hadn't experienced for a while.

"Tulsi?"

Kieran's voice drew her focus. He was walking up to them, Coombs at his side. Looking ragged and thinner than when she'd last seen him, the first thing she noticed was his limp. Tulsi didn't have time to figure it out because someone grabbed her arm and pulled her to her feet.

Looking around, she tried to get her bearings. It was Dam, he had hold of her arm and was pulling her to the side, away from the concrete courtyard. Fearing he'd had a change of heart or was about to abandon the mission, she fought him and shouted, though her words were muffled by the tape.

"Tulsi, what's going on?" Kieran asked, crouching to try helping his brother up.

The siblings struggled against each other; both of them had suffered Merchant's anger.

It was stupid to ask her questions when she couldn't talk, but it wasn't a shock that he wasn't thinking straight. She wasn't either. She was too busy trying to pull away from Dam.

Instead of dragging her back to the car or trying to run, Dam surprised her with a length of rope. Thrusting her against one of the scaffolding poles, he trapped her hands against it, and used the rope to attach her to the metal.

"Hey, she's ours," Coombs said.

The idiot. Whatever Dam was doing, it wasn't stealing her away. By tying her hands to the pole, he'd just made it more difficult for any of them to leave with her in a hurry. Tulsi watched him return to the brothers.

"She stays there until I'm gone," Dam said. "Try anything and I'll put a bullet in her."

"Boss wouldn't be happy 'bout that," Coombs said, once again proving himself a fool.

Baines ignored Coombs. "You're smart," he said, while Dam helped Kieran to steady Rowdy. His eyes narrowed probably on the gun in Dam's waistband. "You wanna tell us why you give a shit about those fuckers?"

"No," Dam called back.

Rowdy was between Kieran and Dam, using all of his energy to walk to the car. Dam opened the back door as he was closest. He and Kieran helped Rowdy into the car, then Dam opened the driver's door to use it as a shield. He nodded at Kieran, indicating he should get in the back too. As he turned, intending to get in, he paused to make eye contact with her.

Tulsi couldn't speak. She couldn't even show him a smile, which was for the best. With Baines and his goons just meters away, showing any sign of appreciation would mess everything up. A tear tracked down her cheek, but it wasn't a tear of sorrow.

Unable to show any expression, Dam dropped into the car and closed the door. He gunned the engine. Baines, Coombs, and Delray had already moved out of the way, which was a shame—watching him drive over those guys might be fun. The satisfaction would be short-lived, it would leave Wreck under Merchant's command and alone.

Gravel sprayed up as Dam disappeared from the lot. The relief was a comfort. For just a second, she was at peace.

Rowdy was going to get the help he needed. Kieran was free too; the brothers had no need to ever return to Merchant's. They'd completed the handover without a hitch.

Sinking against the pole again, she rested her temple on it and appreciated their success. Positive feelings couldn't last. The heat of her thankful tear dried in Baines shadow as it cast over her. He moved in close with Coombs and Delray on either side of him. Tulsi didn't give the other two the time of day, it was Baines who she looked square in the eye.

"Pretty," he said on a sigh and propped his forearm on the bar above her. "You have been naughty… Damn, girl, you need to be taught a lesson."

Knowing Merchant, there wasn't a chance in hell he would've told Baines to end her there. The way the boss hung on every detail of a story being recounted was a real insight into his sadism. Hurting people, or sending others to hurt people, was his MO.

Except this time, Tulsi had been the one to slight him and it wasn't over money or drugs or anything tangible. She'd hurt his pride, refused his love. Merchant wouldn't want to repay that kindness from a distance, he'd want to do it up close and personal.

Baines nodded at Delray who began to untie the rope from her taped wrists. Even when it was loose, and she could leave the pole, Tulsi's still wasn't able to use her hands. The tape on her wrists wasn't bound as tight as Styx's had been way back when, but it was tight enough.

Baines grabbed one arm while Delray took the other. They began to lead her to their car. There was no going back, next stop would be Merchant. Avoiding him was impossible. These were her last steps in the outside; the last time she would breathe fresh air. The end was definitely nigh.

TWENTY-TWO

THE DRIVE BACK to Merchant's wasn't long. Of course that didn't stop Coombs from getting in a few barbs on the trip. He was so proud of the fact that she was back in their hands. Just to shut him up, Tulsi was tempted to tell him her allies had orchestrated the whole thing.

At least he'd done the driving, that was a reprieve. Baines was in the front too and spent most of the journey twisted around in his seat so he could stare at her. Whatever his smirk suggested, she wanted to smack it right off his face.

Instead of losing control, Tulsi switched her own focus to Delray, who sat beside her. The quiet man spent the drive staring out of his window. He couldn't care less about her. He'd been the one to open the door to them at Teal's. Realizing that with Teal dead, Delray's future was uncertain, his silence took on new significance. Kieran hadn't acted like a stranger to Delray and didn't think it was odd to see him at Teal's. If Teal was his employer, maybe his friend, Delray didn't have the same purpose as before. Maybe working for Merchant would be better for him, either way it seemed he was grieving Teal.

Delray gave her hope that maybe some of the thugs had hearts beneath their menacing facades. Even if they did, no one was able to help her anymore.

Coombs drove into Merchant's garage and parked. For some reason, she became hyper-aware of her own breathing. She didn't feel like it was louder than normal, but it was all that filled her ears. Her chest got tighter by the second. Fending off an impending panic attack was not what she needed. In the enemy's lair, Tulsi's head had to be clear. Merchant would want to see her. Maybe. Or maybe he'd want her locked up for a while, leaving her squirming on his hook without an end in sight.

All three men got out of the vehicle. Tulsi wasn't in any hurry to get to wherever was next on the itinerary. Baines opened her door and offered her a hand. It might be a gentlemanly gesture, more likely he wanted to get a measure of how she wanted this to play out, the easy way or the hard way.

With no way to avoid the inevitable, Tulsi took his hand with one of hers. The second hung there in the air without purpose. This was her life, her death, her beginning and her end. Memories of her childhood assaulted her as Baines pulled her out of the car.

The door behind her was closed. She could see Coombs' mouth moving but couldn't hear his taunting. Every second dragged until the whole world was going in slow motion. Thoughts of her mother rose up. Playing when she was a child, talking, enjoying time together. Their fights over her step-father in her teen years. Tulsi relived the low moments and the highs. She remembered the laughter, the tears. The end of her mother's life. Remembered the smile her mom gifted her at the end when they both knew there was nothing else either of them could do.

Wreck was the next to fade up. Briefly overlapping with her mother's end was Tulsi's beginning with him at the bottom of Teal's stairs.

Baines still had hold of her hand. She stumbled, putting one foot in front of the other, panting, subduing her panic as they crossed to the stairwell. Her eyes closed in a slow blink as she thought of Wreck's kiss. Of their first kiss, that night when she'd climbed on top of him and begged him to ruin her.

In their ascent, the stairs grew steeper. At least it felt like they did. Her body was heavy, her heart pulled toward Wreck, wherever he was within the building. She wanted to tell him that Rowdy was safe. Thinking about the question in Rowdy's eyes before she was dragged from him, she sent out a silent plea for him to be okay.

Those people hadn't brought her to the current moment, standing outside the top floor door, waiting for Baines to slip his keycard into the slot.

Merchant. He'd brought her there. He'd wanted something from her, but she'd defended herself.

Baines opened the door. Yanking her hard, he swung her around to push her into the hallway first. There at the end were the double doors to Merchant's office. The room where she'd driven his own dagger into his gut.

Breathing out, moving toward those doors, Tulsi shook her hair down her back as her chin rose. Baines and his goons would be somewhere behind her, but she didn't look back. On her walk to death row, she wasn't going to break down. Tulsi wouldn't beg. She wouldn't cry or plead with her executioner.

Merchant was a cruel bastard with little regard for anyone who didn't conform to his rules. Even knowing that these could be the last minutes of her life, Tulsi kept going, walking with pride and the honor Merchant had tried to steal from her.

At the office doors, she stopped, her eyes trained ahead, her heart pumping against her ribs. Baines moved to one side; Coombs did the same at the other. Both took a door handle and pushed them down to throw the doors open in front of her. In a one shot dose, the office came into view. Empty as it seemed, she knew he was there.

Sure enough, the chair behind the desk began to turn and there he was proud, smug… and definitely alive. His determination was nothing to her resolve. If he wanted to play, they'd play, but she wouldn't give him any satisfaction. Before anyone could utter a command, Tulsi walked forward to enter the office of her own accord. She'd left that room in a hurry but by choice, she planned to enter it again the same way.

Merchant's mouth thinned, not in displeasure, more like he was trying to conceal his joy. He thought he'd won. He thought she was there against her will. Just like Coombs. None of them could know how the situation had been manipulated.

Tulsi wouldn't choose to let Merchant end her life if she had alternatives. The lack of alternatives was the only reason she stood there in front of him, but he'd never understand her choice.

Baines came around her to pick the corner of the duct tape from her mouth. He ripped it off and a surge of pain tried to make her react. But she didn't. Upholding a steely façade that Wreck would be proud of, Tulsi stayed put, her attention fixated on Merchant's.

They stared each other down. Even when Tulsi heard the doors behind her close, she wouldn't take her eyes from his. A fight might arouse him, but it may also free her from his games. Tulsi wouldn't discount pushing buttons to force his hand; she wouldn't discount anything.

"Pretty," he purred the word like it brought him pleasure. "You were naughty."

If that was what he wanted to call it. Tulsi didn't plan to say a word, not until he said something worth responding to.

"I'm disappointed," he said, remaining in his chair. "We could've been something amazing. We were something amazing… But you went too far."

"So did you," she said.

In this room, with this man, Tulsi refused to take all the blame. Yes, she had been the one to hurt him, but his actions had called for a drastic response.

"You knew what we were, where our relationship was going."

Rowdy was free. Kieran was gone. Wreck was in the building. Styx too. Merchant could hurt them in retaliation for any of her actions, but Tulsi was done being cautious. The last thing she wanted was for Wreck to be in pain, but he knew why she'd come back. Tulsi had returned to save his friend and now that was done, her bounds were loose.

"No man has a right to pressure any woman into anything. I said no."

"You think you can justify what you did?" he asked, that amiable façade cracking. "You tried to murder me."

"And next time I'll succeed." They stared into each other again. Her resolve kept increasing even when his lips twitched into a smile. "You think it's funny?"

Slamming a hand onto the desk, he shoved his chair back and shot to his feet. "I think you're deluded! You had a chance," he snapped, thrusting his finger her way. "We could've been a formidable team, a force together! You chose to betray me!"

"I chose to defend myself," she argued. "You betrayed my trust!"

"It doesn't matter anymore," he said, reaching across to retrieve the dagger that she'd thrust into him.

There would be a sense of poetic justice that even she could appreciate if he chose to kill her with the same blade she'd used against him.

Staying still, subduing her emotions, became more difficult when he began to move toward her. Tulsi didn't want to be afraid. Her eyes warmed and she feared tears, feared showing him any iota of weakness.

Wreck would want her to be strong. Closing her eyes, Tulsi imagined herself face-down on the bed in the hotel room with Hillam on top of her. Reliving that moment ensured a potent shot of adrenaline flooded her system. For a second, she was sure the scent of her love hung in the air, just like it had lingered on the sheets they'd shared.

When she opened her eyes, Merchant was in front of her, the knife between them. He touched the point to her throat. Despite the threatening tears, her eyes widened displaying resolve that was fierce, but only semi-genuine. Tulsi wasn't afraid of death, she was afraid for Wreck, of what he would do when he learned she was gone. Her death would herald his and even though it was his choice, she didn't want him to fall because of her.

The tip of the blade slithered lower, toward her

cleavage. Merchant took a small step back, grabbed her arm and shocked her by slipping the point of the knife under the tape on her wrists. With a quick motion, he sliced through it, freeing her hands.

Her fingers hadn't been bound, but she moved them all the same, then ripped the tape from her skin.

Tulsi looked up at him. "Why did you do that?"

"Because you'll need your hands," he said, turning around to walk away from her.

He went back around the desk and opened a drawer to put the knife away. Hiding it was smart of him, which irritated her. All she needed was a few seconds with that blade and his soft underbelly. Rook's lessons came back to her. Tulsi heard his voice in her ear telling her to twist the blade, to drag it through flesh, to inflict as much damage as possible.

She hoped her murderous thoughts weren't obvious on her expression when Merchant faced her again.

"Ask me," Merchant said, behind his desk, but still on his feet.

"Ask you what? Why I'll need my hands?"

"I'm fair," he said, starting around his desk again, slow with a swagger in his step. "I'm going to let you go."

Freedom. That didn't sound right. Tulsi didn't like being off-kilter, but she couldn't figure him out.

"Now?"

"Yes," he said, stopping in front of her. "I'm going to let you go after we have sex."

"What?"

The cruel carnal twist of his smile wasn't benevolent. "You're going to ask for it." Her mouth opened a fraction. "You're going to beg me for it."

A fire of rage stoked her belly. "Never."

He tipped his head to bring his ear closer to her. "What was that?"

"Never!" she asserted and spat at him. Tulsi tried to retreat a step, but he got hold of her wrist. "No! Let me go!"

Pulling her across the office, he flung open the door that led to her suite. While she fought and objected, he dragged her down the short hallway and through the door into the bedroom that had once been hers.

His grip bruised her wrist. When he threw her to the bed, she tried to jump back up, but he pushed her down and wrestled her hand to the head of the bed. Something heavy closed around her wrist.

Tulsi tried to fight against it. The bastard was stronger than her, so he got his way. When his hands left her arm, she tried to move it but couldn't. Tipping her head back, she saw he'd shackled her to the bed with a padlocked leather cuff. He climbed over her to do the same to her other wrist. Tulsi tried to kick and scratch. He fended her off and fastened her other wrist to the headboard.

"You bastard!" she screamed at him.

Her torment was only just beginning.

He grabbed her leg to pull off one boot and then the other. Any assumptions that he only wanted to make her comfortable vanished fast.

From his back pocket, he produced a small switchblade. With one knee on the bed, Merchant went for her skirt next. Using the knife, and in spite of her screeching, he cut the clothes from her body, leaving her naked and at his mercy. The fuck.

With her hands attached to the bed, Tulsi couldn't do a damn thing to stop him taking anything he wanted.

"You're going to hell," she growled.

Smirking again, he closed the knife and slid it back into his pocket. The fucker enjoyed standing over her, admiring her body. He didn't even look at her face and didn't respond. After a few minutes, he retreated back in the direction of his office.

"Think about it," he said, stopping in the doorway to look at her again. "All you have to do is ask."

"Never!"

His smile widened. "Never is a very long time," he said. "Get some sleep."

He flicked off the light and then the door closed.

Once again, her breathing got louder. Ask him. He wanted her to beg him for sex. Damn him. She'd expected starvation and physical abuse. The bastard took his torture to a new level. She wouldn't do it. Not ever. Even if it meant lying there in the dark for the rest of time. Tulsi wouldn't do it. She would not.

TWENTY-THREE

LYING IN THE DARK with her wrists attached to the bed, Tulsi breathed through her anger and adrenaline. Reminding herself that Wreck was close by helped. She had no way to know whether he was in the apartment beneath her or in a cell further down. But he was in the building.

In her attempts to persuade Wreck to get to safety far from Merchant, Tulsi hadn't given enough credit to what it would mean having him nearby. That strength burned in her. It gave her enough fire to stay strong. For that moment, though their time was limited, they were both alive and under the same roof.

After her heartrate climbed back down, she fell asleep. When she woke up in the dark room, with thick drapes blocking out the light from the windows, there was no way to tell what time it was or how long she'd been asleep. So Tulsi lay there, awake, waiting. Time became abstract as she undulated back and forth between awake and asleep.

Eventually, the overhead light came on, jarring her from her semi-slumber. Her instinct was to put up a hand to block the glare, but her hand wouldn't go where she wanted it to. Everything came crashing back. She was at Merchant's.

The intrusion interrupted her solace. A happy dream

had joined her, something she hadn't expected. Given where she was and what may lie ahead, Tulsi had been grateful for the joyous interlude with Wreck, even if it was only an imagined affair.

"Pretty doesn't feel enough anymore."

Blinking her stinging eyes, it took a few seconds to focus. Baines stood at the end of the bed, appreciating her nudity. If Tulsi had the choice, she'd smack him in the head, maybe even put a blade in him, before she'd want him to see her naked.

Stripping her and laying her out was a power play by Merchant and she wouldn't give Baines the satisfaction of trying to hide herself.

"It's skin," she said. "You need to get out more."

He came sauntering around to her side of the bed. When he sat next to her, she tensed. Hiding her true feelings wasn't easy when he was so close. Sealing her lips, she concentrated on breathing through her nose when he laid a hand on her breast. It was difficult not to scream or spit when he squeezed her and ran his hand through her cleavage to the other breast.

"We never got to finish what we started."

"Merchant has rules," she spat out at him.

"He did," Baines said, still caressing her.

When his hand began to drift down, she tensed, balling her hands into fists and drawing up her knees. In an unexpected reprieve, his hand left her body as he chuckled to himself.

"Merch has plans for you, Pretty," Baines said like that was a good thing.

Good was relative. So far, Tulsi wasn't a fan of his plan.

Baines reached over her, pulling a key from his jeans pocket. Both of her hands loosened, so she sat up. He grabbed the chain hanging from one of the leather cuffs around her wrist. He yanked her hand to his lap and fought to gain control of the other.

"Make this difficult, please, baby," he said, pulling her chained hand higher, closer to his groin.

Being close to that part of his anatomy was disgusting enough. Discovering he was hard was a torture in itself.

"You're sick," she hissed. He put a link of the chain through the padlock and then attached it to the metal loop on the other cuff. "All of you are sick bastards."

"Yep," he said, using the chain to pull her onto her feet. Her arms were heavy and began to tingle as the blood rushed back to them. Baines tugged her across the room and shoved her into the bathroom. "You've got ten minutes, then I'm coming in."

The leather cuffs were still on her wrists with the chain connecting the padlocks, giving her about a foot of slack between them. "You want me to—"

He leaned in to grab the door handle and pulled the door to slam it on her words. Alone in the bathroom, the first thing she did was cross to turn on the shower. It gave some cover to her desperate attempt to find a weapon. Everything had been taken out of the room. A bar of soap sat in a tray on the edge of the tub and a towel was folded on the vanity. That was it.

"Damnit," she murmured.

Getting into the shower, Tulsi used the soap to clean her body and hair. A weapon would have limited use. She might be able to use it on Baines, but unless it was a gun, any wound would be more likely to anger him than kill him. Merchant wouldn't like it either, though he'd probably be pleased that he wasn't her victim.

Tulsi used the toilet and drank from the sink before drying her body. Once she was done, she tugged at the chain between her wrists. It was strong, too strong for her to snap or bend.

Baines opened the door, startling her. The way he looked her over suggested that he was disappointed not to find her in the shower.

"That it?" she asked.

"Almost," he said, stepping into the room.

Keeping her expression flat, she didn't react until he slid his fingers into her towel at her breast. With one pull, he yanked the material away from her body. Damn him. Tulsi knew it was unlikely they'd let her keep her towel, but she wouldn't miss a single opportunity to screw with them. Being the meek and sorry victim wasn't going to be in her future. Standing up for herself would either irritate them or arouse them. Whichever it was, Tulsi would keep pushing them to that brink if it meant forcing them to get on with whatever they planned.

The longer she was alive, the higher the chance she and Wreck could be used against each other. With every second that passed, the more Wreck worked himself into a lather. If her lover did anything to enflame Merchant's temper, he could be punished. It was Tulsi's worst nightmare that her love may be forced to relive Sienna's death through her.

Satisfied that he'd reduced her to the object they wanted her to be, Baines got hold of the chain to take her out of the bathroom. Tulsi expected to be returned to the bed. Instead, Baines turned to lead her through the door that only went one place: Merchant's office.

Instinct told her to pull back, to object, to shout. Her body tensed, her elbows bent. The tug on the chain made Baines look over his shoulder. But when she read the smug amusement written across his face, she relaxed. They wanted her to fight. Wanted to make her feel vulnerable.

It was psychological warfare. Merchant wanted to break her down so far that she'd beg for him to bed her on the flimsy promise of her freedom. Since learning about Merchant, she'd heard that he was fair. He believed in one slight being erased by another of equal measure. The only thing that was equal to what she'd done was attempted murder.

Merchant had been unconscious and bleeding when she'd last seen him; she'd left him for dead. At some point, he must have come around and managed to call his people to come back. If he put a blade in her and knocked her out, Tulsi wouldn't have anyone out there she could call to save her.

Baines didn't knock. Merchant's door was already a fraction open. Her keeper nudged it open and drew her into Merchant's office. Once again, he swung her around in an arc to toss her toward the man seated at the desk.

"Afternoon," Merchant said, without looking up from whatever he was writing.

That he sat there like some kind of legitimate businessman was laughable. There was nothing legitimate about him; he was probably writing a grocery list for one of his minions.

Tulsi didn't reply, so Baines jabbed her between the shoulder blades. Turning a glare over her shoulder, she wished Wreck was around to wipe that smug bastard's face clean.

"What?" she said to Baines before turning back to Merchant whose focus rose as he sank back in his chair. "Am I supposed to be afraid now? Oh, I'm naked. Oooh, terrifying… I'm more concerned about my hair frizzing as it dries."

"I wouldn't want you to be afraid, my sweet," Merchant said, nodding at Baines who pushed her again.

"What am I doing here?" she asked. "I haven't changed my mind."

"I wouldn't want you to feel neglected."

Assuming that he only wanted to ensure her decision hadn't changed was a pipe dream. After showing her to her suite the first time, he'd left her alone until she stormed into his office and threw a vase at his head. It missed, unfortunately, but he was using that event against her.

Baines muscled her up the step to the same level as Merchant's desk. He flipped her around and shoved her back to the wall."

"What are you doing?"

Baines reached over her head for something that she hadn't noticed before. A long dark chain, much thicker than the one around her wrists, hung from the curtain rod far above. The padlock on the end was loose. Baines retrieved it and forced her arms straight above her head. Not satisfied that the position was uncomfortable enough, he pulled hard to put her on her tiptoes before using the padlock to attach the two chains together.

The fucker stood back to admire his work. Merchant was already watching. Still in his chair, he had an elbow on the arm and a finger curled on the front of his chin. The two of them appreciated her like they would a painting.

Tulsi didn't want to be inspected by either of them. "Is this it?"

They were both too far away for her to kick out at. With the way she teetered on her tiptoes, she decided it wouldn't be wise to try that anyway. She'd just swing back and hit the wall, hurting herself and amusing them.

"You seem determined, my sweet," Merchant said. "I only want you close." She didn't believe that for a second and let him know by strengthening her glare. But he just smiled and looked to Baines. "Ready?"

Baines nodded. Her imagination went into overdrive. Ready for what? Merchant righted his chair at the desk and Baines went across to the double doors.

A trio of men entered when he opened the door. They saw Merchant first, but didn't fail to notice her. Once they did, she became the most fascinating thing in the room. Stringing her up hadn't been humiliation enough. Apparently, he wanted everyone to see the power he had over her.

Though she despised being ogled by the strangers, Tulsi smiled. "Hello, gents," she said.

"Eyes here," Merchant snapped.

Hanging her in the prominent spot next to his desk tempted those who entered to gawk at her. Asking them not to notice was as effective as asking a dog not to drool. After the command they all took their attention to Merchant, but it kept darting back her way as they stole further looks at her body.

"Give me a report," Merchant said to his men. "What happened last night?"

"Your night couldn't have been as fun as ours," Tulsi said, figuring if she made a nuisance of herself, Merchant would have to send her back to her room. "I had a helluva day yesterday. So eventful. I was kidnapped, bound, traded, taunted, then stripped and chained to a bed. Sounds like fun, right?"

The goons didn't know whether to react or ignore her. Merchant turned his chair around to look at her again.

"Helped me figure you out," she said to Merchant,

still wearing a smile, though it had become ironic. "You force yourself on women because none will give themselves willingly… It's that or you get them young and damaged, and you intimidate them into submission… Or you beat their will out of them… Have you even asked about Svana? Do you give a shit? She's dead, in case you were wondering. Dead. Dead. Dead…" Tulsi sucked in a breath through her teeth. "I sort of envy her that now."

Merchant leaped from his seat and lunged at her, grabbing her chin to haul her head up, pressing it into the wall. "Haven't learned your place yet, my sweet," he hissed, moving his mouth toward hers. "You will. Soon." He didn't let go of her chin, but looked over his shoulder to issue commands. "Get them out of here, bring the others up."

The others. Tulsi didn't want to ask. She recalled how when she'd been at his mercy before, he'd only referred to Wreck and the brothers as "them" and that didn't bode well. The gleam in Merchant's teasing eye confirmed her suspicions even before the double doors opened.

TWENTY-FOUR

MERCHANT BEGAN TO retreat, opening up her view of the room and giving the new entrants an unobstructed view of her. As much as she wanted to win the stare down, Tulsi had more important things to worry about. Just as she'd suspected, Baines had brought Wreck to the office. Not only him, Styx was there too.

Merchant was still watching her, so she couldn't give too much away.

"Now it's a party," she said and sighed. "Should we have another discussion on male pride?"

"Beautiful, isn't she?" Merchant asked, propping himself against the desk to continue checking her out.

Baines was a few steps ahead of the duo he'd brought in. Tulsi had to be careful of what she gave away with her expression, but Wreck's anger was easy to spot. Damnit, he had to calm himself down. His jaw shifted, becoming hard and unyielding. Fury ignited in his eyes. Even from away across the room, she could hear the temperature of his blood rise.

"To be looked at but not touched," she said, though that wasn't a complete truth. "Ilias doesn't want me to be reluctant, we're waiting… You know, until hell freezes over."

The strength of Wreck's sure brow softened to

confusion. Lucky that he'd deflated that fraction because Merchant chose that moment to slide into his chair.

"I should probably pity you, Wreck," Merchant said, rotating his chair to face the room.

The other three men in the room were looking at her. Tearing her attention away from Wreck wasn't easy, but with Baines looking her way, she couldn't be too intent.

"Pity him? He's had the pleasure," Tulsi said. "You should pity me for having to take it."

Laying a forearm on the desk, Merchant swung around her way again. "That's right, your great love betrayed you." His smile enjoyed that statement too much. "How does it feel to know you're nothing to him?"

"I told you I was nothing to him the last time I was here," she said. "Told it to Styx too, which you know 'cause you've got cameras all over the joint."

"That's right, I do," Merchant said, scanning the perimeter of the ceiling.

She wasn't sure where the cameras were exactly. The angle of them would mean everything to the interpretation of what happened the night she'd stabbed him.

"You knew damn well that Wreck didn't value what we were," she said, fixating on the boss again.

"But I knew you wanted it to be more," Merchant said. "I could tell from the way you were after he was in the room."

"No one wants to rehash the past," she said, being glib in the hopes he would change the subject.

No one would benefit from him relaying the events of the night she fled.

"No?" Merchant asked. "Sending him to you was a surefire way to bring you back… You followed like a lovesick puppy. Tell me, did you try throwing yourself at him? Were you hurt when he rejected your advances?"

Her advances. Merchant had laid down the law, issuing instructions that she was hands off. "I don't know, were you hurt when I told you I'd never submit to you?" she asked, landing a smile on him. "Did it hurt when I laughed in your face?" She hadn't exactly done that, but tipping her head to the side, she widened her smile. "You can beg all you like, honey. Won't change a thing. I am not yours. I will never choose you."

Without much of a reaction, he thrust the chair around again, seeking Wreck. "Was she pathetic? Tempted to offer a mercy fuck?"

Wreck didn't react. Tulsi got a better understanding of the position he'd been in trying not to respond to the obstacle between them.

"Want Coombs in here?" Baines asked.

The last person in the world who she wanted to be naked in front of… again. Her humiliation was getting difficult to ignore. Glancing at Wreck, she tried to imagine that he was the only one in the room. Just like the first night Coombs and Hillam had demanded she strip, Tulsi let herself believe that Wreck was the only one who could see her in the vulnerable position.

"No, we have business here," Merchant said, his voice becoming more professional. "The fucker who followed Teal and Coombs, we need to know more about who he is."

"You don't give a fuck about Teal," Styx said. "Can't be thinking about payback."

"I give a fuck about knowing how he found them. We could have a mole. Something is leaking from somewhere. If it was Teal, he deserved what he got."

"And if it was Coombs?" Styx asked. "We gonna repay the favor?"

"Maybe," Merchant said. "For a guy who wouldn't work for me, you've made a helluva turn around."

"Everyone's got to be good at something," Styx said. "Wreck's good at fucking people up, I'm good at killing them."

"Yes, you make an interesting team," Merchant said, then seemed to turn his attention to Wreck. "The man who followed them is the same one who wanted your friends. You know him?"

A surge of panic hit her. Wreck wasn't at the exchange, so he wouldn't have seen Dam. Just as she began to think that Merchant was setting him up, her ruin reminded her of something.

"Told you I didn't when we came back from setting it up."

Yes, Wreck had been with Styx when they'd apparently met Dam to set up the rendezvous. At the time, Tulsi hadn't given it much thought. After hearing the explanation, it made horrifying sense.

"Whoever he was, we can't let this slide."

"The trade is done," Styx said, tipping his chin toward her, though he didn't actually look at her. "You got the better end of the deal."

"Yes," Merchant said. "But my sweet is with me on this. She doesn't like a mystery. And this guy murdered our swan. If there's a new player on the field, we have to take him down."

Tulsi didn't like the direction of the discussion. Telling him that Svana was dead was supposed to give the youngster a chance to flee when this was over. If Merchant was going to pursue Dam or Ripp, he'd find them together. He'd find Rowdy and Kieran too. And they'd be at her place, which would thrust all of them into the spotlight.

"You're asking them to do that?" Tulsi said. "What? I'm not good enough?"

"You are not above suspicion, my sweet," Merchant said, tossing the words her way without turning. "Your emotional reunion with the prisoner wasn't missed."

"Yeah, that's it," she said, licking her dry lips. "I was having a torrid affair with Rowdy. You know, if I have fucked all these guys willingly, it must do something to your ego that you're the only one I keep rejecting. What does that tell you about your manhood?"

"Your little game is not going to work," he said, sinking deeper into his chair. "You think if you goad me enough that I'll just, what? Slit your throat?"

"Poison, gunshot, take your pick," she said. "Styx over there is desperate to finish someone. Bet he could strangle the life out of me in under a minute."

Merchant shook his head slowly. With the angle of his chair, she could only see the back of his profile. "Why would he do that before he's had a chance to enjoy you?"

A chill swept across her shoulders. Enjoy her? Merchant shared Svana with his men. The youngster had allowed it to happen and even given her permission. Was that Merchant's real plan? To turn her into a meek, kowtowed entity supplied to his men for their pleasure? Picked up and put down as their baser needs demanded?

Her smile was far away now. Tulsi wasn't sure she had the strength to pretend anymore. Shrugging off how she'd been flaunted and exposed was one thing. To know that her current position was going to be the highlight of her stay with Merchant was a cruel blow. He'd keep her for what? Days? Weeks? Months? Would he keep her there, in his clutches, for years like Ripp had suggested?

When Baines brought her to Merchant and he'd revealed his plan to wait until she was ready to beg for it, Tulsi had been so sure that it would never happen.

Now she didn't know what to think. Her future wasn't her own.

"Thought you were going to let me go after I begged you for it," she said, the sickness churning in her gut while the rest of her grew numb.

"If you want to leave," he said, his pleasure seeping into his words. "I'm optimistic."

That she would want to stay with him? No. If she had to stay with him for years, there would be no way she'd be able to walk away the same person or with the same conviction. Maybe by then Tulsi would be so conditioned that she would be nothing more than his plaything.

"I will never invite you into my body," she said, fighting to maintain her conviction. "Never."

"You said that last night," he said, peering back at her. "Don't sound so sure now, my sweet."

Her attention snapped from him to Wreck's hand. Something about the twitch of her love's finger grabbed her focus. Even though it was a minute move, her peripheral vision logged it. As his fingers continued to curl, she felt his blood heat.

Just like before, he had that look on his face, he was

waiting for a signal, a sign from her. Tulsi could do it, she could give him permission to take Baines down and Merchant too.

But they weren't alone in the building. As soon as Wreck went for Baines, Merchant would sound an alarm. Even with Styx's help, if he wanted to give it, they'd be outnumbered in seconds. She wasn't even able to help in any way because she was strung up.

No. One thing became clear to her. Tulsi had to separate herself from him. For Wreck's sake, she needed to get the hell out of that room.

"I'm sure the last thing I want is your disgusting body anywhere near mine," she spat out the words. "You repulse me. I need a real man, not a man only capable of chaining women up and beating them down. You're feeble. Pathetic. Nothing to me. You're less than I am. A bug not worthy of my windshield."

Just as she hoped, Merchant vaulted out of his chair and Baines started toward her. Together they unlocked the padlock that held her to the wall. Instantly she stumbled forward. Merchant grabbed her chin to haul her up.

"You need to learn," he growled. "You are going to learn."

"Don't hold your breath," she returned in the same tone.

Anger didn't begin to explain what she felt. Parading her in front of strangers was one thing, but to put her in front of the man she loved, to make him feel powerless. That she would never forgive. Never.

Wreck was a hundred times the man Merchant was. He'd been willing to risk his own life with just a single word from her. She had never loved him more. It took so much strength for him to contain himself.

He wouldn't see it that way, he'd think that he'd let her down. Just by the position she was in. He'd blame himself. None of this was his fault. All of it was on Merchant.

On top of that horror, they'd just learned that Rowdy wasn't as safe as they thought. Merchant planned to pursue Dam… or Ripp… or whoever he found first. One of them had to get out of there. One of them had to escape and warn the others.

Styx might make it, but he was already treading on thin ice. Merchant had noticed his turn around. It hadn't happened overnight, but he couldn't appear too eager or Merchant may ask more questions.

Baines grip on her arm was tightening. Tulsi wouldn't take her eyes from Merchant, who was glaring down at her. The bastard really was the worst of humanity.

Snatching her to the tips of her toes, he got her off-balance again. As Tulsi tried to find stability, he took the opportunity to pull her mouth to his. His grip on her chin increased until he held her with a bruising force.

Tulsi tried to wrench away, but he was too strong. She didn't respond. She did nothing. Not until he stuck his tongue into her mouth. Big mistake. Biting down hard, she got a shot of joy when the metallic taste of his blood flooded her taste buds.

He threw her back; she hit the wall hard. Baines still had hold of her and tried to shake her onto her feet. Sick of him too, she was quick to spit the blood from her mouth up into his face. Seeing the splatter all over him gave her smile an excuse to return.

Merchant's hand moved from his mouth. In a swift sweep, he slapped her across the face so hard that she crashed to the floor. Throwing her hair out of her face, Tulsi noticed Wreck move a step her way. Styx caught his arm and shook his head. Wreck yanked his arm back, making her fear he was going to advance anyway. But he stayed put. Her love didn't like to be touched, and he'd like being restrained less, but she'd never been more grateful for Styx's sense.

Tulsi tipped her chin up, showing Merchant her defiance. It didn't take much to tempt him into physical violence. As far as Tulsi was concerned, she'd made progress.

"Get her out of here," Merchant roared at Baines. "Gag that mouth!"

The words were slurred, probably because the injury to his tongue was still bleeding.

Baines bent down and hauled her up to drag her

across the room. "Tell your guys," she shouted back at Merchant. "That's what happens to anything put in my mouth without permission."

On a laugh, Tulsi didn't fight Baines shoving and prodding. There was hope. Hope that she could take control and steal Merchant's victory right out from under him.

TWENTY-FIVE

SEEING HER LOVE again activated her dreams. Tulsi could feel his hands on her in the dark. In her dream that night, they had already made love. They lay together in her sheets in the apartment where they'd sent the others. Wreck drew his fingertips up and down her stomach, admiring her in his own way. Her sense of peace was at its height. She was happy, content, ready to face the future with the man she loved.

Closing her eyes, she relaxed, concentrating on her breathing, cleansing her soul. The scent of Wreck nearby centered her. With another deep breath, she inhaled him. Except… something triggered the hair on the back of her neck to rise. The scent. It wasn't Wreck.

Fantasy merged with reality. Wreck's scent wasn't the one surrounding her anymore; the hand on her body wasn't his.

On a gasp, she opened her eyes, aware of a form on the bed next to her. Although it was dark, Tulsi knew who it was immediately: Merchant.

After Baines dragged her through to the bed earlier in the day, he'd attached her chain to the headboard again.

So although horrified that Merchant was in the bed with her, Tulsi couldn't do much to get away. Even leaping off the bed wouldn't help. She'd have to bend over the bed at an angle that would leave her exposed to him.

Tulsi tried to pull away, but he curved a hand around her waist and dragged her back to him. Her side pressed into him; his flesh crowded her upper arm. Closing her eyes again, she tried to tell herself that it was just a bad dream; that he wasn't really there.

Her sinuses began to sting, either out of rage or frustration, maybe both. Tulsi didn't like being powerless. That was exactly what he'd made her. A pawn. A playing piece in his ridiculous game of life.

"My beautiful Tulsi," Merchant breathed into her hair above her ear.

She wouldn't open her eyes. It didn't matter from a vision point of view. The room was so dark that she wouldn't be able to see him anyway. *It's a nightmare.* In her mind, with her eyes closed, she could breathe through the torment.

"Mine," he whispered. "All mine… You are so precious."

With the gag digging into the corners of her mouth, she couldn't say anything. She couldn't fight. Couldn't win. A tear slipped from her eye. It tracked down her temple and disappeared into her hair. Tulsi didn't want him to know that she was afraid.

In need of an answer, she shifted her leg to the side to touch his. Finding fabric was only a partial comfort. He was shirtless, but hadn't stripped all the way. Latching on to feeble positives became more difficult when his hand opened on her ribs. Stroking up and down a few times, he was testing her, enjoying her, and it was making her sick.

"Have you changed your mind?" he asked, obviously feeling that her leg had moved to his. "Are you ready to beg for what you want?"

Sex. All he wanted was sex. Tulsi considered that making the request and letting him just get on with it might be the easiest path. Just like Svana told her. If she asked him to screw her, maybe she could walk out before sunrise.

But could she really trust Ilias Merchant's word?

His hand slithered lower, grazing her pubis before

sliding upward and coming into contact with the underside of her breast. Already it was becoming more difficult to take a deep breath. Tulsi didn't want her chest to expand with her breathing too much; it would mean coming into closer contact with the man at her side.

"Such a simple act," he said, still keeping his volume low. "So basic. So primal."

The edge of his finger brushed against her pussy, and reversed to slink back up her body. Wreck came to her mind. The last man to be inside her was her love. The one she'd chosen for herself. The last man she would ever choose for herself.

Merchant stopped with the tease. Losing the subtlety, he took his hand from her ribs to close it around her breast. The bastard took his time about fondling her. His hands didn't feel like Wreck's. They weren't welcome. Glad of the darkness, Tulsi turned her head away, and tried her best to ignore the sweep of his hand and the pinch of his fingertips as he rolled her nipples between them.

The idea of relenting to let him have his way collapsed in one long cascade of truth. She couldn't stomach his hands on her breasts. There was no way Tulsi would be able to disconnect to allow him to put himself inside her.

"You're so beautiful, so soft."

In another situation, the words might be whispered as a middle-of-the-night compliment. They didn't sound that way coming from the lips of the man keeping her prisoner. Tulsi would rather be in a cell taking a beating than be there beneath his caress.

When his hand retreated, she let herself breathe in relief. The reprieve didn't last. In a quick turnaround of emotion, relief gave way to alarm when his mouth replaced his hands. Suckling on her, he circled her nipple with his tongue while pinching and squeezing the other.

Another tear fell, then another. Tulsi didn't want to be his plaything. She didn't want to be used for his sexual gratification. But this was a different kind of torture. He was playing at intimacy. Stretching out the foreplay that would exist between them until she bent to his will. Until she asked, this would be her reality. She'd be laid out there, ready for him, any time he wanted to toy with her.

He hadn't even bothered to remove her gag. Even if she wanted to ask him to get it over with, she couldn't. Tulsi could make noises, but she daren't try to object in case he took the sounds as encouragement.

Kissing her breasts wasn't enough for him, he ran his lips to her throat and began to kiss her neck. They weren't lovers. They weren't in love. All the emotion she connected with Merchant was negative. In fact, he made her sick to her stomach. If it was his goal to win her over or tempt her to actually want him, he'd fail. He could torment her as much as he liked. Kiss her, stroke her, whisper to her, it wouldn't change a thing.

"You taste good," he said, rising to suck her bottom lip into his mouth.

The gag was so tight, it separated her teeth. Biting him had been fun, but he'd learned his lesson, as proved by him removing her ability to protect herself.

"I wonder what other parts of you taste good."

Tension tightened her muscles when he kissed her chin and then her throat. Tulsi panicked. He might use his mouth to assault her further south. She barely noticed that he was sucking her flesh into his mouth. Marking her neck with the bruise of his kiss was a juvenile play meant as a signal to others, not to her.

He trailed his mouth to her shoulder. With her arms stretched up straight above her head, Tulsi took a shot at pushing him away. But he didn't go far. His mouth returned to her breast and he sucked her hard, leaving another mark on her skin.

Wreck would go crazy. The thought kept circling in her mind. Her love would see that mark on her, a mark that he hadn't put there. Getting the message across that Merchant hadn't raped her was easy. Talking of his request was enough to let her allies in on what was happening behind closed doors.

But with the bruises on her skin, even if she tried to somehow signal Wreck that she and Merchant hadn't had sex, it wouldn't matter. Wreck would know the bruises weren't voluntary. He'd probably be more likely to let a punch go than he would intimate injuries.

Sensations churned within her. She hated Merchant. Hated his mouth on her. Hated that he was kissing her breasts like she belonged to him. Tulsi only belonged to one man. Only wanted to belong to one.

Merchant's hand slithered onto her thigh. Her eyes popped open and her lungs stopped doing their job. Clamping her legs together as hard as she could, Tulsi refused to grant him any access.

"You want to play, my sweet?" Merchant asked, his fingers trying to worm their way in. "I love a fight."

Stuck in an impossible position, Tulsi couldn't make a "right" choice. Merchant wanted access to the most intimate corner of her body and she didn't want to give it. Except fighting a woman to get what he wanted turned him on.

She was still trying to figure it out when his hand left her leg. Her lungs finally relaxed to release the breath they had been holding. But she hadn't learned her lesson. Refusing him access hadn't put him off.

Listening to him loosening his belt, Tulsi hoped she wasn't about to be… The head of his hardened penis touched her thigh. He was kissing her breasts again, stroking himself at the same time. The movement of his fingers against her thigh betrayed exactly what he was doing.

Squeezing her eyes closed didn't help anymore. Beyond a nightmare, Tulsi was losing her rage as the cold truth of fear crackled through her. Pushing up, Merchant began to kiss her face and curled his leg over hers to force her legs apart.

Tulsi couldn't fight his strength. She could keep her thighs as close to each other as possible, but with his between them, she was open to him. He kneeled there, straddling one of her legs with his. Still working his dick in his fist, he made sure to rub his head against her inner thigh, taking a pleasure from her that she would never give willingly.

His fingertips touched her lower abdomen and began to slide lower. Tulsi tried to turn away, tried to pull back, but he flattened his hand on her to keep her still.

"Can you feel how close I am?" he asked, rocking forward to brush the head of his dick against her. She stalled, stopped all movement, stopped anything that might stimulate him. "You are here at my mercy. You are mine, Tulsi. Mine forever. My beauty to do whatever I want with."

He eased away, giving his fingertips space to descend to her clit. She didn't feel good when he rubbed her. The sickening truth of his power was beginning to sink in. He was right. The fucking bastard was right. Tulsi wasn't an object, she wasn't a prize, but if he wanted to treat her that way, she couldn't stop it. She couldn't stop him.

His fist began to move on his cock again. All she could do while he stimulated himself was lie there and take it. With her head turned away and her eyes closed tight, she focused on her breathing and ignored the tears that were dampening her face and the pillow. As his hand got faster, he stopped tormenting her clit and zeroed in on himself.

When the burst of hot liquid hit her, she retched, knowing exactly what he'd done. It stayed there, seeping across her skin, reminding her of the marks he'd left on her body, of his violation.

Merchant flipped onto his side, lying out along the length of her again. "I'm sorry, my sweet," he said, touching her face. Tulsi shook her head, trying to get his hand away from her. He laughed. "I know you're disappointed. I should've let you taste me."

Something in her snapped and she kicked out, squirming and screaming at his taunts. But it didn't matter. Her disgust meant nothing to him.

Putting a hand on her breast, Merchant pinched her again. "There will be other chances," he said. "Don't worry, my sweet, you'll get a steady diet from me."

The notion made her retch again, but he didn't notice, or he didn't care. Pressing his mouth into her head like a lover giving an intimate kiss, he stroked her breasts like they belonged to him.

"You are so beautiful, so nice to touch, I doubt I'll be able to keep my hands off you for long... My men will feel the same after you open your body to them."

That was the proof she needed. Merchant had no intention of keeping his word. He wanted her to beg him for sex and then what? He'd demand she begged his men too. Tulsi didn't know all of them, but the ones she did know, she despised. Allowing Merchant's men to touch her would mean giving in to Baines, to Coombs... Her stomach couldn't handle the thought.

"Get some sleep," Merchant said, kissing her cheekbone and then moving to kiss each of her breasts. "You'll need your strength."

For what? To fight him off. If Tulsi had her hands, she'd make a better go of damaging him.

He grazed her nipple with his teeth then rose to whisper in her ear. "How does *never* look now, my sweet?"

It looked a lot further away than he hoped, but too close for her liking. Merchant rose from the bed. The mattress shifted then Tulsi had to listen to him putting his dick back in his pants. He walked away from the bed and went through the door that led to his office.

Alone in the dark again, Tulsi wasn't able to stop the tears from falling. But she couldn't give in to her grief. The bastard would be watching and would take too much delight in that.

Before returning to his mercy, Tulsi believed in her own strength. She wasn't so sure anymore. Merchant held all the cards. She was his. She belonged to a man who made her sick. For the first time, she feared that he could win. If this went on and on, how much of it could she endure? Tulsi needed to take back control somehow or she would lose herself forever.

TWENTY-SIX

CONTROL WAS AN ODD concept. So much of it depended on interpretation. In Tulsi's case, desperation and desire drove her. Desperation to take back some control and desire to spurn Merchant's advances.

On the fifth day of living at Merchant's command, Tulsi was beginning to progress. The days went much the same as the first. Baines would appear at some time in the day, she'd be taken to the bathroom, then dragged into Merchant's office. The gag prevented her using her mouth to aggravate her keeper, but in her fight to regain control, she found a new way to assert herself.

In a change from the first day, whenever Baines returned her to the bedroom, he'd remove the gag and offer her food… Food she refused to eat.

Five days without nourishment were slowing her, clouding her mind, affecting her judgment. Tulsi was tired all the time. Even the nights Merchant slipped into her room to pleasure himself over her body were becoming more tolerable, simply because she didn't have the energy to focus on what he was doing.

That was the key to apathy. The key to taking control. The key to detaching herself from his actions. By her reckoning, it was a race between mind and body. Either her mind would give out, and she'd bow to Merchant's will, or her body would give up and death would take her.

Starvation wasn't a quick or easy way to go. One blessing was it hadn't proved hard to maintain. Any time Tulsi was tempted to take something from Baines, she'd think about the sick bastard who crept into her room at night. Merchant would stroke her, whisper to her, like he had complete rights over her, like they meant something to each other. That was worse than bearing his ejaculate on her skin. Though she despised that he left his mess on her, it was better on her than in her.

Whatever it took, Tulsi would hold onto her resolve.

Once upon a time, she'd promised to never let him win. Tulsi had vowed she'd never break under Merchant's pressure. Holding onto that vow got more difficult as her body grew weaker. Her mind needed all the strength it could rally. The longer she went without food, the more likely it became that she'd slip into delirium. Tulsi would welcome delirium. Her dreams were a safer place to be than reality.

Although she was awake, her mind was playing in fantasy, replaying happier times. Seeking a positive usually meant thinking about Wreck. Tulsi hadn't seen him since that first day. She dreaded to think that something might have happened to him. Twisted as it was, she held onto the hope that if Wreck was injured, Merchant would delight in telling her. The sick bastard would want to assess her reaction to the news. That small comfort was better than none.

As she weakened, it got harder to uphold any kind of impervious façade. On that day, Baines had taken her to the bathroom as normal, but he didn't take her into the office after. Instead, he returned her to the bed and chained her up.

Her life, on her back, staring into nothingness. He'd switched on the light on his way out. In the hours she'd spent cocooned in darkness, there were times she'd wished for light. Now that it was on and more hours were slipping by, she came to realize that it didn't really matter. Nothing mattered.

Tulsi's internal body clock was all screwed up. She had no idea what time it was or how long she'd been lying there since Baines left. Counting the days was a matter of registering how many times Baines pushed her into the bathroom, and how many times Merchant came to her in the night.

The door opened. Although Tulsi didn't think it was night yet, she didn't have much confidence in her judgment. The light stayed on, which was new. Usually, Merchant did his thing in the dark, never with the lights on. Being aware of what he was doing was bad. Having to see it, to actually watch it, would be a whole new repulsive ballgame.

The bed didn't shift as she'd expected it to. Sleep was harder to come by if she anticipated Merchant's intrusion. Before he crept in, she got stuck in a pattern of waiting. Expecting him, never quite sure when he would appear, it was impossible to relax. Tulsi didn't want him to surprise her or to invade her dreams, so she didn't want to sleep before the assault. After he was done, she would lie in the shame of his filth, trying not to let the camera pick up how her confidence took a beating every time he visited. The dark thoughts that circled her in the dead of the still night were growing in frequency and urgency.

Someone slipped into her peripheral vision. She shrugged it off, guessing Baines was about to take another shot at getting her to eat. Tulsi didn't move until someone touched her cheek. At even the hint of contact, she hissed in a recoil. No one should touch her. She didn't want anyone to touch her.

Baines should've learned that the only way to get her compliance was by only touching the cuffs and chain.

The tension of her defense held her rigid. It took a few seconds to recognize Wreck as the intruder standing next to the bed, holding his hands open in surrender.

Tulsi wasn't quite sure what was going on. Looking around for another person, she was confused to find they were alone… She didn't get it.

Using what strength she could garner, Tulsi pulled herself up to sit on the pillow, her chained hands in front of her. She blinked at him, waiting for an explanation. The gag prevented her from saying anything or asking questions. All she could do was wait.

Wreck bent down, keeping his eyes on hers, searching for any trace of reluctance. After he was sure she was calm, he reached to the back of her head to loosen the gag. Her hair tangled in the knot, but she didn't register pain, not while Wreck was so close to her.

The moment the gag was off, even before she'd moistened her lips, Tulsi spoke. "He has cameras in here."

The words were heavy and sore in her throat, but she had to warn him that they were being watched. Wreck glanced around and backed away. A few seconds passed, then he went to a tray on the table by the window. One which hadn't been there before. He retrieved a bottle of water and brought it to her.

Tulsi didn't hesitate to drink with his assistance. He pulled the bottle away before she was finished with it. As much as it pissed her off, she remembered doing the same thing to Styx to prevent him from overwhelming his system.

Each day Baines took her into the bathroom, Tulsi would drink from the faucet. But she had nothing to drink from, so it was a series of sips rather than mouthfuls.

"You're not eating," Wreck said, catching a drip of water on her chin to wipe it away.

"What do you care?" she asked.

Even if she wanted to beg him for comfort or advice, she couldn't, not while Merchant watched them. The chain between her cuffs was around a wide wooden panel, so Tulsi couldn't really put them together. Still, she raised one, which pulled the other around the back of the bed, and wiped her own mouth.

To her surprise, Wreck smoothed a hand down the side of her face, cradling it in one hand while he leaned in to speak in the opposite ear.

"Nymph, you gotta eat," he murmured.

The reaction her body had to his caring whisper was a world away from her response to Merchant's vile attempts at intimacy. Letting herself feel, even for a second, was a bad idea, so she tried to pull away. Wreck clamped her head tighter in his hold, catching her hair between his fingers, forcing her to stay put.

"It's the only thing I can control," she admitted in her own weak voice.

"I know," he said, soothing her. "I understand the why, but you gotta do this. You gotta."

Closing her eyes, she relaxed some of her burden. Merchant would be fuming that they were whispering to each other. He wanted the inside track; that was probably the only reason he'd sent Wreck in. As far as Merchant was concerned, Tulsi was supposed to hate her ruin. That meant there was no way she could give her fear and exhaustion to him.

"We're gonna get outta here, baby."

Tulsi didn't understand. Withdrawing to show him her frown, she envied how he could stay so calm. "I don't believe you," she said, aloud. "Why should I do what you tell me to do?" Giving Merchant some sign of rancor would offset his suspicions about their whispering. "I don't even want you in here."

"I go where Merch needs me."

"Yeah, I know what you goons are… You're an asshole just like him. Worse than him. At least he has the decency to own what he is."

Wreck's arm shot out, he grabbed her hair in one hand and yanked her to him again. His lips moved against her ear. "You are gonna eat because I am gonna get you out of here," he snarled.

Wishing there was even a chance was dangerous. Hope was dangerous. "He wants me to ask for it, beg for it," she whispered.

"I know," he said, his fingers tightening in her hair. "I know what he wants."

"If I give in, he'll let me go… Should I do it? Give him what he wants for our freedom, you, me, and Styx."

His grip grew so harsh that the pain in her scalp became impossible to ignore. The uncomfortable burn webbed from his hand, radiating through her hair. Her mouth opened in silent reaction to that pain. Feeling something, something so real, awakened her dormant determination.

"You're not gonna ask him for it," Wreck said,

turning his head so his mouth was pressed to her skin. "Only guy allowed in your sweet pussy is me, you hear me?"

She did and he was right; but that was in an ideal world that didn't exist. The fantasy wasn't real; she couldn't bring herself to believe it anymore.

"I love you," she murmured, moving her head, rocking it against his.

Asking him to kiss her would be too much. Still, it was all she wanted in the world.

Giving her a shake, he didn't let up. "Promise me, Nymph. Promise me now."

His anger was obvious. From his tension, she could tell he was wound tight. Her man was struggling with seeing her like this, under the control of another man.

She just let the edge of her lips meet his jaw. "I want to believe you."

"Trust me," he said. "I want to hear your word. Say it." But she couldn't. Tulsi couldn't let herself hope. "Nymph…" His agony bled into that word. "I need your help… Help me look after you."

All he ever wanted to do was take care of those he loved. Her heart broke. In truth, there was no way for him to save her. Even if he could, it wouldn't bring his sister back, which was the only thing that would ease his pain.

Merchant wanted something from her that she didn't want to give. Wreck needed to know that. He needed to know that she was strong, that she could look after herself. Though it was far from the truth, Tulsi could give him that reassurance. It was a lie, but he needed to hear it. After she was gone, he'd have that to hold on to. Whether he hated her or not, the lie might make him feel a fraction less responsible for her death when it came.

"I can promise I won't give in to him," she said. "But you are not responsible for me. I choose my demise."

"Not today," he said. Releasing his hold on her to leave the bed, he went to grab bread from the tray and brought it back. "Eat."

She shook her head. "I don't trust you."

Tulsi didn't think there was anything wrong with the

food, not to Wreck's knowledge. Her ruin wouldn't hurt her. The rejection was a smokescreen, a performance for Merchant.

"Fuck trust," he said, tearing off a piece of bread. "You're gonna eat this, 'cause if you don't, I'm gonna hold you down and make you eat it. I'll do it every goddamn day if I have to."

"What do you care?"

"I don't," he said. By Merchant's reckoning, Wreck was the one who'd betrayed her and brought her back… or tried to before she was abducted by Ripp. "But we're not gonna give up. If you don't take it from me, we'll put a tube in from your nose to your stomach, and God knows what sick fucks like us will put in there."

Tulsi didn't even want to think about that. Opening her hand, she expected him to give her the bread, instead he offered it to her lips. Snatching it in her teeth, she deliberately caught his finger in her bite. Despite her obedience, Tulsi didn't like that he was taking her last shred of control.

He fed her the rest of the bread, one small piece at a time. Sitting there with him, staring into his eyes as he stared back, it was ridiculous to be drawn into the same illusion of safety he'd provided for her in the past. Yet, she was.

Wreck. In the last few days, she'd fantasized about being near him. In its own way, her concession was worth it for the opportunity to share air with him again. But learning he had a fantasy about their freedom concerned her.

Getting away from Merchant's lair was unlikely. Holding onto that hope could destroy Wreck. Maybe he could get out, but he'd never be able to take her with him. Tulsi was trying to figure out how she could get him close enough to convey that when a slow clap attracted their attentions.

Just inside the door that led to the office, Merchant stood with Baines behind him. He dropped the applause when he had their focus.

"Congratulations," he said to Wreck. "No one else managed that."

"Not hard to get in her head."

"Not for you," Merchant said, strolling toward the

end of the bed.

Baines didn't need to be there. Tulsi thought it was weird that the lieutenant was observing. Except… Could Merchant be afraid of her? Maybe it was Wreck. Whatever it was, Baines was a beacon of Merchant's weakness. He didn't want to be alone with them so had brought protection along.

"Love to see you bonding," Tulsi said, drawing her knees closer to her chest.

When it was just her and Wreck, her nudity wasn't a factor. With interlopers in the room, she suddenly felt exposed and vulnerable.

Merchant ignored her. "I think we have a new minder for our guest. Wreck, you'll play babysitter for Tulsi. Look as much as you like, just keep your hands off. Bring her meals, stand guard outside the door."

The door to his office? Tulsi didn't get why he would put Wreck there. Anyone coming through that door would be coming from Merchant's office. She hadn't figured out his reasoning before Wreck spoke up.

"I'm a shitty babysitter."

"That's not true," Merchant said. "You got her to eat. As much as she wants to hate you, she's still attracted to you. Isn't that right, my sweet?" Tulsi didn't trust his smile. "We've had this conversation before."

If he was about to bring up the night he'd been stabbed, no beacon would be capable of keeping him safe.

"You're an asshole," Tulsi said. Merchant crooked a questioning brow. "I've wanted to say it for a while, thought I should do it before you put the gag back on."

He nodded once and pointed at Wreck. "As she says, return the gag and take your post." Merchant looked at her again. "Tonight will be interesting."

Tonight? Tulsi didn't like the thread of pleasure that ran through his words. Night meant late visits, meant him spilling himself on her body. If Wreck stayed outside the door, nothing would be different about the experience. Somehow, she figured Merchant wasn't going to make it that easy.

Wreck didn't deserve to go through another trauma. His sister's last hours still tormented him. Merchant might think his orders were enough, but she wasn't so sure. If Merchant ordered Wreck to watch or removed her gag and told her to scream, Tulsi wouldn't have the strength to hold Wreck back.

Merchant was playing with fire. If he got burned, he'd beg for another stabbing compared to whatever Wreck might do to him.

TWENTY-SEVEN

MERCHANT DIDN'T COME to her in the dark. For most of the night, Tulsi stayed awake. If Wreck was on the other side of the door in the corner, she didn't hear him. A foolish fragment of her juvenile mind laughed when she imagined the men coming face to face at the threshold of her bedroom.

As far as she knew, Wreck was unaware of what Merchant did with her at night. In spite of his ignorance, if Wreck encountered Merchant in the dead of night, he wouldn't be understanding. Wreck could just punch him in the face. Given the alternatives, that was the best Merchant could hope for.

The laughter never lasted. Having Wreck so close and being unable to talk to him or to touch was a new kind of torture all of its own. Maybe it was inadvertent, but more likely it was a part of Merchant's sick game. Even if he still believed that she hated Wreck for his betrayal, the reminder of that heartache would be heightened with him nearby.

Being alone in the night, the possibilities plagued her again. Merchant had some kind of plan. Being unable to figure it out made her uneasy. Worries bubbled and bounced around in her brain until she worked up an exhausting anxiety.

When Baines came in, signaling a new day, Tulsi was

dumbfounded. The arrival of the lieutenant confirmed that Merchant wasn't coming to her bed.

Hoping that he was bored with her was premature, but for the first time since she'd arrived back, Tulsi showered with a smile on her face.

In another break from routine, she wasn't taken into the office. Baines chained her to the bed, damp hair and all. But he didn't put her gag back on. The suggestion she might need her mouth brought her discomfort back a hundredfold. None of the prospects put her at ease.

Tulsi was used to the same schedule. Changes made her edgy. Sure, she appreciated not being pawed and played with, but she got the sense that the reprieve wouldn't last. She'd learned her lesson about relief. In her experience, as soon as she relaxed, something worse than the norm crashed down upon her.

So when the door began to open, she held her breath in anticipation, waiting to see who would come into her room. The sight of Wreck relaxed her so much that she almost forgot they were supposed to be at odds.

He carried a tray balanced on one forearm. Food. Right. That was his job. It was his job to feed her. After thinking long and hard about it the previous night, Tulsi hadn't reached a conclusion on whether or not it was positive that they got to see each other. He gave her strength, but being near him was torturous too.

"Good morning," she said in a sarcastic tone as he crossed the room to put the tray on the nightstand. She squinted. "Is it morning?" Wreck shook his head while sitting on the edge of the bed. "Well, good afternoon… or good evening, whatever it is."

"It's about four."

Four in the afternoon. Tulsi turned out her lower lip and bobbed her head. Wriggling up the bed, she sat as she had the previous day: on the pillow, her arms and legs folded, her elbows tucked behind her knees.

A sandwich, water, and orange juice were on the tray.

She blew out a breath. "Did you make it?"

"No," he said, his expression remaining static.

"I don't want it," she said on a shrug.

"I won't go through this shit with you every day," he said, picking up the sandwich to hold it to her mouth. "I'm bigger than you. Eat."

Tulsi leaned in to take a bite. Wreck held it in place while she chewed then gave her another bite before putting it down to open the water bottle.

"Were you on the other side of that door all night?" she asked.

Again, he shook his head. So she'd tormented herself for no reason. Merchant was good. He planted tiny seeds and then scurried away while they took root.

"Had work last night."

That was ominous. Not only did his tone suggest there was more to that statement, but he made brief eye contact. Shit. Work? The last thing she'd heard Merchant talk about with Wreck was tracking down Dam and Ripp.

"Get your hands dirty?"

He raised the bottle to her lips. "No, tip was bogus."

Tulsi hated being attached to a bed. Hated being naked. Hated that Merchant allowed anyone to traipse in and out. She hated every second they spent alone in the dark. But trying to read between the lines of what Wreck was saying brought out a new hatred in her.

"You're a sucky errand boy," she said. Their eyes met. "You're too in charge to be doing someone else's dirty work."

"Trying to manipulate me?" he asked, switching out for the sandwich.

That gave her cover to talk to him like she'd forgiven him. If Merchant was watching, he would assume the same thing: that she'd softened toward Wreck in hopes he might help her escape.

What Wreck had said the previous day about them getting out had been weighing on her mind. With the sheer volume of thoughts and possibilities and anxieties swirling around, it was no wonder Tulsi couldn't sleep.

"If I was doing that, I'd tell you to drop your pants." His eyes narrowed in suspicion, so she smiled. "You might be the bastard who betrayed me, but if I've gotta play with someone's cock, better it's one I know."

"We have rules."

"You don't care about rules," she said, straightening her leg to stroke her foot up his thigh. "Take a risk. Throw caution to the wind."

Putting him in a precarious position was dangerous, but she had faith. Wreck was never going to make love to her while Merchant watched. She just couldn't take hating her love anymore. At least playing with him was some form of communication and contact. What she really wanted to do was throw herself into his arms and beg him to take her out of there.

Wreck pushed her foot away. "Not interested."

"Sure you are."

That voice didn't belong to either of them. Finding its owner didn't take long. Merchant stood in the open doorway, his arms folded, his upper arm propped on the frame.

Wreck stood up, putting some space between himself and the bed. He didn't go so far as to attempt any kind of contrition or fear. It just wasn't his nature to be that guy. If Merchant had been paying attention, he wouldn't have bought it.

"There's something odd about you two as a pair," Merchant said, pushing away from the doorway to stroll farther into the room. "You're both attractive, yes, but there's something I'm not getting."

Tulsi wanted to say, *"Forgive me for not giving a shit,"* because she couldn't care less what Merchant thought of her relationship with Wreck. She kept the sentiment to herself when she noticed how Merchant was scrutinizing Wreck who was still facing the bed.

Watching that man inspect her man gave Tulsi chills. The interest in his gaze was the same sparkle she'd seen in previous times he'd spoken of Wreck.

Merchant came around to sit on the bed between her and Wreck. "Lie down," he said, stroking the comforter.

"No," she said, fearing his reason for not coming to her the previous night.

It seemed that he'd restrained himself while Wreck was out of earshot. He'd waited until Wreck could be present to witness it.

"She is so beautiful, isn't she?" Merchant asked, touching her ankle. Tulsi kicked his hand away, but that just made him laugh. "Maybe we should ask Wreck to hold you down."

He wouldn't. The suggestion hung in the air gathering mass. She didn't dare look straight at Wreck. In her peripheral vision, she noticed how he tensed up. Where Wreck was concerned, tension was never a good sign. For outsiders anyway, sometimes she got the benefit of him being wound tight.

Forcing herself to keep breathing, Tulsi did her best not to give Wreck any signal that she was uncomfortable or afraid. Sure, they were alone in the bedroom, but it was the middle of the day, the building would be crawling with his minions. A quick, discreet exit would be impossible.

"Should we let him watch, my sweet?" Merchant asked, reaching for her face.

Pulling back, Tulsi snapped at his fingers with her teeth when he got closer.

Merchant laughed. "She is passionate," he said. "No man could be uninterested in you." Twisting his head, he spoke over his shoulder. "Have you missed her body, Wreck?"

His jaw was so tight, his teeth could've been welded together. Her love was fighting his instinct and she wasn't sure he would be able to restrain himself for much longer.

"We could share her," Merchant said, running the back of his fingers up her shin. "I wouldn't mind watching you two together… Do you think he would enjoy watching us, my sweet? Would that get him off? To see me enjoying your body with mine?"

Tulsi saw Wreck's fingers twitch before he raised a hand. Her eyes widened when he reached for Merchant's head.

Before he made contact, Baines came stomping through from the office with Styx behind him.

"No one's seen him for a week," Baines said, paying

her and Wreck no attention.

Wreck's hand fell to his side, but from the angle of Styx's eye, Tulsi was sure he'd noticed the intent.

Tulsi didn't care if their ally had seen it. Hopefully when they were next alone, Styx would remind Wreck why it was a bad idea to show Merchant his anger.

"Wreck and I were just talking about Pretty's beauty."

"Yeah, she's hot," Baines said, showing his impatience. "What you wanna do about the motherfucker?"

"He'll show himself eventually," Merchant said, distracted by her legs. His hands kept moving on her skin. "What do you think a man would give up for a chance with a woman this beautiful?"

"His sanity," Styx said, eyeing Wreck whose fingers were twitching again.

"Yes," Merchant said and turned quickly to look at Wreck. "Betraying me for her would be insanity."

Uh-oh, a red alert statement. Did Merchant know the truth? Tulsi couldn't ask and wouldn't look at either of the men.

"I already had everything she'd got," Wreck said.

Good answer. Even Tulsi believed his indifference.

"How can a man ever have enough of her?" Merchant asked.

"You want me to send the guys out, shake the trees?" Baines asked.

"Yes," Merchant said. "Keep the pressure up. Wait for him to make a mistake… And send Coombs in."

Baines nodded to no one and headed out the way he'd come. Tulsi was under Merchant's scrutiny, so she couldn't look to either of her allies. Coombs was the last person she wanted to see. But once again, Merchant was proving his lack of confidence. Having another of his goons in the room was evidence he felt unsafe around Wreck. Some might call it good sense. Tulsi, on the other hand, enjoyed his apprehension.

"Do you miss her?" Merchant asked, curling his fingers around her ankle. "Wreck, do you miss fucking her?"

Glancing past Merchant, Tulsi watched Wreck's mouth open, but no words came out.

"Who wouldn't?" Styx asked, jumping in to fill the silence. "She's a hot little thing."

"She's got a set of balls to go with her fuck-me figure," Merchant said. "That's how you put it."

Coombs came in. He walked right past Styx and continued until he was at the foot of the bed. "Wow, Pretty, nice picture. Been a while since I saw you like this."

"Fucker," she mumbled.

"Wreck is going to show us." That brought all of them up short. Merchant stood up and swept an arm toward her. "Go on."

"What?" Wreck asked.

"Kiss her."

His scowl deepened. "Fuck that," Wreck said and tried to walk away.

Coombs leaped in front of him. The mood of the room shifted. Wreck wanted to end the bastard in his path probably as much as he wanted to finish Merchant. If it hadn't been for Coombs, her first night of intimacy with Wreck may have gone differently. Even more than her, Wreck hadn't forgiven Coombs for his actions that night.

"Please," Merchant said, sidling up to her rigid Wreck. "Show me how she likes to be seduced."

Wreck set a glare on the fucker standing by his shoulder. Merchant made the mistake of laying a hand on his upper arm. Backing off, Wreck pushed Merchant away on instinct.

TWENTY-EIGHT

BOTH SHE AND STYX WINCED.

"He doesn't like to be touched," Tulsi heard herself saying.

And he'd like it even less in this situation with Merchant effectively commanding him to put on a show.

"Fucker," Coombs said, leaping Wreck's way.

Styx jumped to attention too. If there was a fight, he wasn't going to miss a chance to have some fun.

"I'm not your swan," Tulsi said, quick to snap. The distraction worked. The men stood down, probably wondering what the hell she was talking about. "I don't give any of you permission to do anything."

"That means squat, sweetheart," Coombs said on a condescending snicker. "You do what you're told round here."

"No," she said, tilting her head to return a patronizing smile. "You do what you're told because you're a sheep. You can't look after yourself, can't do a damn thing for yourself. That why you were upset I killed your buddy? Need him to wipe your ass for you?"

Coombs bristled. Riling him was so easy. He might not be allowed to hurt her until Merchant gave him the order, but that didn't stop his blood from boiling. Wreck sidestepped putting himself between her and Coombs, blocking the idiot's line of sight.

"Why is he in here anyway?" she asked, shifting her focus to Merchant. "You shouldn't let the riff-raff into my bedroom."

Tulsi wasn't there by choice. As long as she talked, no one was assaulting her… or each other. Yes, she was still naked, but at least she could use her limbs to cover most of herself, even with her hands attached to the headboard.

"You're a bitch!" Coombs called out.

Wreck was still in his way. The idiot had no chance of seeing around him much less getting around him.

"Go stand over there," Merchant ordered Coombs, pointing in Styx's direction.

Styx wouldn't want to be near Coombs, but Merchant was obviously worried about what Coombs might do and say. She offered a finger wave to Coombs. Though Tulsi had to push herself back against the headboard to give him any chance of seeing her hands, the effort was worth it to witness him fume.

"Wreck," Merchant said. "Kiss her."

"I don't want him to kiss me," she said. "Remember what happened to you when you tried that?"

The swelling in his tongue had improved in recent days, but Tulsi was confident that she'd left her mark on him. The bruises he put on her skin would fade, her mark on him would scar.

"You won't hurt Wreck," Merchant said. "Because if you try it, I'll give him permission to hurt you."

"Wreck won't hurt me just because you order it."

Merchant smiled and edged around a fraction. "Not Wreck," he said, turning his attention to Coombs.

Just the hint that he might get a chance to be near her speared the idiot with unrestrained delight. He was practically salivating.

"Yeah," he said, his fingers moving quickly like they were itching to get onto her. "I'll scar that pretty body up good. Won't be so beautiful after I'm done with you."

Something Svana had said came back to her. *"Merch doesn't mind bruises, but the swelling can get in the way of our beauty…"* They were both sick. Probably every man in the building was sick and deviant. Tulsi had felt pity for Svana in the past, but getting a look at the goons through a new microscope was increasing that compassion. Svana thought she gave men permission to be intimate with her. Merchant had brainwashed the youngster; Tulsi would not let that happen to her.

Merchant began to walk around the bed. She watched his every step as he watched her. Her chain kept her closer to one side of the bed than the other. In the dark, in the night, she didn't see Merchant come and go. He always chose to be on the open side next to her, and that was where he was heading.

"Do we need a weapon?" Merchant asked. "How do I make your dog perform?"

"He's not my dog," Tulsi said. "You're the one holding his leash…"

Merchant sat on the opposite side of the bed, fixated on her. "I'm not sure I am. I think you still have power over him."

"Even if I did, I wouldn't use it for you," she said. "Why should any of us do what you say?"

"Wreck and Styx are here by choice, aren't you?" Neither could look less convinced, still, they mumbled in vague confirmation. "Did you tell him?"

After toeing off his shoes, Merchant got on the bed pushing up to sit on the pillow at her back. Tulsi couldn't twist all the way around. Not being able to see him was unnerving, it reminded her of the nights he'd come in and used her at his will. Her time was running out, he was getting closer to his threshold.

Merchant swept her hair from her back and must have taken it to his nose because she heard a deep inhale. Squeezing her eyes closed, Tulsi didn't want to show any weakness. Coombs was drinking it all in. She didn't want an audience present to witness her fear in action.

"You armed?" Merchant asked, his voice deeper in its

professionalism.

Coombs stepped forward, producing a gun from his waistband. "Want me to put one in her?"

"Better a bullet than anything else," Tulsi said, finding it easier to locate her confidence when the prospect was death.

Losing her life was an attractive option when compared to giving herself to Merchant. Being naked in front of these men hurt her less than Wreck's pain. Her ruin didn't carry himself with conceit and his pride was well-placed. He didn't like to be powerless. Tulsi hated Merchant for taking her love's dignity. That was what he wanted from Wreck, a performance that would reduce their love to a party piece for the enjoyment of others.

"Give it to me."

Coombs did as he was told. Once Merchant had the gun, he waved Coombs away. He retreated to stand next to Styx, excitement still shimmering around him.

"Who you gonna shoot, boss?" Coombs asked.

"That's up to Wreck," Merchant said. She heard Merchant check the clip and load the chamber. Not long after, the unyielding weight of the barrel pressed into the back of her skull. "Would you like me to shoot her…" The gun moved away from her head. In her peripheral vision, Tulsi witnessed him aiming the weapon at Styx. "Or him?"

"Ilias, there's no—"

"Shut up," he hissed at her, pressing the end of the barrel into her head again. "Wreck's going to show me exactly what you like."

"If you wanna shoot someone, shoot me," Styx said, opening his hands at his sides.

"Didn't know you cared about her," Merchant said. "Want to play the hero?"

"No one wants to be a hero," she snapped. "This is sick. What is wrong with you?"

The barrel moved in her hair like he was using it to caress her. "Don't get emotional, my sweet. You are what men want… You're unattainable… At least that's what they think."

"Just get it the hell over with," she said, throwing the words at him over her shoulder. "Put a bullet in me. Do us all a favor."

Because if she was out of the equation, Wreck and Styx would have a better chance of freeing themselves from Merchant. They could slip away while out on a job for him. In that time, they could get to her place, collect the others and get out of the country. If that was what they needed to do, Wreck had confirmed he knew contacts who could do that.

Imagining Wreck free of this torment, free of her, free to be who he always had been, was a comfort. But it was an illusion. He'd watch her die in front of him, just like he'd watched Sienna die. After that, she didn't know how much of his spirit would be left. Rowdy would be his only hope of salvation. His friend would support him, he'd do his best to bolster Wreck. Still, it might not be enough. Either way they were in an impossible situation.

The gun stopped moving. Merchant obviously strengthened his arm because the weapon pushed harder into her scalp, forcing her chin down.

"Jesus, all for a fucking kiss," Wreck said, storming to the bed.

He didn't even give her a choice, he sat down, grabbed the back of her head and forced his mouth over hers. His fingers stayed in her hair, he gripped it tight, like he had during their last time together. But he wasn't trying to remind her of that. From the way he scooped his hand around her skull, insinuating it between her and the gun, she sensed his powerful grip was his way of offering some protection. It wouldn't be enough to stop a bullet, but he did what he could.

The Wreck who was kissing her for Merchant's pleasure, wasn't the same one who kissed her by choice. She didn't do much to encourage him. Without her hands and in front of an audience, Tulsi couldn't relax enough to enjoy it. Not that she couldn't relax. Losing herself in the taste of her wonderful man was an ecstasy so enticing that she almost gave into it.

Luck was on her side, or rather Wreck was, he pulled her mouth away from his and stood up. "Now can we get some fucking work done?"

"Yeah, we gotta track this Ripp guy down," Styx said.

Tulsi kept her head tipped down. Being so specific was his way of telling her what was going on. Styx and Wreck knew where Ripp was, or at least they knew where the man had been sent. Covering his ass meant covering Rowdy's. Whether it was true or not, she liked to think there was a camaraderie between those who had come together to save the brothers.

"We're not finished here," Merchant said, shifting his position so he was farther down the bed.

Tulsi could see the gun. In his new position, she could twist to see him too, which she did to show him her glare. "No," she murmured. He waved the gun in her face. "I told you to do it, pussy."

"Hey!"

That unexpected shout came from the only man in the room she couldn't see. The others were just as startled as her that Wreck had called out. His focus was on her, no one else, and he wasn't happy.

"Stop telling him to kill you," Wreck growled.

"Why?" she asked. "You want to do it?"

"He's going to do something better first," Merchant said, grabbing her ankle to yank her down the bed. With a scream, Tulsi fought as best she could, but Merchant overwhelmed her. "He's going to do what you wouldn't." He glanced at Wreck. "What did you first notice about her? What attracted you to her?"

Merchant kept hold of her ankle, so she couldn't sit up again. "No," she said, her head moving side to side.

"She's still so attracted to you," Merchant murmured, running the barrel of the gun up the front of her leg. "Even after what you did to her, she's still attracted to you."

The wonder in his voice was less forceful than the questions he'd asked on the night she stabbed him, yet the sentiment was the same. He was curious about her and Wreck's relationship.

"Don't," she said to Merchant. "You don't want to do this again."

"I didn't get to do it the first time," he said, switching the gun into his other hand as he lay down at her side. "Do you think he wants to know what we do at night?"

There was no "we" at night. Tulsi was usually gagged and was never a willing participant in his violations.

"I think you should go to hell," Tulsi said, trying to pull away.

Merchant dropped one of his legs over hers and used the barrel of the gun to caress her chest. Better the weapon than his mouth, though she didn't like being so close to his mercy.

"She fought me because of you," Merchant said. Though he was talking to Wreck, he was more interested in what the gun was doing to her chest. "Because she wanted to protect you."

"Stop it," she said, yanking at the chain that restrained her hands. "Stop talking."

"I knew you would find her," Merchant said. "I knew she would trust you. She can't help herself. Even now, she is protecting you." Boosting himself higher, he pressed the weapon against her upper chest. His lips hovered near hers, just an inch or two away. "What would he have to do? What would he have to do to hurt you?"

Being hurt didn't change her loyalty. Just like the night she'd put a knife in his gut, Merchant was pushing the boundaries of what she could tolerate.

"Stop," she said, gritting her teeth.

"If you'd just answered my questions… If you'd just told me the truth…"

"You wanted something that didn't belong to you," she panted.

"Him?" Merchant asked. "Do you think he belonged to you? We could've been everything. We could've been such a force."

"And now we're nothing," she hissed, raising her head from the pillow. "You want to kill me? Kill me. I will never submit to you."

"Will you submit to him?" Merchant murmured. "If I leave you alone together and let him do whatever he wants with you? Will you submit?"

TWENTY-NINE

TULSI DIDN'T WANT to answer him. Merchant would like that, he'd get off on watching her and Wreck together with his little camera. But with so many constraints and variables, they couldn't be them. Not the real them.

Merchant would probably get mad if they didn't put on a convincing show. In spite of that, she couldn't care about his response like maybe she should. A familiar thought kept asserting itself ahead of that concern. Just like on the night of the stabbing, Tulsi didn't want to give any of their intimacy to a man who didn't deserve to witness it.

"You'll never know," she whispered, sensing Wreck's shadow approach.

Merchant wasn't as astute. "He'll do whatever I tell him to do. Wreck works for me. He'll do it or I'll have other men do it for him… I'll learn everything about you. Everything, my sweet. I'll watch every man take you, every man use you for his pleasure. By the time they're through with you, you'll beg to belong to me."

Wreck stepped up to the edge of the bed. He grabbed the back of Merchant's shirt, pulled him up and punched him so hard that the bastard immediately went limp. The fucker hadn't even known what was coming.

"Not on my watch," Wreck muttered.

Coombs began to bounce around like he was walking on hot coals. "What the fuck do you think you're—"

Coombs exclamation was cut off when Styx hooked an arm around his neck and yanked him back. Tightening his muscles, their ally cut off the idiot's air supply. While Coombs hung there, clawing and trying to breathe, Styx looked to Wreck.

"Finish him?"

Wreck shrugged. "Sure," he said, retrieving the gun from the bed.

"Wait," Tulsi said. "You can't kill him."

Styx didn't let up and actually appeared disappointed. Wreck put the gun on the tray and sat next to her to check out the padlock on one of her cuffs.

"He'll squeal," Styx said, hauling the idiot higher.

The gravity of the moment suddenly hit her. "You just knocked Merchant out," she said, absorbing their predicament. "What's happening?"

Retrieving something from his back pocket, Wreck was quick to begin picking at the padlock. "How long d'you think I'd let him near you?"

"Ruin, you can't—"

"What?" he asked, pausing to look at her. "Protect you?"

"I'm surprised he lasted as long as he did," Styx said, contributing to the conversation while still cutting off Coomb's air supply. "What we doing? Is it now?"

"Yeah," Wreck said, returning his focus to the padlocks again. "Finish him."

Satisfied he was getting his way, Styx smiled before pulling back on his arm, closing Coomb's windpipe for good.

"My Ruin," she whispered, but he kept concentrating.

The padlock popped open just as Merchant began to groan. Wreck tried to get the other padlock, but she pulled away from him.

"Nymph—"

"No, wait," she said, searching Merchant's pockets.

If Wreck intended to attempt escape, they needed tools. Tulsi had experience; it wouldn't be her first time making a run for freedom. Merchant's security card was in his pants, which was what she had been hunting for. Their luck was in because she found a key too.

Wreck snatched the key from her and unlocked her other cuff, freeing her from the restraints. Tulsi wanted to kiss every inch of him. Even if they went out in a hail of bullets, at least they'd tried. She handed Merchant's security card to her love.

"Go find some clothes," Wreck said, giving her a push.

Clothes. Yes. They had to get out of there. Tulsi jumped over the end of the bed just as Styx let go of Coombs body. It collapsed to the floor, prone, gone. The world was a safer place.

Looking from the corpse to Styx, Tulsi smiled. "Thank you," she said, much to his surprise.

Merchant groaned again. The sound kicked her into gear. Gratitude could come later. Tulsi ran into the closet. Most of the things Merchant had bought were still there. She dressed, found the most sensible shoes in there, and gathered her hair up on her head in a messy bun.

The hardest part would be getting out of the building. She would like to think that Wreck's actions were part of some master plan, but his response to Merchant seemed more instinctual than strategic.

Sounds of a struggle drew her out of the closet. Coombs was still on the floor where he'd fallen. Styx was at the end of the bed. Wreck was off to the side. Merchant was the one who got her attention. Lying on the bed in her previous place, the leather cuffs encircled his wrists, attaching him to the headboard with the same chain Wreck had taken from her.

A smile rose on her lips. Merchant wasn't so lucky. Although he was conscious, a length of fabric acted as a gag. Once closer, she noticed it was part of the sheet beneath him. Stopping next to Styx, Tulsi folded her arms and looked down on the man who'd kept her prisoner.

"Funny how quick fortunes can change, isn't it, my sweet?" she asked, sneering at him.

Wreck came to her side and bowed to nuzzle his face against her. Looping her arm around his waist, she tipped her head up to welcome Wreck's mouth when it lowered to meet hers.

Their kiss was nothing like the one they'd shared earlier. Tasting and appreciating each other, they let Merchant see exactly what he'd requested. Wreck grabbed her ass in both hands and dragged her higher, pinning her to him.

It took a lot of willpower to break the kiss. Tulsi sucked in a breath of semi-free air and threw her head back in elation. Her man was holding her. They had each other.

"Nymph," Wreck said, angling his chin toward the bed.

She caressed his face and brushed her lips across his. "Let it be the last thing he ever sees."

Wreck lowered her onto her feet. Raising a hand to her face, he looked into her eyes. After a slight nod, she turned her head to kiss the side of his thumb.

He backed away. Although his expression didn't change, she read a renewed determination in him as he turned to stride up the length of the bed with purpose in his gait.

Choosing to turn her back, Tulsi wouldn't give Merchant any satisfaction of comfort or triumph. His dying breath belonged to the man he'd stolen from. The man she'd given her heart to.

"We've gotta get outta here," Styx said, putting a hand on her shoulder.

The gargling sounds of a desperate man accompanied their conversation.

"How?" she asked.

Sneaking out wouldn't be simple. Being the only female captive Tulsi was aware of, and the only female who had tried to murder Merchant, even her gender made her conspicuous. Although most of the goons she'd interacted with were dead, plenty of the others had seen her in the past week. Hanging around in Merchant's office had left her exposed to many of them. All she could hope was that her boobs had distracted them from paying too much attention to her face. Though that didn't take care of the female part.

"We gotta just go for it," Styx said, glancing around. "Office might be a dangerous way out."

Tulsi spun around to point at the other door. Her attention snagged on the lifeless man on the bed. Merchant was gone. Wreck was feeling for a pulse. When he was satisfied there was none, he stepped back.

Tulsi couldn't grieve the man. For months, she'd believed he was already dead. Her ruin had followed through; he'd finished what she started. Just like he'd said he would.

Taking Coombs out of the world made it a safer place. Taking Merchant out made her feel good. She wouldn't miss him, but his absence would create a power vacuum in the city. Whatever happened next, they'd have to take some element of responsibility for it. Keaton was free to run the gauntlet, which probably made Ripp's life more difficult.

Still, when her focus floated up, and she found Wreck assessing her, Tulsi smiled. "Thank you, my Ruin."

"It's my job," he said, raising his arm to hold his hand out for hers.

Tulsi went to his side and clutched his hand in both of hers. Something would change in the next few minutes. Either they'd get out and begin a race against Baines or they'd be confronted by Merchant's goons and would fall together. Better to fall together than to live apart. Tulsi breathed in, her eyes matched to his. Somehow, she knew Wreck was reaching to the same conclusion.

"This intense staring thing is great," Styx said, crouching to search Coombs' pockets. He plucked out a few bills, a pack of gum that he tossed aside, and a car key. Styx stood up, showing them the key. "We got a ride. Wanna blow this pop stand?"

"I'm ready," Tulsi said, nodding to the door behind Wreck. "We can get from there into the hallway. Bypassing the office."

"Works for me," Styx said, striding across the room.

The door was unlocked. Of course it was. With her chained to the bed, she couldn't exactly get close enough to use it.

Styx opened it as Wreck grabbed the gun and handed

her the security pass. "Put it in and step back before you open the door. Styx and me deal with the obstacles."

Obstacles being anyone they met. Regular goons they would be able to deal with. Baines might be more difficult. He was bigger and stronger than most of the guys at Merchant's beck and call. More than that, he'd know just by Wreck and Styx's urgency that something was wrong. If he caught sight of her, that would be it. Over. He wouldn't have to check on Merchant, he'd declare war.

Styx led the way. Wreck stayed a few feet behind, gun in one hand, her in the other. The dining space was dark. The drapes were closed and no candles burned. Styx went to the only other door and stepped back to make eye contact with Wreck.

They had no idea what they were about to run into. Sometimes Delray and others hung around in the hallway when they were waiting to be called into the office. Styx put a finger to his lips for her benefit. Tulsi almost rolled her eyes, she didn't need to be told this was a covert escape.

Squeezing Wreck's hand tight, Tulsi sealed her lips to breathe through her nose. Styx didn't have a weapon, but Wreck was close enough to provide cover if things got dangerous. Merchant told her that Styx was known for killing with his bare hands. That didn't offer much reassurance. To kill up close, he had to actually get close to someone. If the thugs in the hallway had guns, Styx could be a quick casualty. She wouldn't leave him behind, couldn't; he'd put everything on the line for her and Wreck's cause. Tulsi wouldn't forget that in a hurry.

He was slow to push down the handle. On the other side was a security lock, this side just looked like a regular door. Anyone outside might see the handle move. All of a sudden, Styx opened the door and threw it back.

It took her a minute to register that there was no one on the other side. Styx crouched, putting himself at a different height to peek out, left and right. Still looking out, he gestured for them to follow. Someone could be in the office. The doors were closed, but if they made a sound, whoever was in there might come to check what was going on.

Styx had a stealth mode that was truly impressive. The first security barrier they had to deal with was on the door to the stairway at the end of the corridor. Styx stepped aside, keeping his attention on the double doors. Wreck let her close enough to slide the security pass into the handle. It beeped when it flashed green. Wreck tugged her around to his back and held the gun near his shoulder while Styx opened the door, still scanning everywhere around them.

Finding no one in the stairwell on their floor was another gift. As they descended in silence, the danger became more real. Merchant's goons hung around on lower floors; some of them lived in the building. All it would take was a fortuitous confluence of timings to put them in the path of someone coming or going.

Neutralizing someone feeble would be easy for the guys. But her blood pressure didn't seem to take that into account. They picked up the pace the lower they got. Moving in near silence, the trio were relying on each other not to make mistakes. If one of them fucked up, all of them would die.

While passing the steel door of the cells floor, Styx didn't so much as look up. Tulsi had met him on that floor in one of those cells. Seeing what he went through, it wasn't difficult to figure out why he'd been so eager to end the lives of Merchant's people. He'd killed Coombs without any regret or remorse. From what he'd told her, Coombs wasn't his first victim.

On their approach to the first floor, only a few steps before getting to it, the door to the stairway opened. All three of them stopped moving in unison. Tulsi's first thought was retreat. But if they went back up, they may never get out. It was just as likely that they'd meet someone going up than they would going down.

This could be it. The moment they'd have to face their fate. They were together, but if bullets started to fly, Wreck wouldn't be able to protect her and Tulsi didn't have any way to defend herself. Even if she had a knife, she would have to make a target of herself before she got the chance to throw it.

Inhaling, she closed her eyes and waited to see who

heralded their end.

THIRTY

WRECK WAS QUICK to yank her in at his back as someone emerged. Tulsi didn't have the chance to see who it was. For a few tense seconds, there was silence, probably as everyone assessed each other.

"Putnam," Wreck said.

Her face fell against his spine. Why did they have to meet a man who had reason to hate her ruin?

Most of the guys under Merchant probably didn't like Wreck. He brought dislike out in men he intimidated. Tulsi thought it said less about Wreck and more about the weakness in others.

Despite her initial thought, facing Putnam was fortuitous next to whoever else they might meet. Other goons might try to macho it out. To prove themselves. Putnam, on the other hand, had reason to fear Wreck from personal experience. Wreck reminded Putnam of his ability when he let go of her hand to load the gun.

"What the hell is going on?" Putnam asked. "Where are you going? Who is that behind you?"

"Wanna go back in there and forget you saw us?" Styx asked, though she wasn't sure they could rely on him to keep his mouth shut. Putnam had no reason to cover for them. He must have given some hint of that because Styx exhaled. "Yeah, I didn't think so."

"Any last words?" Wreck asked, aiming the weapon.

"Let me do it," Styx said like it was just something to check off the list. He descended another couple of stairs. "Won't make as much noise as a gunshot."

"Wait," Tulsi said, realizing that they did have a way to get through to him. When she leaped out from behind Wreck, Putnam's eyes widened in surprise. "You remember who I am?"

"I know who you are," he said. "You stabbed Merchant... killed Hillam."

"That's right," she said, slow to descend a stair but staying out of Wreck's way. "Are you in love with Svana?"

Putnam had been the one to raise Svana's hopes of escape. Not so long ago, the pair had made their own break for freedom. They'd made it too. For a while anyway. Merchant hadn't let them go forever.

Coombs once told her that Merchant never forgot, that he always had to be in control. The lifeless figure laid out on the bed wasn't in control. Whether he remembered or not, he wouldn't be a direct harm to anyone ever again.

Baines was a different story.

They'd met Putnam after he helped Svana escape Merchant. Rather than give her up, he'd tried to protect her by keeping her location a secret. From that, Tulsi could only surmise that Putnam's feelings for the swan were real.

"What?" he asked, wary of her question.

Talk of Svana in front of Merchant's other thugs would be a reminder of what he'd done, so Tulsi understood his reluctance to get into it.

Holding up a hand to calm him, Tulsi kept her tone as unthreatening as possible. "Do you love her?"

"Let's just kill him," Styx said. "He's been Baines lackey for weeks. He's not even allowed out the building. He won't step up for us."

"Not for us," she said, running a hand down the back of Styx's arm when she reached his side. "But he would for Svana."

His trepidation lessened to show he was a defeated man. "She's dead."

That was Tulsi's line. The news must have trickled through to the goons.

She smiled. "We can take you to her."

Putnam frowned. "She's dead."

Tulsi edged closer. "Is she? If you trust me, I'll take you to her... or you can die here in the stairwell."

"I don't care anymore."

"She will. I know she still cares for you," Tulsi said. "Take a chance. What have you got to lose?"

The last she'd talked to Svana about Putnam, they'd ended up discussing Merchant instead. She couldn't know for sure that Svana's feelings for Putnam were real. But the youngster wanted someone to love her. Love had been missing from her life. Putnam might not be the ideal man, but he'd put himself on the line to secure Svana's freedom. That spoke to Tulsi. That was love.

"You're... you're saying she's alive?" Tulsi didn't answer, she just smiled again. "Why would I trust you?"

"Death is your alternative," Tulsi said, stepping aside to clear Styx's path to him. "All you have to do is stay quiet and come with us."

Svana could take news of Merchant's murder hard. Telling her they'd killed Merchant *and* Putnam might be more than the blonde beauty could take.

Putnam was still thinking about it and they didn't have a lot of time. For every second they lingered, they increased the chances someone else would happen upon them. They were out of aces too. No one else would have a reason to let them go or to join their crusade.

"Nymph," Wreck said.

His warning betrayed he wanted to get going, even if that meant killing the obstacle.

"It's okay," Tulsi said, keeping her attention on Putnam who was considering her offer. "He knows that if he steps out of line, one of us will end him." Tulsi was the only one of their trio who hadn't killed, but Putnam didn't know that. "Come with us."

"I'll see her? You swear she'll be there?"

Tulsi nodded. In complete honesty, she couldn't be sure that Svana hadn't pushed her luck too far. Ripp might have ended her already or his periods of long silence might have frustrated Svana to death. Either that or the swan might be sleeping with one or all of the guys holed up in the apartment. But if it came to killing Putnam as soon as they got there, they would. At least the guy would get to live a while longer.

"I…" Putnam glanced at the men behind her. "Okay."

"Good," Tulsi said, grabbing his arm. "Go down the stairs."

Putnam began to descend. Styx rolled his eyes at her as he passed to follow Putnam. Just as she was about to go too, Wreck caught her wrist to pull her back.

"This is a bad idea," he said.

She shrugged. "We can reunite them and they can have a chance together," she said, aware that her opinion on relationships was flavored by her experience with Wreck. "What's the worst that happens? We have to kill him?"

Wreck still didn't appear convinced but he locked their fingers and pulled her to the next flight of stairs. They made it to the lower floor; the basement where the vehicles were stored. On Tulsi's last escape, she'd used the security pass to get out of the building through one of the side doors. Styx had car keys, so they'd need to get out in a vehicle. The two men had been working for Merchant a while, so she was confident at least one of them would know the way out.

Wreck folded his arm around his back to tuck her behind him when the four of them stopped at the stairwell entrance to the garage. Upstairs, before Merchant's death, Baines had asked his boss for permission to send some of the guys out. If they were unlucky enough to be going out as the men came in, the jig would be up.

Styx took the keycard from her and used it on the door. That time, he opened the door quickly. She heard it rather than saw it and guessed everything was clear when they began to move again. The door closed itself once they were in the concrete space. Several spaces in the lot were empty, which suggested the goons were still out with Baines.

Her heart hammered hard; they were exposed. Anyone could drive down one of the ramps at any second. Out in the open, there was nowhere to hide. Putnam wasn't supposed to leave the building either. If Baines came back and spotted one or both of them, he'd order his guys to shoot first, ask questions later.

Styx held up the key he'd taken from Coombs and pressed the button, making the lights flash. The beat up once-black car was in the corner, near one of the exits. He turned to gesture them all in the right direction. Tulsi didn't hang around, she wanted to get out of there as quickly as possible.

"In the back," Styx said. "You and him."

Putnam went around to the other side and got in the back as ordered. Wreck got in the driving seat while Styx went to the passenger side. The men made an exchange, key for the gun.

Styx was still on high alert. "Down in back, both of you," he said. "If they see us driving out, they might not follow."

Because Styx and Wreck had run errands for Merchant before. If Baines saw them, he might just figure Merchant had instructed them to go somewhere.

She crouched in one of the foot wells while Putnam flattened himself on the seat. It wasn't a guise that would hold up to close scrutiny, but it should do against anyone driving who glanced their way.

"This is nuts," Putnam hissed as Wreck backed out of the space and took them to the exit.

"Shh," she said.

They couldn't distract the men in front who were the only thing between them and discovery.

Tulsi didn't like the setup any more than Putnam did, but they were alive and they were free from Merchant. The burst of light that filled the car when they got outside surprised her. Tulsi winced and tucked her head down, hiding from the evening light. It was dwindling, but it was more natural light than she'd seen since arriving at Merchant's.

After a few seconds, when she guessed they were leaving Merchant's block, she picked up her head and looked to the window opposite. Light. The sky was overcast, but even gray clouds were beautiful to someone who thought they'd never again see anything except the inside of their tomb.

"Stay down," Styx said under his breath. "Know where you're going?"

"Nowhere now," Wreck said. "We're gonna drive for a while, ditch the car, switch it out."

"Smart," Styx said. "We need to put some distance between us and them."

"We have to go to mine," she said, even though it wasn't wise to draw anyone's attention. "We have to go to Rowdy."

"You know where he is?" Putnam asked. "What the hell is going on? How do you know where he is? How do you know Svana is alive?"

"Stop asking questions," she said, with no idea how much they should tell a man they weren't sure about yet.

His loyalty could lie with Svana or he could just want to stay with them until he could report back. Putnam didn't know that Merchant was dead. He didn't know that Baines would be the one in charge and the one who would want all of their heads.

"Why did Merchant let you go?" Putnam asked.

To his credit, he was whispering and was talking to her, so no one in the front had to turn or reply. Someone in the front switched on the radio. The volume wasn't loud enough to draw attention to them; it was loud enough to smother Putnam's questioning.

The danger wasn't gone; it wouldn't be for a while. Life was going to be tough until they made a decision on what to do about Baines. He'd want to take them down as payback.

If word got back to Ripp and Dam that they'd escaped and they hadn't shown up, the two might think they'd abandoned them. That could lead to them abandoning Rowdy, whose strength would still be low. He wouldn't be able to cope with a life in hiding alone. Baines could decide that Rowdy was the key to getting to Wreck. If it had worked before, there was no reason to believe that it wouldn't work again.

Kieran wouldn't know what to do and wouldn't have the skills to support his brother. Chances were high that Kieran had already deserted him. Nothing other than his brotherly connection would keep him with Ripp and Dam. The two men supporting Rowdy didn't deserve to be subjected to Kieran twenty-four seven. If they'd kicked him to the curb, she wouldn't blame them. Kieran was a lot to take at the best of times. Talking to him, or hearing him talk, in the rough times would just highlight that he was a liability. No one should ever doubt that Kieran was a liability.

If Wreck wanted to grab Rowdy and run, she'd support that. But if Kieran was still around, she wasn't sure she'd be comfortable taking him too. Rowdy would want to, even knowing that he was likely to get them into a precarious position. The whole mess had sprung from Kieran getting mixed up with Merchant in the first place.

A bunch of decisions lay ahead of them. Tulsi would choose to be with Wreck, no matter what that meant for their future. Rowdy had suffered for her mistake, she'd do whatever he needed, but the prospect of Kieran being part of the deal brought out a sigh. Kieran Rigby was an accident waiting to happen, and she had a feeling he wouldn't be the one to pay for his own mistakes.

THIRTY-ONE

THEY DROVE OUT of the city, acquired another car and headed back in. They dumped the vehicle and then got in a cab. It took them closer to her place, but they didn't take it all the way there. Leaving a direct trail could be dangerous.

While Tulsi was locked up at Merchant's, no one had any reason to check her old place. With her on the street, free, Baines might think to check her apartment. Being close by, he'd guess she might just be stupid enough to go there. Which, given where they were, it turned out she was.

After finding Merchant and Coombs dead, Baines wouldn't take long to figure out that Wreck and Styx were gone too. Then he'd know they'd been played.

Baines wasn't the type of guy to let anything go. Beyond the fact that he delighted in murder, as he'd proved with Alexis, he wouldn't have any purpose without Merchant giving him orders. He'd track them down and given half a chance would pick them off one by one in his own depraved way.

They walked toward her place from where the cab dropped them off. They didn't take a direct route either. It had been hours since they'd left Merchant's. Tulsi didn't think word would've gotten back to Ripp yet, but she couldn't be sure because she didn't know anything about his network or who he trusted.

Dam knew a lot of people, though Tulsi didn't know if he'd put out the feelers for information or if he was keeping a low profile instead. Their group was vulnerable. While Rowdy was weak and reliant on them, she guessed he wouldn't be doing much networking.

She and Wreck walked a good twenty feet behind Styx and Putnam. The streets weren't busy. Still, two pairs seemed less conspicuous than three men walking with just one female.

"What will we do if they've moved on?" she asked.

They could've decided that being in her apartment was too dangerous. Maybe they were spooked by something, or they'd got word of Merchant's death and scarpered.

"Deal with it," Wreck said.

He'd been distracted ever since they got out. Guiding their joined hands to her free one, she stroked his knuckles. "My Ruin," she whispered. "What's wrong?"

"Nothing," he said. "We're out."

"Yes," she said. "But you haven't relaxed since we left. I need to know what's on your mind."

"Keeping you safe is on my mind," he said. "Keeping you and Row safe is what I'm thinking 'bout. We can't stay here. It's not safe."

"Merchant hurt a lot of people, maybe it won't be as bad as you think."

"He helped a lot of people too, kept them in work, kept paying them. All that stops… because I killed him."

"Are you sorry?" she asked. "That you did it? I asked you to do it, so if you—"

He stopped. "He hurt you. No matter what, he was on borrowed time."

Tulsi smiled. "We're together," she said, stroking his jaw. "We never thought this would happen. I thought he would kill me for sure. His stupid game was what killed him. If he'd just raped and killed me, we wouldn't have had the time to—"

"You want me to thank him? Fuck that."

"I want you to see that even in spite of the danger, we're in a better position now than we were when we woke up."

As a couple, they had issues to work through. They'd need to support Rowdy too. But Tulsi would choose this life over any with Merchant still in it.

"You're dreamin' again."

"No, this is reality. You are my reality."

"Did he fuck you?"

"Ruin—"

"I gotta know."

"No," she said, wondering what he'd do if she said yes. It wasn't like they could kill him over again. "He didn't."

"What was all that shit about at night? What did you do at night?"

A whistle from further up the street distracted them both. Glad to see Styx's subtle gesture for them to hurry up, Tulsi began to walk in step with Wreck who didn't have to work hard to keep up with her.

Tulsi's store was just up the block. From where Styx stood, she guessed he intended to go into the alley that ran along the side of her building. Styx and Putnam disappeared into the alley, so she did her best to pick up the pace to catch up to them.

There was one window from the apartment that looked out on the alley, so it wouldn't be smart to loiter for long. If Ripp and Dam were up there, watching what was going on below, they'd see two shadowy figures conversing in the cover of the alley. If they weren't taking any chances, or were edgy enough to be trigger happy, they could injure their own allies.

On reaching the alley, Tulsi pulled Wreck in with her. Styx and Putnam were flat against the wall, beneath the second floor apartment window.

"Is there a way in back?" Styx asked.

She nodded. "There are two ways in," Tulsi said. "The front that customers use and one in the back. I use that one the most. The stairs to the second floor are inside, right by that door."

"That's the best way," Styx said. "Any keys hidden around?"

She shook her head. "If there were, I'd have told Dam about them."

"We're with the only smart, wary property owner in the world," Styx murmured and looked to Wreck. "If they haven't heard we've made tracks, they could shoot before we pick the lock."

Tulsi hadn't considered that. The front of the first floor was glazed, but entering that way would be conspicuous. Especially if they had to pick a lock or break a window to get in. Cops might be easier to deter than Baines' people, but Tulsi wasn't sure how she'd explain seven men in her apartment with just her and Svana.

"Gotta take the risk," Wreck said, taking a step back to look up. "Leave someone here, in case they come to check it out… Just gotta be quiet."

"Yeah, we wanna be quiet to stay alive," Styx said, moving away from the wall. "But if we can get in without being detected, that means someone else can do it too."

Fair point.

"Can't we just ring the bell?" Tulsi asked.

The benign suggestion startled the guys. "Ring?"

"Sure," she said. "They're not going to expect Baines to knock."

"Will they hear it upstairs?"

"It's connected upstairs. The stairs lead into the kitchen, the living room is at the front," she said. "There's a hallway off the living room, that's where the bedrooms are. Bathroom's opposite my room. The bell rings in the hall, so no matter where they are, they should hear it."

"But will they answer?" Styx asked.

Though he'd asked the question, he hadn't expected an answer. Styx started to move, going through the wooden gate that they had to go through to get to the rear entrance. All of them went with him. At the back door, he rang the bell, and stepped away from the door.

Wreck and Putnam stayed away from the door too. She guessed they were being wary in case those inside started shooting or something. Resting her head on Wreck's arm, Tulsi waited to see if her genius plan was going to work.

The kitchen windows were above them. She tipped her head back to look up and was sure she'd seen the blind move. Though in the night, it wasn't so easy to be sure.

"How long do we stand here?" Putnam asked, his gaze darting all over the place like he was expecting a sniper to take them out.

Being back at home was odd. The only time Tulsi thought about the building was when her dreams put Wreck in her bedroom. Those dreams were some of her favorites, but she had never believed for a second that he would ever be this close to her sheets.

Curling her arm around his, she threaded their fingers together again. The danger on the horizon was their first priority, but she and Wreck would have to have a conversation sometime soon. They had never addressed having a future together, so she had no idea what it might look like. With Baines on their tail, it was likely to be nomadic, just as Merchant once told her.

Tulsi didn't hear any sound from the other side of the back door, which made her think she'd been wrong about the blind moving.

"If Rowdy's not here, would you know where to look for him?" she murmured, peeking up at Wreck.

Before he had the chance to even look at her, the backdoor opened. Just a crack, but it was enough to show that Dam was on the other side.

"What do you fuckers want?" he asked.

While standing around in the cold darkness, jokes weren't really appreciated. Dam must have picked up on that, or been scowled at, because he stepped back to open the door to let them all in. Once they were in her workshop, Dam closed the door and locked it. He slid the bolts into their slots too. Security was more important than he probably even realized.

Wreck didn't wait for an invitation. Pushing between Styx and Putnam, he took them up the stairs into the kitchen. She'd given him a lay of the land on purpose, so he knew what he was walking into.

The wide square arch between the kitchen and living room didn't have a door. They had a clear view of Ripp who was sitting in an armchair, weapon in hand, resting on his thigh.

"What the fuck happened?"

"You hear about Merch?" Styx asked.

Styx was just behind her and Wreck as they walked through to the living room. Wreck crossed to the loveseat in front of the window and pushed her down onto it.

He didn't sit with her and instead turned to Ripp. "Where's Row?"

"In there," Ripp said, bobbing his chin toward the hallway.

Wreck didn't hesitate to go to his friend. She got it, they were like brothers. Wreck and Rowdy had enjoyed less alone time than she'd had with her love. They needed to catch up. Wreck would also be concerned about Rowdy's injuries and how he was feeling.

"Someone fucking talk."

Ripp's demand distracted her from wondering about Wreck and Rowdy's reunion. Dam leaned on the wall by the arch to the kitchen, as interested in the story as Ripp.

Tulsi looked to Styx to fill them in.

He exhaled. "Merch is dead."

"I know," Ripp said. "Him and a few of his guys."

"One of his guys," Styx said, sauntering over to drop into the armchair closest to hers. "Today anyway. We could count the one you finished."

"And the one she finished," Ripp said without looking at her.

Being the only woman in the room, Tulsi didn't have to wonder who he was talking about. It seemed like forever ago that Hillam had been killed. Wreck and Rowdy knew the truth, she had no idea who else they might have told.

Dam hadn't said anything, but lowered to sit on the high arm of the pull out bed, which was unmade, strewn with crumpled sheets.

"He deserved it," she said, thinking her friend might

judge her for the murder. "They all deserved it."

"Are you okay?" Dam asked. With his simple question, he erased her fear for their friendship. "Did they hurt you?"

"They can't hurt anyone else," she said. "That's what's important. I won't shed any tears for Ilias Merchant or Coombs."

"Wasn't part of the deal."

Ripp's deep, slow growl was unexpected. It was then she noticed the darkness in his gaze. There were no lights on in the room, which she guessed made sense if they didn't want to draw anyone's attention to the fact that her apartment was occupied. But the lack of illumination made it more difficult for her to figure out what was behind his angry glare.

"You're mad?" she asked. "That we killed Merchant?"

Tulsi had thought about him, about his feud with his uncle that would be affected by Merchant's demise. Keaton would want to step in. Either Ripp had already had word about his uncle's plans or he knew the man so well that he could predict what would happen next.

"It wasn't part of the deal," Ripp said, slower, as though he was containing himself.

"There is no deal," Styx said. "Things changed, you can fuck off if you want to, makes no difference to us."

Their deal had included a swinging axe. If Ripp walked away or betrayed them, Styx had threatened to reveal all to Merchant. That didn't matter anymore. With Merchant dead, they didn't have anything to hold over him.

"Baines will step in," Tulsi said. "He'll want to pick up where Merchant left off... Styx can still tell him about the shipment."

Her tone didn't suggest that she was threatening him. After the words were out, she realized how sinister, and ungrateful, they sounded.

"You don't want him to stick around," Styx said. "Wreck will want to move soon. The fewer in the group, the faster it can move."

Made sense. If Rowdy was in a bad way, he could

slow them down. They didn't need to worry about numbers making them conspicuous too. Kieran wasn't around. Just as she was about to ask if he was still there, Putnam spoke from the threshold of the kitchen.

"I don't see Svana. Where's Svana?"

"Who's he?" Ripp asked.

"Svana's lapdog, I think," Styx said. "He walked in on us leaving."

"He came with us because he wanted to see Svana. If she's not here—"

"He knows where we are," Ripp said, not impressed by their tagalong.

"I can kill him," Styx said, shifting to the edge of his seat. "No big deal."

"Then we gotta get rid of the body," Ripp said. "Or it'll start to smell."

As unpleasant as it was for Tulsi to hear them talk about murder and corpses, it was no doubt worse for Putnam who was listening to them plan his demise.

"Just tell us where Svana is," she said, hoping Ripp had some idea.

"Other bedroom," Ripp said.

Putnam scurried away up the hall to locate the woman he'd been promised as a prize. His need for her was admirable. Tulsi just hoped that Svana was pleased to see him.

"Does she know?" Tulsi asked. "About Merchant?"

"Maybe heard us talking, I don't know," Ripp said, extending his legs out to cross his ankles. "You fucked up."

"Nope," Styx said. "Might fuck with your little game with Keaton, but we're out. It was us or them."

Not exactly. Coombs was pathetic. He needed to be finished so he wouldn't sound the alarm on what they'd done with Merchant, but he wasn't actually a physical threat to them. Merchant had been chained to a bed. They could've left him there alive. Wreck had knocked him out and taken the gun, so killing him was sort of an indulgence. Despite that, Tulsi wasn't sorry and wouldn't ask Wreck or Styx to be either.

"You think you can end a guy like Merchant and just walk away?"

"No," she said to Ripp. "But even if the consequence is death, it's better than living with Merchant."

Better than living naked, chained to a bed, waiting for Merchant to come through from his office to violate her. She and Merchant would've lived in a stalemate, probably for a long time. She would never have asked him to screw her and that was the only way to break the pattern. Either he'd have gotten bored and killed her, or he'd have sent her off to one of his brothels to be taken against her will. Whichever way it went, Tulsi ended up dead.

So even if Baines caught up with them and killed them, the outcome would be the same as not killing Merchant. Better to have him off the streets and have a chance at enjoying some time together than just lying down and waiting for death to come.

"Nymph," Wreck said.

Tulsi hadn't seen, or heard, him coming. But he was at the end of the hallway, looking at her, ignoring the others.

"What?"

He tipped his head to the side, indicating she should follow as he retreated into the darkness. Leaping up to follow, Tulsi wasn't sure what he wanted to say. Something could be wrong with Rowdy or the friends could've come up with a plan. Whatever the reason, any time Wreck asked her to follow, she would always jump to attention.

THIRTY-TWO

TULSI WENT INTO her bedroom behind Wreck who went to stand at the end of the bed. Rowdy was sitting up, leaning on pillows against the headboard. With the covers over his lap, she could see there were bruises on his torso, arms, and face. They weren't as angry as she'd imagined they might be, although it was obvious he was skinnier and weaker. Guilt forced her to pause just inside the room.

"I'm sorry," she said. "I'm so sorry that… What he put you through because I—"

"Don't care about that," Rowdy said, lifting an arm her way. "Get over here."

Tulsi's guilt hadn't gone anywhere. Tiptoeing across the room, she wasn't quite sure what to do. Tentatively, she sat on the edge of the mattress.

Rowdy lunged over to grab her hand. "All the way here," he said, wearing a smile as he tried to haul her across the bed.

Still not really sure what was going on, Tulsi kneeled on the bed to shuffle closer. As soon as he could reach, Rowdy let her go to throw both arms around her. In Rowdy's confusing embrace, she twisted to seek Wreck out, hoping he'd be able to offer an explanation.

"What did you tell him?"

"Everything," Rowdy said, answering for Wreck. "You were gonna die to get me out of there."

"It's not a big deal," she said, sinking back on her knees to sit on her feet when he let her go. "It was the right thing to do."

"Not everybody does the right thing."

He'd said that Wreck told him everything, but she doubted Wreck had filled him in on their discussion in the motel parking lot. Rowdy wouldn't be so chilled and optimistic if he knew his best friend had encouraged her to leave, to save herself and screw both of them over.

"Do we have a plan?" she asked, eager to progress their focus.

Wreck had tried to make her go; he'd tried to save her. Given all she'd learned since that conversation, Tulsi doubted either of the friends would be alive if she hadn't returned. The only reason they had the ability to escape was because Merchant's ego gave them the opportunity. He could've finished her as soon as she walked into his office. In the hours she'd spent chained up, he could've raped her if sex was what he wanted. His compulsion to break her was their savior.

"Kieran's in the shower," Rowdy said. "When he's out, I'll clean up. We'll pack and be ready to go."

Rowdy wasn't in a terrible state, but he wasn't himself and definitely wasn't at full strength.

"Do we think that's a good idea?" she asked, glancing from one man to the other. "If we run now, we could be running for a long time."

"We'll wait and get word from the street. If the heat's on, we've gotta get away," Rowdy said. "Find somewhere to lay low."

The first place she thought of was Fox Den. They could protect themselves there and would have considerable support if they needed help. There were issues with that plan though. Dam didn't like to be in Florida at that time of year, and he wasn't Wreck's biggest fan. Dam was important in Fox Den, valued, it wouldn't take much for him and Wreck to come to blows. If that happened, the others in Fox Den would choose Dam over Wreck.

"Do you have any ideas?"

"Some," Rowdy said. "We've got friends out there."

She turned a smile to Wreck. "I didn't think you had any friends outside Rowdy."

"Yeah, well," Rowdy said. "I have friends, even if he doesn't."

"Have you got along with Dam?" she asked.

Rowdy could be the key to the safety of Fox Den. He acted as mediator between Wreck and Kieran when he had to, and he was much better at keeping a level head. If he and Dam got along, Rowdy could fill that role in Florida.

"Kieran's not a fan, but he seems okay," Rowdy said, then narrowed his eyes. "You thinking about Fox Den?"

It seemed he and Dam had been talking. It was that or Wreck had talked really fast.

"They have security and there's a bunch of guys if we need back-up. It's really down to Dam, if he says it's okay, then we're set."

"And if he doesn't..." Rowdy didn't finish the sentence, but he didn't have to. "Thought he had the hots for you."

Tulsi only just managed to restrain her groan. "That's what other people say. He's never made a pass at me."

"But I'm guessing he and Wreck aren't best buddies."

On a shrug, her gaze fell. Tulsi didn't want to look at her love or to remind him of how it had been when he'd found her in Florida.

"That's not our biggest problem," Wreck said.

His statement sort of confirmed Rowdy's statement without being explicit.

"What's our biggest problem?"

Kieran came striding in, nothing but a towel around his waist. As soon as he registered there were others in the room, he paused. For a few seconds nothing happened, everyone just assessed each other.

Soon a smile formed on his face, which quickly became a grin. "Tuls!"

Rushing over, he snatched her from the bed. Wreck wasn't so relaxed about the semi-naked guy hugging her. From his loose, relaxed stance, he straightened up and frowned. Half a second before she thought he was going to storm over and punch Kieran out, Tulsi pushed away from the embrace.

"I'll let you get changed," she said, climbing off the bed and sneaking around Kieran.

"Wait," Kieran said before she got to the door. "What happened? Why are you here?"

When Tulsi turned around, she noticed the wound on his leg. It was sealed, but still an angry red. The circle with its jagged edges was evidence that Merchant had ordered him shot. More guilt. Just when she thought Rowdy's forgiveness had assuaged it, she was hit by another dose.

"Excuse me," she said, quickly leaving the room.

People occupied most of the other rooms. Tulsi headed for the only room she knew was free: the bathroom. Steam still lingered and the mirror was fogged, but she didn't care. Dropping to sit on the toilet lid, she caught her face in both hands.

"What's the problem?"

Without taking her head from her hands, she exhaled at the sound of Wreck's question. "So many people were hurt because of me," she said. "I don't know if I can face that every day."

Going anywhere with Wreck meant going with Rowdy. Rowdy would want to keep an eye on his brother, so that meant going with Kieran too. Every day she would have to see the men who'd got hurt because she wouldn't give in to Merchant.

"You think they're perfect? Fuck, baby, we met because Kieran screwed up with Merchant."

"He didn't though," she said, lifting her head to find him leaning against the closed door. "Ripp took the shipment."

"Yeah. He only knew where it was because of Kieran."

"He was afraid," she said, sort of surprised at herself for defending Kieran. "Ripp is an intimidating guy. He pressured Kieran. He scared him. That's why he told Ripp what he wanted to know, not out of malice or stupidity, he was scared."

Wreck surprised her by sinking into a crouch and laying both hands on her thighs. "Why did you stab Merch?"

"Why did I… because he attacked me."

"How did you feel about that?"

"That he tried to force me?" she asked. "I was angry… I was upset—"

"You were scared."

The simplicity of those words blanked her mind. Yes, she had been scared that Merchant would force himself on her. Even though that couldn't happen, Tulsi still feared how Wreck would react when he found out what Merchant had done to violate her. Once he knew, he may never look at her the same way again.

Cupping his jaw, she smiled. "I was. Scared for me and for you."

"Why for me?" he asked. "What happened, babe? He talked about us."

Merchant's comments before his death had revealed more than she'd ever wanted Wreck to know.

"I can't—"

"Trust me, Nymph," he said. "We have each other. We're set."

Easy for him to say when he didn't know the full story. Wreck wanted to know, he'd asked her before and she'd wriggled out of telling him. Tulsi wanted to protect him; she didn't want him to live through what had happened.

Yet, if she wasn't honest, it could mean the end of them. The unknowns would hang like weights around their necks. Wreck would keep asking any time he thought there was an opening, maybe whenever they argued. Secrets would drag them down. They would never be able to move on.

"He said I was still attracted to you," she murmured. A flicker of surprise in his eye betrayed he hadn't expected her to open up. "Just like he did today. It wasn't a question, he just stated it."

"You confirmed it?"

"No," she said. "I made up some lie about him being all I wanted. I was scared he'd hurt you. I already knew he was jealous. That whole dig about pride was something he'd said before. How pride is important to a man… I couldn't let him think that I still wanted you. If I dented his pride, I had no idea how he'd react… I worried you'd end up in the firing line because of me. You'd always said that we were nothing—"

"We weren't nothing."

She laid a hand on his cheek. "I know. I just couldn't let you be hurt because of me."

"That's it? That what you were afraid to tell me?"

"I wasn't afraid," she said, her hand sliding from his face to her lap where his hands still rested. "I don't want to hurt you. I didn't want you to feel responsible. He wanted to know about us. He asked what it was like…"

"What what was like?"

"Sex," she said, toying with his fingers. "He wanted me to talk about having sex with you. He wanted details."

His fingers closed around hers, gripping them tight to stall their movement. "Did you?"

Although he was trying to disguise his anger, she could hear the rumble of it in the back of his throat.

"No," she said, quick to frown. "I wouldn't. I wouldn't ever talk about us like that to anyone."

"Why did he give a shit about us?"

She shrugged. "You intrigued him and he liked to hear details from Svana too, details of her with other men. He got off on it. You'd just walked out of the office. Somehow, he knew that I still wanted you, even though I tried to tell myself we were over and that you didn't want me. He was right. I was attracted to you; that never went away." Her lips dried as she admitted her own guilt. "I put both of us in danger because I couldn't hide my feelings for you… He pushed for sex because he saw that in me. It aroused him. I don't know why. But he got turned on. Really turned on. He didn't want to wait. He wouldn't wait… I tried to say no, but he—"

Wreck scooped both hands around her ass and slid her from her seat to bring her onto the floor. He brushed her hair away from her face. "I killed Hillam for touching you."

Tulsi nodded, afraid that if she opened her mouth, her sorrow would overwhelm her. "If I'd heard you fight, I would've come back to end Merchant too."

"I couldn't even do it right," she mumbled. "I'm an idiot. If I had really killed him…"

"What?"

On a blink, she made herself meet his eye. "Rowdy wouldn't have been chained up. Kieran wouldn't have been shot. You wouldn't have been left in the impossible position of choosing between me and your best friend."

"Baines would still want blood. He fucking hates Kieran," Wreck said, and she could almost hear him saying *"like the rest of us"* in his mind. "Baines would've put one in his skull, not his leg."

Like he had with Alexis. Wreck was right that Baines didn't have much in the way of restraint.

"But Rowdy—"

"Wouldn't have got off easy."

"So you're saying that the only way I could've stopped anyone being hurt was to sleep with him," she said. "That I should've let him have what he wanted." Tulsi exhaled a laugh of irony. "Wow, Svana really is smarter than me."

Wreck was trying to make her see that everyone was in the path of hurt. Tulsi knew that she couldn't prevent everyone's pain. But she didn't want to be responsible for it. Her actions had caused Rowdy, Kieran, and Wreck to be hurt.

Svana had been right. If Tulsi had just breathed through and let Merchant have her, no one would be hurt because of her. Wreck took responsibility for things outside his control. But this had been in Tulsi's control. She'd had the ability to protect others and had chosen to be selfish instead.

THIRTY-THREE

"YOU WANNA KNOW what it did to me to think of you with him?"

Wreck's gruff words were more than angry. His guttural tone shivered all the way through her, leaving her cold.

Tulsi pushed her hand into his. "I never was… I was always yours."

"What did he do to you at night?"

Oh… that question chilled her into silence. What Merchant did to her at night couldn't be prettied up. At the time, it had been a matter of breathing through his abuses. In the light of where she was and who she was with, suddenly those abuses felt different.

Wreck was the man she loved. The man who she wanted to be with. If he heard what Merchant had done to her body…

Having been sure that Merchant would kill her and that she wouldn't see freedom again, Tulsi hadn't considered telling Wreck or how he might feel on learning what another man had done on her skin. Skin Wreck used to enjoy touching, teasing, kissing. If he knew the truth, he wouldn't want to do any of those things ever again.

Before Tulsi even found the words, she was shaking her head. "I can't."

Anger collided with his impatience and the tension in the room flew up a dozen points. "You can't what?" he barked.

"If I tell you, you won't want to be with me."

"That what he tell you?"

"That's what I'm saying," she said, rising to touch her lips to his. "I love you so much."

Taking her face in both hands, he eased her away from their kiss. "You gotta tell me, baby. You gotta trust me."

"I do," she said. "It's selfish, but I… just want you to keep looking at me the way you do… I want to feel safe, be like this with you."

"He touched you?" She nodded. "Nymph, I thought you were having sex with him before you split. Soon as I found you, what was the first thing we did?"

They had sex. He made a good point. Until their conversation in the motel parking lot, Wreck believed she and Merchant had been sleeping together. Ridiculous as it may be, she felt that Merchant using her body against her will was more intimate than them having consensual sex. Wreck wouldn't want to be near anywhere Merchant's spunk had spilled on her body. Tulsi still felt dirty if she thought about it too much.

"This is different," she said, hating Merchant for coming between them even in death.

"Different how… You said he didn't fuck you."

"He didn't," she said, squirming under his oppressive scrutiny. "He kissed me… My body."

"He went down on you?"

"No," she barked, horrified at the disgusting thought. "It was never about my pleasure. I never climaxed anywhere near him, I swear it."

"Then it was about him," Wreck said. "You suck him off?"

Breathing in as her head rose, Tulsi couldn't think of any other conversation that she'd want to have less. "Wreck, why do we have to do this? Can't we just—"

"I wanna know," he snapped.

"Why? It won't change anything. Can't we just forget about him and move on?"

Though with Baines on the warpath for vengeance, they couldn't forget about Merchant completely.

"No," Wreck said. "Why the fuck won't you tell me?"

Not telling him was setting them up for a fall. Just like she'd worried about the story of the stabbing tearing them apart, concealing this truth had the potential to do the same.

Wreck left the floor and strode toward the bathtub. It was only a few feet away, but she didn't like the distance, or his tension.

Getting to her feet, Tulsi gave him his space, but couldn't think of how to calm him. "Wreck—"

"What the fuck did he do to you? What the fuck did that bastard—"

"He jerked off on me. A lot. All the time. Every night." The words just tumbled out of her. "He used my body, okay? He used me as his own personal…" Thinking of it made her nauseous. "The bastard would come in at night and whisper about how I was his and ask if I was ready to beg for it. He taunted me, Wreck, and I let it all happen. I let him touch me and talk to me, and I did nothing to stop it."

The gag had held her objections in. The chains had bound her to the bed. Still, she felt responsible. The only way Tulsi could live with herself was not to think about it. Except she *was* thinking about it. About how his breath felt on her skin, about the scent of his body as he lay beside her. Her eyes closed when she relived the sensation of his tongue on her chest and his fingers as they caressed her skin.

Wreck's fingers slid onto her jaw. The unexpected contact sharpened her next inhale. Given the shame that lived deep inside her, she expected to read disappointment in his eyes. But she didn't. Something else burned within him; something she couldn't identify.

He tipped up her chin and descended to brush his mouth across hers. The gentle kiss wasn't like him, he was usually forceful in taking what he wanted. Sinking into the rhythm of the reassurance his mouth gave to hers, Tulsi inhaled through her nose and curled her fingers in his tee-shirt. Holding it in her fists, she dragged him down, begging for more without words.

Her love read her need and slipped his tongue between her lips. Their urgent desperation gathered pace. Their panting and pawing built to a frenzy that took her to the edge of desire. Then all of a sudden, Wreck took her shoulders and forced their bodies apart.

Was that it? The reality of what she'd told him must have caught up with him. She was dirty and he knew it.

One of the things that always upset her when she thought about Wreck while they were apart was that they hadn't had a chance to say goodbye. Standing there, trying to settle her heaving chest and hammering heart, Tulsi couldn't find the words. If Wreck was finished with her, if he couldn't bring himself to be with her, they would have to say goodbye. Only, she didn't know how to do it.

"I can't be around you and not be with you," she said, licking her damp, tingling lips. "I wouldn't know how to do it… and if I had to see you with someone else…" Shaking her head, she lowered her chin. "I'll talk to Dam. If you think Fox Den is safer—"

"What shit you talking?" She looked up. "I don't give a damn what the bastard did to you, it doesn't change this, doesn't change us… I just needed to know so I didn't fuck up."

Tulsi was so shocked that she was left at a loss. "What?"

"I don't want the fucker anywhere near our bed. I don't want him in your head; I don't want to take you back there." He touched her cheek with just his fingertips. "Whatever you need, Nymph."

Dumbfounded, she could only blink and gawp for half a minute. "You don't want to leave me? You don't think I'm dirty?"

"Nothing changes this but us… Nothing and no one."

Just when Tulsi thought Wreck had no more tricks to stun her with, he pulled a whopper out of his hat. He didn't care. He truly didn't. No matter how long or how hard she looked, she couldn't see a glimmer of judgment or revulsion.

After taking a good minute to gather herself and appreciate how freeing honesty could be, she looped her arms around him and sighed.

"What now?" Tulsi asked. "We run from Baines?"

"Maybe," he said, curling a loose tendril of her hair around his finger. "We need intel first."

"What kind of intel?" she asked. "And how do we get it?"

"Ripp knows people. Others respond to Rowdy. There are ways it can be done."

"What do we want to know?"

"How many Baines has. Merchant's lost a couple of guys, that'll spook the rest of them. Anyone loyal to Baines will stick around, but anyone who wanted free of Merch will run."

"You said Merchant kept people in jobs, that he paid them. You thought his thugs would hang around."

"And they might," he said, tugging her hair as he freed his finger from it. "Rowdy thinks we don't assume nothing. We find out if there's a chance we can take Baines."

"Rowdy's still weak," Tulsi said, bringing her arms around from his back to lay them on his torso. "He can't do much, not until he has his strength back. I'm worried if he rushes in, he won't realize his own limitations."

Wreck sneered, offended by the suggestion that Rowdy wasn't at full strength. "And that could get us all killed?"

Tulsi stroked him in an attempt to soothe his pique. "It could. Someone has to say it. I know you trust Rowdy with your life, but how do you think he'll feel if he isn't quick enough or strong enough to help you? Someone could get hurt. Look at everything he's put up with from Kieran. It doesn't matter how much he fucks up, Rowdy still feels responsible for him." She slid her flat hand up his chest until her fingers touched his throat. "You two have a lot in common."

"And you?" he said. "Taking responsibility for the

fucker's crimes?"

She smiled and rose onto her tiptoes. "Maybe it's catching."

When the strength of his grip tightened on her waist, she inhaled his need and let it fuse with her own. Tulsi recognized the way his eyelids grew heavy and how he got closer without ever moving. She scratched his throat and leaned in to drag her teeth across his bicep before he had a chance to kiss her. Watching the light in his eyes grow to an inferno, she opened her mouth wider to sink her teeth in, reminding him of her claim on him.

The moment she released her jaw, Wreck began to sink down. They were seeking each other, seconds from a kiss when a shout from beyond the bathroom interrupted their moment.

"No!" That shout was close by, right on the other side of the door. "No! Shut the fuck up!"

The voice belonged to Kieran. She and Wreck moved away from the door as he opened it. They bundled out into the hall. Rowdy stood in her bedroom doorway wearing a pair of gray sweats.

"What's going on?" Wreck asked, laying his hands on her shoulders so she could lean into them.

"I told him about you."

"Me?"

"No," Rowdy said. "You."

He moved his head at the same time his focus jumped back and forth between them.

Tulsi didn't immediately catch on, but when she did, astonishment assaulted her. "He doesn't know?"

"Why would he know?"

As far as Tulsi was concerned, the more relevant question was why *wouldn't* he? In Wreck's version of the story, Merchant had hauled all three of the men into his office after she disappeared. There must have been whispers about what was going on among Merchant's men. Kieran did have a habit of being self-involved, which meant he couldn't see past the end of his own nose most of the time. It didn't help that he would've been nursing his bullet wound, or someone would've been nursing him.

Svana faded into her thoughts. The guest room door was closed. Tulsi couldn't hear anything coming from the other side of it. Giving Svana and Putnam time alone was right, they'd need it to adjust to their new reality. Both of them had relied on Merchant for far longer than the rest of them. Their lives had been connected to the man for months, maybe years. Tulsi didn't know much about Putnam's back story.

"Where is she?"

Startled by the booming insistence of Kieran's voice coming from the opposite end of the hallway, Tulsi forgot about the guest room when she saw him storming toward them from the living room.

"Calm down," Rowdy said. "Just calm down."

"Are you shitting me? You're telling me that your best friend stole my girl and I'm supposed to calm down?" Kieran asked, throwing his hands in the air.

Somebody had to tell him sometime. Tulsi was glad Rowdy had made the decision to put it out there… and that he'd waited until Kieran was dressed to break the news. Everyone else knew. Kieran finding out by witnessing her and Wreck touching or kissing could've led to a much more public explosion. Her apartment wasn't big enough to handle his bruised ego.

"Is it true?" Kieran demanded.

At something of a loss, Tulsi wasn't sure why he was so emotional about the news. "Is what true?" she asked.

Kieran sort of nodded in Wreck's direction even though he didn't go so far as to actually look at the man standing behind her. "That you're with him! Are you with him?"

"Yes," she said. "I am. Not that it's your business."

"My business?" Kieran asked, prodding his own chest with an indignant forefinger. "We were dating!"

"No, we weren't," she said, jumping in before he worked himself into more of a lather. "I told you more than once that there was nothing between us, that we weren't going to be together, that we were finished."

Like she hadn't said a word, he carried on. "When did

it start?"

The hallway had never felt so small. Being surrounded by three tall men who took up more space than her, Tulsi was dwarfed. Even in his weakened state, Rowdy still proved to be an imposing figure in the narrow space.

"I don't know why you're upset," Tulsi said. "We haven't seen each other for months."

"Doesn't mean that we were finished! I can't believe this. I can't believe you would do this to me!"

His voice was loud, his rage apparent, which may have been why when he swayed her way, Wreck's hand left her shoulder. He straightened his arm to hold a flat hand in front of her, blocking Kieran from getting any closer.

"Settle down," Wreck grumbled.

"You don't have any right to tell me what to do! You don't have any right at all! You stole her!"

"Tulsi isn't property," Rowdy said. "You didn't even have one full date. The first night you took her out, you got her kidnapped. Are you surprised the relationship didn't work out?"

"It didn't have a chance!" Kieran argued. "That's all I wanted! A chance!"

At what? Tulsi wondered. To get into her panties most likely.

The two of them had nothing in common. She didn't even enjoy his company. It wouldn't have taken long for him to realize he didn't enjoy hers. Tulsi wouldn't have swooned or pandered to him every time he walked into a room or when he talked about his newest workout routine. They were opposites, always at odds. They had different values and valued different things.

All Kieran wanted from her was sex. He just couldn't admit that to himself while he had this chance to be indignant. If he wasn't careful, Wreck would give him something else to be stressed about; something like whether or not he wanted to keep breathing.

THIRTY-FOUR

STANDING IN THE HALL listening to Kieran come apart was getting them nowhere.

Tulsi exhaled. "Take all the time you need to figure this out," she said to Kieran, knowing he would be of little use when it came to making a plan for the newest potentially fatal disaster awaiting them. Taking Wreck's hand, she looked to Rowdy. "Will you come talk with us?"

Rowdy shrugged and used his arm to ease his brother aside, giving her space to walk past with Wreck in tow.

In the living room, Ripp and Styx still sat in their armchairs at opposite sides of the room. Dam hadn't moved either and remained on the high arm of the pull out couch.

Wreck led her over to the loveseat and pushed her down, just like he had earlier. Only instead of leaving, he stood beside her. Tulsi didn't see Wreck signal his friend, but Rowdy came over and sat down next to her.

The most injured had the right to sit, especially when they didn't know how long the conversation was going to last.

"You can't just walk away from me," Kieran said, marching into the room. "I deserve an explanation! An apology! You can't just leave me for some other guy, a guy you don't even know! You don't know what he's like!"

"What do you think happened?" she asked, so offended by his attitude that she had to switch her anger to amusement. If she didn't, Tulsi was in the perfect mood to join a club that Styx, Wreck, and Ripp were a part of, possibly Rowdy too. "I told you that we were through when Merchant sent me to the apartment."

"Merchant ordered you to say that."

"Merchant knew I was with Wreck. He knew about us. Everybody knew!"

"Except me," Kieran said. "Because you knew it was wrong—"

"Because it was none of your business! I didn't want to be with you. I never wanted to be with you. Just the fact that you never listened when I said that was a good reason for me. You never listen. You don't take on information. You don't understand anybody except yourself. Half the time I don't think you even do that.

"Important things are going on. Lives are at stake. Our lives. Throwing a ridiculous hissy fit about something that means nothing is an indulgence we don't have the time for! If we all make it out of this alive, you can yell as much as you like. You can be dramatic and stamp your feet, but it's not going to change anything."

Leaning back in her seat, Tulsi folded her arms and peered across the room at him. "Do you think this is attractive?" she asked. "Do you think I'll see you acting this way and beg you to be with me? You think I'll just ditch Wreck and throw in with you because… what? You make the most noise? You whine the most? Trust me, that's not gonna happen." She turned her attention to Ripp. "What have you come up with?"

"Fuck you all!" Kieran said, throwing his arms toward them before stomping off through the kitchen and down the stairs.

No one said anything until after they heard the back door slam.

Rowdy's brows rose. "That was harsh," he said, casting his attention up to Wreck. "Should I go after him?"

"Your call," Wreck said.

One outburst shouldn't answer another. Tulsi didn't know what to say. Her response had provoked Kieran into storming out onto streets that weren't safe for any of them.

Styx had an opinion too. "One less body to worry about. Kieran can handle his own mess; he always falls on his feet anyway."

That was true. Even though Kieran had been through an ordeal, it wasn't as bad as it could've been. If Kieran had gone to Teal's apartment by himself without his brother and Wreck, without her, he'd probably be dead already. Other than the bullet wound on his thigh, Kieran hadn't suffered much.

Rowdy and Wreck were the ones who were forced to work for Merchant. Styx had endured torture and starvation. Tulsi had been chained to a bed and violated. All things considered, a bullet to the thigh wasn't that horrific. The rest of them would've begged for that over what they'd survived instead.

Kieran was set up in an apartment. Fed. Watered. Not required to do anything except tell the truth. The more Tulsi thought about it, the more it irritated her. Kieran enjoyed playing the victim, the martyr. He liked to claim he was so hard done by that he deserved sympathy and praise for what little he actually did.

Tulsi wouldn't praise him. Wreck wouldn't either.

"Sure know how to make friends, Patch," Dam muttered.

"He'll come back," Styx said. "He knows where we are and will end up shitting the bed out there on his own. He'll have a bullshit excuse about why, but he'll find his way back."

"Can we move the fuck on?" Ripp asked, unimpressed and impatient.

Styx filled them in. "Ripp's plan is to kill him."

"Kill who?" Tulsi asked.

"The one who killed Alexis," Ripp said.

So Rowdy had filled him in. That was good. It showed they were willing to follow through on their promises. Kieran could've been the one to tell the story. Though that was doubtful. Ripp wouldn't have put up with Kieran's tone for the length of time it would take to hear the whole story.

"What was the deal with you two?" Tulsi asked Ripp. "All we heard was that she was one of Keaton's favorites."

"She was. Doesn't mean he was a favorite of hers."

"So you were sleeping with her too? Sleeping with your uncle's girlfriend?"

"For information on the fucker? Sure. Not much I wouldn't do. My vendetta's my job. Taking him apart is my living."

Ripp was glib about it. Not that he was making a joke, but just laid back and matter of fact about it. His vendetta, as he called it, was his life. All he had was time to think of ways to hurt his uncle and enact the plans he came up with.

"Did she know who you were and that you have this vendetta?"

"She knew," Ripp said. "She was smart, knew how to play both sides."

Something most of the men in Tulsi's life had told her to do at various times over the past few months.

The pieces weren't difficult to fit together. "Then Merchant's shipment went missing and the bottom fell out of her world."

"Did Keaton go looking for her?"

Ripp shrugged. "Who gives a fuck?"

Because Keaton wouldn't have to take down Alexis' murderer. Ripp already had the inside track and planned to do it himself. Losing the woman must have meant something to him. He was letting it distract him from his usual mission to disrupt his uncle's life and business.

Though she was interested, Ripp was right. Other things were more important.

"Should we leave now?" Tulsi asked. "Put some distance between us and Baines?"

"We don't know what he knows yet," Rowdy said. "I say we stick until our intel comes through."

Tulsi looked to Ripp. "What do you say?"

"I don't run, Pretty," he said. "This is my city. I don't tuck tail."

Strong or deluded, it could go either way. The city wouldn't be as high on his list as Keaton. Leaving the city meant giving Keaton a break, something he didn't want.

"They were looking for you too," Tulsi said, sliding a hand onto the arm of the chair. Continuing to the edge, her fingers brushed Wreck's. "Merchant was looking for Ripp, wasn't he?"

"Yeah," Wreck said.

"Merchant said you came back into town," she said. "So you haven't always been in the city."

"Keaton gets product from elsewhere," Ripp replied. "Sometimes it pays to go after the source."

So he didn't run, but he did take trips for business purposes. Tulsi was sorry that they didn't have more time to get to know each other. Everyone had been thrown together. Trust was tentative. But these men, most of them, had supported her when she had few options. They'd protected her and protected Wreck. She wouldn't forget any of them or what they'd done for her.

"Best thing we can do now is get some rest," Rowdy said.

"Yeah," Styx said, pushing his hands down his thighs as he leaned back before boosting onto his feet.

"Where you going?" she asked.

"Someone's gotta check downstairs is secure."

As Styx crossed into the kitchen, Dam stood up. "I'll go with him."

He didn't wait for a response and disappeared in Styx's wake.

Tulsi laid a hand on Rowdy's knee. "You should lie down."

He shook his head. "You two take the bedroom. I'm gonna wait, see if little brother comes back."

Having left in a fit of temper, Kieran had once again raised his brother's concern. Even when he wasn't present, he was causing problems.

Wreck snagged her hand and pulled her onto her feet. There weren't many places to sleep. Though there were plenty of pillows and blankets, she didn't have many beds. That didn't seem to bother Ripp who slouched in his chair and closed his eyes.

Her mind was racing. All her jumbled thoughts bounced and pinged from one thing to another like a pinball hitting the bumpers at high speed. Tulsi was still thinking, trying to imagine how the situation might play out. At least she was until she noticed Wreck at the end of her bed reaching to the back of his neck to pull off his tee-shirt.

A smile rose on her lips. He tossed his tee-shirt to the chair in the corner and started on his belt.

When he noticed her expression, he paused. "What?"

"Nothing," she said, slinking his way. "I dreamed of this."

"Of what?"

"This," she said, drawing a fingertip down his sternum. "You and me here, in my bedroom."

"You dream about everything," he said, sitting on the end of the bed to untie his boots.

"This was different," she said, kicking off her own shoes.

After his boots were off, he stood up to shove his pants from his hips. Tulsi hurried to get ahead of him. Once naked, she crawled onto the bed and sat in the middle. Wreck didn't take his underwear off before he joined her.

On his back with the covers loose at his hips, he laid a forearm on his forehead. With everything that was going on, it shouldn't be a surprise he wasn't in the mood. Tulsi, on the other hand, couldn't help herself. Being so close to her love and all alone with him was more than she could resist. It was a treat she wouldn't take for granted.

By the way he fixated on the ceiling, she could tell that his mind was full too. Climbing on top of him, she lay there with her head on his shoulder for a while before saying anything.

"Are you worried about Kieran?" she asked.

"The weasel? No."

She didn't think that he'd be angry about what she'd said. "Are you worried about Rowdy?"

That question, he wasn't so quick to answer. Maybe what she'd said was beginning to sink in. Rowdy wasn't at his peak. That put pressure on Wreck to keep him safe, maybe without being overt about that protection.

Most men didn't like their strength to be questioned. The men couldn't be at odds, especially over something like that, something that proved their connection to each other. Rowdy was a sensible guy, but that didn't mean he wouldn't run into danger if he thought Wreck or Kieran needed him.

Nothing Tulsi could say would ease his concerns. Instead of trying platitudes, she took her head off his shoulder and kissed him instead. He ran a hand over her hair, reminding her that it was still mostly on her head. While pushing harder to speed their kiss, she fought with the hair tie to free her locks. It cascaded down over both of them; Wreck growled in appreciation.

Wrapping both arms around her, he flipped her over to put himself on top. Tulsi's hands slithered down his body and into his underwear. She hooked her thumbs over the elastic to push them down as far as she could.

Wreck cradled her head with a supporting arm that kept his weight from her body as he rid himself of the last shred of clothing between them.

"Nymph," he said, his breath coming hard and fast when he forced himself to break their kiss.

"It's okay," she said, stroking his face. "I want you… I need you… Please don't leave me wanting."

He brushed his lips over hers and then plunged down her body to bury his mouth between her thighs. The sensation of his mouth kissing and licking her most intimate corner gave her the strength to be confident in their triumph.

Wreck was with her. They were together. He sucked on her clit and circled it with the tip of his tongue. Flickering it over her, taking her to the edge of orgasm, Wreck reminded her of the power they had together. No matter what, as long as they were together, they'd go to any lengths for each other.

"My… My Ruin," she gasped, her eyes closed, her hands lost in her own hair.

He delved deeper to push his tongue into her. Fucking her with his mouth, Wreck showed her just how much he valued her. Tulsi wanted more, she wanted him always, wanted him hard and fast, wanted him soft and slow.

Even in the times she didn't know what she wanted, in the times she couldn't think straight, Wreck knew what to give her.

Just as she sucked in a breath expecting to slam into orgasm, Wreck's mouth left its post. He surged up to join their mouths for a breath as he positioned himself to slide into her.

Her lips parted to whisper his name. He pulled out and drove in deep; the man knew what he was doing. He'd been inside her for less than a minute, but orgasm seized her with such force, she had to scream. It was the only way her body could process the cascade of feelings that hit her all at once.

Blinking through the stars he'd put in her eyes, Tulsi sought him out. In the dark, beneath the man who'd screw her to within an inch of her life at the same time he protected her existence with his soul, Tulsi felt blessed.

Not so long ago, she'd believed they'd never be alone again. That they would both lose their lives. But they'd been given a gift.

"Wreck," she whispered and yelped as he took her to the edge of another climax. "My love… Oh, my… My Ruin."

She just managed to finish the words before another scream signaled her climax. Taking her to this happy place, showering her with the optimism of possibilities, Wreck devoured her. Tulsi wasn't only safe, she was alive. With Merchant, there was no alive. She hadn't wanted to breathe. Near Wreck, thoughts of life overwhelmed her. For as long as they could, she wanted both of them to hold on to it.

"My Ruin," she panted, warmed by shimmers of aftershocks that vibrated through her in time with his own release.

Wreck stayed there over her, even after both of them were satisfied. "If the shit hits—"

She touched a fingertip to his lips. "We're never going to say goodbye to each other again. Never. Whatever it takes, whatever we have to do, Wreck. I love you. I don't want to be without you."

He opened his mouth to catch her fingertip between his teeth. With a gentle bite, he tickled the end with his tongue and then let go, granting her freedom.

"It could be dangerous."

"When is it not," she said on a laugh. "I don't want to think about Baines or anything except this. Can we just think about us? We're in my bed, together and alive."

That seemed to appease him. He rolled onto his back, though he locked her in the circle of his thighs, putting her on top of him again.

"If we have to leave here in a hurry—"

"Then we leave," she said. "There's nothing to keep me here. Not if you're not here."

He ran his fingers through the ends of her hair. "Sleep."

On his command, she closed her eyes. Something would change when their intel came through. Tulsi trusted the feelers that had been put out and expected when she woke that they'd know more. Even if they didn't, she would wake up with Wreck. That was all she needed.

THIRTY-FIVE

SHARING A BED with Wreck lulled Tulsi into a deeper sleep than she'd enjoyed for a long time. That was maybe why when Wreck eased her onto her back to free himself, she hadn't stirred. A chill tingled in her shoulders, piquing her awareness. She didn't remember hearing anything, but when her eyes relaxed open, she saw Wreck on his feet in a crouch. That was the first Tulsi knew of him being out of their bed.

"Ruin?" she mumbled, pushing onto her elbows. He put a finger to his lips. She didn't know what he was shushing her for. They'd had loud sex. He hadn't cared about anyone hearing that. Her confusion only grew when she noticed he was wearing jeans. "Baby—"

"Someone's downstairs," he whispered.

Alert in an instant, Tulsi threw off the covers and rushed to grab a pair of jeans from her dresser without making a sound. Wreck had a gun in his hand, Coombs gun maybe.

"You got any weapons?" he asked in a whisper, edging closer to the door.

Tulsi shook her head. There were things that could be used to hurt people, but no guns. Her knives were in the kitchen. The stairs opened out to the kitchen, which would be the first room any intruders would come to if they ascended.

Still in stealth mode, Wreck opened the bedroom door. With the gun pointed up, he extended an arm back toward her. Tulsi pulled a shirt over her head and was still fighting to put her arms into the sleeves when she took his hand.

The bedroom wasn't a great place to be stuck. Any of the rooms that led from the hallway would leave them cornered.

Clutching Wreck's hand, she was as quiet as she could be while following him down the hall to the living room. Styx was the first person she saw, standing at the mouth of the hallway, like maybe he'd been about to come and rouse them. Dam appeared at his side.

"Got ammo?" Styx murmured.

"Just whatever's in it," Wreck said.

"Take it to them?"

Dam held something toward her. Tulsi took it and smiled when she recognized her knife. He nodded and retreated to the far corner where Ripp was standing with a gun in hand and another on the back of the chair. Dam took the gun and the clips of ammunition Ripp was handing out.

Styx handed a couple of clips to Wreck. "We don't know how many there are."

They edged into the living room. Instead of being in his armchair, Rowdy was behind it, a weapon in his hand too. All the furniture had been shifted to offer the best cover between them and the kitchen.

The creak of the stairs startled her. Wreck dragged her across the room and around to the back of the loveseat they'd been sitting on earlier. He pulled her down to a crouch and hunkered down with her.

"Stay here," he said. "No matter what you hear, stay here. Stay low. First chance you get to get the hell out, go."

Shaking her head, Tulsi wouldn't let go of his hand. "I won't leave you."

The burst of a gunshot ended their conversation in one beat. Another was returned.

"Nowhere you can hide!"

That was Baines. Wreck knew it too, their eyes locked

and the silent acknowledgement passed between them.

Tulsi couldn't figure out how he'd have found them so fast. Not until she heard another voice.

"Don't fucking hurt my brother," Kieran said.

While Tulsi was hit with shock, the first thing that hit Wreck was rage. The clamp of his jaw revealed his fury in an instant. She tried laying a hand on his face to soothe him, but it didn't work. He pushed her hand away and rose from his crouch to peek over the back of the couch.

When he aimed and fired, she dropped her knife to stick her fingers in her ears. More gunshots were returned.

"Just come out and we won't hurt you," Baines said.

He couldn't keep a straight face while saying it, his words were giddy in their anticipation. Baines had been threatening to hurt them for a long time, since the night she first met him. Finally, he had his chance.

"He's got four guys," Rowdy shouted. "Six total."

Six if they were counting Baines and Kieran. It couldn't be easy for Rowdy to admit that he and his brother were on opposing sides.

Their enemy already knew their numbers, so Rowdy didn't have to worry about revealing any secrets.

"Yeah, and how many more do you think I've got downstairs?" Baines asked. "I can stay here for days, motherfuckas. I have more men, more weapons, more ammo."

"If you're so sure, big man, come charge us," Styx snarled, his voice more menacing than usual.

"Why would I do that when I can just wait you out? You made alotta enemies, throwing our kindness back at us."

Tulsi couldn't believe what she was hearing. "Kindness?" she called. "You're deluded!"

"Ah, Pretty, can't get away from us, can you? We always track you down."

"You didn't track me down. The weasel gave you directions, he led you straight here!"

"I'd have found you eventually. Why don't you come out? We'll all sit down and talk."

Only an idiot would trust him, which might explain

why Kieran had done it. All he'd seen was red. While fuming over Wreck's apparent betrayal and smarting about her humiliating rant, Kieran had gone to the one place, to the one man, who wanted the same thing as him.

"Wreck did it!" Kieran exclaimed. "We're here to take him down."

"You never see the big picture, Weasel."

"What big fucking picture?"

"Sure, Wreck took Merch down, but hurting him means taking out his brother or his girl. You wanted good, old-fashioned revenge, this is it!" Baines volume ascended. "Who can tell the weasel more about that? Ripp? They got you too?"

"Get the hell out of here," Tulsi shouted.

"Can't do that. You took down the man I answer to, there won't be any peace for any of you until I return the favor."

"Rowdy wasn't a part of it," Kieran argued, desperation flavoring his words. "He didn't know anything about their sick plan, how could he? You kept him locked up all this time."

"You still don't get it?" Baines said. "I don't give a shit about your brother. You don't give a shit about him either, fuck, you brought us here with guns. We give a shit about hurting the fucker who killed Merch. It's blood for blood. That's our code. Merchant's code. For me, he was worth ten men, so I'll keep on killing until I've evened the score."

"You'll try," Tulsi said. "But you'll fail. You always fail. How many times have we got to prove we're smarter?"

The blast of a gunshot came a fraction of a second before a hole exploded in the back of the couch between her and Wreck. Wood and fibers spurted out to scatter on the floor. Wreck looked from the back of the couch to a small hole in the wall beneath the window.

While she was still in shock, Wreck grabbed her head to force it down onto the floor. There wasn't much space. Dam, Styx, Ripp, Rowdy, didn't have much better cover. They'd have to take down Baines and his guys without losing any of their people.

"I'll keep coming at you 'til I'm cold in the ground!" Baines hollered. "You want freedom? You'll have to kill me first."

"Done," Styx said at the same time Wreck edged to the side of the couch to peek around it.

From the direction of the kitchen, another gunshot sounded. In close succession, two shots rang out from the living room, though she couldn't place who'd fired.

"Now there's two with him," Rowdy said.

Two and Baines. So Tulsi's allies had taken out two of Baines' men; Rowdy was no longer counting Kieran. Either that was a message to their side that he didn't want his brother shot or that the weasel had made a run for it.

Tulsi lay with the side of her face pressed against the hardwood floor, listening for footsteps on the stairs, expecting Baines' reserves. But none came.

"Where are your men, Baines?"

"Couldn't keep as many of them as he thought," Styx said.

"Few of them on the fence?" Rowdy asked.

"Or switched to Keaton's camp?" Ripp added.

In the hours Tulsi had spent hanging in Merchant's office over the last week, she'd seen many of the same faces. By her estimations, Merchant had more than a dozen men on site, and probably far more on his books. Guys who didn't live in his building, but worked as outside contractors. Those men wouldn't sign on with Baines until they saw how the power shifted, and who got the most of it. Merchant's territory was up for grabs. Maybe some of them thought they had a chance at grabbing power.

Teal was dead. Coombs was dead. Of those who did live in Merchant's building—who would be the men at Baines' fingertips when Kieran burst in with his information—only four of them had joined the quest to avenge Merchant.

"Last chance!" Baines called. "Stand up and show yourselves or I start shooting."

Pot luck shooting would be dangerous for both sides. Even if everyone thought the same thing, it didn't stop them.

Someone broke the ceasefire. Tulsi didn't know who shot first, she was still lying on the floor. Gunshots popped and banged everywhere all at once. Keeping track of who was shooting and who may be hurt wasn't easy. Closing her eyes, she pressed her palms to her ears, trying to block out the battle.

THIRTY-SIX

HER COWARDICE only lasted a few seconds. The danger wouldn't go away just because she buried her head in the sand. Tulsi opened her eyes to see that there, just a few inches away, was the glint of her blade. Her finger slid across the floor and curled around the handle. Wreck was intent on his task, catching glimpses over the back of the couch and around the side, returning fire whenever he could.

Shouting joined the gunfire and a door slammed. All of a sudden, the shooting stopped. Tulsi pounced onto her knees to peek over the back of the couch before Wreck could notice and stop her.

Baines tucked himself against the wall in the kitchen and stole the occasional glance around it into the living room. Tulsi registered his position and that his attention had shifted from the living room to the hallway. Putnam and Svana were in the guest room, she hadn't seen them yet. If they were smart, they would stay there until the fighting was over. But it turned out they weren't so smart.

"Putnam!" Baines called and chuckled to himself. "You in on this too, asshole? Not fucking surprised you picked the losing team."

Without thinking about the process, Tulsi rose higher

in her crouch, adjusting her grip on the weapon. In one slick move, she threw her blade across the room, imagining the target Rook had used to train her. That it hit such a sweet spot surprised her, but not as much as it surprised Baines who howled in pain.

Tulsi was static, dumbfounded to see that the knife had gone through his forearm and embedded itself in the wall behind, pinning him in place. His hand opened, releasing his gun, which clattered to the floor.

Her team followed her opportune lead. One shot followed another, one hit his back, the other his shoulder. With Baines incapacitated, Tulsi searched for the men he'd brought. All she saw were bodies on the kitchen floor and the sheen of liquid around them... blood. One of the bodies could've been Kieran, Tulsi couldn't pick out specifics in the dark.

Baines had his back to the living room, his arm still connected to the wall. He tried to twist to reach for the knife, like he wanted to pull it out. Except whenever he tried to stretch, the shot in his shoulder squeezed another pained cry from his lungs.

In her semi-crouch, she watched Ripp leave his cover to cross the room, the injured Baines in his crosshairs. He went into the kitchen to look Baines straight in the eye as he raised the barrel of his gun to his forehead. Without saying a word, he pulled the trigger.

Baines drooped. The knife in his forearm only kept him up for a few extra seconds before his own weight pulled it free and he collapsed to the floor. Gone. Dead.

Wreck stood up before Tulsi had processed that it was over. Truly over.

Styx was already in the kitchen, checking for pulses. "I'd shoot 'em again just to be sure, but I don't want to make more mess." He looked across the apartment at Wreck. "Got a preferred method?"

"One or two," Wreck said and put his arm around her.

Tulsi was still fixated on Baines crumpled body, trying to process all she'd seen.

Kieran stepped out of the shadow of the kitchen. Her view of him erased her daze. Anger fizzed and bubbled in her guts.

She didn't even want to see him, so she looked up at Wreck instead. "What do you need me to do?"

Rowdy wouldn't let anyone kill Kieran, even though he probably deserved it. What happened to him was a matter for the men to discuss and decide. Having made a big deal about her business not being his, Tulsi couldn't decide his business was hers just because it suited her.

"Go back to bed," Wreck said. "Stay there."

"I can help."

"I don't want you to leave the apartment."

"We're safe… aren't we?" she asked. "Are we safe?"

"Maybe, but this is a dirty job. I don't want you involved." He curled a finger under her chin and elevated it to press his mouth to hers. "Go on."

Tulsi wouldn't be much help with the bodies anyway. She didn't have the strength to lift and carry and didn't know anything about dumping corpses. When it came to concealing murder, she was a novice.

In the midst of doing what Wreck had told her to do, the movement of Rowdy's arm drew her eye to the kitchen. The smack of his right hook on Kieran's jaw sent the weasel straight to the floor. Tulsi smiled. They'd been worried that Rowdy couldn't take care of himself. Kieran might not be the most dangerous of targets, but Rowdy wasn't going to let what he'd done slide.

Tulsi stopped when Wreck went striding into the kitchen. The purpose of his gait was clear. He bent down to pick Kieran off the floor, and that's when the stuttering started.

"I'm sorry!" Kieran said. "I am. Look, I was wrong, I was mad—"

"I wanna kill him," Wreck growled.

"Yeah, you're not the only one," Styx said.

"You know what I woulda done to you if Tuls was hurt?" Wreck snarled. "Death's too good for you."

"We're not gonna kill him," Rowdy said, standing at

Wreck's shoulder. "But he is gonna get the hell out of here while he still can."

"Wha… what? What?" Kieran said, the stuttering fear in his tone mangling the words. "Yeah! Yeah, I'll go, I'll leave, let you calm down and—"

"No, you're gonna go for good," Rowdy said, which brought them all to a stop. "You're gonna fuck off out of our lives. Go back to the rich mom and dad who took you in. Go live your fancy lifestyle with them."

"No, but—"

"It's that or I let Wreck take care of you."

"No! I'll go, I'll go!"

Wreck spun him around and threw him across the room. Kieran skidded and crashed into the side banister of the descending stairs. After lying dazed for a moment, he used the wood to pull himself up. Although he glanced back, he didn't loiter and was quick to run away down the stairs, just like he had earlier.

"I said bed, Nymph," Wreck said without turning around.

Tulsi didn't know how he knew she was there, but she jumped to action and continued to the hallway. Putnam stood at the opposite end, next to the open guest bedroom door. He must have seen what had happened. Tulsi wasn't going to rehash it for him, so she went into her own bedroom without a word and sat on the end of her bed.

"Putnam!" Styx called from the kitchen.

Although Putnam had missed the gunfight, he wasn't going to wriggle out of the cleanup. He was another pair of capable hands. With at least five bodies to dispose of, they'd need as much help as they could get.

A few minutes after seeing the movement of Putnam's shadow pass by, the bedroom door began to move on its hinges. The men would be busy, so it wasn't a surprise to see Svana in the doorway.

Tulsi exhaled. "What can I do for you?"

"How did he die?" Svana asked.

"Gunshot. He shouldn't have come here shouting the odds, talking payback. How many people has he hurt—"

"Not Baines." She came a few steps further into the room. "Ilias."

"Oh," Tulsi said, wondering if those were tears glistening in Svana's eyes. "I didn't watch. Either Wreck strangled him or smothered him… He could've broken his neck."

She wasn't sure what method Wreck had used and wouldn't make assumptions. Though she probably wouldn't ask either.

"It's funny," Svana said. "I don't know what to feel."

"He was a part of your life for a long time."

"You were right. You told me that I could get away from him and… You were right."

Tulsi put her hands behind her to support her weight on straight arms. "I didn't know what I was talking about back then. I thought I did, but I could never have predicted this."

Svana came over to sit on the bed at her side. "He wants to take me home to his mother. He comes from small town somewhere or something."

Tulsi didn't quite see Putnam in a small town. "Putnam?"

Svana nodded. The youngster twisted her whole self around, lifting her feet from the floor to fold her legs in front of her. "I'm free. I don't have to worry about anybody chasing me. I don't have to worry about who could be coming for me or what they might want."

On a nod, Tulsi exhaled. "It's completely up to you what you do. He's offering you something. If you want to take it, take it. If you don't, then don't. You don't want to be beholden to a man you don't care about."

"I do care about him," Svana said. "At least, I could… I think. I don't know. All I wanted was a chance to make my own decisions. Now that I have that chance, I don't know how to make them."

"You'll learn," Tulsi said. "It'll take time and you'll make mistakes. We all do. But you'll learn."

Svana smiled and snatched Tulsi's hand. "We really are friends… You're the only friend I have."

Friends was a strong word. Not so long ago, Tulsi had

been talking about how untrustworthy Svana was. In a quick turnaround, she was accepting the woman's touch and sharing secrets while advising her about the future.

The blonde was bright and beautiful. Tulsi didn't like a lot of the things she'd done but couldn't bring herself to hate the woman. Svana was a victim of her upbringing and environment. Of course, it was easy to feel that way when they'd be parting ways soon.

"Give it a try," Tulsi said. "With Putnam. What's the worst that happens? You don't like it and you leave? At least you'll know. You can take care of yourself. Just steer clear of Vegas and rich men who promise you the world. Stand on your own two feet. I guarantee you'll be stronger for it."

Tulsi hooked her heels onto the end of the bed and pushed back until she could lie down to rest her head on Wreck's pillow.

"You're going to rest?" Svana asked. "How can you go to sleep?"

With the adrenaline wearing off, exhaustion was creeping in. The guys were still working, still moving, but the enemy was gone. No monsters lurked waiting to jump out on them. Tulsi folded her hands under her face and closed her eyes.

Svana had asked the question as though it was the last thing she wanted to do. Yet, less than a minute later, the swan crawled up the bed and lay down beside her.

Her life had become like a dream mixed with a nightmare. The nightmare might be over, but there would be a few obstacles in the future. They'd eliminated the enemy and destroyed the threat, now Tulsi could only wait to find out what happened next.

THIRTY-SEVEN

WRECK WOKE HER with a kiss. Tulsi hummed in satisfaction and tried to put her arms around his neck, but he caught her hands to trap them in his. On a yawn, she blinked to bring him into focus.

"Time to say goodbye, Nymph."

Her love wasn't in the bed at all, he was standing beside it, bent over her. When she twisted around to check the other side of the bed, Tulsi found it empty.

"I thought we weren't doing goodbyes," she said, rolling toward him while trying her best to tuck his hands in against her chest.

With little effort, he freed his hands, and brushed hair away from her face. "Not us. Come on."

Tulsi yawned again, but followed when he pulled her from the bed and onto her feet. Wreck led her out of the room and into the kitchen where everyone else had gathered. Everyone except Ripp.

"Where's Ripp?" she asked.

Styx answered. "Gone. He did his bit. Think he wants to get a jump on what's happening with Keaton."

Sorry that she'd missed him leaving, she understood that his fight wasn't over. Their fight had delayed him from his vendetta for longer than he probably wanted.

"You're going to stay, right?" she asked Styx.

On a smile, he boosted himself away from his leaning post against the kitchen counter. "Remember what I said, Prize?"

She raised her brows. "About what?"

"Those balls of yours," he said, laying a straight arm on her shoulder. "Don't lose the fight, okay? Stay optimistic."

Tulsi hadn't really thought of herself as optimistic. But compared to the others, she guessed it wasn't a high bar.

"You should stay a while. You don't have to run away."

"Nah," he said. "I got places to be. Think maybe Ripp inspired me."

She frowned. "What does that mean?"

"I've got a home to go to," he said then angled his head. "Less of a home and more of a base... Been a while since I checked on my brother."

"You have a brother?"

Styx smiled. "With a chip on his shoulder."

Thinking of Styx with a family was difficult. As sorry as she was to see him go, she understood his need to connect with his kin. They were probably worried because Styx had been MIA for a while. Tulsi wasn't sure why they hadn't tried to track him down, but didn't have time to ask.

Styx bowed to kiss her, just a quick one. After, he held up both hands and backed off, showing Wreck a smile. When he offered a hand to Wreck, her love slapped his against it and they did a sort of handshake, which Styx then did again with Rowdy.

"Take care of her," Styx said, backing toward the stairs. "She'll get herself in trouble again if you don't."

Rowdy offered a two fingered salute and then Styx was gone.

"We're going to go too," Svana said, showing Tulsi that her hand was joined with Putnam's. "I'm going to learn about baseball and apple pie and all things American." Just like she'd probably dreamed of when coming to the country. "Putnam says his mom has a white picket fence."

Could be true, but Putnam had got himself mixed up with Merchant somehow. Svana's life might not be plain sailing.

Wreck and Rowdy retreated from the room as Svana offered her a hug. They hadn't been close and she supposed they were still wary of the blonde.

"Take care of yourselves," Tulsi said. "Remember what I said."

Svana nodded. It was nice to see the smile on her face as she disappeared down the stairs with Putnam in tow. The poor guy was going to have his work cut out for him. Tulsi had no idea if the relationship would stand the test of time, probably not, but it was a change of scene. One that Svana was in desperate need of.

"Guess asking you to come with me would be pointless," Dam said.

The sound of his voice made her turn away from the stairs to look at him. At the top of the kitchen, leaning against a counter, he wore a simple smile.

"I have things to do here."

"Sure you do, Patch," Dam said, sauntering toward her. "You've always got a home at the Fox Den." She nodded. "Don't forget."

He put both arms around her and held her close. As her eyes closed, a tear fell. Her friend had supported her when she needed someone.

"Will I see you again?" she asked, still buried against his chest.

"Don't know. Maybe… I'll check in."

"Promise me," she said, pushing back to look up into his face. "Promise you'll come and see me again."

"You know where to find me," he said, swiping a tear from her cheek. "I go south in winter."

If he didn't come around to visit once in a while, Tulsi would go to Fox Den in winter and drag him across the coals.

"Thank you," she said. "It doesn't really sound like enough, but… I'm grateful."

"Yeah," he said, touching her chin. "Remember what Styx said, okay? Keep that fire burning."

"I will."

He cradled her head in his hands and with closed eyes, bowed to press a kiss to her forehead. Less intimate than Styx's kiss, yet a thousand times more powerful.

"Be good," he said, and kissed her again quick before striding away.

Tulsi spun around to see him approach the stairs. "Amsterdam?" He paused, one hand on the banister. "I wouldn't have made it without you."

Offering a smile and a wink, he nodded once and then carried on down the stairs. After the back door closed, Tulsi took a deep breath. She wiped her cheeks and headed into the living room.

Rowdy sat in the armchair closest to the loveseat where Wreck was.

"You guys must be exhausted," she said, going to the pull out bed to strip off the sheets. "I'll move all the junk out of Rowdy's room after you get some rest."

"Rowdy's room?" Rowdy asked.

With the sheets bundled against her, she turned to look at him. "You want the master? It's not much of a master... the closet's bigger, but we all have to share a bathroom."

He smiled. "I didn't know I was staying."

"Of course you are," she said, glancing at Wreck. "Both of you are... We don't have to live here forever, but for now it will do... don't you think?"

The two men shared a look then Rowdy sucked in a breath. "Okay, I'm going to *my* bed then." He came over to kiss her cheek. "Don't be too rough with him."

Rowdy went along the hall and into the second bedroom. Tulsi was still standing looking up the hallway when Wreck came over to join her.

"Nymph, Row and me aren't squeaky clean."

"Oh wow, what a surprise," she said, smiling when he crooked a brow at her sarcasm. "I love you... and I love him... For now, you come as a package deal." She dropped the sheets and kicked them aside so she could get close enough to wrap both arms around him. "I don't mind taking a backseat during daylight… So long as you're mine in the dark. You've earned me, Wreck. I'm all yours."

"You sure this is what you want?" he asked, pushing her hair away from her shoulder. "Things were intense. If you regret—"

"I only regret that it took me this long to find you." Wreck took her hand from behind him and began to lead her away. "I have clean up to do." Not as serious as his, but it needed done. "You should sleep and—"

Wreck glanced over his shoulder. "I gotta sleep with you against me."

"So I can't get away or so no one can steal me?"

"Both."

When they started their journey, neither could have known where they'd end up. People were dead. Others were freed. Lives were changed forever. Not all for the better.

Just breathing the same air as Wreck was a thrill. Tulsi had lost hope that her fantasy really existed, yet there he was, leading her into their bedroom. She didn't have to picture what life could be anymore. She was living it with the man she loved. As long as she had him, it was enough.

Wreck was all she wanted. Her fantasy existed in him. As far as Tulsi was concerned, they'd spend the rest of their lives basking in their dream life. After all they'd been through to get there, they deserved it. Nothing would come between them; they'd battled the odds and made it through. They'd fought for each other, proved their love, and Tulsi planned to enjoy every second of it.

**Styx, Wreck, & Tulsi feature later in
Scarlett Finn's To Die for Series!**

Thank you for reading this tale!
If you can, please take the time to review.

~

Ask your local library for more Scarlett Finn
novels!

~

For all things Scarlett Finn
check out:

www.scarlettfinn.com

CHECK OUT

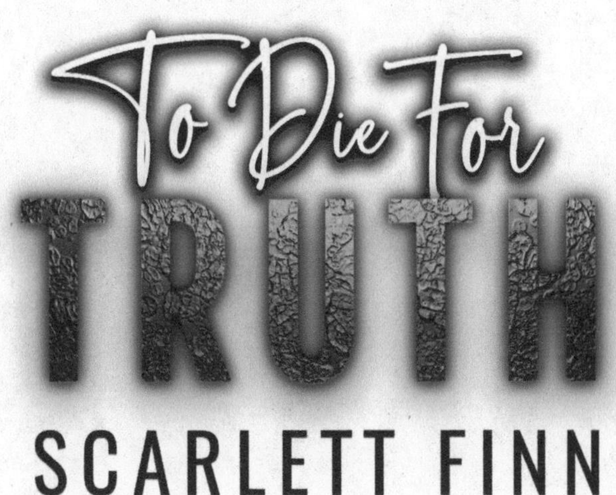

AVAILABLE NOW!